THE WYVERN, THE PIRATE, AND THE MADMAN

THE CELWYN SERIES BOOK 5

THE WYVERN, THE PIRATE, AND THE MADMAN

Lou Kemp

4 Horsemen
Publications, Inc.

Table of Contents

❖   ❖

VII

Acknowledgements:

MANY THANKS AND LOVE TO MY daughter, Charmaine, who has supported me no matter what, even when I got a third cat. Thank you to friends for their help and feedback: Nikki, Debbie, Peggy, and Karen. To authors and bloggers who have done their best to help me: Anita Dickason, Sue Costner, Gina Ray Mitchell, Norm Backstrom, Benjamin X. Wretlind, and Bob Van Laerhoven. Also, well-deserved praise to Joseph Mistretta for the final editing of this series.

Cast of Characters:

Jonas Celwyn: Immortal magician and provocateur

Professor Xiau Kang: Automat, medical man, skeptic, and scientist

Bartholomew: widower from Juba, friend to Kang and Celwyn

Pelaez: Celwyn's immortal and immoral magician brother

Qing: mechanical bird & lover of all things shiny and wonderful

Annabelle Pearse Swayne: heiress and ward of Uncle Celwyn

Captain Patrick Swayne: Friend to Celwyn who is married to Annabelle

Mrs. Elizabeth Kang: tolerant and beautiful wife of Kang

Zander: an orphan rescued on the way to Prague

Otto: an orphan who joined them on their journey to Singapore

Edward Murphy: driver and in charge of security at Tellyhouse

Tara McFein: good witch and good vampire Celwyn is enamored with

Simone Redifer: good vampire

Valentine Soriano: uncle to Tara & Simone, head of their family

Captain Nemo: Captain of the *Nautilus*

Granger: Nemo's Lieutenant

Captain Emilio Dearing: pirate king and confederate of Talos

Talos: devious, deceased automat and brother of Kang

Wolfgang Augustus Griffin: Father to Celwyn and Pelaez

Thales: Father to Wolfgang, demi-god and capable of saving other immortals

Jakow: Pirate who is second in command to Dearing

Gaspard: automat in league with Dearing, who stayed behind in Prague

PART I

Preface

The North Sea off Margate
1869

A S THEIR CAPTIVE LAY UNMOVING on deck, Celwyn trussed the pirate captain like a Christmas goose. He even stuffed an apple in Dearing's mouth before asking Bartholomew, "Do you see anything out there?"

"The fog is gone," the big man replied. He leaned over the rail of the *Primero* and shielded his eyes. In the distance, the sea roiled and from just below the surface, a flash of metal glinted at the sun. As he watched the churning water, something streaked through the sea, heading directly toward them.

Jonas Celwyn joined him and smiled when he saw it, too. Right on time.

"It appears our visit aboard Dearing's ship is about to end."

"It's—it's—the *Nautilus*!" Bartholomew shouted as the realization of what was about to happen dawned on him, but he couldn't move. He was frozen in fascination and the horror of the moment.

"I suggest that you brace yourself." Celwyn grabbed the rail and held on.

Bartholomew did so, his eyes on the water.

Like a sleek and enormous whale moving incredibly fast, the submarine grew larger as it closed in. Bartholomew pointed out the iron horn extending from the nose of the *Nautilus* as she dove below the waves.

Long seconds went by, and when the impact came, it seemed to last forever under the deafening rending that shook *Primero*. After it subsided, Bartholomew leaned over the side and saw the seawater gushing into the ship's hull as she keeled over.

An ominous crack shook the deck behind them. The big man whirled. With a deep groan, the mainmast began to fall as the ship tilted starboard. Bartholomew and the magician scrambled to hold on to the rail, and Dearing rolled by them toward the center of the ship. The magician brought him back to where they stood. The mast cracked again and slammed onto the deck, smashing everything underneath it.

Celwyn drew Dearing closer and kicked him. "I should have put you in your hold, along with the rats. You'd be dead by now." *Tara wouldn't have been hurt if it weren't for this bastard.* He kicked him again. The pirate would eventually receive exactly what he deserved. "Annoying Captain Nemo does have its consequences," Celwyn informed Dearing, and without touching him, tossed him overboard. He turned to Bartholomew.

The big man's eyes grew wider. He gulped.

"I'll keep him out of the water for now. We've got to jump." Celwyn felt the ship shift, and he slung a leg over the rail. "Nemo is turning around and coming back to pick us up." He patted Bartholomew's arm. "This tub will sink in another minute. I promise we will float downward like a feather and stay above the waves."

"Do we have to—"

"Yes."

Bartholomew muttered an imprecation to a god and hoisted himself on top of the rail.

"God damn it, Jonas!"

Chapter 1

SEAWATER SLOSHED UP THE SIDES OF the *Nautilus* as she cruised to a stop beside them. Feet away, the shattered timbers from the hull of the *Primero* drifted in a widening circle with the other debris from the destroyed pirate ship.

Wine bottles and dead bodies bobbed in the wreckage like morbid toys in an aquatic bathtub. None of the dead were automats, causing Celwyn to grin. The mechanical men couldn't swim, and with the impact of the collision, hundreds of those nasty things must have sunk to the bottom of the North Sea. If the murderers of Mercury (the vampire who helped Tara on occasion) were among the automats wandering across the sand hundreds of feet below, it would be most fitting.

As promised, Bartholomew hovered with him above the surface. Just beyond his left foot, Dearing floated face up in the frigid sea, causing Celwyn to wonder if sharks swam in these waters. If not, it could still be arranged. A nip here and a nip there would keep the bastard entertained. The magician had promised Nemo he would bring the pirate to him alive, and he found giving Dearing a scare and a good dunking just plain amusing after their ordeal this afternoon.

While they waited for the hatch on the submarine to open, Celwyn asked Bartholomew, "How are you doing, my friend?"

The big man's eyes opened long enough for him to say, "I am upset, Jonas. But pleased we survived." His gaze moved to what remained of the prow of the *Primero*. With a drawn-out hiss of displaced air, she disappeared under the waves. "That was a huge ship."

"We will be inside the ship in a few minutes," he assured the big man.

Bartholomew managed to look at their surroundings. Across miles of choppy waves, the boardwalk of SouthEnd on Sea could barely be seen. Bartholomew waved his arms in the air to rotate 360 degrees and back again. He'd learned that trick when he last experienced one of the magician's aerial displays.

"There are hundreds of dead pirates. This isn't how they thought things would turn out."

Celwyn agreed. A wave of expelled air hissed from the submarine as she surfaced beside them, and the hatch on the bow opened. Nemo's men wasted no time. In minutes, they straddled the platform, using poles to push bodies away from the ship. A crewman held a rifle steady while he scanned for unfriendly survivors.

"I trust your magic, Jonas. I must—because I cannot swim." The big man closed his eyes again.

The magician didn't find that surprising. Bartholomew had spent most of his life in the Sudan, only venturing beyond Juba a couple of years ago. When he had joined the magician and the Professor in their adventures, he could never have predicted how interesting things would become. Celwyn smiled. The big man's life had been rather exciting ever since.

The hatch on the stern platform opened. After several of the *Nautilus* crew climbed topside, Professor Xiau Kang joined them. First came his elfin ears, the too-long hair, and then the leathery skin. His dark eyes moved with the precision of the machinery behind them as the automat tilted his head back to study Celwyn and Bartholomew hovering a dozen feet above the surface. The magician took the big man's arm, and they descended to the platform. The crew pretended that they didn't see anything unusual as they fished Dearing out of the water.

Xiau patted Bartholomew's back and rolled his eyes at Celwyn. He couldn't help smiling, too.

"I am glad you both are not hurt."

Celwyn confronted his friend, the automat, not one of the evil ones they had just destroyed. "How is Tara?"

"Fine, considering. She will recover."

Celwyn sighed with relief and followed the others into the belly of the submarine. He motioned for them to continue down the corridor. "I want to be sure Dearing receives a proper welcome aboard the *Nautilus*."

As the crew maneuvered Dearing inside the hatch and to the top of the spiral stairs, Celwyn woke the pirate up; he should see this. Flanked by his lieutenants, Captain Nemo arrived at the foot of the stairs and stared, his expression full of satisfaction at what he saw. It had been a long hunt.

Now on his feet again, the pirate towered over the crew. He had gall. Only minutes ago, his ship had been blown to pieces underneath him. But still, the pirate twisted out of the grasp of one of Nemo's men and tried to stomp the other.

"Allow me." Celwyn elevated Dearing and dropped him off the stairs. He rolled to a stop at Nemo's feet.

Captain Nemo, a man of medium size with a dark complexion and hooded eyes, rarely showed emotion, except when Jules Verne made illogical and wishful bids during their nightly bridge games. But at the sight of his enemy lying at his feet, a broad smile filled Nemo's face.

He placed a boot on Dearing's neck. "I could do worse, sir, because of what you did to my crew and those villagers. Hundreds of deaths are on you." Dearing growled a profanity, and Nemo used Celwyn's method and just kicked him.

The magician addressed the Professor, "Are you sure about Tara?" At Kang's nod, he added, "I want some tea and Tara."

"I know you do."

The magician addressed Nemo. "Sir, may I suggest that your crew hose this bastard down before they put him in chains?" Although the hunt for Dearing had been a long one for Nemo, it had been a short but intense game for Celwyn that had ended as quickly as it had begun.

"An excellent suggestion." Nemo made a face of distaste. "I do not think he has bathed since we encountered him last year." The Captain motioned to his crew.

Dearing's eyes bulged, and he tried to yell an endearment around his gag. Celwyn couldn't help it; the gag became a furry mouse that crawled into his mouth. When the point had been made, the magician put the man to sleep again. It would be easier for the crew if they didn't have to contend with him on the way to the brig.

"Excuse me." Celwyn bowed and left them to make his way down the corridor to the study. As he entered, he searched for Tara, instead finding Bartholomew, Jules Verne, and Valentine Soriano; Tara's uncle. He was a most dangerous vampire and temporary guest on the *Nautilus*.

"*Where is she?*"

Xiau followed him into the room and said, "Come with me."

Celwyn trailed the automat toward the bow. In front of the last cabin, a crewman stepped aside for them to enter.

"Quiet. I gave her a sedative." At the magician's nod, he added, "She needs rest." Kang gripped Celwyn's arm and warned him, "Her wound was deep. It was most brave of her to throw herself in front of you."

"To save me." He blinked away his emotion and peered inside.

This cabin was smaller than his own, just a bunk, a chair, and a desk. Miss Tara McFein lay unmoving under several blankets. The magician could have reminded Kang vampires did not mind the cold, but it was probably a medical habit. She looked as beautiful as ever, if perhaps a bit pale. Some of the charcoal she'd rouged on her cheeks for her earlier disguise remained. Celwyn wiped it away.

"Allow me." Kang lifted her eyelids and checked her pulse. Not only a doctor and scholar, but the automat also had many other talents. "If nothing else occurs, she will be back to normal within a week." Kang rubbed his chin. "It is hard to predict medical outcomes with vampires. I did not study them at university."

"I doubt many do." Celwyn knelt beside her and stroked the black curls off her forehead. "She saved me, Xiau."

"I know. I was there when she did it."

Celwyn's lips twitched, despite his worry. "If she knew of the condition of her hair, she would wake up much sooner." He sighed at his friend. "Does she need my help?"

"No. It was a clean but deep cut. I have repaired it. She needs rest, and she will sleep for hours." He stretched. "Let's leave her alone for now."

With another fond caress, the magician stood and said, "Then, by god, it is teatime!"

Chapter 2

P ROFESSOR KANG RETURNED TO THE study after making a stop in the magician's cabin for someone he would want to see. Verne covered his notebook and ducked as Qing squawked and flew as fast as he could to the magician. It had been a month this time. "I missed you, too." Qing rubbed his beak on Celwyn's ear while he stroked the mechanical bird's back. "Have you behaved?"

Qing stopped snuggling and left him to flap his way to the crystal decanters on the bar. The sound of pecking on glass reached them.

"The Captain doesn't like that," Bartholomew said.

With a sigh, Kang sat heavily on the sofa next to the others. "Nemo will join us soon, I imagine." The aquatic window in the study took up nearly the length of the room, and on the other side of the glass, a school of mackerel lingered. There had to be a thousand of them displaying their shimmering scales in the low light. Beyond the fish, one of the drowned pirates drifted from side to side downward like a macabre leaf from a tree and arrived a bit late to the party of the dead below.

In the window's reflection, Kang's elfin ears looked the same size as the mackerel. The seawater gave his skin an otherworldly glow of blue-green, overlaying the pale alabaster from his makers. His expression seemed a bit more harassed than usual. Celwyn knew the automat well and wondered what bothered him. Possibly, his wife Elizabeth had demanded that he return to Prague instead of participating in another adventure with Nemo and the others.

"That bird only listens to you and the Captain." Bartholomew watched Qing peck a tune on the crystal decanters. The big man relaxed next to Celwyn with his tie askew and a general air of dishevelment after his experience on the *Primero*. He was a strong man, fleet of foot, educated, and brave. Bartholomew had many choices, and for now, he chose to be with them.

Celwyn grinned. The big man was also most attractive to any woman they met, including Miss Simone Redifer, Valentine's other niece. The magician laughed as quietly as he could to himself; what if someday Bartholomew suddenly acquired the most dangerous vampire they knew as an in-law?

Valentine's mane of silver hair shone under the soft lights of the study. He, too, had smudges of charcoal on his aristocratic face from their earlier disguises. In the hour since Captain Nemo had destroyed Dearing's vessel, he hadn't had time to tidy up, and in his torn street clothes, he reminded Celwyn of a tawdry, but dignified, Darwinian character.

The magician produced his tea service and inhaled the heavenly steam. It had been months since he had ordered Earl Grey from the ship's crew, and they'd stopped sending him curious looks when it appeared. Good grief, he was tired. The euphoria from their battle with Talos and Dearing had worn off, and the exertion from his magic set in. He needed to rest.

As he floated a fresh bottle and glasses around the room, Celwyn said, "I visited Tara. Xiau has probably told you she will recover."

Valentine nodded. "That was very brave of her." His eyes did not appear friendly. "Too bad you removed that witch who attacked her before I could—"

"The witch is feeding the fishes. Personally." Celwyn assured him.

"Possibly." The vampire's long nails scraped the arm of the sofa. Months ago, Valentine Soriano had introduced Tara and Miss Redifer to them when they joined forces for a foray into the catacombs in Palermo. That it had been a memorable experience did not properly describe what happened. In the end, Captain Nemo rescued them before backing the *Nautilus* out of an underground river for miles until they reached the sea. Throughout it all, Bartholomew's claustrophobia remained as strong as his superstitions; he had not enjoyed the experience at all.

"Your luggage did not come aboard with you," Kang observed, as ever the voice of reason, distraction, and diplomacy. Celwyn was convinced he and Bartholomew practiced it.

Valentine shrugged. "No, it did not. As far as I know, it's still at my hotel in London or in Talos's lair."

"I need to clean up." Bartholomew studied his clothes. "At one point, I found myself on the filthy deck of that ship." He stood and told Valentine, "I have some extra things. You are what … a bit over six foot? The trousers will be too long, but Jonas will make the adjustments."

"Thank you."

One of the crew escorted them out, probably to find Valentine an empty cabin. Celwyn grinned again to himself. The two things Nemo didn't want on his ship had occurred again: vampires and women. The magician sent a tailored dress and shoes to Tara's cabin. On second thought, he also provided a brush, comb, and pins, knowing she would not be pleased when she saw her hair. If he could have reproduced her special perfume he found so intoxicating, he would have done so. When he tried to before, his version had not turned out the same.

As Celwyn poured his second cup, he felt eyes on him and encountered a sarcastic stare from Kang.

"Yes?"

"Are you going to tell us what happened?"

From his perch at the chess table by the aquatic window, Jules Verne tugged on his little beard. "We are most curious!"

The magician asked, "Shouldn't we wait for the others?"

Before the automat could answer, Captain Nemo strode in, purposefully and in a great humor.

"A wonderful afternoon! Jonas, I am delighted that you and Bartholomew prevailed."

"So am I, and I imagine that seeing Dearing tied up at your feet was a most pleasing sight." The magician regretted not doing something more entertaining to their captive.

"To be sure." Nemo stood between the sofas and the window, savoring his thoughts. He grabbed the whiskey bottle and glass as they went by. After he tossed a shot back, he stared at the curtain of kelp just outside the window. The magician refilled his glass without getting up. The action had occurred so many times over the last year, Nemo no longer wondered how it happened or hesitated anymore.

"Sir, where are we?" The little author pointed his nose at Captain Nemo.

"I took us over to the coast. We're submerged about a hundred feet." Nemo glanced around the room. "Where are the others?"

Kang said, "Miss McFein is resting. She will recover from her wound." As he spoke, Valentine and Bartholomew walked in. "And now we are all here."

Bartholomew's prediction came true; his clothes almost fit the vampire. Celwyn shortened the pants and sleeves and made a few adjustments for the big man's wider shoulders.

Valentine walked up to Nemo and bowed.

"Once again, it appears we must request accommodation on your ship, sir."

Nemo did his best. Formal, but not unfriendly, he replied, "I am pleased you are here. You and your niece were instrumental in today's successful activities. We have a common purpose in hunting down the rest of the villains."

It seemed like a good time for an announcement. "Talos will no longer be a problem." The magician fished in his pocket and tossed a metal disk to Kang. "I took care of your brother."

Kang's broad smile was not a pleasant one, filled more with revenge than happiness. "Ah. A memento." He examined the disk that had powered the other automat. "Let's hope he stays dead this time. What about the others with him?"

Celwyn checked the room's interest. "That is part of a much longer story. We can begin it now if everyone is ready."

Nemo said, "Certainly, especially while we're waiting for the crew to set the table. What all happened?"

"As expected, Mr. Soriano and Miss McFein donned disguises and followed Dearing's man out of London." Bartholomew told them, "Just as I did, staying in front of him, with the intent of getting onto the pirate ship. It worked very well. Talos's automats attacked and took me aboard. What we hadn't planned on was that when they confronted Jonas, they also assaulted Miss McFein and her uncle." He inhaled. "Nor did we expect that the witch Ginnie would be in league with them." He waved a hand at the magician to take over the tale. "She did not die with the others at the compound in Turkey."

"After Ginnie had been subdued—" the magician began.

"My niece sat on her and questioned her," Valentine said.

Celwyn enjoyed the memory, then continued, "I enhanced the boat we used to follow the pirates, and as we drew closer to the pirate ship, they shot cannon balls at us. We could also see them hauling Bartholomew up the side of the ship. Then the witch got free and flung a knife at me. Tara threw herself in front of it, and in saving me, she sustained a severe wound. I realize some of you know these details, but am assuming Jules does not."

The author nodded. "Please go on." Verne uncapped his fountain pen and sent the magician a brave look. The author knew the consequences of his fraternization with reporters but probably hoped Celwyn was too distracted to pay attention.

Kang eyed him with distrust. "When Jonas saw that I could take care of Miss McFein's wound, with his usual subtlety," he paused for an eye roll, "he changed into a raven as big as a train car. Most likely, the size was intended to frighten the pirates." His voice grew quiet. "The last time I saw that raven was in the forests where ... where..." He swallowed several times. "It was a memorable experience."

"I was there too, Xiau," Bartholomew said, and told Valentine, "And we barely survived." The big man shook himself and his voice became stronger. "It is my turn to finish this story, perhaps while we eat." The silverware sparkled and as the candlelight flickered against their faces, the aroma of garlic from the soup reached them.

"Shall we?" Nemo gestured for them to take their places.

After the wine had been poured and water glasses filled, Bartholomew took up the tale again.

"Once I reached the pirate ship, Dearing attacked me, and Talos joined in. There were several hundred automats and just as many pirates. I couldn't see where they had taken Miss Redifer. When the situation became violent, Jonas arrived and subdued them." The big man inhaled his fears and turned to his soup.

"How?" Verne asked.

Bartholomew laughed. "He swept most of them into the sea and had a bit of fun with Talos and Dearing."

Captain Nemo's eyes twinkled in anticipation. "Do tell."

Celwyn did so, describing the surreal but artistic scene where he transformed the deck of the pirate ship into a ballroom floor and forced Dearing and Talos to perform a waltz. "We couldn't enjoy it very long, though; I had made arrangements for the Captain to give us exactly twenty minutes before he destroyed the *Primero*." It was his turn to laugh. "You should have seen Bartholomew's face when I told him we had to jump over the side."

"It was hundreds of feet down to the water!" The big man exclaimed.

Kang sampled the soup and nodded to himself. "I'm sure Jonas told you about that gently. He is so considerate."

The magician snorted.

Bartholomew's eyes still bulged. "From that high up, you wouldn't believe how it looked with this ship racing right toward you!"

"Anyhow," Celwyn tamped the air, "I'd already dispatched Talos. We tossed Dearing over the side so we could take him with us. He floated just fine." He watched the big man nod confirmation. "I kept us above the waves until the *Nautilus* picked us up. In total, it was a wonderful afternoon."

With a satisfied twist to his lips, Verne capped his pen and pulled the basket of rolls closer. Celwyn wondered how the little author would use what he heard here tonight. In the past, it hadn't always gone so well.

"Sir, why save Dearing?" Kang asked Nemo.

Valentine guessed, "To help us find my niece?"

Nemo motioned the crewman to serve the main course. "Yes, and for my own purposes. We will kill two birds with one stone."

As evidence he understood some words, Qing escaped from Celwyn's collar to fly to the aquatic window and greet a handful of clown fish bobbing against the glass. While Qing did a little dance of joy, Celwyn experienced his own euphoria as he finished the soup. He loved the taste of ginger!

"What do we know about my missing niece?" Valentine asked. "When I asked earlier, no one knew."

Celwyn chose his words with care. Everyone thought he had trouble controlling his anger, but Valentine was worse. "The pirates captured her, and she is on another of Dearing's ships. I do not know where yet."

From Valentine's expression, he wanted to visit the brig to find out right then and there and had to be talked out of it. Kang could talk fast without breathing, quite an advantage in negotiation.

If the vampire had prevailed, it would have been a mortal visit; the pirate would not have survived. Celwyn reminded him that they did not know enough yet from Dearing, no matter how Valentine stewed. After a long moment, the vampire nodded at the others to continue. By the time they moved on to the dessert course, he still growled under his breath.

Because they sat at the table, Celwyn thought it best not to mention they faced another challenge. If the vampires were to remain on the submarine, they needed to obtain a supply of fresh animal blood. Celwyn assumed the ship had an excellent refrigeration system, which segued into a need to discuss something most serious. The Captain must have thought the same.

"We need to assess our situation and make preparations," Nemo said.

"I agree." The automat nodded.

"I normally do not discuss our plans; however, our interests are unique and intertwined, making it proper to do so." Nemo sampled the fruit ice in front of him and continued, "Everyone is aware of what has recently occurred; however, we need to back up a bit and discuss details." He raised a brow at Valentine and transferred it to Celwyn.

The magician complied. "Until recently, we had two sets of villains after us. Both probably sought the Professor's work on atomic theory, not the flying machine. As of this afternoon, the automats are no longer a threat because they are at the bottom of the sea. Talos has been eliminated, and Captain Dearing is in our brig." He smiled. "Right under our feet." The magician made a mental note to reinforce Dearing's cell and add a few disturbing gifts to welcome him aboard.

Verne finished his ice and sat back to pat his round belly. "What happened to the automats exactly?"

"I assume they sank to the ocean floor after I removed them from the deck of the *Primero*." The magician checked with Kang.

"Yes, they would have. They are mostly metal, and would not have been buoyant, nor known how to swim." The automat shrugged.

"I will not forgive them." Valentine's grumble grew louder. "During their operation against us, they killed one of our family, and after attacking my other niece, kidnapped Miss Redifer." His gaze could have lit the tablecloth on fire.

"Which brings us to the first goal we have; finding Miss Redifer," Celwyn said. "The second objective belongs to the Captain."

Nemo carefully replaced his spoon and lined up his bowl just so, before glancing at Verne. "This is confidential, Jules."

Verne opened and shut his mouth before shooting a look at Celwyn. "I understand."

Nemo reached and extinguished one of the candles. "The reason I asked Jonas to not kill Dearing is because that bastard has something of mine. I'm hoping Jonas can use his talents to extract the location of it from him." He made eye contact with the vampire at the other end of the table. "We will put all our efforts into finding your niece first."

Celwyn hid a grin. Kang caught it and glared. "What *is* it?"

"Xiau, you worry." The magician smiled again as he considered the possibilities. "From what I heard in Dearing's thoughts, and the hints the Captain has given us, there is a chance both purposes will coincide nicely."

Everyone considered the prospects, both the obvious and some that required speculation.

The magician told Valentine, "It sounds like we will be leaving this area shortly. If you need a supply of your form of nourishment for the next several weeks, perhaps the Captain could send someone ashore before the butcher shop in town closes." At Nemo's nod, he added, "Or if you prefer to hunt game yourself, you may want to accompany them."

Valentine said, "I will go with them. There are some fields to the west of that town that should prove fruitful."

Captain Nemo stood. "My lieutenant will accompany you. He is discreet and level-headed."

Chapter 3

After Valentine and Lieutenant Granger departed, the others settled in the study of the *Nautilus* with coffees and expectant faces.

Kang voiced the first question.

"I believe you wanted Valentine out of the way for at least an hour or two?"

Celwyn paced behind the sofas, an uncharacteristic action. He felt not only angry but disgusted with what he must say.

"Just spit it out," Bartholomew suggested.

"Captain, without yet knowing details of your interest here, can we assume it is somewhat urgent?" The magician asked.

Nemo's growl rivaled one of Valentine's. "Yes." He regarded Celwyn. "But ... maybe not as much as what you know of Miss Redifer's predicament."

Celwyn dropped onto the sofa by the automat and put his hands on his knees.

"True. Her situation is dire. I wanted to tell you of it before telling her uncle, or Tara. There is no use in upsetting them, and I do not relish battling Valentine in a full rage."

"Explain?" Bartholomew asked.

"We won't be able to control Valentine's reaction if there isn't a solution when we tell him." Celwyn sighed and moderated his voice. "When I entered Dearing's mind, I discovered he had sold Miss Redifer to Sultan Mahmud. The pirate ship carrying her sailed five days ago."

"Oh, my," Kang said.

"Just like the Barbary pirates used to do." Verne frowned.

Bartholomew said, "That news alone is troubling, but I suspect there is more."

Tea time. In an instant, he inhaled the steam from a wonderful blend and offered cups around. When everyone declined with grace, the automat just rolled his eyes. The silence grew again until Celwyn continued. "There is. I can't describe how I felt when I found out, knowing I couldn't rip Dearing apart. At least, not yet." He indicated Nemo. "Not only had I promised to deliver the bastard here, but he may still have further information buried in his worm-ridden brain."

Kang patted his shoulder. "Good call. Tell us. It must be bad for you to get Valentine off the ship and keep this from him."

With a sigh he felt all the way to his boots, Celwyn looked at them. "The sultan intends to breed Miss Redifer to make superior, unstoppable soldiers for his army. She is one of many female vampires he has bought."

Silence reigned over the room. Qing's nails sounded too loud as he clicked his way across the ledge under the window.

"Not only is that terrible," Captain Nemo cleared his throat, "but it will not occur. We will set off as soon as Mr. Soriano and Granger return." To Kang and Bartholomew, he asked, "Should I drop you off at Findbar or near Prague?"

"Or, do we prefer to go with you?" Bartholomew shot a glance at the Professor.

The automat pursed his lips and asked Nemo, "Could you dispatch another boat ashore to send a telegram to Prague? We will all be going with you."

After Nemo gave the order, he left his hand on the intercom for several seconds before rejoining them, pacing, and seeming to have another decision to make. The others sensed his turmoil and waited. Celwyn sipped tea. If only Attila the Hun, Richard the Lionhearted, and Napoleon had drunk their weight in savory leaves, they would have never worried about their battles.

Nemo took a last turn to the window and back. He stood at attention in front of them, his uniform as pressed and pristine as if he had not already had a remarkable day. His voice sounded just as clear.

"Dearing has, for years, enslaved and looted villages from Espanola to the far east and all lands in between. His main occupation is as a slave trader, and he destroys those he doesn't enslave. He has also plundered many of the world's museums for the most beautiful art ever created." He slammed one fist into the other. "I intend to free the people he has captured and retrieve the artifacts and artwork."

Bartholomew nodded. "It will be most rewarding to attempt this."

Kang added, "Findbar Island and the flying machine will be waiting for us when we return."

"I must map our course and get the ship ready." Captain Nemo stood. "At dinner, I will tell you of other crimes by Dearing." He clicked his heels together, saluted, and marched out.

As soon as he left, Kang popped up and crossed over to the newest feature of the study. Next to the chessboard, a square table had been added. Its sole purpose? To display maps—Kang's idea of heaven. The automat selected several of them and returned to the sofas.

"Here we are." Kang unrolled the charts. "I am not an expert at sailing, either above or below the waves, but have noted some of our activities over the last year."

Bartholomew spoke. "I have also. If we are not in a hurry, we average about 160 to 200 miles per day. If we are in a rush, such as when Jonas was dying, we traveled nearly double that non-stop for days to reach Thales."

Celwyn had missed much of the trip, being unconscious at the time. He had left Thales's island feeling nearly back to normal. In fact, he'd been given a few extra abilities that had since then mostly faded.

The Professor and Bartholomew exchanged one of their silent scientific question-and-answer glances. "So," Kang said. "You may assume that we'll be in a hurry due to the danger to Miss Redifer. Because of the urgency, we estimate we'll average about 325 miles per day."

"Do you know where Nemo is going?" Celwyn asked.

"Yes," the automat answered as he and Bartholomew continued to study the map.

Verne had pulled out his ever-present notebook. When he found the magician's eye on him, he hurried to say, "Nothing here about Nemo's purpose. Only finding Miss Redifer."

"All right." Kang squinted to measure different points on the charts. "A rough estimate, and with time to recharge the ship's batteries and other things, plus obtaining supplies, is that it will take about two to three weeks to reach Bintan Island and the Sultan's palace."

"That will provide plenty of time to explore Dearing's thoughts for clues and anything else we can use." Celwyn felt some relief.

Kang raised a brow. "Would it hurt the Captain's feelings if you searched Dearing's thoughts without him?"

"Probably not. We must explore many avenues. Nemo will want some specific information, and if I must, I'll scare it out of Dearing." The magician's smile could be described as revengeful. "If he didn't need information from him, the Captain would probably prefer to draw and quarter the bastard right now."

"He'll have to fight Mr. Soriano for the privilege," Verne said.

Bartholomew laughed, hesitated, and eyed the magician. "I agree. While we have time to discuss it, do you want to hazard a guess as to why your new pet joined you on the *Primero* earlier today?" He shook his head in wonder. "The pirates and automats were already scared of the enormous raven circling their masts, and then a big fat wyvern with lots of teeth appeared up there too."

Verne sat up, his ears practically wiggling. "A wyvern?"

Kang grinned. "Tell him, Jonas."

The magician sent the automat an irritated look. Verne didn't need encouragement to meddle. Then he thought better of it—this could be useful.

Celwyn told Verne about Wye. The creature had adopted the magician months ago, and none of them knew why. So far, he seemed rather harmless. Just a large, and odd, mystical pet.

"What does it look like?" Verne inquired, pen ready.

"It resembles a corpulent dragon." Celwyn shrugged. "Mostly it is a brilliant green, and scaley with iridescent wings and short legs curled up near its body."

"Wings, you say?" Verne scribbled fast. "Interesting."

"Yes. During Annabelle's wedding, it visited us and bared its teeth at Francesca." He waited for

Verne to catch up on his note-taking. "Yet, how and when we see it seems to vary. Sometimes Wye, that is his name, is only a few feet long, such as when he joined us on our trek through the catacombs. Other times, he is as big as this ship." Celwyn spoke slower. "If someone irritates me, Wye shows his displeasure."

Verne paled. *Yes*, Celwyn thought. *It was a good idea to tell the author about Wye.*

Bartholomew shuddered, and the sofa shook underneath him. "Let us not talk about the catacombs, please. I say ... it seems you are out of tea, Jonas."

Celwyn recognized the diversion and thanked the big man. He sent a tray of whiskies around the room and poured himself a fresh cup.

Verne recovered fast. "The wyverns are usually large, then?"

"We saw a man-sized version of it a few weeks ago," Kang told him.

"This afternoon," Bartholomew started and swallowed, "on the pirate ship, it had to be scores of times bigger, just like Jonas' raven. It flew between the top of the masts and weaved in and out of them at speed."

"I think," Verne licked his lips, "but I'm not sure that I would have liked to have seen that."

He would? Celwyn decided to see if his connection with the wyvern was still strong, and perhaps growing. He concentrated on the table between them, willing Wye to appear. Unlike his own magic, with the wyvern, he couldn't predict what would happen. A minute passed, then another while Kang and Bartholomew discussed their favorite subject, the flying machine. Verne listened a bit and then his attention drifted to Celwyn and the table between them. He squeaked, and his eyes opened wide behind his spectacles.

A wispy halo of green became distinct, thickening as it spread and covered the table. Wye took shape as his scales became defined, and his eyes gleamed a greeting to them above rows of pointed teeth on full display. The creature lay curled on its side, wings tucked tight to its chubby body. Wye blinked adoring eyes at Celwyn and flopped his tail, knocking both glasses off the table.

Kang covered his surprise and exclaimed, "Well, well."

Bartholomew climbed backward over the sofa. Verne wanted to run too, but couldn't. "Look—look—"

A commotion in the corridor reached them, and then Valentine arrived, his cheeks rosy with health, a sign of successful hunting ashore.

When the vampire saw the wyvern, he stopped short and stared. "I see your wyvern has returned." He cocked his head to the side. "I wondered if I'd see it again."

"You saw it before?" Verne asked, and Celwyn heard envy in his voice.

"Yes." Valentine approached and stopped a few feet away. Wye tracked him, but seemed otherwise unconcerned, preferring to stare at the magician.

Celwyn asked Valentine, "What do you know about these creatures?"

"Unpredictable, devoted to whoever attracted them. They're known to inhabit objects. Where did you get it?"

"Apparently from a painting in a museum near Palermo."

"How fortunate for you." Valentine smiled with a perfect set of teeth that appeared much sharper than a wyvern's. "They are loyal, very much so. I hear they can be fanciful, and sometimes destructive."

Verne glanced at Bartholomew, who waited over by the chess table. "How old are they?"

"I do not know, but they have been depicted in artwork for thousands of years." Valentine shrugged.

The author licked his lips. "Jonas, have you tried to touch it?"

"Err, no." The magician looked at Wye and offered his hand.

Without hesitation, a red tongue shot out of its mouth, and it licked his palm.

"It feels rough, like Qing's beak—oh, hell—"

Celwyn turned in time to see Qing flying full speed straight at Wye. Before he could do anything, the wyvern dissolved.

"Thank god," the automat breathed.

Verne said, "I totally agree."

When everyone had regained their composure, Kang said, "I wonder if the wyvern reacted to your fear for it, or to Qing?" He hesitated. "To help you ... as if he was so much a part of you that when you were alarmed ... he was..."

Bartholomew said with fascinated slowness, "It feels what you do."

"Like showing his anger at Francesca at the wedding when I couldn't," the magician said.

Scientific fervor gleamed in Kang's eyes. "Can you imagine how behaviorists would love to study the two of you?"

"I can. To understand their connection, and how it works," Bartholomew's interest was written across his face.

Celwyn stroked Qing's back as the bird rubbed his beak on the magician's chin. "I suppose it is possible."

"It would be just like the connection between a dog and its owner," the big man observed.

Celwyn thought about it a bit more. "We do not know much about Wye at all. Or what he is capable of."

"Jealousy is possible," Valentine repeated.

Bartholomew regarded the table where the wyvern had been. "What will it do if it sees Miss McFein in your close vicinity?"

The magician got to his feet and shook his pant legs down. "I do not know, but I'd like to be in her vicinity right now, and preferably, her sedative has worn off."

Chapter 4

H E HEARD AN INVITATION TO COME in, and when Celwyn opened the cabin door, he found Tara sitting on the bed and combing her hair with her left hand. She wore the clothes he'd made for her, but her right boot and stocking lay on the floor, probably where she'd kicked them when she couldn't put them on. Her buttons had been buttoned, if somewhat haphazardly.

"I can't use my right arm yet." She said in a confidential tone, "Don't tell the Professor, but I took off the sling he provided."

"He wanted to keep you from moving your arm too much on that side." Celwyn waved a hand and replaced the sling, redid buttons, and shod her foot. "Although I have done something similar, I am not sure Xiau would think it is permissible for you to be out of bed." He sent a kiss to brush against her lips.

After she enjoyed the sensation, she said, "You could do that in person if you wish."

Before she finished speaking, Celwyn had her in his arms and whispered in her hair, "I am so relieved you will recover."

She kissed him. "I am also."

"That was foolhardy." He held her chin. "You saved me."

"I would do it again." She reared back. "Why do you look so worried?"

The magician thought he had hidden the news of Miss Redifer's predicament rather well ... until now.

"Tara." He held her at arm's length. "There are things you need to know, but should you be out of bed?"

"There certainly are things I should know." She appeared determined, and color had come back to her cheeks, some of it from impending irritation. "While you decide whether to tell me or not, could you help me with my hair, please?" She stood, and he grabbed her elbow to steady her.

"I will do my best." He noticed she had only arranged one side of it, and even then, not too well. He produced a hand mirror, and it hovered in front of her.

After a few suggestions, she laughed. "Thank you, but you don't know what you are doing, do you?"

"Correct." He tucked her hand into his arm. "A short visit to the study, with my assistance, and then you'll come back and rest. Agreed?"

"Would I lie to you?"

Celwyn hadn't considered that possibility. "You could probably do it convincingly." He kissed her.

As they entered the study, the magician beheld a homey sight; Verne and Valentine played chess as Qing stood on the author's shoulder and watched. Celwyn suspected the bird's interest lay in the chess pieces that were usually put away if not under observation. When Qing saw the magician, he obediently flew to him, landing on his free arm. He squawked a greeting and studied Tara.

"I think he remembers you," Celwyn said.

"Or my glittery hair clip." She told Qing, "I'm sorry I do not have—" As she spoke, Celwyn put one in her hand. "It appears I do. Would you like it?" She opened her hand, and Qing wasted no time snatching his prize and flying back to the aquatic window.

From his position on the sofa, Kang drawled, "Jonas, she shouldn't be out of bed." He yawned. "But, considering you'd do the same thing, what else should I expect?"

Beside him, Bartholomew laughed and put down the atlas he'd been studying.

Time to change the subject. As Celwyn settled Tara on the other sofa, he sighed; he must tell her and Valentine about Miss Redifer's situation. If he didn't, Kang would certainly bring it up. With a glance, he caused Verne's queen to move into mortal jeopardy. Minutes later, the older vampire thanked the author for the game and joined his niece on the sofa.

"I also wonder if you should be out of bed," Valentine told her.

She patted his hand. "It's all right, Uncle. As soon as Jonas has told us about whatever is bothering him, I will rest."

The magician wondered if she was using blackmail or...

Valentine noted her seriousness. "Is it a private conversation?"

Celwyn gazed at the others. "No, it concerns us all. I waited to tell you until Tara looked well enough to hear it. I had also hoped to provide a solution." Nemo's offer to set sail as soon as possible would have to do.

While everyone stared at him, it didn't take long to describe the conditions Miss Redifer was kept in, and what all Dearing had done. The pirate's thoughts had been in vivid color. After Tara had calmed her uncle down, the magician told them of Nemo's intention to leave for the Sultan's lair as soon as he could. The *Nautilus* would perform her maintenance tonight so she could travel all day tomorrow.

Valentine shook off Tara's restraining hand and leapt to his feet. He growled loud enough to make the guard at the door back up several steps. "Where has Nemo put the pirate?" As he started for the corridor, Celwyn blocked the door. When he couldn't go any further, the vampire swung around with a scorching glare at the magician.

"Uncle, let him finish," Tara requested with a labored breath, reminding Celwyn that she didn't need to be in the middle of this.

He squared off in front of the enraged vampire. "We plan to question Dearing so that we can successfully retrieve Miss Redifer. We can't do that if you tear him up first. *Think* about it."

As he spoke, Valentine inhaled, and his temper subsided along with his high color. He retook his seat next to his niece. "You look pale and should rest, my dear."

"I know."

Valentine grumbled to himself. "They would have taken you too if they hadn't been using you to get to the Professor."

Tara sighed, getting air, and acknowledging the situation, too. "I realize that now."

Satisfied he wouldn't have to chase Valentine through the bowels of the submarine, Celwyn said, "We have about two weeks to plan our attack while we travel to Bintan Island. With luck, we'll make up some of the head start the pirate ship has on us."

Verne said, "If they ran into a storm along the way, that would help."

"We can hope for it." Tara patted her uncle's hand. If she intended the gesture to be soothing, it did not work.

Valentine's brows lowered over a stormy expression. "How dare they!" His nostrils flared, and he started to get up. His niece pulled him back.

While Tara calmed him down, and Kang finished scrutinizing his maps. He announced, "When most of you were out of the room, I verified our route with the Captain, and can talk about where we'll stop along the way." The automat measured something with a caliper he'd borrowed; a sign they'd soon have another map room in here, too. "Thank god we sent Elizabeth a telegram before they closed."

"Are we stopping in Seville?" Bartholomew asked, most likely daydreaming about empanadas.

"We pass by from a distance." The automat shook his head. "Nemo plans to leave during the night, travel due south, and circle Gibraltar. Our first stop will be Algiers three days from now. While there, we'll have time to telegraph and pick up supplies." He frowned at the map. "We'll recharge our batteries near there, and then continue the next day."

"Do we need assistance?" the older vampire asked. "I have family members in Capri, and they would be ready to assist by the time we reach that city if I telegraph them. Ever since Barbarossa's time, they have hated pirates and would welcome a confrontation."

Celwyn, Bartholomew, and Kang exchanged a silent look. The automat said, "We need to know what we're up against before answering your question." He asked Celwyn, "When are you going to explore Dearing's thoughts?"

"Now." The magician brought Tara to her feet. "First, I'll escort Tara to her cabin." He smoothed the hair off her brow and continued, "And I assume Bartholomew would like to accompany me to see Dearing, since Nemo can't spare the time." To Valentine, he said, "You will have several turns with the bastard as we go along, but it would just infuriate both of you if you saw him right now. We need him thinking he is crafty."

The vampire held back a remark and then nodded.

"I had thought about a spot of revenge too, but understand the need to wait." Bartholomew stood.

Kang regarded Celwyn down his nose. "I could go with you."

The magician ushered Tara to the door, saying, "If Bartholomew doesn't sufficiently irritate Dearing, you will be welcome to try."

"Fine," Kang pouted. "I like maps better, anyway."

Chapter 5

THE *NAUTILUS'S* BRIG LAY DIRECTLY below the study and consisted of a quartet of cells. Only a few feet away, the noise from the turbine room probably made sleeping a bit tedious.

Captain Emilio Dearing filled the first cell with no room to spare. His booted feet hung off the end of the cot and grazed the bars of the cell. Celwyn sniffed the air, detecting the scent of soap. Nemo's crew must have soaped him up and hosed him off; Dearing's mane of red hair still glistened with water.

The pirate tracked Celwyn and Bartholomew as they approached behind a pair of guards. Nemo had sent his regrets but had his duties preparing the ship. He also agreed they might require several sessions with Dearing to extract all the information stored in his devious mind.

"There's no need to open the cell, thank you," Celwyn told the guards. They saluted and left.

The crew had removed the pirate's scabbard, knives, and decorative gold chains, but he still looked like a nasty thing. Although not quite as big as Bartholomew, the man had even more muscle mass. A family of birds could have nested in his fluffy beard and probably had at some point. Above it all, a pair of blue eyes radiated guile and controlled rage.

The magician produced a pair of comfortable armchairs and a table for their beverages. He bowed to Bartholomew, "After you."

"Thank you." Bartholomew made himself comfortable.

Dearing stopped glaring to stare at the chairs, and then the bottle.

"Shall I pour?"

"Please." Bartholomew executed a yawn.

"Ah, life is good, is it not? A spot of Earl Grey, a pleasant afternoon, and a dastardly villain in a cage." Celwyn asked the big man, "What should we do with him?"

Bartholomew rubbed his chin and sipped. "I believe he enjoyed your musical interlude before Nemo sank his ship."

With a roar, Dearing threw himself at the bars of the cell and shook them.

The magician waved a hand and brought forth a full orchestra. "Nothing is too good for our guest." He confided to Bartholomew, "I hope he enjoys Mozart." He lifted a hand and conducted for a moment. "So precise and balanced."

Bartholomew sipped and smiled. The big man loved a good show, especially with someone of the pirate's temperament.

"Would you care to ask him a question?" By prior arrangement, they had decided that with the magician monitoring the pirate's thoughts, the truthful answer would float there, even if he lied, or said nothing.

Bartholomew regarded Dearing. "What does the ship carrying Miss Redifer look like?"

The pirate laughed at him, while his eyes traveled back to the liquor bottle. Celwyn noted a slew of details from a ship called the *Quarto* sailing across the pirate's memory, including the interior of the cabins and the lockbox he kept there. It wasn't clear, but his gaze beyond her deck seemed to reveal a flock of canvasses from the other ships sailing with her.

"When did she leave London?" the big man asked and touched the whiskey bottle with a fingertip.

Dearing watched the gesture, as fascinated as if he'd touched a woman.

Again, the pirate confirmed what they needed to know without saying a word. Celwyn found the space in his thoughts surprisingly clean at the moment: no scraps of erotic thoughts or avarice-fueled tidbits. When Dearing turned his back on them and retreated to his cot, Celwyn floated another bottle into his cell to hover above the man's head. The pirate licked his lips, glanced at Celwyn, and reached for it. His hand closed around nothing.

Celwyn silently summarized what he had found so far to Bartholomew. "What else would we like to know?" the magician asked the big man.

Bartholomew pretended to think and tapped his lips with a fingertip. "Is the *Quarto* manned by automats or pirates?"

Dearing began shaking his head and stopped.

"You know the name of my ship." It was a croak.

Bartholomew yawned again.

"How?" Dearing lunged at the cell bars, his voice rising with his fury. "How?" He thundered, *"How?"*

Celwyn yelled back, "How many pirates are on the *Quarto*?"

Dearing stuck out his bottom lip. "I answer nothing until you give me something."

"Such as?" Bartholomew asked.

While he waited for Dearing to think of his ships again, the magician noticed the pirate's arms had so many tattoos he had no unmarked skin. A picture of one of the beautiful and poisonous snakes of Borneo covered his forearm, but the magician couldn't remember the name of it. Celwyn remained in Dearing's thoughts for another few minutes, having gathered enough for now. When he was sure he had the pirate's attention, he dissolved the chairs and bowed Bartholomew ahead of him toward the stairs.

As they reached the upper corridor, Bartholomew asked, "What do you think?"

"We received confirmation of many things." Celwyn enjoyed their success, having not expected so much so soon. "I left the bastard a small, but furry, present to remember us by until we return. It sings."

He held the door for Bartholomew. "And added a block around the cells in case Dearing overpowers the guards."

The crew had just finished setting up the dinner table when Celwyn and Bartholomew arrived in the study. To Celwyn's surprise, Tara sat on one of the sofas, looking much more like herself. However, she would need a larger mirror to repair her hair. Perhaps her dress needed something ... *ah* ... he added an emerald necklace to complement her graceful neck. She thanked him with a look as she touched it.

"Should you be out of bed?" Celwyn asked with a sidelong glance at the automat, who appeared ready to say something sarcastic. "I, of course, always obey Xiau's medical advice." He blinked at the automat with feigned innocence and Bartholomew roared with laughter.

"For a while," she said. "The Professor escorted me here. He is pleased with my progress."

With a nod at Celwyn, Kang said, "You are a much better patient than Jonas, my dear. Yes, you are doing well. Are you able to sit with us at dinner?"

"Certainly. My uncle and the crew brought a variety of nourishment from their trip ashore this afternoon. It should last at least as far as Algiers."

The crew lit candles and filled water goblets. As everyone took their places, the Captain rushed in, his tie untied. Celwyn fixed it with a gesture and greeted him.

Nemo stood behind his chair and addressed them. "Good evening, everyone. I have excellent news. We will be able to leave the area about midnight and head south."

As he held Tara's chair for her, Valentine said, "Thank you, sir. The Professor has given us a general timetable. We're hoping the weather has changed for the worse and will slow the pirate ship down."

"With luck, we will arrive before them." When everyone had been seated, Nemo sampled the wine and nodded to the crewman to pour. "Before we reach Tripoli, we should be able to make up all but a day of their head start."

"That is better than I hoped," Tara said.

"Same here." Bartholomew still grinned from their teasing of Kang. "I see we moved a few hours ago and are stationary once again." Everyone gazed out the aquatic window. Only a handful of stars twinkled at them above the waterline.

Nemo said, "Yes. We're topside just off the Hastings coast, near an uninhabited area. The crew is performing our maintenance now, so we can depart as planned." He sampled the appetizer and scrutinized Bartholomew with speculation. The big man's less-than-adventurous approach to seafood had expanded over the last few months, and he enjoyed most of it.

"I like this," Bartholomew told Nemo and chewed. "What is it?"

"Eel stewed in sauce."

The big man maintained a fixed, pleasant expression. "It is quite tasty."

To save Bartholomew from any further bad acting, Celwyn addressed Valentine, "During the time we've been together, we have evolved to where our dinner conversation is not dictated by polite society." He looked at Tara seated directly across from him. "A feminine presence would normally preclude most of our usual table talk."

Bartholomew kept an eye on the Captain as he waited for the crew to offer the platter of eel again. The big man declined.

The Professor told Tara, "Jonas is leading up to telling us what he discovered during his visit with Dearing, but he doesn't want to shock you, my dear."

"Noted, and I will be fine, especially if it helps rescue Simone."

"We will find Miss Redifer, I assure you," Nemo said. "Please pass the butter."

After he handed over the butter, Verne pointed his nose at Celwyn. "I have been in my room writing all afternoon. What have I missed?"

While the crewman ladled soup, Celwyn scanned those present, thinking. He might as well get it over with. "Bartholomew accompanied me to visit Dearing in his cell. There will be many visits. We think the most efficient way to obtain information is for me to already be in his thoughts while whoever is with me asks him questions; he will think about what he is asked, and we'll discover whatever he doesn't say."

"Ah," Verne murmured. "Clever."

"Just so. We are not letting him know how we find out information. If he knew, he could direct his thoughts elsewhere, making this harder to do."

The Professor drank off his wine and gestured for more. "That would certainly drag this out."

Celwyn paused for another bite before saying, "We now know the following: Miss Redifer is on the *Quarto*, a three-masted barque a touch smaller than the *Primero*—Dearing's main ship that we destroyed yesterday, and there are only pirates aboard the *Quarto*, no automats." The magician finished his soup and continued. "I saw enough so that after dinner I'll be able to draw a detailed picture of all the decks of the *Quarto*. Including her guns. If Dearing's memories hold true, we will know exactly where they have confined Miss Redifer when the time comes to rescue her."

What Celwyn did not tell them was that they were keeping her in the ship's bottom, wrapped in chains. Valentine and Tara did not need that image to upset them further.

"This assumes we catch them at sea." Kang switched to Captain Nemo. "Which is preferable."

Nemo returned their look as enigmatically as a satisfied owl and finally nodded.

Celwyn grinned. He had his own version of that which annoyed the automat to no end.

"We didn't ask Dearing any questions about what you want to retrieve." He eyed Nemo. "I'll assume I will be with you for your questions."

"Yes."

"What else?" the automat asked.

Celwyn finished chewing. A fine sauce had accompanied the eel. Nemo's chef had talent. "There are times when Dearing's mind is as disorganized as you can imagine. One minute he is wallowing in carnal pleasures, the next reliving setting a village on fire."

When the crew placed a large platter of swordfish nearly four feet long in front of them, the magician controlled a whistle. As they withdrew, he said, "Luckily, we were there when his thoughts cleared for a few minutes and verified the date that the *Quarto* sailed—it is as we thought. Also, we confirmed how many pirates are aboard her. As mentioned before, we now have the type and number of guns on their ship; approximately twenty-four on each side."

"Is the hull of standard construction?" Nemo inquired.

Celwyn could imagine why he asked. "I will find out."

"How does she sit in the water?" Nemo asked and dabbed his lips with his napkin. The action displayed the contrast between the civilized atmosphere of his table and the violence of the subject at hand.

"Again, I will confirm that before making the picture of what Dearing thinks it looks like."

When their desserts arrived, Verne did not hesitate and dug in. After he'd eaten half of it faster than a bunny would, he asked the table, "Would you care to hear some background on Sultan Mahmud?"

Valentine eyed Tara, who said, "Yes, please."

"The only thing I know is that for years he has either courted the Cossacks or fought them," Kang said.

Verne whispered a request to one of the crew, and another piece of cake appeared in front of him. "The Sultan of Mahmud supplies mercenaries to the highest bidder. His forces are known for their ruthlessness in battle. However, he has been known to attack those same armies he had rented his troops to."

"Quite an unsavory individual." Bartholomew said, "It is most interesting that this is all about war, and it touches us here."

"Like Pelaez said, 'The horrors of war envelop the air we breathe. Each new invention of war bloodies our souls.'" After the magician quoted him, he remembered his brother's other words and deeds. How could he have been so wrong about him?

"We can't change what he did." Kang patted his shoulder. "But I understand it now."

"*I don't.*" Nemo's growl exceeded the vampire's ire, and the fire in his eyes could have lit up Albert Hall.

Time to change the subject. Celwyn said, "Sir, it sounds like you will attack both at sea and on land, correct?"

"Yes." Although it still sounded like a growl, not as bad of one. Nemo resented Celwyn's traitorous brother, who had destroyed the first flying machine and murdered his guards and house staff. At least, they assumed Pelaez had done it. Celwyn couldn't rule out Ginnie, the witch. Would they ever know? She had participated in the plot with Talos. But now? Perhaps she could wave at the automats walking across the sand to nowhere—as of today, she had become a part of the debris at the bottom of the sea.

"Do we want further information about Talos?" Kang raised a brow at each of them. "I ask because it would be useful to know why he attempted to capture me and tried again in the last few weeks. Who was he working with?"

"Or for?" Tara said, "Possibly it is someone of wealth or a warlike government."

Several of them nodded.

"It may have taken that long for Dearing to find Talos's power source where we left it in the Artic, and then enlist someone to reconstruct him." Celwyn tracked Qing as he hopped across the chess table and knocked pieces to the floor. Only the pawns. Verne had forgotten to put them away, and his playful little friend didn't hesitate in case someone else noticed.

Bartholomew asked, "Xiau, was it just fraternal jealousy between you and Talos?"

"Possibly. Or it was all done for an unknown reason." Kang shrugged.

"I see. It is not too fanciful to assume Talos told Dearing why so that he could enlist his help." Celwyn thought a bit and added, "Or he promised Dearing something."

"I agree." The automat placed his napkin on the table. "Let's go have a chat with him."

The magician checked on Tara, who looked a bit drawn.

Valentine saw it, too. "I will escort her to her cabin. The Captain has kindly provided us with more elaborate accommodations."

"Just down the hall," Tara told Celwyn and tried a tired wink.

Kang tugged on his sleeve. "Let's go."

"All right, all right."

Chapter 6

IF DEARING HAD FOUND CELWYN'S earlier visit irritating, the magician wanted to be sure that this time, his annoyance knew no bounds.

Before they reached the cell, the magician silenced the hum of the turbines and brought forth a full complement of cellos. They played the same waltz that had accompanied Dearing as he unwillingly led Talos across the deck of his ship. By design, the music grew in discordance and volume until Dearing covered his ears and bellowed curses. When he opened his eyes again, Celwyn and Kang stood in front of him.

It was like someone had turned off a switch; the pirate stared and approached the bars of his cell as if pulled by an invisible string. If he hadn't been so muscle-bound, he could have reached through and tweaked the automat's nose.

Dearing frowned in confusion, while Kang returned the regard as if inspecting a new breed of monkey. When the magician entered the pirate's mind, he found a few surprises, including Dearing's most immediate thought; *This is him? He is what this is all about?*

Kang yawned and said, "Where did you meet my brother?"

"Jakarta."

Celwyn nodded at the truth of the answer.

Without being asked, Dearing said, "When he didn't return after his mission to capture you, I scouted the area where I expected him to be." The pirate narrowed his eyes at Celwyn. "And found debris from my ship that he borrowed... that was you?"

The magician just smiled at him. Dearing sneered and pivoted until he again studied the automat—with intensity, like he expected him to sprout wings.

Celwyn murmured in Kang's ear, "Just now, Dearing recalled how he lost nearly a hundred men diving the Arctic Sea to retrieve Talos's power source. He must know of someone who builds automats."

"It would seem so," Kang whispered back.

They withstood Dearing's regard for several minutes, with only the faint sounds of the submarine keeping them company.

"You rebuilt Talos," Kang told the pirate.

Dearing's eyes dropped, and he studied the floor of his cell. The magician caused a bottle of wine and a platter of succulent steak and vegetables to appear beside the pirate. When the aroma reached them, the magician wished he hadn't eaten so much at dinner.

Dearing sucked on his lips for a scant second before grabbing a handful of meat and stuffing it into his mouth. They watched as juice ran off his chin and into the mysterious recesses of his beard.

"What did Talos promise you?" Celwyn asked in a purr.

Dearing shook his head and continued to stuff meat in his mouth.

"Come now, he would have told you, certainly," Kang said.

In Dearing's thoughts, his sensory appetite stayed at the forefront. The magician explored further until he found what they needed to know.

"Interesting."

Kang said, "Oh?"

"I'll tell you upstairs." He switched to Dearing. "Where are your other worm-eaten little ships?"

"*Little*?" The pirate snarled like a dog and pictured his ships, as expected. Again, Celwyn discovered many of the answers they needed but was constrained by not knowing what else Captain Nemo wanted to know.

Luckily, Kang had his own questions as well.

"Where did you rebuild Talos?"

The pirate had begun to eat again, but at the question, the food fell from his fingers, and he wouldn't meet their gaze. While the silence built, Dearing's thoughts moved fast and could be picked like ripe tomatoes.

The magician winked at Kang. With a most satisfied smile, the automat asked, "Who rebuilt him? Was it Minsky?"

Dearing's head jerked up, and he dropped the plate. The magician dissolved it and the remains of the meal. The pirate couldn't keep the glint of fear out of his eyes, and the picture utmost in his thoughts was of a gnarled, gnome-like man standing in profile while his crabbed hands moved quickly—as if electrified, as he hovered over a workbench. Although the magician silently sent several hints and suggestions for the pirate to think of the gnome's face, he wouldn't—or couldn't—do it.

"Does Minsky still have his glass eye?" the automat asked.

No answer, but at last Celwyn was treated to a clear picture of Minsky's face and the eye.

Kang tried again. "Have you seen Sultan Mahmud's palace?"

Dearing slammed chest first into the cage and shook it. "Why do you ask?"

Celwyn couldn't help it. He laughed. "Because that is where you sent the vampire you captured and sold." He bowed Kang ahead of him as they headed toward the stairs leading upward again.

"What should I leave for Dearing to remember us by? A small crocodile with blue eyes like his own?" Celwyn glanced back at the pirate, who still raged and shook the bars of his cage. "Or something slithery?"

"Your choice." Kang chuckled. "Better yet, make sure it has Talos's face."

When they entered the study, the improvised dining table had been removed, Tara had retired, and the bridge game had started. Verne had drawn Bartholomew as a partner and blinked disarmingly at him. The big man acknowledged them as they walked in, and glared at the top of Verne's head.

After Celwyn floated a tray of whiskies to the others, a separate tray brought Valentine a bottle of strong claret. The magician had noticed that neither vampire cared that much for whiskey.

"Who is winning?" Kang asked.

Bartholomew selected a card and threw it on the table. "Don't ask."

Valentine seemed content with the Captain as a partner. Their relationship would never be warm, but their common purpose united them.

Outside the aquatic window, a thin line of stars twinkled above the water line, and the clock behind Captain Nemo chimed the ten o'clock hour. *Goodbye England, and to my favorite trunk languishing at the Claridge's Hotel,* Celwyn thought.

"The next time I'm in Britain, I must continue north and visit the family home."

Kang raised both brows at the magician. "It still exists?"

"Of course." Celwyn grinned at him. "The aunt of my third cousin on my mother's side was the con-sort of the Earl of Orange. One of their offspring still resides there."

Bartholomew laughed. "If they knew your father was still alive and nearby, the Earl's descendent would lock himself in the basement and hide inside a trunk."

The magician joined him in the joke. "Probably." He poured another cup, thinking that if so, they should run far instead.

Meanwhile, Verne raised his chin, and with a determined look, like he expected to battle the others for the bid, said, "Four spades."

Celwyn checked. Bartholomew had nary a spade. Beside him, Kang smirked as only another victim of Verne's bidding habits could.

"Tell us about your visit with Dearing," Bartholomew said. "The story can't be worse than my hand."

Celwyn regarded Captain Nemo. "Sir, have you had enough of this for the day?" Nemo's face sagged with fatigue, and he would probably be at the helm when they powered out of the North Sea at midnight.

"Two hearts." Nemo expelled his breath. "Go ahead. It will complete the picture before we resume our discussion tomorrow."

"As you wish," Celwyn said. "First, having questions asked of Dearing with my simultaneous monitoring of what he really knows is working."

"It is." The Professor chuckled without humor. "Also, Dearing looked quite surprised to see me."

"Yes, as if he was expecting someone not only mysterious but recognizable." Celwyn tapped a nail on his saucer. Qing's head popped up from behind the library books. He was either hiding something there or chewing on something he knew was not allowed. "Wonder why Dearing was so startled."

"I do also." Captain Nemo covered a yawn and blinked at his hand. "Mr. Soriano, you have the bid." Nemo laid his cards out for Valentine to use and joined the others on the sofas.

"What all did you learn?"

Kang said, "Dearing initially met Talos in Jakarta, and months later, as we thought, he retrieved Talos' power disk from the Arctic Sea."

"What is so amusing?" Valentine asked Celwyn as he took his first trick. The magician tilted his head at Kang, thinking it best to let the automat tell them.

Kang leaned back with a faraway look of remembrance in his eyes. "It takes a rare and specialized skill to build a functioning body around an automat's existing power source. The disk has memories, skills, speech, and other things, and needs to be intricately blended with the physical body." He caressed his chin. "Also, the particular 'skin' that we use is unique. I am amused because Dearing is afraid of whoever they used to rebuild Talos."

When the bridge game ended, the others joined them on the sofas, including Qing, who had been spying on them from the bookshelves. Without any sign of guilt, the mechanical bird pushed at the porcelain cup he'd heard earlier, probably hoping to hear the pinging again.

"Whoever can build an automat can make birds like Qing and other animals?" Bartholomew asked.

Kang nodded.

"I found the name 'Minsky' utmost in Dearing's worries." The magician relived the pirate's thoughts. "He showed a distinct measure of fear when he heard us say it."

"I wonder why." Valentine rubbed his chin.

Captain Nemo humphed. "I didn't think the bastard had any."

"Minsky's talents are not a free service. My guess is the pirate either tried to cheat Minsky out of his fee or attacked him. The Russian is not to be trifled with." The automat studied Celwyn like a prize at the fair. "Could you duplicate Minsky from Dearing's memory of him?"

"But, of course."

"It might prove useful at some point," Kang said.

Bartholomew pretended he didn't hear the exchange about effigies, which he was terrified of, stretched his legs, and yawned. "Lots of nice possibilities, I'm sure."

Captain Nemo frowned as the clock struck the eleven o'clock hour. "Very much so. Is Dearing the only one who is afraid of this Russian?"

"I heard of him long ago." The automat shrugged. "Minsky is a craftsman. He is not immortal, but very old. It is said he knows how to call up the dark powers. That could be what Dearing is really afraid of, not just paying his fee."

"Or he saw an example of Minsky's ire," Celwyn said.

"Perhaps." Kang blinked at them a moment before speaking again. "He also has served the Romanoffs for centuries, and if they become displeased, Dearing's pirate activities could be hampered, or worse."

"I think worse has just happened to the bastard." Bartholomew laughed. "We have him."

Celwyn agreed. "It turns out Talos only told Dearing about the Professor's atomic secrets. He didn't know about the flying machine."

"That is wonderful news." Nemo stood and shook his trousers down. "Please continue. I must leave you soon."

"There is some excellent news. Dearing has been to Sultan Mahmud's palace. I saw some of it pictured in his mind, and we'll be able to extract details from him." Celwyn asked Nemo, "Sir, perhaps you could accompany me on the next visit to the cells? I do not know the questions you need answered." When a low growl escaped the vampire, the magician hurriedly told him, "As long as you don't hurt Dearing until we're done with him, of course, you would be welcome to join us."

The growl subsided. Valentine pulled down his vest and tried to look virtuous. "Better that I go than Tara. She wouldn't be as restrained—or as lenient—as I can be."

The magician smothered a laugh and wondered about that.

A series of gongs resounded in the submarine's belly and the floor under their feet vibrated.

"It is time." Nemo saluted them and departed.

Chapter 7

B Y NOON THE NEXT DAY, CELWYN had produced a passable drawing of the interior and exterior of the *Quarto*. To help direct their efforts, and prepare the vampires for bad news, he depicted the details of the darkest and dreariest part of the ship where they held Valentine's niece. Yesterday, he had found a contingent of pirates in Dearing's mind parading in front of Miss Redifer in various stages of inebriation. It didn't appear they did anything else, probably because their payment was tied to delivering the merchandise in perfect condition.

On another front, the magician had also been busy. As an adorable fly, he visited Dearing's cell long enough to plant a few thoughts. Before he flew back, Dearing unwittingly rewarded him with the information to work on something else they would need.

Tara arrived in the study and crossed to the chess table. The magician had just finished coloring in the various rooms of the Sultan's palace, which had taken a while. Not using magic was tedious, but necessary, so that the drawing would last if he left the ship. Dearing's memory did not include any of the service rooms, storage, or kitchen. The pirate also had not visited the adjoining village or the coastline. Instead, his carnal activities took up his time. No matter. Celwyn had caught enough glimpses of the guards to record where they were deployed.

Tara pointed. "Is that the main room where the Sultan conducts his business?"

"Yes. In Dearing's memory, the room is nearly the width of the palace; just one long, wide hallway with Mahmud's entourage at one end. At the other are his army of accountants and clerks. It seems he lacks trust."

"Where are his generals and military?" She leaned closer to the magician to study the drawing. Celwyn didn't mind at all. She smelled like spices, flowers, and danger.

"From what I have discovered, the generals report to the Sultan but are headquartered elsewhere." Celwyn laid a finger on the north wing. "No clue as to how many total guards there are, only how many Dearing saw on duty."

She took a step toward the aquatic window. "Where are we right now?" On the other side of the glass, a variety of yellow fish hovered in large numbers, suspended in the water as if in a painting. Behind them, a cloud of flotsam swirled, extending in rings outward into the shadows as the ship moved away.

"About three hundred miles into our journey. If I had to guess, we are nearing the Iberian Peninsula." Celwyn studied her. "How is your side?"

"Much better, thank you." She smiled fondly at him. "I let the Professor in on a secret; vampires heal fast. I am almost back to normal and can move my arm without pain." She demonstrated by using it to tilt his face toward hers. "You should have told me how terrible my hair looked." She kissed him. "My new cabin has a much larger mirror."

He kissed her back. "I should also replenish your wardrobe. I hear it will be an additional two days until we stop in Algiers and where you can obtain anything."

"Please keep the clothes serviceable in case we run into the pirate ship before then."

As the *Nautilus* moved through the water, scattering masses of fish, she gazed out the window with interest. From what Celwyn could determine, the submarine traveled about fifty feet below the surface—low enough to avoid sailing ships, but high enough not to worry about submerged obstacles, such as shipwrecks, deep trenches, and shelves. Their journey illustrated the purpose of the underwater maps that Nemo created, and that the automat drooled over.

"The main shipping lanes are above us. From what the Professor said, in several hours, we'll ascend closer to the surface and pick up speed."

The water above them refracted little light. Tara followed his gaze. "That means it is at least a partially sunny day above us, correct?"

"Perhaps." The magician looked down at her, enjoying her so much he couldn't remember what he had planned to ask. "It … is nearly the luncheon hour. Do you know where the others are?"

"Yes. Valentine is in his cabin. The Professor and Bartholomew are supposed to be in the map room, but I do not know where that is."

"Two doors aft toward the spiral stairs. Xiau thinks of it as heaven and his personal playroom."

She laughed. "And he's corrupted Bartholomew into this nefarious activity?"

"Of course."

As he spoke, Verne trotted in with his notebook and a fistful of pens. He stopped short at the table.

"I assume this is the Sultan's palace." The author studied Celwyn's drawing for a moment. "Ah. I have heard of this place. Most interesting." He continued to the chess table. "Do you think our luncheon will be early?" He rubbed his stomach.

Celwyn grinned at him. "We can hope."

Tara took the chair opposite the author and arranged her skirts. "We have not had a chance to talk very much, Mr. Verne. I would love to hear about your most recent book."

The author's eyes twinkled with happiness, and as he began talking about his passion, his fear of vampires evaporated into the world of books. No matter his annoying habits, Verne had a wonderful imagination. Celwyn added glasses of wine to their table and moved to the sofa. When Qing joined him, he walked up his leg and hopped onto the cushion to sit there like a person would, seeming to wait for something.

After a few moments, Celwyn realized what was missing and brought a dozen flutes and a melancholy cello into the room. The magician held a finger in the air, directing as the music wove around the key of F before settling into the minor keys. When the automat and Bartholomew walked in, they continued to debate something from one of the maps they had found. Qing moved over before Bartholomew sat on him.

Kang perched across from them and bestowed a wistful look on at the table; his unsubtle way of requesting a plate of cookies. Celwyn decided against it since their luncheon drew near. Instead, he enlarged and floated the picture of the pirate ship and the palace to hover in front of them. From any angle, they had an excellent view. To the magician, the perspective appeared perfect, and the details real.

Verne exclaimed, "Unbelievable! Your magic is very useful."

"I drew them without magic so that they will last a long while. Note that when I am not here, they will appear one-dimensional only."

"Incredible, Jonas," Bartholomew marveled. He touched the nearest picture and wiggled his fingers through it. "You saw all this in Dearing's mind?"

"Yes." Celwyn indicated the shadowed areas. "These darkened locations are the ones the bastard has either forgotten or never saw."

Kang said, "We will have more opportunities to mine Dearing's memory. There are many things the Captain wants to ask him."

As he spoke, Nemo joined them and stopped still in the doorway to stare at the floating drawings that spanned the floor to the ceiling. He approached, and a most satisfied expression spread across his stern face.

"Very useful, Jonas." Captain Nemo said, "Though I am not sure how yet."

As the crew arrived to set up the table for their luncheon, the Professor pointed out some details to Bartholomew. Nemo continued to study the drawings and note the distances to the entrances and the location of the guard shacks on the grounds.

After their questions, Celwyn brought the drawings down to size, and asked Nemo, "May I?" Indicating the wall between the bookshelves and the window.

"Yes, please."

While the crew served the soup, Nemo tried to cover a yawn. Although he looked a bit drawn around the eyes, his speech and movements seemed as quick, or quicker, than usual. Verne occupied the chair to his left. Tara and Valentine sat on Nemo's right. When Celwyn's stomach growled loudly, he wondered if they could hear it. Of course, someone did. At the other end of the table, the automat's head jerked up, and he grinned at the magician.

Nemo regarded them like he was hesitant to say something they may not want to hear. That could cover many things. While they waited for him to speak, the magician checked the crystal decanters on the bar. Qing hadn't been pecking at them lately. If only Nemo's problems were as simple as a misbehaving bird.

"We are all aware of our situation, and I wanted to speak with you." Nemo watched as the last soup bowl was filled, and when the crewman withdrew, he continued, "It will take about eighteen days to reach the island of Bintan and the Sultan's palace. This timeline assumes we enter the Red Sea at Suez." He glanced at Bartholomew.

The big man put down his spoon with a stifled groan. "I presume by way of an underground river?"

Nemo shook his head. "Actually, it is a canal. Perhaps better for our purposes."

"They began work on that nearly twenty years ago, you know," Verne said.

Nemo rubbed his spoon on the tablecloth as he tracked the serving cart entering the room. "Traveling this route is partially how we'll catch up to the *Quarto*—if we don't find her sooner. Hopefully, she will be delayed by the weather before then."

Valentine asked. "Wouldn't they be arrested by the Suez authorities? Why would they allow a pirate ship in the canal?"

"Bribery," Captain Nemo answered.

Verne nodded in agreement. "The pirates would change their flags to legitimate ones before they passed through and probably be towed by steam-powered tugboats." Several at the table frowned, picturing how that would look.

They ate in silence for several minutes before Nemo spoke again. "Over the next several days, we will develop our plan of attack, whether on land or sea." He tilted his head to the side and back. "Isn't it fitting that the weather will dictate how this will occur?"

Kang said, "It is. I can see several advantages to confronting them either way."

The Captain's expression gave nothing away. "We will know more after we visit Dearing this afternoon."

The anticipation in the room escalated and caused Celwyn to smile. Nemo had waited a long time for this.

As the crew served the fish, he spoke. "You have all probably wondered about my past with Dearing, and why I pursue him. It isn't a pleasant story. For now, I will only say that the world would be better without him. Ships full of passengers will be safer. And thousands of slaves and villagers from Seville to the Bay of Bengal will rejoice when he is gone."

"We are traveling that far?" Bartholomew asked.

Nemo shrugged. "I do not know for certain yet. It depends on what we discover from Dearing." To Valentine and Tara, he said, "I beg your indulgence. After we retrieve Miss Redifer, we may need to take a short detour before returning to Italia or wherever you would like to go. If that is not convenient, I will arrange for your transport."

"I understand, as does my uncle." Tara locked eyes with the Captain. "We will be in your debt after this and most grateful for her return."

"I second the sentiment; however, I would be even more grateful if I am the instrument of Dearing's demise, along with all his men." This time, Valentine stopped short of a growl.

Celwyn suggested, "Perhaps we can draw straws? I also wish him ill for his treatment of Miss McFein."

Tara murmured through a grin, "Miss McFein is right here and reserves the right to destroy him, also."

Bartholomew chuckled and reached for his water goblet. "Can you imagine how many contenders there are in various lands for the honor of killing the villain?"

"Well, to provide reparations to his victims ... we could auction off the privilege." Kang wiggled a brow. That usually meant he was serious, not being fanciful, but he also seemed thoughtful—as if the idea would work.

"Professor, that would be a lovely gesture, but perhaps illegal," Verne said.

Valentine's growl won. "When I am done with him, there will be nothing left to bid on."

Nervous laughter followed that statement. "Just so you know, I have placed a block around Dearing's cell to protect the crew, and to avoid surprises," the magician told the Captain. As a hint to Valentine to leave Dearing alone, this would do for now.

Nemo nodded his thanks and went back to his lunch.

"What do you know of Dearing's background?" the older vampire asked the table.

"He is the son of Sir Robert Dearing and the daughter of the King of Spain," the automat answered. "That news accounts for the blue eyes, but not the villainous intentions."

After they finished their coffee and tortes, the Captain sighed with satisfaction and patted his stomach. "We will arrive in Algiers tomorrow for supplies and a quick trip to the shops." He nodded at Valentine and Tara. "And for those needing additions to their wardrobes. It will be a short stop. Tomorrow night, we will stay off the coast for our maintenance during the night."

"Excellent." Valentine said, "Mr. Bartholomew has graciously loaned clothes, but I hope to pick up a few things."

The author spoke up. "I can direct you to a tailor who keeps some pre-made clothing on hand for travelers in need such as ourselves."

"For women, too?" Tara's voice held hope.

"I do not remember, but on Herbeuse Street there are many *l'habillement* shops."

Chapter 8

I T LACKED A FEW MINUTES BEFORE four in the afternoon when Nemo and Celwyn descended to the lower deck. As they walked, a companionable silence accompanied them.

When they reached the cellblock, they found Dearing asleep, his snoring sounding like a nasty fairy snorting around in a pigsty. After they reached the cell, Nemo studied the pirate; his first intimate view of the man. He took his time. It had only been two days, and already an unpleasant aroma drifted out of the cell.

The Captain removed the pistol from his belt and cocked it, the click loud in the cavernous room.

Dearing jerked upright and flung a log-size arm in front of his chest. He glared at Nemo.

"Who are you?"

Since he didn't know, the magician didn't intend to tell him. Instead, he entered Dearing's thoughts and toured.

This time, he found the bastard concerned about his fate. The bravado still ruled, but Dearing toyed with what information he could sell to gain his release, or if he could trick them into releasing him. *Not likely*, Celwyn thought. When an unexpected worry flitted across the man's mind, Celwyn didn't hesitate and noted the bank numbers and locations of Dearing's banks.

It only took seconds for the magician to gather other choice tidbits about Dearing's wealth, including gold stored in banks in Macau and Hong Kong and his stockpile of loot at his compound in the Sulu Islands. The last item was what they'd been hoping to find. Dearing also speculated about Celwyn and what the magician would be interested in. Jewelry? Women? The magician wrinkled his nose, finding the pirate's aroma grew with each moment.

Captain Nemo holstered his pistol. With a hooded expression, he regarded Dearing like a dung heap. As the seconds became minutes, the magician wondered if the pirate would cooperate more or less if he knew this was Nemo.

"In 1850, you plundered Plymouth Museum. You stole many paintings and murdered the employees there." Nemo looked ready to spit.

Dearing stood. With undisguised curiosity, he gazed down his nose at Nemo. His expression confirmed that he still did not know who Nemo was; otherwise, his response would have been different.

"Some of it was yours?" He asked as if they were fellow thieves and murderers.

The pirate's thoughts swelled with pride as he pictured ornate hallways with sculptures on pedestals in front of gilded frames. Without any break in his internal picture show came a sudden close-up view of Dearing running a guard through with his long knife that was repeated several times. Then he stepped on the man he had killed as he followed his men further inside the museum. *How much of this was wishful thinking?* The magician wondered. In room after room, the pirates smashed artifacts while others ripped paintings from the walls. The remaining guards ran, only to be shot in the back by the pirates.

Celwyn made sure Nemo saw him tap the side of his nose, a prearranged signal confirming the bastard's actions at the Plymouth.

"Where are the paintings you stole from the Abbaye de Graville museum?" Nemo named the renowned museum in Le Havre.

When Dearing's lips compressed, his thoughts crystallized around a windowless storage room. The magician sent Dearing a hint to turn his viewpoint slightly, so Celwyn could see the way the room had been set up, and who guarded it. What the magician discovered went beyond the expected. *How interesting...* The pirate's memory shifted to a panoramic view out an open door to a horseshoe-shaped bay under the pinkish skies of dusk. Celwyn would remember that exact scene and the vibrant jungle surrounding the water.

They now had further confirmation. The magician sent Nemo a silent message. *"I have noted where he stores the paintings … and the bay nearby. There are buildings with flat red roofs and huts on the north side. Perhaps you can confirm which bay? I think it is in the Sulu Islands."*

Nemo barely nodded amid his growing annoyance. His brows nearly touched, and he frowned.

"Manuk Bay, eh?" Nemo asked as if it was already known.

Dearing's face burned with anger, confirming the guess, and the pirate reached for Nemo through the bars. The Captain grabbed his wrist and twisted.

"Apparently so." Nemo's eyes flicked to Celwyn to be ready. "Too bad you don't have enough guards."

The pirate roared and shook the bars of the cage. Celwyn turned them hot. Dearing's hand flamed, but not before the magician caught a swift and telling glimpse of Dearing's guards at his compound. *Nicely done*, he told the Captain. The magician would arrange several visits with the pirate until they had a complete accounting of the guards.

"Excuse my reaction, but he obviously needed to learn his manners." Celwyn stared at Dearing, totally understanding Valentine's urge to eliminate him without ceremony.

"Not a problem, I would react the same if I could." Nemo faced the cell. "Perhaps he would like to earn a bottle of wyine for his dinner."

Celwyn shrugged. "He probably has nothing to trade."

When the magician removed the burn from Dearing's hand, the pirate stopped massaging it and shot Celwyn a sullen glare.

"Well, sir? We don't have all afternoon." Nemo waited for a beat, and swiveled, ready to leave. "So be it."

Celwyn preceded him, and they had almost reached the staircase leading upward before Dearing called out.

"Tell me, where is this dungeon?" He rattled the cage he stood in.

Silently the magician reminded Nemo that he had knocked Dearing out before they brought him on board, and he had only seen the bottom of the spiral stairs.

Nemo told the pirate, "Perhaps later." He started upward.

"What do you want to know?" Dearing yelled.

From halfway up, Nemo leaned over the rail and asked, "Where are your ships?"

The pirate flopped back on his bunk and laughed. Of course, he imagined the ships in his mind, and Celwyn took his time exploring. He nodded at Nemo as he told Dearing, "It seems you only have a few vessels left, what with three on their way to Bintan Island and the Sultan."

"Ha!" Dearing's laughter reached them as he pictured all four ships and a panorama of even more ships at his compound.

When they reached the top of the stairs, Celwyn concentrated on Wye, asking him to sit outside the

pirate's cage and keep him company for a while—
with his teeth on display, of course.

Chapter 9

After dinner, everyone remained in the study to plan and exchange information. Tara yawned twice but shook her head when Valentine suggested she retire for the night. Celwyn wished she would rest, but knew she would stay longer if he tried to insist. If nothing else, his hundreds of years had been a learning experience in the world of women. He smiled at her, most appreciative that she walked with him in it.

As the *Nautilus* traveled at speed just below the surface of the Mediterranean Sea, the last rays of sunset reflected across the water above them. The Professor reminded the more nervous members of the room that Nemo kept someone on the periscope when they traveled in this manner.

He had told no one, but, at times, Celwyn felt some anxiety if they traveled too deep. The submarine had a sensory mechanism that sounded an alarm if it neared objects such as other ships, wrecks, or undersea mountains. For their safety, the ship had sensors that sounded an alarm if they encountered overly warm water from an undersea volcano, for instance. The magician didn't understand how it worked, but Bartholomew and Kang did. The big man's word for it was "fascinating."

Captain Nemo welcomed everyone as they gathered around the sofas and made themselves comfortable. "We need to talk."

Even Qing left the aquatic window to perch on Nemo's chair as he and Celwyn related highlights of the information they'd gleaned from Dearing. Tara's hand tensed next to Celwyn's as she listened, but she said nothing.

"Once we find Dearing's horde, I need to study some of the paintings in detail." Nemo's voice did not sound annoyed, instead concentrated as if the subject was somehow crucial to him. "Jonas will tell you what else he discovered in Dearing's thoughts."

"As you wish." Celwyn cleared his throat. Time for his after-dinner tea. He gestured, and a service sat on the table in front of them.

"You go right ahead," Kang drawled with a teasing grin.

The magician resisted the urge to decorate him in bright colors, instead saying, "There are four of Dearing's ships accompanying the *Quarto* to the Sultan's palace. They appear to be built for speed and each has a complement of more than two dozen guns. Two of the ships have double decks of cannons." He tilted his head and said, "Sir, wouldn't it be entertaining if the escort ships disappeared, one at a time?" Celwyn also wondered why the pirates had so much security for just one vampire.

Nemo's eyes danced without humor. "Very much so, and it can be arranged."

"It is sounding more and more as if we would prefer to encounter the ships at sea." Bartholomew blew out a match and puffed on his cigar.

"Yes, we would," Nemo said. "My men can acquit themselves on land if necessary. But I would prefer to use this ship. It would prevent many casualties."

The Professor jumped to his feet and retrieved the drawing of the ship from the wall. "Tell us things we do not know about the *Quatro*."

Celwyn once again enlarged the page until it stood greater than eight feet tall and wide, the details visible to them all. Tara's glance at him confirmed she had dreaded this moment.

"I'm afraid there isn't good news. On the *Quatro*, Miss Redifer is kept in the bowels of the ship and covered in chains."

A low snarl escaped Valentine. "Go on."

Nemo left them to answer a call on the intercom. When he returned, he said, "We will be most careful not to attack that ship without verifying your niece's location."

"I will be a delicate, but swift fly visiting the *Quarto* before then," Celwyn said.

Kang snorted his opinion.

Verne asked, "What else did you learn?" The little author remained at the chess table, and Qing had joined him, watching the room with glittering eyes.

"We confirmed Dearing's men took paintings and artifacts when they raided and burned the museum in Rotterdam, just one of a dozen museums he has destroyed and stolen from. It seems he has as strong an affinity for artwork as he does for gold. Because we had success with our interrogation today, we know exactly where his loot is located." After Kang raised a fist in approval and Tara nodded hers, the magician continued. "The Captain intends to retrieve the treasures from Dearing's headquarters on Manuk Island. That is part of the Sulu Islands. Today we gathered many nuggets from our guest, but we need further information."

"We will learn that when we rescue Miss Redifer." Nemo puffed, filling the air with the scent of sweet tobacco.

Gongs resounded across the lower deck but were not repeated. Celwyn had learned that the amount and spacing of the gongs signaled many things. The ones they had just heard indicated a change of shift of the crew, nothing more.

Nemo tapped out his pipe and stood. "When we arrive in Algiers, my Lieutenant will inquire at the docks about Dearing's ships. By this time tomorrow, we may have a much better idea of how far behind the pirates we really are."

Chapter 10

Prague

FILTERED LIGHT STREAMED through the parlor window overlooking the rose beds and lawns of Tellyhouse. Outside the front door, the carriage and team of two Arabians waited. Edward, their footman, driver, and head of security, relaxed in the cab, and his top hat shaded his eyes while he waited.

Annabelle stood in front of the parlor window, her thoughts inward, not on the flowers outside. She wore a most feminine lace dress while she smoked a long cheroot and blew smoke rings at the ceiling. Although still young, as the mistress of Tellyhouse, the responsibility made her feel old at times. Especially when she worried about the Professor, Bartholomew, and Uncle Celwyn. They were supposed to be here, too.

From the desk behind her, Patrick replaced his pen and asked, "Do you feel well?"

"Yes, dear," she said with a frown that wrinkled her fine skin like a ripple on a tennis ball. "I'm just worried a bit."

Patrick joined his wife at the window. They seemed a perfect match. Blonde complimenting blonde. Patrick was always quiet and thoughtful with a bearing military, while his beautiful wife Annabelle had an unconventional and free nature. Years ago, she had bribed Celwyn and the Professor to smuggle her from Singapore to Prague to escape an arranged marriage. By the time they'd arrived, all she wanted to do was marry Captain Patrick Swayne. Her wilder tendencies faded once they established Tellyhouse, and she became responsible for two orphans.

"What worries you?"

Annabelle shook a telegram at him. "Uncle Celwyn sends us this," she raised her eyes heavenward, "which says they are dropping everything to sail off on another adventure!"

He put an arm around her shoulders. "They tend to do that, I've noticed." From the conservatory at the rear of the house, the echoing notes of Otto's piano lesson continued, rather discordantly. "Otto's substitute teacher doesn't seem as good as his regular one." Another string of tortured notes reached them. "At least it is almost over. What did Sully say this man's name was?"

Annabelle thought. "I do not know... it sounded like Gasper ... Gaspard ... something like that."

"You are correct. I heard it as Gaspard," Patrick said.

Mrs. Elizabeth Kang entered the room, dressed for town and her errands. She studied her hat in the mirror above the hearth and tucked an errant strand of flame-red hair behind her ear. Although older than Annabelle, Elizabeth remained a most striking woman in both appearance and bearing. As she put on her gloves, she transferred her attention to Annabelle. "What is wrong?"

Annabelle faced her friend and confidant. She patted her stomach, and said, "Everything here is fine. I am just worried about Uncle and Bartholomew and, of course, the Professor because they are haring off across the world again."

"I am also—" Elizabeth finished fussing with her hat and, at a noise, turned toward the hallway.

"Excuse me." Through the open door, a medium-sized dark-haired man stood in the shadows holding his hat. "The piano lesson has finished. I have another starting soon on Pearl Street."

Elizabeth said, "Why, that is very near where I am going. Would you care to ride there with me?" She glanced at the grandfather clock. "It is almost eleven now."

The man bowed. "I would be honored, madam."

Minutes later, Annabelle and Patrick stood at the parlor window as Gaspard escorted Elizabeth to the carriage and followed her inside.

"Doesn't that man remind you of someone?" Annabelle could only see his profile... still...

Patrick pursed his lips. "I suppose. Of all things, he reminds me of the Professor."

"That is probably why Elizabeth offered him a ride."

After a lunch of roast beef sandwiches and American potato salad, Patrick herded the boys ahead of him to the stairs leading to their classroom.

"Where is Miss Elizabeth?" Zander demanded. "She usually does our history lesson." Worry was written across his young face.

On their way to Prague, Bartholomew, Professor Kang, and Celwyn had found him starving on the streets of Pushkari, and in the last two years, he had grown taller and more confident. Another lost lad, Otto, had joined them last year on their way home from Singapore and became Zander's brother. Orphan to orphan in spirit, and fast friends.

Patrick leaned against the banister and made sure they did not see the worry in his eyes. "Never fear, I am well-versed in history. We may talk about the Napoleonic War if you two can prove you've done your homework."

Otto nodded with the confidence of the prepared. Zander yelled, "Cannons!" and raced ahead up the stairs.

Annabelle followed them to the hallway and checked the front door.

Where is Elizabeth?

By late afternoon, everyone was worried and hiding it from Zander and Otto with nervous smiles and vague answers. Their charges were older than young boys, but still impressionable, and not yet young men. An argument could be made that because of their traumatic early years, they should be protected from dangerous situations for a while longer.

Conductor Smith usually drove their train but maintained the Tellyhouse garden while in Prague. He'd been sent out to look for the carriage. As the two-seater calèche rolled down the driveway, it leaned to the side with the weight of the Conductor, and Annabelle wondered if it would make it downtown and back.

While a little voice in her head whispered that Edward would not be gone this long without sending a message, she picked up her embroidery and gazed out the picture window. Their driver had a knack for punctuality and displayed absolute steadfastness in everything he did. It made her worry grow in leaps and bounds; the errands Elizabeth had gone to do were the same ones she did every Wednesday. Annabelle's heart raced when she saw the calèche return without them.

As dinnertime neared, Patrick announced he would go with the Conductor to the police and see what could be done. The entire time he was gone, Annabelle paced in front of the entrance to the parlor; a location from which she could watch out the window and the front door at the same time.

The boys came downstairs and stared at the door. When she tried to give Otto and Zander an explanation, she faltered. Mrs. Thomas, their housekeeper and the ultimate authority over everyone in the house, stepped up and insisted the boys help her move everything out of the summer storage room. The disquiet in the housekeeper's eyes confirmed Annabelle's worst fears.

Patrick and the Conductor came home without Elizabeth, or Edward—or any news at all.

Chapter 11

THE NEXT MORNING THE DAMN BIRDS woke Annabelle as usual, and when she realized Patrick wasn't asleep beside her, and with dread realized why, she dressed as fast as she could and went downstairs. As she reached the last step, their footman Sully rushed by on the run and on out the front door.

Annabelle ran after him.

Overnight, the carriage had come back. Patrick and the Conductor stood on the running board and backed out of the cab holding something, while Sully struggled to pull Edward off the driver's seat from atop the carriage. Blood poured off Edward's head and over everything. Annabelle let out a cry as she reached them.

Patrick tried to block her view as he laid Elizabeth on the ground. When Annabelle reached for her friend, she saw her sightless eyes and slashed throat.

Annabelle sank to her knees. Patrick pulled on her arm, but she wouldn't let go of Elizabeth's hand.

Patrick grabbed Sully. "Take her inside to Mrs. Thomas. Go, man!"

As Sully ushered Annabelle inside, Mrs. Thomas charged toward the door, and the younger woman blurted out what she had seen. The housekeeper's face drained of color, and she lifted her chin in resolution. "Stay here." She about-faced and marched up the stairs to the boys.

Annabelle fought back her sobs as she addressed the maid. "Flossie, please ... please fetch Abe and Andy. Hurry—" She gave the girl a little push toward the side door leading to the garden and stables. As the door closed behind her, Conductor Smith came through the front entrance and stood quietly beside her, holding his hat.

Soft thumps and creaks filtered down from above them as Mrs. Thomas moved around. That floorboard in the classroom protested every time anyone walked across the room... *Elizabeth had mentioned it months ago...* Annabelle started crying again and glanced through the glass on the front door and at the body. *I have to do something*—she wiped her tears and rushed through the parlor to the dining room. Ripping the cloth off the table, she ran back to the front door. She covered the glass as best she could— when they came downstairs, the boys shouldn't see what was out there, especially until Elizabeth had been taken away.

A set of weather-beaten hands took over covering the window. The sympathetic voice of the Conductor seemed to come from far away. "It's going to be all right, Missus."

"I ... I ... can't have the boys see her..." she stammered. From the commotion at the side door, she knew Flossie had found the others.

"Then they won't," the Conductor said. He nodded at Abe, one of his assistants on the train and a fine gardener for Tellyhouse. "Don't let Zander and Otto come down these stairs, and don't let them look out any of the windows."

"Yes, sir." Good-natured Abe always followed orders.

"Mrs. Thomas is upstairs with them now." Annabelle inhaled and held onto the stair rail to regain her composure. "She is trying to keep them from seeing ... outside—but I want to be sure." She checked the front door again. The commotion from horses arriving and the creaking of coach wheels reached them.

"Don't worry, Missus." The Conductor's voice sounded infinitely kind, and so strange right now. He switched to his other assistant. "Andy, go up there and guard the windows on this side of the house. Block the boys from them."

Like his twin brother, Andy obeyed orders well. "Yes, sir." He took the stairs two at a time. When he reached the top, Annabelle swallowed and faced the front door.

"I must go outside again. I must."

The Conductor offered her his arm, and they stepped outside.

The coroner's wagon blocked the Tellyhouse driveway. Three more police wagons encircled their coach, Edward, and the body.

Along with Sully and a pair of uniformed policista, Patrick had been shuffled off to the side by the roses. When he saw Annabelle, he rushed to them. "You shouldn't be out here, my dear."

"I have to."

"If you are sure." Patrick held her close, and over the top of her head, sent the Conductor a nod of understanding.

The older man returned the regard, and his eyes strayed to the open carriage door and the sheet-covered form on the ground. Feet away, a well-dressed and corpulent policeman had cornered Edward while he sat on the running board of a police wagon and a doctor examined his head.

"That isn't a doctor. It is a damn coroner," Patrick said in an aside to the Conductor. Annabelle leaned into him, crying softly while he patted her back. His shirt grew wet, and he searched his pockets for a handkerchief.

"Here you go, sir." Conductor Smith passed one of his own over. "You'll need several, I imagine."

Patrick blinked back his own tears. "Yes. Thank you."

"What happened, sir?" Sully asked.

Patrick eyed Annabelle and saw her nod. He still hesitated before saying, "As you know, yesterday Mrs.

Kang left to run errands but didn't return. For hours we searched for her, then went to the police, and nothing—until this morning."

The coroner jerked his chin at Edward, who wasted no time escaping and crossing the driveway to them. A large bandage encircled his head. At six feet tall, he looked Patrick directly in the eye.

"I am so sorry, sir."

Annabelle cried harder. "It isn't your fault… I should have gone with her."

Patrick inhaled and held his breath. "Please, dear, stop saying that. It won't help." He didn't want to think what would have happened to her, too.

Annabelle's eyes flared and her voice rose. "She was my *friend!*" She pummeled her fists on her husband's chest and then collapsed in his arms. "I'm not going inside until I hear what happened—"

"Tell us quickly," Patrick said to Edward.

Their driver eyed the well-fed policeman who squatted over the body and examined Elizabeth's neck. Patrick turned Annabelle the other way.

"I'm so sorry." Edward wrung his hat in his hands.

"Tell us, man," the Conductor said with the authority they knew well.

Edward's face crumpled as he fought not to cry. "Mrs. Kang brought a man with her when she left here." He pointed to Tellyhouse behind them. "They acted friendly enough and talked about Otto's piano lesson. I drove to Pearl Street. After I parked, I held the door open to help Mrs. Kang out, and something slammed my head." He touched the bandage above his eye.

The fat policeman stood, and they heard his back crack even from twenty feet away. He would be with them soon.

Edward hurried to say, "I woke up in the back of the coach. The man was gone." He gulped. "Mrs. Kang's body was lying on top of me."

The policeman stopped to study the front end of the carriage.

Patrick said more to himself than the others, "This is horrible." Annabelle heard him and cried harder.

Edward said, "She was dead, blood still running off her... I saw ... that it was dark outside. We were in a forest." They watched as the policeman searched under the carriage and sent them inquiring looks. "I found my way out of the countryside and back here. This doctor," he jerked his chin at the coroner, "told me I was hit a half-dozen times, probably every time I woke up." He winced. "He says whoever did it knew how hard to hit a man, but not kill..." His eyes strayed to the body.

"You found your way back here," the Conductor prompted him.

Edward tried to nod and stopped with a grimace. "Yes." He pointed with his eyes. "She was still a little warm when I woke up and found her. Like they kept us someplace until about three or four in the morning."

"Why?" Patrick demanded. "Why did they leave you alive?"

It wasn't as cruel as it sounded, and from his expression, Edward not only understood but knew why. "Probably because whoever did it wanted me to pass this along." He handed a folded page to Patrick, who read it aloud.

"Tell Professor Kang we will meet soon."

"I'll take that." A pudgy hand ripped the paper out of Patrick's fingers. Unmemorable eyes regarded them with hooded suspicion. "Major Jardin of the city's force, at your service. You must be Mr. Swayne, the owner of this house."

Annabelle wiped her eyes on Patrick's shirt and cleared her throat. "I am Mrs. Swayne. Elizabeth's friend—" she wailed and buried her face in Patrick's shirt again. The Conductor handed him another handkerchief.

"Shall we go inside and talk?" Jardin asked.

Patrick squared away in front of him, still holding Annabelle. "No. We have children who shouldn't see or hear any of this."

The Conductor said, "If he is up to it, Edward or I will bring the Mr. and Missus to you after they feel better. We have another coach."

"Who are you, sir?"

"I am employed by Captain Swayne. My name is Smith, and I am the Conductor of their train."

"Why are you here?" Jardin eyed him.

"I work the gardens when the train is not in use." The Conductor crossed his arms.

Patrick could have added a dozen other things that he did without being asked.

Jardin stared at them a moment and waved over one of his men. "Fine, we'll take this coach and the body. One hour—" He glared at Patrick. "One hour, the downtown station on Charles Street."

Chapter 12

Algiers

A S USUAL, THE *NAUTILUS* DROPPED them off a few miles outside their destination on an uninhabited part of the coast. Besides the magician, Bartholomew, and Kang, their party consisted of Verne, the vampires, Lieutenant Granger, and his men.

From their view over the low hills above the city, Algiers bustled with activity as the markets opened for the day. The braying from complaining donkeys reached them clearly. To Celwyn, it felt good being on land again, and he celebrated by adding a field of daisies next to where they gathered, ready for town.

Granger had to urge some of his crewmen into the carts in front of them. They'd hesitate even more if they knew the pairs of horses had been made from the healthier rats the magician found in the bushes.

Once in town, most of the crew would obtain supplies for the larder, while Granger intended to investigate the docks for news of the pirates. That left everyone else a bit of time to shop before the submarine traveled east.

As for gathering news from the docks, Nemo had warned everyone not to get their hopes up. Algiers, with its history of harboring the Barbary pirates, continued to allow a parade of pirate ships to pass through unmolested. Spotting scoundrels at the docks would not be unusual, but knowing a particular ship's name and description would help.

Celwyn eyed Tara beside him. "Finding you acceptable clothes is our most pressing errand." He took the opportunity to survey her. "Although I do make quite fetching garments."

The cart hit a hole, and they bounced and settled again before she touched his hand. "Yes, you do. I need new boots too, by the way." Her eyes clouded. "I will buy a few things in Simone's size, too. She likely will have nothing when we find her."

On Tara's other side, Valentine paused in his search of the nearby brush—probably for tasty game—and said, "Good idea, my dear."

From his position behind them, Bartholomew called out over the noise of the carts and horses, "You do not remember us stopping here on the way to Thale's island, Jonas? It was a quick visit." They hit another hole in the track and veered toward a dead dog before Celwyn got control of the horses again. The canine corpse had been there a while.

"That is correct." The magician asked Verne, "How do we get to the district where the tailors or cobblers are?"

Verne strained to see the buildings in the distance. "If I remember correctly, they will be south of the market area and set back from the water." A light rain pattered the dusty road and the carts. "I hope you can do something about the rain, Jonas."

"But, of course." He waved a hand and added awnings to both carts. "You'll also find umbrellas at your feet for when we arrive at our destination."

The sun had begun its descent to the western horizon by the time their party once again piled into the carts to return to the ship. The magician made a third and fourth cart to haul the ship's supplies. Books, packages of clothes, and what looked suspiciously like a cake box had been piled in the back. For his part, Celwyn had bought a bag of iridescent marbles for Qing; everyone loved presents, even naughty birds. They were also useful for when the magician had to leave the ship for an extended time and Qing needed more toys than usual.

Tara had managed a stop at a perfumery and smelled divine, like a whiff from a mysterious casbah hidden in fields of wildflowers. She also seemed pleased with her new blue dress with ruffles. Celwyn silently told her what he thought, and a satisfied smile crossed her lips.

For their return trek to the ship, Bartholomew drove. Celwyn asked, "Does anyone know if Granger found out anything at the docks?"

The big man shrugged, and the Professor said, "Unknown. I wouldn't suggest invading his thoughts to check. It would only upset him."

"Ha." The magician checked behind them. "Granger's cart is too far away, or I would."

The earlier showers had dissipated, and the Alboran Sea glimmered below them as they neared the rendezvous point beside a grove of cypress trees. After seeing Tara safely on the ground, Celwyn excused himself and approached Nemo's lieutenant, who shook his head.

"I learned nothing this morning," Granger told him. "There is only one avenue left to us, a man named Gunst. After dark, he is supposed to be at a tavern near the cannery."

Of course, the saloon would be disreputable and next to a cannery. Celwyn had never seen one on the docks that wasn't. "That is only a few hours from now. If properly disguised, I would like to accompany you."

Nemo's lieutenant regarded him. "From what the Captain has said and what I've seen, I would welcome your assistance. The less of us, the better, though." His eyes darted toward the others. "They seem to attract trouble instead of repel it."

"Yes, they do." Celwyn tried not to laugh; he couldn't have described his friends, despite their enthusiasm and good intentions, any better. He caught Kang watching them and turned his back on the automat. Kang could read lips. Celwyn pointed at the water, so Granger would look that way also. "Let's not tell anyone, for now, so they won't try to go with us."

"Agreed. They would not blend in well." He kept his attention on the waves. "I'll be in the transport boat by eight tonight, just before the dinner hour."

"Perfect. The Captain can distract the others from following us. If I used magic to do it, their suspicions would be aroused."

Celwyn could imagine the hissy fit the Professor would throw, while Bartholomew would just wish he were going with them. Tonight wouldn't be just an opportunity to tease the automat; during a quiet moment, last night, the magician had agreed with Nemo they should minimize threats to both Kang and Bartholomew. Their value went beyond their friendship and the flying machine—no matter their desire to participate.

Chapter 13

A CLOUDLESS SKY, HEAVY WITH stars, accompanied Celwyn and Granger as they walked into town. Lights from the commercial district guided them, along with the saltiness of the bay. The magician sniffed the air, preferring Tara's perfume by far. Smoke from charcoal fires and the stench of dung heaps mixed with the miasma of spices from the markets. Above it all, the promise of intrigue seemed so tangible he could touch it.

They passed a pen of horses and then a dilapidated brothel, deserted except for a discarded stocking next to the road. Next came a long, narrow brick building with a crumbling façade that must have been there since before the Carnatic Wars. It had no windows and a metal door.

"Makes you wonder what is inside," Celwyn said.

"It does." Granger craned his neck to check over a fence and down the alley between the buildings.

"There are a few men down there. Right after the shadows take over." They kept walking, mutually deciding not to stir things up if it didn't apply to their objective.

"Tell me about yourself?" Celwyn asked. "You have worked for the Captain for a long time?"

Dark-haired and of average height, Granger displayed more than average muscles that strained at his uniform jacket. At about forty years of age, he still retained an American accent, mixed with some interesting phrasing commonly found in London. His mustache had been trimmed with preciseness, just like everything else aboard the *Nautilus*.

"I left the Navy about twenty years ago and fell in with some shady sorts in Marseilles. One day, I tried to hijack some goods destined for the *Nautilus*."

"And Nemo caught you."

"He certainly did. We talked. He made me an offer." They headed down another dark avenue leading to the water, and the pervasive brininess increased tenfold, along with the reek of rotting fish. "Over the years, we have had many adventures. I wouldn't trade this life for anything."

The magician could completely understand. He'd thought about the *Nautilus* and the others and the adventures they had experienced, and the ones they would have. Would he only remain in Prague a short time before wishing he were aboard the ship again? A small sound interrupted his thoughts, and the magician whirled. The hair on his neck had risen—a sign of danger ... and not from a supernatural source. Although not as good as Bartholomew in spotting a threat, the magician recognized the three men following them as not particularly friendly.

Granger spied the men, too. "I understand you have extraordinary talents, Mr. Celwyn. We may need them soon."

"Call me Jonas, I—"

A dagger zinged by the magician's nose and banged blade first into the door they just passed. Celwyn swiveled and Granger crouched low. In a rush, the three men jumped them brandishing knives and clubs.

Granger brought one of them down by his hair as the magician tossed the other hard against a wall. With the third one, he used an old-fashioned punch in the face and backed up for Granger to finish the job by bashing him with a chunk of the fence. It wouldn't do to appear to be anything more than a victimized tourist in case someone communicated with any of the pirates passing through here. The magician cursed under his breath as he remembered something; these ruffians could also be brethren to the Mafioso. For months, everyone on the *Nautilus* had assumed that they had hefty bounties on their heads since the altercation with the vermin last year.

One hoodlum started to get up, and another punch from Granger put him down again.

They made haste down the street.

◦◦◦

Coquillages, the bar of ill-repute, was difficult to find. Dirt covered most of its sign, but the noise from inside confirmed they had found the right place. Only steps away, the Bay of Algiers lapped trash against crusty pylons dating from the Greek raiders.

Granger pushed through the swinging door, and the magician followed, holding back a curtain of beads as they stepped into a dim and smoky room.

English Cockney, gutter French, and several dialects of Spanish predominated in the conversations along with strong Chinese tobacco. The room seemed like any pub anywhere. Celwyn noticed the bartenders all looked alike, natives of Algiers with full beards and turbans. One of them couldn't have been over four feet tall and had to climb the shelves of bottles to reach the upper tiers.

Sitar music emanated from the farthest corner, heightening the noise level. The magician did not recognize the mysterious music but found it wonderful, so he imitated it, causing the melody to echo over the heads of the patrons.

"What does Gunst look like?" he asked as they reached the bar.

Granger requested two beers. The labels were German, and the beer a variety the magician had never tried. After the barkeep uncapped the bottles, they faced the crowd until Celwyn thought better of the idea. It would be easy, even for the short barman, to crack a bottle over his head. He adjusted his position to oversee both directions.

Granger said, "Our quarry is of Persian descent. He is supposed to be roughly your height, with a stoop, bald, excessively thin, and a reported opium user."

"All right." With care, Celwyn perused the room. Nearly all the tables were occupied by Europeans, sprinkled with a few from the Far East. Most patrons kept their conversations hushed and private, except for a few drunks holding forth as if they alone occupied the place.

"Do you see him?" Granger said, "Between the smoke and the lack of light, I can't tell."

"Not yet." Celwyn listened to the conversations, hearing thieves conspire, a smuggler bragging, and a Royal Navy officer peddling a massive amount of nutmeg. Perhaps someone wanted to bake a cake the size of a ship. He spied a man sitting alone in the back. The magician nudged Granger and nodded at the man.

Granger squinted. "It could be."

"Let's move closer so I can verify his thoughts."

They took their time wending their way between the drinkers to the table next to the man. This close, he did indeed fit the description. Nervous hands and a pair of haunted raccoon eyes confirmed the opium preference. Gunst's fingers trembled as he played with a pair of coins on the table. When he dropped one and bent over to get it, Celwyn entered his mind. A moment later, he backed out and met Granger's gaze with a slight nod. Yes, they'd found him.

Aware of the man's need for the drug, Granger had brought some along to trade and stretched an arm to place it in front of him.

"Good evening."

Gunst's eyes flicked at them, both hopeful and afraid, and he wet his lips with a pallid tongue. As they settled onto the chairs on each side of him, Gunst's fingers beat a rat-a-tat on the table, and he sidled closer to the package.

"What d'you want?"

Granger leaned closer to him, keeping his voice low. "We want to know if the *Quarto* has stopped here."

As he spoke, Celwyn checked the other nearby tables and then expanded his inspection to the whole room. His inner alarm of impending danger came alive, and he sat up straighter. No one close to them could account for his reaction, but when he verified the entrance again, two men with fore-arms the size of tree trunks pushed the beaded curtain aside.

"Yes." Gunst slipped the opium inside his jacket and began rising.

Granger laid a heavy hand on his shoulder. "When?"

"I want—"

"*When?*" Granger squeezed the man's shoulder.

The men in the doorway headed toward them and were joined by two additional brutes of the same size. *Damn,* Celwyn thought, *not using magic is a problem.* However, one must break the rules sometimes.

The magician blocked the men, who found tables suddenly moved in their way. He whispered in Gunst's thoughts, "*Tell us.*" Gunst paled and swayed in his seat before naturally thinking about what he didn't say.

"Got it—let's go!" A shot rang out, right past the magician's ear, and splintered the post behind him.

A second shot hit Celwyn in the shoulder as he and Granger dove behind the bar and on through the service door. Celwyn felt blood soaking his best shirt as he took the lead, and they ran. *Damn it.* As soon as they burst into the alley, both he and Granger appeared as mangy dogs slinking through the shadows and sniffing pieces of trash. Seconds more, and the four men ran out, looking in all directions and jabbering in Spanish. He caught the words for "gold" and "ship."

The most muscular of the men, and the one who wore the most gold chains, sent a pair of his companions chasing up the alley. The rest headed south toward Rue de Zerrak.

Celwyn cut in front of Granger, steering him the other way. As they neared Rue Anassers, the avenue that would take them north to the ship, the magician lagged and found controlling his pain and the bleeding taxing. The magician didn't change them back to their normal appearance until they entered the trees outside of town as they flitted through the moonlight toward the sea.

Chapter 14

CAPTAIN NEMO MET THEM AS THEY climbed out of the transport boat and up to the platform.

Granger saluted.

"We were successful, sir. However..." He indicated Celwyn's bloody shirt.

"How serious is it?" Nemo asked.

"I'll live," the magician answered. "We expected success, not an attack." He dissolved the blood on his shirt. "I would prefer the others not hear of this." He straightened his cuffs and collar. "I will look normal when I go inside."

Nemo asked, "The bullet?"

"I'll remove it."

"Sir, we found our man at the pub but had a spot of excitement first. We were attacked on the way there." Granger glanced at Celwyn and added, "Then we were shot at as we talked with Gunst."

"Do they know of this ship?"

"No. More likely we were just fresh game to them," Granger said. "They talked about a ship and gold. It could be a simple robbery."

"I made sure they didn't see any magic, or get close enough to recognize me," Celwyn said.

"They may not have seen magic." Granger's eyes twinkled. "But I experienced it for the first time."

Nemo raised his brows and asked, "And the *Quarto?*"

"She stopped here for supplies two days ago." Granger's voice changed to steel. "We have almost caught up to her."

"Most welcome news. Dismissed. And thank you."

Granger scratched his side—which caused the magician to privately smile—saluted, and swung down the stairs into the *Nautilus.*

"If we don't go down below soon," Celwyn rubbed at his bullet wound, "Xiau will be up here within a minute."

Nemo's lips twitched despite his seriousness.

"What did you do to escape your attackers?"

"We ran away." Celwyn shrugged. "As a pair of stray dogs."

Ha! Kang would have voiced a choice comparison if he'd heard that description, and Celwyn would not have to hear it tonight.

Moments later, Celwyn settled in the study with a tea service as a crewman arrived with a dinner tray.

Fresh bread, baked sea bass, and a variety of greens filled his plate. With a thank you, the magician dug into the fare.

"Take your time," the automat drawled with as much sarcasm as he could muster.

Bartholomew's shoulders shook as he giggled and lit a cigar. The others, including Tara, regarded the magician with a measure of impatience as the automat asked, "Was there an altercation? You have a smudge on your brow."

Celwyn chewed. He was ravenous. "Yes, two of them." He sampled his salad and approved of the dressing. It had a tang to it, probably from lemons. He loved teasing Kang, but not Tara, so he said, "Lieutenant Granger and I went into town to talk with an opium addict whose sphere of social life is the docks. Before we reached our destination—" He shifted position as his shoulder commenced to throb. He'd been able to remove the bullet, but the pain seemed to be growing worse. "When we were a block away, the first attack occurred. Granger can handle his fists quite well. Anyhow—" He cut off a bite of sea bass and stifled the pain. "—after we dealt with that, we went into a pub and found the opium addict. His name is Gunst."

Qing chose that moment to sail off the bookcase and land on the magician's wounded shoulder. It was all Celwyn could do not to cry out as he moved the bird to his other shoulder. "I missed you, too," he told him. Qing rubbed his beak on Celwyn's ear.

"And?" the automat asked with growing suspicion.

"Oh. Well, Granger questioned the man while I kept an eye on the room. A quartet of thugs followed us in." Celwyn asked the nearby crewman, "Is there any sea bass left? There is? Yes, please."

Verne chuckled at Kang's expression, while Valentine had grown as irritated as the automat and a low growl rumbled in his throat.

"The ship carrying Miss Redifer is two days ahead of us. We've made up five of the seven days of their head start."

Captain Nemo had entered the study a moment ago and kept his face neutral while Celwyn toyed with the Professor. "Which means we will arrive at the Sultan's palace before them. We also have improved our odds of intercepting their ship at sea."

"You appear most satisfied," Bartholomew said.

"I am."

The automat rubbed a finger on his chin as he thought, finally asking, "Wouldn't it be fortunate if we came upon Dearing's other ships late at night, while they were sleeping?"

"It certainly would," Valentine agreed. "Captain, what would you do if we did?"

"Jonas would use subterfuge to visit the *Quarto* and determine exactly where Miss Redifer was located. The next step would be our rescue of her."

Verne said, "Then you would sink those ships."

"Without a doubt." Nemo bowed. "Or before that. I must get back to the bridge. We'll be traveling near the surface after our maintenance tonight." He touched his cap and departed.

Celwyn felt the room grow dark.

"You're bleeding!" Tara exclaimed as she rushed toward him along with Kang. "Oh, my god!" She held his coat open, exposing his blood-soaked shirt.

The Professor reached him next. "God *damn* it, Jonas!"

"His shirt is—" Tara stopped, and her tears started.

"Bloody," Bartholomew said as he joined them in a circle around the magician.

Celwyn opened his eyes and tried to smile.

"A momentary pause … is all."

Bartholomew growled. "You were shot and tried to cover it up." He carried the magician over to the sofa. Tara brought pillows.

As Kang began his examination, Captain Nemo rushed back into the room. He said nothing as the automat peeled off the magician's shirt with a running stream of curse words.

"You sound worried, Professor," Valentine said with a sardonic eye. He was beginning to know the interplay between them all very well indeed.

Kang intercepted Bartholomew charging across the room with his medical bag. "I am. Let's see how bad this is, this time."

Verne leaned over the back of the sofa and watched Kang work. He patted Tara's arm. "Jonas is strong, my dear."

"And stubborn." Kang used an instrument to lift the skin around the bullet hole.

Nemo watched them. "He told me he would remove the bullet."

"He prevaricates, too." Kang aimed a glance at Nemo. "He did remove it, but missed fixing the part that is bleeding."

"You fuss too much, Xiau."

"I do?" The automat pressed his lips shut and managed, "All around where the bullet went in, it is bleeding, Jonas. Fix it."

The magician nodded and winced. "I was in a hurry. Hungry and—"

"Don't say 'tea.' Fix this." After a long wait, Kang said, "That is better." He lifted the ragged side of the wound and nodded. "If this had been a few inches lower, you wouldn't have had time to fix it."

Celwyn sighed. "It is done."

Kang leaned toward him. "Don't try to get up, or I will shoot you myself."

<hr>

By midnight, Celwyn had watched Bartholomew and Valentine triumph at Bridge, much to Kang and Verne's chagrin. Without leaving the sofa, he serenaded Qing and Tara where they sat side by side at the organ. Both enjoyed watching the keys as they moved until Qing decided he preferred her new hair clip. She grabbed it back from him just as the automat addressed Celwyn.

"Are you better?" he asked and settled beside him. "According to the Captain, after another two hours, our maintenance will be complete, and we'll be underway."

The magician nodded.

"Where are we now?" Verne asked.

Bartholomew bent over the map table and stabbed a finger on a quadrant. "We're on the leeward side of Munsee Island, east of Algiers. There isn't any maritime traffic here, per Nemo. So ... we can stay topside while the maintenance occurs."

Valentine joined him and stared at the map. "Where will we be by dawn?"

The Professor found the question too much to resist. He popped up to cross over and help Bartholomew with the maps. They did some measuring with a caliper and compass, conferred, consulted another map, and then the big man said, "At 325 miles a day, if pressed for speed, like we are now, six hours from now would put us after Jijel and before Bizerte."

Tara asked, "Is the weather in the pirates' favor?" With a look he wouldn't forget, she had let Celwyn know she was quite annoyed at being left behind. The magician had explained that no women had been inside the bar. A majority of Algiers were Muslim, and women would not have been allowed there at all. She had retorted that he could have disguised her. Celwyn had the presence of mind not to argue.

"Interesting question," Kang said. "This stretch of the Mediterranean is known for some fine storms this time of year. One thing to consider, though—" he hesitated.

Celwyn prompted him, "Yes?"

Kang shrugged. "A good-size squall could fill their canvasses and propel them forward. Or ... it could cripple their ship."

"Or both." Bartholomew lit a cigar. "The escorting ships could become separated from the one carrying Miss Redifer."

Valentine asked, "Do we know what the *Quarto* looks like?"

"Completely." Celwyn added, "I will finish the drawing of it tomorrow morning." He shifted position to a more comfortable one but did it with circumspection to keep the automat from noticing. If the Professor saw any discomfort, he'd loudly insist the magician go to his cabin.

"Couldn't you do it now?" Valentine asked.

"If, for some reason, I am not close by, the drawing must be done without magic so that it will last."

"And the escort ships?" Tara reminded him.

The magician inhaled. "Those are not as clear in Dearing's mind."

"Tomorrow, Valentine and I will go with you to the cells and see what we can learn about them."

Chapter 15

BREAKFAST BECAME A JOVIAL OCCA-sion after Celwyn submitted to the automat's re-examination and promised not to do anything strenuous.

For the first time since they left the waters off the southern coast of Britain, the atmosphere in the study swelled with hope and the expectation of pirate blood in the water.

"Did you send Elizabeth and the others their letters yesterday?" Celwyn asked.

"I did while you were immersed in that tea shop. You were in there so long I thought they had offered you a position at the counter."

The magician smiled. "That wouldn't be a hardship at all."

"What did you find there?" Tara still hadn't forgiven him for leaving her behind, but her worry over his wound kept her from saying so.

"Pu'er, Rishi rose, and Da Hong Pao ... the leaves of Pao are considered rare, and extremely hard to obtain. They come from China's back country."

"What does it taste like?" Bartholomew asked as he buttered a piece of toast.

"I found the Rishi a bit muddy." Celwyn reached for the butter. "However, the Da Hong Pao tasted divine. I must not become too attached to it, considering how difficult it can be to come by."

The Professor sent him a fond, but worried, look. "Did you have fun at the docks last night?"

"Yes, and before you are offended, Granger and Nemo agreed that the fewer of us who approached Gunst, the better." He offered them a conciliatory bow. "It worked out."

"No, it didn't!" Bartholomew was aghast.

"You were shot!" Kang exclaimed.

"Yes, you were!" Tara joined them in outrage.

When Bartholomew realized the magician was jesting, he tamped the air. "Do you believe what the man told you?"

"Granger does, and I think so, too." To the automat, he said, "Do you have a crewman on the bridge that we can quiz, without pestering Nemo, about the expected weather for the next few days?"

"I do." Bartholomew asked, "Where is the Captain?"

"I spent most of last night in here reading." Valentine said, "The Captain had his breakfast hours ago."

Verne asked himself more than the others, "I wonder what all Dearing has done."

The room fell quiet for several minutes until Celwyn said, "Think of all the years where he has plundered hundreds of ships and killed people. Then killed again while he looted museums and palaces."

Kang eyed him. "We could start a journal of what you can glean from his thoughts. Then turn it over to Interpol or Scotland Yard."

"It would entertain you, Jonas," Bartholomew suggested.

"Yes, it would."

The magician told Valentine and Tara, "They think that when I am bored, I amuse myself by using magic on them. How silly." He blinked innocently. Of a sudden, Kang had dozens of carrots in his hair with tiny ears and frog faces. "Whatever do they mean?"

Verne giggled and covered his plate as he ate.

"You have made your point." The automat pulled one of the carrots out of his hair. "Do you have other ideas?"

"Just talking to Dearing. Tara and Valentine will enjoy doing that later today." Celwyn sipped. "What else?"

"We are thinking a few good old-fashioned bombs to sink his ships are in order when we arrive at his compound. Nemo can only ram one ship at a time and needs room to stop and turn around, and then at least a mile to get up to speed to sink another one."

"All which he couldn't do in a confined bay, or similar," the Professor said.

Tara asked, "Does the Captain agree with these conclusions?"

"We think so," Bartholomew said with a frown. "Or, he is humoring us."

Valentine said, "We should remember that the pirates won't take kindly to our rescuing Miss Redifer, or whatever Nemo has in mind at the pirates' compound."

They all considered that until Bartholomew speculated with the kind of anticipation that entertained them all, "Nemo would probably lead them out into open water and then have a spot of fun."

Verne nodded, and the others did the same.

"After all this is done, Dearing is mine." Valentine snarled the challenge to anyone to disagree with him.

"Please pass the butter," Kang asked. "When this is over, I look forward to our return to the flying machine and never seeing a pirate again. Or smelling one."

"I want to return to Findbar, also," Bartholomew said with the kind of thoughtfulness that gave the magician pause. He wondered what the big man's plans included.

"When this is over, we will hopefully have stopped Dearing's slave trade permanently." The Professor chewed slowly, and his thoughts drifted elsewhere.

"Single-handedly?" the big man asked.

Celwyn considered the question. "Yes, or..."

"Or *what*?" Kang's thoughts came back to the present, and he jumped on what the magician said.

Celwyn grinned at him. "What if Dearing renounced slavery and set everyone free?"

"Ha!" The automat slapped him on the back. "You would make an effigy of Dearing. But, what about the voice?"

"I'll practice."

Kang sobered. "I assume you will heal from your wound between now and when we find the *Quarto*. We will need you, especially at first, to locate Miss Redifer."

Chapter 16

B Y AGREEMENT, CELWYN SPENT THE rest of the day resting. Occasionally, he would practice his imitation of Dearing on anyone who happened to be close by. If they appeared frightened, then it had been a good test. If they just looked annoyed, he had work to do. In between pots of Earl Grey and watching Kang and Bartholomew play chess, he finished the drawings from the information he'd siphoned from Dearing.

Verne helped, not only by inking the final captions but providing colorizations of various rooms and passageways of the sultan's palace. When Verne insisted on mounting the drawings on the wall with the others, Celwyn couldn't resist a spot of fun. While Verne balanced on a stool to attach the drawings, his trousers threatened to fall off. Tara saw what was going on and pointedly faced the other way.

The magician's entertainment didn't last. Celwyn yawned several times. There was no reason for that... he directed a suspicious stare at the automat... Xiau was more than capable of slipping him a sedative in his tea...

When Bartholomew pulled on his sleeve and asked him about the Sultan's armory, he jumped a bit, feeling foggy. It neared four in the afternoon, and the magician hoped Kang's cure would wear off soon. Celwyn wasn't sure what it would be yet, but the automat would find something floating in his soup tonight.

At the end of his third yawn, Tara swiveled to study him. "How do you feel?"

"Bored."

She called over to the chess table. "Professor, is your patient strong enough for a short visit with Dearing?"

Kang moved his queen back a spot and sent Bartholomew a yawn. "Yes, if you take Valentine with you, in case he needs help."

"I assume you mean with walking or climbing stairs." She stood up. "I won't need any help dealing with Captain Dearing."

From her tone, Celwyn could well believe it.

⁕

Despite Kang's prediction Celwyn might need assistance walking, probably from the sedative he'd slyly given him, he had no problems. As a good host would, he floated the three of them down the stairs;

he saw no purchase in expending energy needlessly until he was fully healed, although he wouldn't tell the automat that.

Dearing leaned against the bars of his cell, staring at Celwyn and the others as they arrived. A pair of guards had been standing on the other side of the cells. When Celwyn nodded to them, they touched their caps and headed upstairs.

The magician provided velvet-covered chairs in front of the cells; the type most appropriate for watching a drama. He added a table of wine bottles and crystal glasses.

"Thank you, Mr. Celwyn." Valentine took his time uncorking the bottle and pouring the rich red liquid as slowly as possible, just for the pirate. Dearing couldn't look away from the act, so Celwyn added a third glass and sent it through the bars.

The pirate backed away as the glass hovered in front of him. He probably remembered a few instances when something he saw transformed into a member of the rodent family. It didn't take long until Dearing drained his portion and stared at him for more. The magician dissolved the glass—no sense in leaving him a weapon.

While that transpired, Tara studied the pirate with hard eyes. She looked too angry to speak, but Valentine didn't have that problem. He showed the pirate his teeth.

"You have committed an attack on my family."

Dearing sneered and sat on his bunk with his back to them.

"He wouldn't have done that if there weren't bars between you," Celwyn said.

"True." Valentine eyed the pirate.

And then there were no bars. Valentine realized it at the same time as the pirate did. The vampire moved faster, and his nails snagged Dearing's throat before Celwyn could blink. When he pinned the pirate to the floor, Dearing struggled at first and then stopped.

Tara found her voice.

"We're going to ask you some questions. If you do not answer, I can't predict what my uncle will do."

Celwyn couldn't either, and he would prefer not to have to wrestle an enraged Valentine. He sent the older vampire a silent reminder that for now, they needed Dearing alive, for Miss Redifer's sake. Valentine's growl echoed in the chamber as they all watched blood trickle down the side of Dearing's throat.

"What is the name of the island where your compound is located?"

Celwyn checked the pirate's thoughts and nodded to Tara.

"All right, then. What do the ships escorting Miss Redifer look like?"

When Dearing started to shake his head, Valentine leaned over him, inches above his face, and a drop of saliva dripped off his teeth and ran down the pirate's cheek. Celwyn took the opportunity to verify Dearing's thoughts. He found some details foremost that he hadn't expected. The magician made a silent suggestion to Tara as Valentine climbed off Dearing with a last fond kick. The vampire resumed his seat and drank his wine.

Tara waited for the pirate to get to his feet again before saying, "I understand your ships are all painted black, and they are flagless at times. They travel in an upside-down V formation in front of the *Quarto*."

Dearing swiveled and gave his full attention to Tara. He licked his lips and kept his eyes on her, unwilling to look at Valentine anymore. Celwyn watched the pirate's hands, which tensed and flexed with each breath. Just to be sure he didn't attack her, the magician wrapped Dearing's wrists in bonds. The flexing stopped, and his attention flickered to Celwyn. The magician bet the bastard had deduced that Celwyn was the main reason he was alive at this point, even if restrained.

"Well?" Tara raised her beautiful brows.

The magician discovered a pictorial tornado whirling in Dearing's flea-ridden mind; picture after picture twirled by, from a hank of roasted lamb to someone hacking off a man's hand, and a beautiful sunset in the Bay of Biscayne.

"They travel from sunup to sundown?" Tara asked. On the way down here, they'd decided a few innocent questions in between what they really wanted to know would be wise.

Dearing executed another slight nod, splitting his attention between the wine bottle and Valentine. A yearning verses a fear—which would win?

"Thank you. Where will they stop on their way to the Sultan's palace?" She regarded him as if she expected an answer. They had assumed with that many men, at least two hundred per ship, they had to stop frequently for supplies.

Dearing touched his bloody throat, eyed the wine bottle, and said, "What you'd expect, and anyone knows; Cagliari, Tunis, and Kalamata."

"Then through the Suez Canal," Celwyn stated it as a fact, not a question.

When Dearing said nothing, Valentine was on him again in a blur, knocking him down and pinning him, his superior strength evidenced in the sudden capitulation by the pirate. This time Dearing didn't even twitch under the vampire's hands.

"I'm tiring, and need to replace the bars on this animal's cage," Celwyn told them.

Valentine shook Dearing hard and backed off him. Once he cleared the cell, the bars were in place once again. The pirate scrambled up, yelling, and shaking them.

Tara touched Celwyn's sleeve. "You look a mite pale."

"I suppose we should go, then." He made sure he had Dearing's attention. "I wonder what the best way is into your compound on Manuk Island?" He had purposely named the exact location. In the next second, the pirate confirmed it as rage filled his face, but not before Celwyn received a clear picture of the beach, the bay itself, and places he did not expect. *Oh my*, the magician thought. The bastard really was worried! There was a weakness in the pirate's defenses. On the far north side of the docks, his ships blocked the view of the rest of the bay, and Dearing dithered about it.

By the time they reached the study again, the magician felt glad of Valentine's support. He leaned on him a bit more before striding into the room as normally as he could. Tara preceded him and pointedly shook her head at Kang. Celwyn sighed. Just what he needed; the automat acquiring a confederate in nagging him.

He sat heavily beside Kang. "I assume the Captain is on the bridge?"

Bartholomew had taken the prime spot at the map table and looked comfortable. He'd even removed his boots. "Yes. Do you have news for us from Dearing?"

Celwyn nodded.

"I'll see if the Captain would like to hear it before we have our luncheon so we can discuss something more pleasant while we dine." The automat sailed out the door.

By the time Nemo joined them, Celwyn had poured his third cup and replaced Valentine's empty wine bottle. As Nemo sat next to him, the crew entered the room carrying the dining table. It could be a coincidence, but Verne also arrived with an expectant look across his studious face.

"We now know additional details of how the pirate ships travel." Celwyn described the formation and added, "Dearing didn't mention it, but proudly thought about his cannons. Three of the escorting ships have the newest ones."

"Paixhans guns?" Nemo asked.

"I think so, but I'm not an expert on these things. I can duplicate what I saw." Celwyn waved a hand, and a transparent replica of the ships and their cannons appeared in front of them.

"Those may be Paixhans, but they seem different." Bartholomew studied the image.

A short discussion on the range of cannons ensued among those who knew about them. When it ended, Tara asked them, "How can the inverted V procession protect a ship both front and back if it is behind the V?"

"From what I have heard, their crows' nests have lookouts to the rear. It is a known defense." Bartholomew stood to get a closer look at the replicated guns.

"Thank you." Tara nodded and addressed Celwyn. "Please continue."

The magician handed Nemo a list and a copy to Kang to pass around. "Those are the cities that we can expect Dearing's ships to visit for supplies. Contrary to what he told us, the *Quarto's* first stop will not be Cagliari. It will be the smaller city, Annaba."

"When will we reach there?" Tara asked.

"In another day or so," Nemo answered. "It is debatable if the pirates will still be in the area when we arrive." To Celwyn he said, "You list Tunis as their next stop."

Celwyn nodded. "Yes, according to what Dearing thinks, but there's no telling if that is true."

Tara said, "They could have altered their initial plans."

"Possibly." Kang ignored the others while he thought.

"But not by too much. Dearing expects them to follow a pattern and schedule so he can find them if needed," Bartholomew said.

Nemo frowned and took off his hat. He played with the emblem as he spoke. "No matter the port, the pirates will most likely stay offshore and send a single ship into a city to avoid any notoriety. Even in the smaller outposts of lawlessness, people on the docks romanticize the bastards and vie for the privilege to supply them what they need."

Tara eyed the magician. "This time I could dress the part and investigate the docks with you."

Celwyn gasped but didn't say anything. When Tara began laughing, he joined in, more in relief than humor.

The automat sobered. "Agree. The men on the docks are easy targets for anyone with coins. Just like Gunst, they can be bought one way or another." Kang glanced at the others. "Does Palermo have a telegraph system?"

Nemo said, "I'm not sure. Tunis does, though." He observed his crew while they set the table, and he made up his mind. "We prefer to attack before the *Quarto* reaches the Red Sea."

"Because?" Bartholomew asked.

"The water there is not as wide as I'd prefer in spots," he told them. "And the Suez, at its highest point, is not deep enough for us, depending on the tides. Our timing must be perfect."

Of all of them, Bartholomew was the first to catch his meaning. He swallowed and seemed to shrink in his seat. "Oh..."

"You would take us underground by way of the Nile instead, and then another river to the Red Sea?" the automat asked.

"Yes."

"Or ... we follow the ships through and beyond the Red Sea ... before we attack." Kang eyed the big man while he speculated.

As the crew pushed carts of food into the room, Nemo crossed over to sniff the dishes. "Unless we find them sooner, that is the plan."

"It sounds like we will not invade the Sultan's palace then. Such a shame," Verne commented as they took their places at the table. "I wanted to see it."

"The Sultan should still be dealt with after we have Miss Redifer back," Valentine said. "He won't stop collecting vampires for his purposes."

Nemo's eyes glinted like the *Nautilus* in the sun. "Perhaps we can prevent that."

"Sir, there is one last tidbit from our visit with Dearing." The magician unfurled his napkin. "At his compound in the Sulu islands, there is a weak point in his defenses he worries about. After we dine, I'll draw what I saw so that you can see it, too."

Chapter 17

OVER THE NEXT TWENTY-FOUR hours, the stress of their mission filled the air, illustrated best in the short tempers of both Valentine and the Professor. For Celwyn's part, he could be patient when he had to be and did not hesitate to remind the automat of his comparative virtue. He also noticed that his wound healed at an exceptional rate this time, and he neared normal status now. Could this be Thales' gifts were resurfacing again? *Why?* That was a troubling thought.

As the days went by, everyone reacted differently. While the anticipation of attacking the pirates dragged on, it put Valentine in a filthy mood. Yet, it left Verne in a buoyant one. The magician understood; impending mayhem can have that effect.

Their arrival at the port of Annaba had been a disappointment to everyone. The *Nautilus* cruised offshore, beyond prying eyes as the sun set over the bay, casting broad ribbons of blue, gold, and red across the water. It also covered the overwhelming misery and squalor on shore. There was no sign of the *Quarto*.

At dinner, Nemo confirmed the pirates most likely sailed a few days ahead of them, heading toward Malta. Disappointment reigned in the long faces Kang and Bartholomew wore, and in frustrated anger from Tara and Valentine. When the evening bridge game began, Celwyn had felt well enough to serenade the room with new compositions at the organ, his way of lifting the spirits of everyone. He also had a premonition that the night would not be a complete disappointment.

He had just kissed Tara goodnight outside her cabin when the lights blinked twice, and a series of gongs resounded from the belly of the submarine.

The gongs grew louder, abnormally so, and they did not stop.

"Yeehaw!!" Celwyn exclaimed, just like the American cowboys did. He took Tara's hand, and they ran back to the study and up to the aquatic window.

"We have surfaced—" Tara breathed as they gazed through a mass of bubbles at the scene above the waterline.

A full moon painted the sea silver under a twinkling galaxy of stars. Without going topside, they couldn't see more. Kang trotted back into the room with his tie askew, and Bartholomew thudded to a stop right behind him, still re-buttoning his shirt.

Verne had remained at the chess table writing. "I must finish this scene." He waved a hand around them. "I've witnessed this before."

"This?" Tara asked.

Valentine walked in again, still smartly attired all in black and every hair in place. "What is going on?" As he asked, the lights in the study blinked and went dark. Tara found the magician's hand and held on.

"I guess I will finish later." Verne sighed.

Qing squawked and flew to Celwyn, who tucked him inside his collar. "No biting."

Kang left them to pace to the sofa and back with his eyes glowing in anticipation. "This situation appears very similar to when we sank Dearing's other ship."

"He is—" Valentine started.

Granger ran in, verified they were all there, and spoke, "The Captain requests that everyone remain seated until the gongs stop." He saluted, clicked his heels together, and ran out again before they could question him.

The *Nautilus* revved her engines and surged forward, sinking below the waves. For the next few minutes, they waited amid the roar of the engines and darkness. The only light came from a blue glow emanating from the hallway sconces.

"The pirates won't know what happened," Verne said.

"I need to reinforce Dearing's cell—" Celwyn shot to his feet, caught Valentine's attention and pointed to Tara, and ran. Kang and Bartholomew fell in step behind him.

The magician threw light ahead of them as the ship dove, and they bounced against the corridor wall before continuing down the stairs and to the cells.

When they arrived, they found Dearing roaring and shaking the bars of his cell. Fear, or trying to escape? Celwyn didn't care. He slammed Dearing flat on his bunk and strengthened the cell all around. As he and Bartholomew caught up on their breathing, the automat, whose mechanics had nothing to do with breathing, tapped his foot and waited.

"Should we stay here?" Bartholomew asked.

"We're midway between the stern and the bow," Kang said. "Nemo will attack head-on." He patted Bartholomew's shoulder. "We're safe here."

"Then, I suggest Jonas make us something to hold on to, or we sit on the floor."

They dropped to the floor and waited. Seconds ticked by with the only sound—the roar of the engines vibrating the ship. To the magician, it seemed as if the submarine ascended somewhat and slowed. They held their breath and waited.

The *Nautilus* shot forward at full speed, her engines straining. Seconds went by. When the impact came, she shuddered all over and continued forward again. Even through the walls of water and iron, the noise had been incredible, echoing like a train crash within the chamber.

"Depending on the target, Nemo may, or may not, go in for another pass by," the automat said.

"It only took one hit for the *Primero* the other day." Bartholomew rose to his knees and then his feet. "We're slowing now."

Celwyn stood. "Let's verify everything is solid down here."

Although he tried to hide it, Kang frowned at him. "You are still moving slower than normal, Jonas."

"But I'm better than yesterday."

"So, you say."

They examined the engine and turbine rooms for leaks, finding a few crewmen inspecting things, and that all seemed well. When they peered at the cellblock, Dearing remained quiet and unconscious, as the magician intended.

The trio headed upstairs. A quick stop at the bridge revealed no leaks, no panic, only a sense of triumph in the air. Nemo stopped issuing orders long enough to give them a thumbs up.

"No leaks on the lower deck, sir," Bartholomew reported. "We made sure Dearing stayed put."

"Any breaches around the bow?" Celwyn asked. He assumed all was well, but asked anyhow.

"We checked, and everything is fine," Granger told them and returned to his gauges.

Celwyn bowed to Nemo and saluted Granger as they tramped out and down the corridor to the study. The aquatic window had been opened again.

An eerie glow from the moon filtered through the water and painted the debris as it fell through the sea all around them. Chunks of wood, several bodies, and pieces of pottery and crates floated by the submarine on their trip downward. An entire canvas brushed against the side of the ship as it danced in the current and drifted side to side like an enormous leaf in a slow drain. Another body fell after it, with the drowning pirate still flailing his arms.

"Close the window please, Jonas." Bartholomew crossed himself. "They were evil men, but I do not wish to watch."

Celwyn didn't know how it usually closed, but he closed it. "The fortunes of the sea do not always favor evil, and the men of these pirate ships signed up for evil acts," he said, more to himself than the others.

"As just one example, those blood-thirsty bastards killed scores of patrons and guards at the Bingham Museum," the automat said. He rubbed his chin in thought. "Still, on a human level ... this is hard to watch."

"It was necessary." Celwyn felt a strong measure of satisfaction knowing that the pirates wouldn't kill again. He reserved guilt for himself as needed, which was often, but not in this instance.

With a raised did-you-know brow, Kang told Bartholomew and Verne, "Over the last 500 years, the attitude toward death has evolved. Life seems to be worth more in modern times, yet, in this instance, there was only one solution to prevent additional horrific acts."

"Interesting perspective. I wonder if the Captain will sink another of their ships tonight," Verne said.

Bartholomew said, "No. He will want them nervous and thinking it was a sea monster ... or the weather."

Kang nodded his agreement. "The other ships might assume that ship's magazine blew up."

"Attacking at night has its advantages," Valentine said. "If they are superstitious, so much the better, wouldn't you say?"

Everyone appeared wide awake, including Qing. Celwyn let him out of his collar and the bird flew to the automat to be admired. When that had been accomplished, he walked across the back of the sofa to Bartholomew, who shook his head.

"Move along, bird."

While they stared at each other, Celwyn asked, "Tea, anyone?"

"No. I know what it tastes like. I need something else." The automat eyed Celwyn. "Elizabeth rubs my feet when I felt anxious."

"Pfft." As the magician poured whiskies and passed them along, the others made appropriate comments about the automat's feet.

Tara refused a glass of wine. "You still look tired."

"I agree." The automat nodded.

"I won't be up too much longer."

She frowned at him. "I understand the Professor's point of view better now."

From his position at the chess table, the author said, "We will follow the rest of the pirate ships throughout tomorrow, most likely."

Tara stopped frowning and her face became animated. "Tomorrow, we rescue Simone!"

"Perhaps." Bartholomew gazed at the magician.

"It is possible, and it depends if I find her on the *Quarto*," Celwyn said. He cupped Tara's chin in his hand. "I won't promise you success and then disappoint you."

The older vampire paced. "I want to be the instrument of Dearing's demise and that of the rest of his men." Valentine glared around the room, daring anyone to disagree with him.

"From what I can tell, you will be able to at least participate," the automat said. "When we arrive at the Sulu Islands, we will be outnumbered by hundreds of pirates, perhaps a thousand. To help balance that, the Captain is picking off their ships before then. It is part of the process."

Captain Nemo strode in, his eyes alive with victory and revenge. After he poured a single shot, he stood by them, regarding the closed aquatic window.

"The debris..." Bartholomew waved a hand.

Nemo shrugged. "I understand."

"Tell us about tomorrow," Kang said.

"As you wish," Nemo drained his glass. "I'm not sure where the other escort ships are. However, we will find them."

"And then?" Valentine asked, his restrained anger choking his voice.

"It depends on what Jonas discovers when he visits them. Ideally, we take Miss Redifer off the *Quarto* and then sink them all." With an eye on the magician, he added, "You should all retire for the night. It will be an exciting day, and we'll get underway early."

At the automat's request, Qing spent the night in Celwyn's cabin. It was either that, or the automat informed him he would sit at the magician's feet himself all night. He expected Qing would beat a rat-a-tat on the metal door if Celwyn needed help.

The magician prepared for bed and purposely kept his thoughts on Tara, not worrying about Wye or Qing. He considered her much softer and prettier. It had been over a month since Qing had slept in his cabin, and he suspected the bird would celebrate by keeping him awake all night. He made a dozen cuff links that shone and twinkled in the low light.

"This is all you are getting if you wake me up."

Qing squawked at him. The magician tossed the trinkets in the air and caused them to circle the room just under the ceiling. Celwyn climbed into his bunk, and sleep claimed him immediately. His last thought was the suspicion that the automat had slipped him another sedative.

Damn it.

When Celwyn awoke, he heard the usual activity in the corridor and felt the vibration of the submarine's engines as he stretched and glanced at the clock on his desk.

In its place, he saw Wye curled up like a cat, with Qing nestled under his chin and chewing on his scales.

Chapter 18

Prague

PATRICK SUPPORTED ANNABELLE IN his arms as she sobbed. After an incredibly sad minute where time seemed to stop, he regarded Sully standing beside the shrouded body of Elizabeth. He wrung his cap as big, fat tears rolled down his face. Patrick waved him over.

Sully moved aside to allow the coroner and his assistants to reach the body. As they laid a stretcher on the ground, one of the men stood on top of the seedlings Elizabeth had planted only a few days before.

"Please take Miss Annabelle to the kitchen. You and Ricardo are to stay with her. Abe and Andy are to remain upstairs with the boys to make sure," Patrick took a deep breath, "that they don't see this."

"What will you be doing, sir?" Sully asked as if he hoped it would comfort him as well.

"I'll be at the police station. Take her inside, now—" Patrick kissed Annabelle's forehead. "Go with him and wait for me. No arguing."

After Sully led her away, Patrick addressed the Conductor, "Would you get the calèche ready, please?"

"Certainly." He eyed Edward. "I don't think he can drive. He needs to stay quiet and rest."

Patrick agreed. Blood seeped from Edward's bandage. "Yes, but he must go with us. The police want to question him."

"I'll bring the first aid kit." Conductor Smith could move fast for a large man. He trotted down the driveway to the stables at the rear of the mansion. With this tragedy, he might be wishing they were aboard their train and traveling—anywhere.

Patrick led Edward to the garden bench facing away from the spot where the body had been. After leaving his underlings with a list of things to do, the fat policeman climbed back into his wagon. Patrick listened to him, hearing their last instruction; to take the coach that had held Elizabeth's body back to the police station and inspect it.

"Sir—"

Patrick put a hand on Edward's shoulder. "No, just rest. We're going to redress your wound before we go." He sighed and couldn't help another glance at where the corpse had been. "Just rest."

An hour later, with the Conductor driving, Edward sat in the calèche next to Patrick as they pulled out of the driveway under a dreary sky. The gloominess seemed like a portent for the horrible events and sadness yet to come.

As they entered the downtown district, Patrick again verified Edward's condition. He appeared marginally better; a bit more color showed in his cheeks above his muttonchops. But he remained as miserable as could be.

"If Jonas were here, he'd fix your head and torn clothes," Patrick told him. "We'll make this quick, and get back so you can rest."

"Yes, sir." Edward's tone indicated his intention to do no such thing. Self-recrimination swam in his eyes, and he couldn't stop clenching his hands.

The Conductor took the corner in front of the Mercantile Bank at a crawl to avoid the pedestrians, shook the reins, and sped up again. Patrick said, "From what I can tell, you could not have prevented it. The attack was planned."

Edward wagged his head, and with a wince, stopped. "No disrespect, but Miss Elizabeth was *my* responsibility."

The calèche gained speed, causing the standing water to splash high behind them. The Conductor clucked at the horses, urging them forward. On the sidewalks, Patrick noticed everyday people talking, holding hands or packages, smiling and laughing; every one of them unaware of the heartbreak at Tellyhouse.

"I'm not going to argue with you," Patrick told Edward. "However, know that I, Annabelle, and everyone else do *not* blame you."

"Same here," the Conductor called over his shoulder as he pulled on the reins, and they clattered onto the cobblestones of Charles Street.

⌣

"You're late," the fat policeman said as an underling ushered Patrick and Edward into his office.

Besides an inkwell, a lone placard decorated his desk. Major Jardin seemed pleased with himself and probably expected visitors to admire the certificates on every wall. His framed picture must have been from a few years ago; now he sported only a fringe of hair around his ears and several more double chins … and an obnoxious attitude. Patrick knew he normally wouldn't be as critical, but Elizabeth's death weighed on him.

After he propped his walking stick against the desk, Patrick took his time removing his gloves and getting comfortable. Edward stood beside him and was only a few feet from a guard who avoided looking at them. Patrick urged Edward into the other chair.

For minutes, Patrick said nothing, then measured his voice with enough irritation behind it to leave Jardin no doubt of how he felt, and who controlled the conversation.

"Sir, I came here as a courtesy." He glanced at the underling taking notes. "My name is Captain Patrick Swayne, most recently discharged from the Queen's

Army after a tour in Punjab. I will not put up with insolence from you or any other man."

Jardin said nothing, but his expression hardened, and he dropped his gaze.

"Mrs. Elizabeth Kang was a dear friend of mine. She and her husband resided with us at our mutual home. We have two adopted sons, and..." For the first time since the murder, Patrick realized he would have to tell the Professor and the others. "And Mrs. Swayne is with child. I will not allow her to be disturbed. We will answer your questions now. If there are other questions, you may make an appointment."

"Fine." Jardin lit a cigar and blew the smoke at Patrick. "Tell me in detail what you know." He pulled a pad from his pocket and added, "Your Mr. Murphy here will do the same."

Patrick sighed. "Please send for some coffee. I am sure you were about to offer the courtesy."

Jardin nearly smiled. He nodded at the guard, who departed in search of coffee. When the door closed behind him, he said, "Go ahead."

"Mrs. Kang left the house about eleven yesterday morning to run some errands."

Jardin scribbled a note. "Where?"

"Hall's Toiletries, and Cherov's on Alsinov Street."

Without looking up, Edward said, "Near the butcher shop..."

Patrick resumed his tale. "She and Mr. Murphy did not return as expected. We became worried and by late afternoon, another of my employees began looking for them at both establishments. Still nothing. We also visited this station to report them missing." *If only they had searched longer, asked more questions,* Patrick thought. He cleared his throat. "By the time we retired last evening, we were seriously concerned. Again, our footman went looking."

Two guards entered, one of them bearing a tray he placed on Jardin's desk. He saluted and left. The other guard remained in front of the door at attention.

"Send someone over to Alsinov Street. Have them ask at all the shops and street vendors. I want to know if anyone saw the victim." The Major glared. "What are you waiting for?" The guard scrambled a salute and left.

Jardin faced Edward. "Now, Mr. Murphy. What is your story?" His tone lacked even less respect than he used with Patrick.

If only Jonas, Bartholomew, and the Professor were here. Patrick knew this wouldn't be as painful. Edward refused coffee and spoke, his voice strong as he returned the policeman's stare.

"We reached Hall's about 11:15 yesterday morning. I say 'we' because a man had come along with us." Edward couldn't have sounded more miserable.

Patrick slapped his forehead. "I'm sorry. Yes, we had a visitor. Rather, he was a substitute piano teacher for our son Otto. I was told his name—a Mr. Gaspard. After Otto's lesson, he said he had an appointment near Alsinov Street, so Elizabeth invited him to ride with her."

"Had she ever seen him before?"

"Not that I could tell."

"Describe him."

Edward said, "Medium build, dark hair, and eyes. Dressed all in black with a string tie. Perhaps forty years old."

Patrick debated whether to mention the man had reminded him of Kang and decided against it.

"Had you ever seen him before?"

"No. He just appeared at the door when Mr. Baylord should have for the lesson."

Jardin made a note and ordered Edward to continue.

"When we arrived at the shop, I couldn't find a place to park, so I drove into the alley around the corner. It is only a few steps from there to the street." He swallowed and had trouble getting the words out. "I opened the door to help Mrs. Kang out of the carriage. When I turned around, something slammed my head."

"Go on."

"A long time after that, I woke up." Edward squeezed his eyes shut. "I discovered I was in the back of the coach. It was dark. Then—" He stopped and checked with Patrick.

"Her body was left on top of him." Patrick patted Edward's shoulder. "He could tell she was dead."

Jardin made additional notes before asking, "What time was this?"

"I don't know. It was completely dark." Edward blinked and thought. "No people around at all, nothing nearby I recognized. Just trees and some lights in the distance. The sun was coming up when I made it home. Mr. Patrick was out front when I got there."

"Your coroner examined him, as you know." Patrick's anger grew. "He had been hit many times, probably every time he started to wake up."

The policeman finished writing and admitted it. "Yes. So, he has stated." He flipped pages in the notebook. "The victim had been dead for a few hours when we examined her." Jardin shrugged. "We'll know other details by tomorrow." As he drank coffee, he asked as if it didn't matter, "Who hated Mrs. Kang?"

Over the next half-hour, they answered questions about Elizabeth, about everyone else, and who would attack her. The questions became about her husband, the professor. Patrick answered everything he could but offered little else. The police now knew Kang and the others had traveled to Singapore, but nothing about Findbar Island.

Finally, Patrick stood and retrieved his walking stick. "You'll excuse us. We must send a telegram to her husband to come home. He needs to know his wife is dead."

For a long moment, the Major stared at him and then waved his hand in dismissal.

A few minutes later, Edward followed Patrick out of the police building and into a somber drizzle. As they walked, Patrick kept his thoughts to himself; the police didn't need to know about his worries.

Was the murder caused by an enemy of the Professor's ... or Bartholomew or Jonas? Was this about the flying machine? An answer to any of that opened so many other questions. For the police, it could be a serious line of inquiry. Or send them down dozens of rabbit holes. Gaspard must be the killer... *poor Elizabeth.* Patrick concluded the heinous act indeed had nothing to do with her. She was just a tool in some macabre game.

In the next second, Patrick realized he had several things to do, urgently. When they stopped in front of the calèche, he studied Edward.

"How are you?"

"Much better, sir. The police doctor told me not to go to sleep for the next twelve hours because of my head."

Patrick regarded him. "You do look better. More color in your cheeks." And the fire of revenge in his eyes.

"I am. You have a plan, Mr. Patrick? I want to get my hands on whoever did this!"

"I do also, but we have things to do first." They greeted Conductor Smith and climbed into the back of the calèche. "A telegraph office, please; we must send the Professor the news." As he spoke, the Conductor jiggled the reins, and they rolled into the street. "Francesca's coven is next. We need to order as much security from the witches as possible."

Edward rubbed his face and touched his bandage. "That will be interesting. You haven't been there before, have you, Sir?"

"Err ... no," Patrick said. "We also have two other things to do." He reached and tapped the Conductor on the shoulder.

"Yes, sir?"

"As an alternative, take us to the nearest stable, please. We need to rent a family-sized coach."

"Until the police release ours," Edward guessed.

"Yes." To the Conductor, Patrick said, "We'll leave you to drive it home while we take this rig to the telegraph office."

The Conductor nodded and turned down a side street leading back downtown.

"What else, sir?"

"We will meet back at the house. It is a sad affair, but my anger at whoever did this is growing, and that helps immensely."

"Same here," the Conductor said.

Edward echoed him. "Same here."

Patrick appreciated them both right now. It helped to share the anger. He addressed the Conductor.

"On the way home, please stop for Mrs. Pearse, Miss Annabelle's aunt. Edward will give you the address. Tell her we wish for her to come to Tellyhouse for an extended time." Patrick only tolerated the aunt at the best of times. But right now, they needed her in their house of mourning.

⌣

As Edward took the Conductor's place driving the calèche, he said, "The nearest telegraph office is on Scorcinsky Street. It is also on the way to the coven."

"Are you sure you are up to driving?"

"Getting better by the minute."

"Should we stop and find refreshments?" Patrick asked. It wouldn't do for Edward to extend himself, considering his condition.

"I want to do my job." Edward shook his head and winced. "I have to remember not to do that." He steered the calèche onto a busier street. "The doctor also told me not to drink any alcohol for a few days."

Patrick realized something he hadn't before, and it caused his heart to race: *who was to say that whoever had killed Elizabeth wouldn't come back?* He had to warn everyone at Tellyhouse and tell them about the new protection from the witches.

"On second thought, Annabelle will worry. Swing by the house, please. Then we'll continue on."

Chapter 19

AS TESTIMONY TO A LONG VIGIL IN bleak silence, when Patrick burst into the house, he found all the residents of Tellyhouse had gathered in the parlor.

Their chef, Ricardo, and both scullery maids hovered by the arch leading to the dining room. Jackson, porter for the train and second in command of the kitchen, stood beside them. The red-headed twins, Abe and Andy, sat like statues in front of the fireplace flanked by Flossy, the upstairs maid. The remnants of a coffee service lay on the table in front of them.

From her favorite spot next to the fireplace, Annabelle hugged herself and wept softly while staring out the window. Otto and Zander perched on each side of her. Both boys had been crying and looked lost and miserable. Zander patted Annabelle's shoulder while Otto held her hand.

The misery extended to the other side of the room, where Sully and Mrs. Thomas occupied the other sofa. His glances at the bar indicated he wished for something much stronger than coffee. Mrs. Thomas dabbed at her eyes; her expression so forlorn that Patrick wondered if she had ever faced a violent death before. This bothered him because if their formidable housekeeper was not in charge, surely all would be lost.

Patrick crossed the room in three strides and hugged both boys before lifting Annabelle into his arms. A moment passed, and then another before he faced the others. Edward joined them and removed his hat. Every one of them stared at the white bandage around his head.

"We all share in the horror of what has happened." As he spoke, Patrick met their eyes with the same calm conviction he used for his troops before going into battle. "We will mourn Miss Elizabeth, believe me, we will, but this may not end with her."

"Excuse me. What do you mean, sir?" Andy asked.

"We know little about what happened, but my money is on someone who is after the Professor, or Bartholomew, or Mr. Celwyn." Patrick felt anger constricting his throat. It had to be... "Perhaps as a message."

Sully grumbled to himself. "They didn't have to kill her, by God."

Tears streamed down Mrs. Thomas' face, and Otto arose to offer her quiet empathy and his handkerchief. Patrick had never seen this before; the boys' pain mirrored the others' pain.

"Do we know that for certain, sir?" Ricardo asked.

"No." Patrick settled Annabelle back on the sofa and remained at her side. "No, but we have to be prepared and on guard."

With some of her usual forcefulness, Mrs. Thomas said, "I understand. What do you want us to do?"

They had reached the point where Patrick's worst fears would be realized, but he had no choice.

"For those of you who do not already know," he took a deep breath, "since we have lived in Prague, we've had a series of unfortunate events. They led us to employ extraordinary measures to ensure everyone's safety."

"But Miss Elizabeth is dead." Zander's bottom lip quivered.

Patrick said gently, "Yes. And the villain who did it is miles from here." *At least I hope so.* As he spoke, Otto wiped his eyes, once again living through the death of someone he loved. God knows what the boy had seen before they found him.

Damn. Patrick couldn't take much more of this. He hurried on. "The measures used to protect everyone were spells from the local coven. The witches put them over this house and accompanied many of you as needed."

Otto blinked fast behind his spectacles, and his lips tightened in resolution.

Flossy's eyes bulged. Of everyone present, she was the least likely to know about Francesca and her coven. Jackson murmured comforting words to her. She bobbed her head several times and kept her eye on Patrick in case he turned into something fantastic, or worse.

"In a few moments, Edward and I will depart," Patrick told them. "We'll go to the coven and arrange for additional help." When Mrs. Thomas emitted an outraged squeak, Patrick plowed on, saying, "I'll also hire guards."

Their murmurs grew until Patrick held up a hand.

"We'll send telegrams to the Professor and the others on our way across town." Patrick cleared his throat. "I intend to keep you all safe. This means using anything and everything I can think of. You must begin telling Mrs. Thomas every time you leave the house. One of the guards will go with you on your days off." He regarded each of them. "This is not negotiable."

Patrick accepted a cup of coffee from Ricardo, sipped, and thanked him with a look. He went on, "There is a great deal to do. I know I can rely on your help. But, please..." He paused to emphasize his next words. "Of even greater importance, I must count on your alertness and caution."

"You have it, guv'nor," Sully said.

"Mine too, sir." Ricardo waited until the others under him chimed in, some in fear, some in confusion.

Mrs. Thomas demanded, "Who did this to Miss Elizabeth?"

Edward stepped forward and related the events. "When I woke up, Miss Elizabeth was dead. Gaspard was gone. I drove straight here and arrived at dawn."

"The police took over. We have just been interviewed by them. They might ask you questions also." Patrick gazed around the room. "Answer as best you can. Hold nothing back."

Annabelle burst out, "Oh, no—" She brought Otto back to her and studied him. "You were alone with that man. Did he hurt you?"

Otto wrote fast and Zander leaned over to read his tablet aloud.

"'No, he just oversaw my piano lesson. He didn't listen as well as Mr. Baylord.'"

Patrick didn't voice the horrible thought that rushed into his mind: was Mr. Baylord still alive? He didn't know what the police found when they checked. Had Gaspard killed him to take his place?

"What did this man look like?" Mrs. Thomas asked. "I was next door when he was here."

Annabelle glanced at Sully. "I didn't see him except in the hall when he left. And he stood away from the light."

Their footman pursed his lips and shot the whiskey bottle another yearning glance. "Well ... medium size. Funny duck. Dressed real fine, and reminded me of the Professor, but I can't say how."

As he spoke, an older, full-size coach they hadn't seen before drew to a stop in front. Like he drove the rig every day, the conductor sat in the cab up top. They watched as he swung to the ground and opened the carriage door. A plump, short, grey-haired woman in a flowered dress and outlandish hat allowed the conductor to hand her out of the coach.

"I thought it would help if your aunt stayed with us for a while." Patrick prayed it wouldn't have the opposite effect.

Annabelle nodded. "Thank you, but I do not want to be the one to explain the witches to her. Will you?"

Chapter 20

In the waters off Tabarka

AS CELWYN AND QING ENTERED THE study, the bird escaped the magician's collar to squawk his way across the room to the aquatic window, ready to greet "his" fish. This ritual included a piercing and energetic rat-a-tat-tat on the glass.

Bartholomew cringed. "That damn bird is loud."

From his position on the sofa, Kang said, "And so early in the day. You spoil him, Jonas. But, of more importance, how is your gunshot wound?" He stood. "I can examine it if you like."

Celwyn bent to peck Tara's cheek. She smiled at him, just a smile from her to him. It made him wish they were the only ones aboard the ship.

"I am fine, and ready for our adventures today." He undid his jacket buttons, and they stepped out of the room. "Here you go. You'll find I am healed and back to normal." As he submitted to Kang's examination, he asked, "Do you think that is because of Thales?"

The automat froze in surprise at the thought and then shrugged. "Unknown, but I'm glad it is getting better."

By the time Celwyn put his jacket back on and returned, Bartholomew had finished pouring coffee and handed a cup to Valentine. "It appears we're moving due east, just below the surface. Judging from the ruffling of the water, there is a storm above us."

"Good. It will slow them down." The older vampire's scowl smoothed out.

"It must be cloudy because by this time of morning, there should be streaks of sunlight penetrating the water to this depth," Bartholomew said.

Qing paced back and forth under the window, and beyond him, folds of water undulated outward from the ship. The *Nautilus* moved so fast; the schools of smaller fish couldn't keep up. Qing pecked at the glass in frustration.

"Do we know where we are?" Verne asked.

Kang moved to his favorite location—except in front of a cookie plate—the map table. He adjusted the lamp and said, "Nemo sank that ship about here." He stabbed a quadrant of the chart with a forefinger. "The other ships would have stayed close by the rest of the night, looking for the ship, or for the wreckage."

"Or attempting to," Bartholomew said.

Valentine poured a cup and offered the coffeepot to the automat, who shook his head. "First light occurred about six this morning. It is eight now."

"So, at what seems to be a medium traveling speed and possibly stormy conditions, we're between fifty to seventy-five miles from Tunis." The automat frowned. "If … that is their destination."

Tara asked, "Are there any islands between here and Tunis they would stop at?"

The automat didn't seem ready to move out of the way, so Bartholomew went to the bookshelves and pulled down an atlas. "One moment."

While they enjoyed themselves, Celwyn produced his tea and settled beside Tara. After he poured her a cup and she accepted, it took will-power not to enter her mind to confirm if she only drank his tea to please him. With a martyr's shrug, he poured a second cup and leaned back to listen to Bartholomew.

The big man grunted. "The only island before Tunis with possibilities is Spellman Island. They purportedly export rubber and cinnamon. Of course, there would be supplies for the settlers and workers there."

Tara raised a brow. "But … probably not enough for a collection of pirate ships."

"It wouldn't stop the pirates from murdering whoever was there and taking what they could find." Bartholomew shook his head. "Such bastards."

Valentine asked, "All because they do not want to go to Tunis?"

"Or," the automat rubbed his chin, "because they want to save a few days of travel and go directly to the Suez Canal. That tactic would also deceive anyone looking for them."

Celwyn crossed the room to stand at the window with Qing. As the ship moved forward, they studied an undersea sandstone wall with perfectly graduated steps that paralleled their path. Then another identical wall became visible. Possibly a sunken city? As the wall faded into the murky water, he said, "So Nemo is tracking them right now. Probably to get close to the *Quarto* without alerting the other pirate ships."

Valentine rubbed his hands together. "I think you are right. The pirates are avoiding Tunis and sneaking away. What do you think, my dear?"

Tara said, "It is fortunate that the Captain is craftier than they are."

Celwyn agreed and patted Qing's back. The action caused him to remember something. "For those of you who have developed an interest in the wyvern, you will be pleased to hear that Qing and Wye have become friends."

"No?" Kang grinned. "How fascinating!"

"Yes, Qing enjoys chewing on Wye's scales. Wye likes to watch Qing. Both are happy."

Tara laughed. "At least he isn't pecking at the decanters, as usual."

The Professor told the magician, "Nice to know, but I hope your new acquaintance doesn't complicate the situations we encounter." He got to his feet and headed to the door. "I must finish my letter to

Elizabeth before breakfast. We stop again very soon." From the speed at which Bartholomew patted his pocket, he verified he'd written his letters to the boys.

"Good to hear," Valentine said. "Our supply of nourishment is running low." He asked Bartholomew, "Is Spellman Island forested? Perhaps there are small game?"

Knowing the probable fate of the small game, the big man tried to pretend he didn't. "I do not know, but will look." He went back to the atlas. Qing flew to him and walked onto the page. Bartholomew wiggled the book, but the mechanical bird held on.

"Come here." Celwyn opened his collar. When Qing obeyed, the magician sent Kang an I-told-you-so-look; Qing was not spoiled. "I should finish my letters to Tellyhouse also. While we're gone, I hope the boys are keeping up with their lessons..." His thoughts drifted to the future as he glanced out the window at the mysterious and serene sea. Someday, with Nemo's permission, the lads would visit this ship and their eyes would light up with wonder as they looked out that window. He patted Qing's back. His little mechanical friend would have to learn to share his fish.

Valentine told Tara, "If we're traveling to the Sulu Islands to finish off Dearing's organization, we could invite some help from the family."

"I will think about it, Uncle," Tara told him, but her quick frown at Celwyn showed she didn't like the idea.

There were other reasons to hesitate. Although Celwyn would welcome the help, having more vampires aboard might push Captain Nemo's hospitality a bit too far. From Tara's reassuring wink at him, she probably thought so too and would talk her uncle out of the idea.

Breakfast was a jovial affair, with Nemo expansive in his mood and answering their questions. He even addressed Valentine in a pleasant voice instead of with his usual hesitation. The magician appreciated the improvement, but wouldn't want to be between them if an argument broke out.

"Yes, it is as we discussed. We are following the ships with the intention of getting close to the *Quarto*." Nemo buttered a piece of toast and continued, "After Jonas goes aboard her, and reports back, I want to be ready and facilitate getting Miss Redifer away from them. Then we will position ourselves underneath that ship."

"This sounds promising ... but complicated," Tara observed.

Nemo nodded his agreement. "The weather will be in our favor. If it holds, we may attempt this tonight."

"We could use Dearing to feed the sharks while we wait," Valentine suggested.

Tara sent him an indulgent look and asked Nemo, "Captain, do you agree that they are heading to the Red Sea, not Tunis?"

"I believe so." The Captain pushed his fruit away. "We'll know by noon when they turn slightly south toward Spellman Island or continue east toward Tunis."

He could not help it; the magician started to laugh. As he thought about his idea, the more he liked the artistry and irony of it, his amusement grew.

"*What?*" Kang demanded.

Bartholomew said, "I wish to know too, Jonas."

It wasn't his intention to tease the big man, just the automat. Celwyn enjoyed the entertainment and revenge dancing in his head. "What if the other ships guarding the *Quarto* followed an illusion of it, and we followed the real thing?"

Nemo's own rare smile surfaced, as broad as his own. "It would be most appropriate."

"Where would the misdirection occur?" Verne asked.

"Let's find out." Nemo stood, and the others followed him to the map table.

As they gathered around, Kang produced another chart from the various bundles piled there. A hushed moment went by while everyone held their breath.

Finally, Nemo said, "The misdirection should occur here." He pointed to a spot perhaps a hundred miles southeast of Tunis.

To the magician, he said, "I would assume you can't maintain the illusion if it is too far away."

"Correct." Celwyn considered the situation. "To produce the illusion of the *Quarto* is one thing, and to block the other ships from seeing the real ship is another. All the ships need to be close by and not see each other, at least initially, and any noise coming from the *Quarto* silenced until you can eliminate the ships guarding her." He frowned, debating whether hiding one of the ships behind a bank of fog would be easier.

"What is wrong?" Tara asked.

"Well..." Celwyn said. "I would also have to expend energy to get into the hold of the *Quarto,* possibly fight Miss Redifer's captors, and get her away from them." He shrugged. "I might not be able to do that and maintain the illusion of the ship at the same time."

"I wondered if it would be too much at once," Nemo said.

"Please don't give up on this idea." The Professor switched to Bartholomew, whose fierce expression indicated he was anxious to shoot a few pirates. "We will think of something."

"I have confidence in your imagination, Professor," Valentine said.

"At least my ideas are less risky." Kang arched a brow at Celwyn.

The magician snorted. "Let's hear it."

"We could assume two things: before our attack, Jonas will verify Miss Redifer's exact location and condition. Then, under the gloom of dusk, when the pirates are already drinking and ready for their evening, they follow the illusion ship." He opened his hands. "Which will cause them consternation.

"Why?" Verne asked. He had been so quiet, Celwyn had forgotten he sat there scribbling in his notebook.

The automat answered, "Because, just as in a chess game, the queen normally stays back until she attacks, or is attacked. The pirates on the *Quarto* will not be pleased. They will follow until they know."

"Agreed." Captain Nemo paced to the window and back, deep in thought.

"We will figure out a way," Celwyn said. "Sir, you are an expert at military tactics and planning."

"Just not working with a temperamental magician." Kang grinned.

"Ha!" Celwyn smiled back.

Nemo rubbed his chin, enjoying the possibilities, ignoring the automat baiting the magician, and vice versa. "Yes, the ships guarding the *Quarto* will be concerned and follow what they think of as that ship."

Kang relished the situation another moment and said, "At this point, depending on Jonas' skills and the condition of Miss Redifer, we can either board the *Quarto* cloaked in his invisibility, or he goes in and brings her out. He could also cause a diversion to distract the crew. It depends on many things, including how many pirates there are."

"Think of the pirates' reactions if Jonas suddenly deposited my uncle and me in their midst," Tara suggested with a gleam in her eye.

Verne blinked rapidly. "It would certainly get my attention, my dear."

The magician enjoyed the ideas and enthusiasm, although he did not particularly think he needed any help.

Bartholomew rubbed his hands together. "After we retrieve Miss Redifer, we descend under the waves again. If the pirates are superstitious, that is even better. They would hesitate." He regarded Celwyn. "It all depends on you."

The magician twirled the man-sized globe beside him.

"It certainly does." In the silence that followed his words, Celwyn considered that he couldn't do that many things at the same time but wondered how to adjust circumstances to where he could.

"Like the Professor said," Nemo stood and straightened his cuffs, preparing to leave for the bridge, "I am not used to planning an attack with a secret weapon. When the cut-off for Tunis has been reached one way or another, I will inform you."

Chapter 21

"I T IS TIMES LIKE THIS THAT I WISH we traveled above the waves." Bartholomew made the pronouncement a few hours later as they smoked and waited. "I want to see the ships we're following." He pushed a pawn forward and stared at Verne. The author licked his lips and removed his knight as carefully as if it had been made of robins' eggs.

"You are distracted," Kang told the big man. "As we all are." He covered the short distance between the chess table and the aquatic window and back. "What time is it?"

Tara glanced at the wall behind him and went back to studying the atlas in her lap. "Almost eleven."

"At least we'll know about Tunis soon," Valentine said as he tapped his foot in irritation, "but I am not clear why it is important."

It surprised Celwyn when Verne answered him. The author paid little attention to logistics, as a rule, only being concerned with his writing and the menu for dinner.

"If the pirates veer away toward the Red Sea, there are several island chains along the way, including Spellman Island." Verne watched Bartholomew take his rook. "Really? Anyhow, I believe the Captain would find the area around the islands conducive to our attack."

"I hope so," Tara said.

Qing buzzed the room, flying as fast as he could around the perimeter of the ceiling. Bird exercise. As the magician observed the aviary show, he flexed his hands while saying, "I hate waiting." Qing landed on the back of the sofa and waddled closer to rub his beak on the magician's chin. It felt like a metal file rubbing off his beard. Celwyn said, "You do too."

Minutes of terse silence went by until Granger marched in and announced, "Professor Kang is wanted on the bridge."

"I wonder what is happening?" Verne asked as Kang trotted out. The author turned his attention back to the game in time to see Bartholomew move his queen forward two spots. The big man's satisfied expression said he'd just chopped off Verne's queen at the knees. After connecting that image to something similar in the ballroom at Findbar Island, Celwyn dismissed the thought as fast as he could.

"Unknown," Bartholomew said.

"I do not know either." The magician was more interested in his foray onto the *Quarto*. He gazed through the water and the darkened surface only feet above them. If they weren't so far from the pirate ship, he would go now.

He grinned; he'd already added a few features to his planned illusion of the pirate ship, ones sure to entertain the pirates after they'd been separated from the *Quarto*. For instance, the illusion would feature half-skeletons manning the masts and canvasses. One side of their faces with flesh, and one without. At times like this, Celwyn could picture himself as an artist painting the surreal. Perhaps a watercolor, too, with small apples for eyes, and a few gold teeth that wiggled with life.

"I wonder what is so amusing." Tara joined him at the window and hooked an arm through his. Her look grew serious. "My injury has completely healed. There is no reason I can't participate in rescuing Simone."

If it were anyone else, the magician would let his emotions rule the moment and dissuade her, but he respected her opinion too much to do so. "Understood."

"Now," she laughed, "are *you* recovered from being shot?"

The magician wondered if Kang had put her up to that. "Yes, I am in no pain at all."

The automat reentered the room in time to hear him.

"Jonas often fibs about his health. Did he tell you of our previous adventure, when he became so ill that we had to seek out Thales?"

"I—"

Tara eyed the magician and said, "No, he hasn't. I just knew Thales saved him."

"Maybe we don't have time for all that right now." Celwyn glared at the automat. "What did Nemo want?"

Kang shrugged. "We talked about the weather patterns, and how far it is to Spellman Island. He thinks most of the bad visibility that will favor us will occur about five hours from now. The pirates have deviated from their path to Tunis completely."

"Wonderful!" Bartholomew slapped his thigh. "How fast are they going?"

"Nemo let me use his periscope for a minute. Those ships are designed for speed and move fast, but the ship they are guarding is slowing them down. At the moment, there is a storm sitting over the area, keeping them here."

"Are we far from land?" Celwyn asked so softly, Kang swiveled and tried to look through him.

"Yes, why?"

"Just inquiring. What else did you see?"

The automat continued to study him, trying to guess his motive. "The pirates are having a time of it with the wind and rain."

"How far away is the ship with Simone?" Tara asked.

Kang gentled his voice. "I couldn't see well because the waves were high, and they kept swamping the periscope. However, I think the ship is about a quarter mile away, no more."

"What are we waiting for!" Valentine jumped to his feet.

Nemo strode in and up to where they'd gathered by the sofas. He stood at attention, his face inscrutable, and hands clasped behind his back as he addressed them.

"The waiting is over. The storm is worsening, and the pirates are preoccupied."

A series of gongs resounded in the bowels of the submarine, like a portend of ancient horns heralding troops into battle. "In ten minutes, we'll surface about three hundred feet north of the *Quarto*." He eyed the magician. "Reconnaissance only."

"I understand, sir."

"Good." Nemo slammed one fist into the other. "Let's get on with this."

Chapter 22

THE SUBMARINE RESTED JUST BELOW the waterline as the hatch leading in and out of the ship opened a scant inch. Seawater sloshed in, and Celwyn flew out—they couldn't afford to be seen. Yet.

The magician hovered long enough to spot the pirate ship and headed straight at it. *At last.* A small thrill raced through him as he got his first look at the *Quarto.*

She floated under a heavy cloud, squat and heavy as the wind whipped her canvasses and the waves swirled high up her sides. Even in the gloom, she looked nasty: formidable, mysterious, and a tool of evil men.

Although not an expert, Celwyn identified her as a four-masted barque spanning greater than 400 feet. He found it interesting that she sat so low in the water, nearly half of her lay below the surface. She might be loaded with cargo, which would account for why the *Nautilus* had caught up with her.

As the magician drew closer, he stopped counting the cannons that ringed her deck and the pirates that crawled over every inch of the ship. They must have retrieved scores of the bastards as the other ship sank.

No matter. None of the pirates would be interested in a handsome fly unless he tickled them with his wings. Celwyn flew higher to tour the ship, buzzing in and out of the masts until he spied the entrances to the lower decks. As he watched the pirates on the bridge, he thought of several possibilities... *what if their keel no longer functioned? Or what if their mainmast wouldn't move? How unlucky for them.*

As he neared the starboard side of the stern, he discovered a black man of no more than twenty years on his knees and chained to a post. His back had been flayed open, and a bloody cat-o'-nine-tails lay next to him. With a growl, Celwyn flew closer. The lad was dead. The magician controlled his reaction and elevated himself higher to see further. He located three more butchered black men nearby. It took all his control not to wipe the deck clean of the pirates right now, lighting them afire as he did so. Between Kang insisting he learn self-management and his promise to Nemo, he contained his anger and flew on.

In the center of the deck, the door leading to the lower levels opened, emitting a blast of foul odor reminiscent of rotting meat and sweat. Celwyn held his breath and dove by a pirate scratching his ass and down the stairs.

If the upper deck had seemed murky and dark under the storm clouds, the hold hadn't any light at all. He flew aft toward embers from a pipe that glowed like a cluster of animal eyes in a cave.

Heavy smoke hung below the ceiling of a hallway that opened toward an immense area filled with barrels and crates. They leaked, producing an overwhelming smell of sap and oily tar overlaid with the tang of gunpowder. Barrels and barrels of it. Yet, a pirate leaned over them, smoking. Celwyn wiggled his nose, and the pirate's cigarette dissolved amid his surprised curses.

The magician's eyes adjusted, and as the hold broadened further in front of him, he discovered other details. The *Quarto* was a huge ship. Thousands of pounds of cargo spread out before him; no wonder this tub sat so low in the water. Feet away, dozens of makeshift bunks had been scrabbled together, even now filled with the extra pirates they'd picked up.

Center of the hold, between towering stacks of wood, another set of stairs led down to the orlop, the lowest deck of the ship. The magician zipped by a gaggle of pirates to the final set of stairs. He kept to the wall, just under the timber ceiling, and inhaled hints of what lay below.

An overpowering mixture of raw rubber and kerosene predominated along with spilled vinegary wine. Celwyn hovered above the last step and gazed through the haze at stacks of rubber for as far as he could see. He flew toward the stern, following the stench of rotten wine, and stopped. Of all things, he heard singing that grew louder as he went … until he discovered a pile of dirty pirates, discordant and drunk, and wallowing among their wine bottles and waste in front of an iron cell. One of them lay on a rifle and snored. With a look of pure disgust, the magician put the rest of them to sleep and flew into the cage.

He had found Miss Redifer.

If he hadn't expected to find her here, the magician wouldn't have recognized the beautiful blonde vampire. Dearing had lied when he said they wouldn't harm her. They had. Even unconscious, she shuddered in agony.

She had been stripped naked and covered in bruises, and her hair hung in bloody strings around her aristocratic face. In seconds, the magician removed the mounds of chains twisted around her and applied something to help her pain. He located her clothes in the corner, and with a flick of his hand, dressed her, including her boots.

"Miss Redifer," he whispered, afraid to scare her or alert anyone else nearby. "Please wake up. Tara sent me." He repeated it again.

One icy blue eye opened, and then the other. Pain filled both eyes, and she moaned. Once more, Celwyn added his type of relief. As himself, he landed in a crouch on the filthy floor in front of her.

"You met me. Jonas Celwyn, the magician."

She blinked her understanding.

"We must get out of here."

"No—others—" Concern, not fear, filled her eyes.

Concern for who? As for the fear, Celwyn had expected it, well remembering when he had been rescued after the Siege of Rhodes. "It will be all right," he whispered as he put her into a deep slumber. He pivoted to face the rest of the hold and listened. From her reaction, there had to be other prisoners. *God damn Dearing.*

With care, he made her small enough to fit on his back, and as a sparrow, he flew out of the cage and continued toward the stern where the rest of the towering stacks of crates stood like mountains. Seconds passed, and then he smelled human waste and heard whimpering as he flew over the last of the crates.

What he saw made him stop. And cry.

Small children huddled in groups, their mothers sheltering them and trying to keep them quiet. Babies wailed. Able-bodied men had been separated into cages and chained together, away from their wives and children, yet kept where they could see each other. Rivers of tears flowed over their black skin.

The last of any hesitancy the magician had about killing the pirates evaporated.

Celwyn couldn't detect any food or water. He waved a hand, sending scores of hampers full of supplies and milk into the cages. Bundles of blankets followed. Before he could do anything else, he stopped dead. In a cell by herself, a woman bled from a fresh gash across her face. She lay there sobbing and trying to hold up her torn clothing. Feet away, on the other side of the cage, a pirate sat on the floor playing with a knife. Blood smeared the blade.

The magician gritted his teeth. Nothing fancy, he told himself. He widened the bars behind the pirate, and pulled him through, across the floor behind the nearby crates, and slit his throat. The rest would soon be dead, too. He repaired the woman's face and her clothing and dosed her in a balm of calmness as he erased whatever she remembered in the last while. He didn't know what else to do, except make sure she was back with her family. With a gesture, he blocked what anyone could see, and also broadcast a silent suggestion to check the hampers for food.

There was much to think about. How to rescue the hundreds of others imprisoned here? They needed a plan. It would be one thing to remove them from the ship and then take them ... where? And he had the casualty on his back to deliver as soon as possible.

Time to return to the submarine.

All the way up the stairs, he tried to shake the anger and sadness overwhelming him as he rose hundreds of feet to the top of the canvasses. He soared between them and then higher onto the crow's nest, realizing that it was a good thing Miss Redifer could not see anything.

As the magician searched for the *Nautilus,* the rain bashed him, and the wind tried to swat him into the roiling sea. Inch by inch, he scanned the sea, expanding his search until he caught a flash of metal off the leeward side of the ship.

The magician dove into the water and to the *Nautilus's* bridge. He pecked on the glass of the aquatic window until Granger jumped.

Celwyn surfaced and waited for the ship to ascend a few feet, bringing the faint sound of the gongs. Once again, the hatch opened just enough for him to squeeze through before the ship sank below the waves again.

Chapter 23

T HE MAGICIAN FLOATED DOWN THE spiral staircase, and by the time he reached the bottom, he crouched there as himself. He laid Miss Redifer on the floor as if she had been made of glass.

As running steps resounded down the hallway, he called out, "Bring the Professor and his bag—" The magician shook his head at Valentine and his niece. The older vampire held Tara back.

Nemo marched up the corridor to them.

"I had a feeling you would have to bring her with you, Jonas." He motioned, and a pair of the crew placed a folding stretcher on the floor. As Tara struggled to reach her, he said, "We'll take her to sickbay."

Kang skidded to a stop and bent over his patient.

"There are specialized medical supplies in sickbay," the automat told Tara as he dug in his medical bag. Although he tried to keep his face as closed and

174

neutral as possible, he couldn't control the worry in his eyes. He held a stethoscope to the victim's chest.

Tara broke free of Valentine and knelt beside the stretcher. She stifled a cry of horror. "Professor … you will need my help."

Kang jerked his chin at Celwyn. "Keep her asleep and then join us in sick bay in half an hour."

"I will." He leaned against the corridor wall and breathed deeply. Although he had told Kang and Tara differently, his wound still bothered him, and he tired much sooner than he should. "Nothing wrong—" He waved Bartholomew back. "Just need … to rest."

"Of course, you do." The big man held out a hand and pulled him up. "I would tell Xiau, but he's busy. Lean on me." The magician did so, and they followed Captain Nemo into the study while Kang and the crew continued toward the bow with the stretcher. Once through the door, Nemo faced them.

"I just took the ship down another thirty feet. They won't spot us. When the squall is over, they'll have time to notice what you did."

"I didn't do … too much." The magician inhaled, catching up on his breathing. Nemo eyed him and must have decided he would stay upright, for he said nothing.

As everyone settled around the sofas, Nemo remained standing while the magician gave them an abbreviated account of his trip to the *Quarto*. He finished with a description of how badly hurt Miss Redifer had been when he found her.

"*How could they?*" Bartholomew demanded.

"This is horrible. Will she survive?" Verne asked.

"I think so," Celwyn said. "We'll know more when Xiau finishes examining her. I am due in sick bay to help soon." He felt like punching something, but they had to know what else he found on the pirate ship. After he gave them a shortened report—with the inhumanity illustrated in detail—his audience fell silent. "I'm not sure we can discuss the slaves while we wait. I am too angry to think about it right now."

Verne's eyes grew as big as the breakfast eggs he coveted. "I'd hoped the slave trading had stopped years ago."

Bartholomew jumped to his feet again and took two strides to the door before whirling around and saying, "Let's go back to that blasted ship—"

"There are a good three hundred pirates on it," Celwyn told them. "Probably closer to five hundred. We need to keep the pirates running that ship until we make other arrangements for those unfortunate people."

Bartholomew's mouth opened and closed, and he sank onto the sofa.

Nemo tore off his cap and rubbed his face. "This is a fine mess." The angry silence in the room agreed with him. "We will do something!"

"If the Professor were here, he would say that the amount of slaves precludes transferring them here," Verne said. Bartholomew nodded his agreement.

"Some will need medical attention if left in the pirates' hands any longer. They already killed several of them." The magician shook off the last of his exhaustion and sat up straighter.

Nemo asked, "How long have the pirates had them?"

"From what I could see—" Celwyn considered it. "—and what I didn't see, perhaps a week. I left them food and water, just in case."

"Most likely they picked them up in Zeralda, just before Algiers." Nemo glanced at the liquor bottles, then decided against it. Minutes passed, and their silence indicated they were thinking about evil and the various forms of avarice that fueled it.

"Dearing arranged this abomination months ago." Bartholomew pivoted to Nemo. "What are we going to do?" His eyes held a sadness that went beyond anger. That would return later.

Celwyn checked Nemo's expression and said, "I think the Captain will decide after we learn the facts. One idea; we could have Tara put a spell on the pirates, impelling them to take the ship back to Africa. We'd have to go with them so she could be close enough to maintain it."

"How would the slaves get from the coast to the interior?" Bartholomew asked.

Nemo shook his head. "We would not leave them there without knowing."

The magician felt refreshed by the tea and poured more. It always helped.

"Is there a church in Damascus or Jerusalem that would take in the slaves and help them?" Bartholomew asked.

"We could ask the monks of Monastère Sainte Claire if they will harbor them," Verne said. "They are in Beirut."

"I've heard of them. Beirut is closer at this point … and possibly safer," Nemo said.

The clock behind him struck the hour, reminding the magician he was due in sick bay soon. This day had become one full of changes and spelled a turning point in the plans of those aboard this ship.

"We should ask the slaves if that is what they want. To go back to Africa somehow, or stay with the monks at first, and then resettle elsewhere." Bartholomew sighed. "If most of them are from one village, they will have a leader we can work with."

"That helps." Nemo nodded.

"They have immediate needs. Such as being rid of the pirates," Celwyn said. "And much better conditions."

"A conundrum." Verne fiddled with the buttons on his vest. "Which comes first?"

"I do not know." The magician stood, refreshed and ready to go again. "Xiau is ready for my help with his patient. She is in a terrible state."

"For now, I'll irritate but not alarm the pirates," Captain Nemo said. "Many of them will disappear without being noticed."

Bartholomew's satisfaction showed. "Especially with the storm raging."

"Sir, I think we talked about disabling their keel?" The magician mused as innocently as he could.

"Of course," Nemo said with a nod. "I'll send divers to do it so that you won't have to continue the 'adjustment.'" He rubbed his hands together. "I still like the idea of the escorting ships following a ghost ship out to sea."

⌣

As he walked into sickbay, an atmosphere of heart-wrenching sadness gave Celwyn pause. He inhaled a bit of courage and squared his shoulders.

Under a halo of strong light, two examination tables lay in the center of the room, surrounded by cabinets along both walls. The rest of the unoccupied beds had been positioned behind curtains, ready for casualties. It made the magician wonder about some of the *Nautilus's* adventures and the outcomes.

Because of the patient's nature, the medical officer, Lieutenant Tiddle, had been excused.

Tara leaned over Simone and whispered words like "safe" and "Valentine and I are here," repeatedly. Kang had peeled back the torn dress to reveal her blood-soaked undergarments and damage to her upper body.

"They beat her savagely, Jonas. I think she has a collapsed lung and broken ribs in addition to what you see here." He lifted one of her hands. "They smashed her fingers and tore off her nails. There is a deep knife wound, too." Kang pointed. From the damage to her arms, she had fought back.

Tara stifled a wail and looked away.

The magician patted her shoulder and told the automat, "I'll start with her lung. Tara, as soon as she starts to wake up, alert me."

"I will," Tara told him and wiped her eyes.

It took a while. As he finished the lung, he asked Kang, "Do you agree that she will need nourishment as soon as possible?"

Kang examined the deep wound in her forearm that went all the way to the bone. He cursed. "Yes. She is severely dehydrated, so it is doubtful they fed her either." He aimed a thumb at the refrigerated box against the wall. "Can she have a little bottled blood for now?" he asked Valentine.

The older vampire's expression looked so forbidding, Celwyn doubted he could speak. Tara smoothed Simone's hair back and answered. "Too much will make her sick. But, yes. When she can have the variety we use, you'll let me know."

Kang retrieved the bottle of blood, and the magician went back to working on the damage to her ribs. "Do you want to hear what I found on the ship?" He didn't have to add that it would help them ignore the horror of what the pirates had done to the once beautiful vampire.

Valentine and Tara both said "yes" at the same time. She added, "As long as Simone can't hear or relive it."

Kang nodded his concurrence as he continued to clean the vampire's wounds. "She can't hear anything right now."

When the magician saw the dirt and other debris covering the vampire, he realized all her open wounds should be cleaned, not just wiped clean. It would take a while to be sure it was done perfectly;

another example of why the automat handled any-thing medical.

Celwyn repeated the story of what he'd seen on the *Quarto,* and what he had done.

"*Hundreds* of slaves?" Kang repeated.

"Yes. Probably about three hundred, give or take a few. There are at least that many pirates on that ship, too."

Valentine stared at him, his anger and high color growing to the point of an explosion. Tara tugged on his sleeve and pointed at Simone with her eyes.

The magician went back to repairing Miss Redifer's ribs. "I only killed one pirate who had attacked one of the female slaves. The other villains won't know how it happened, and will probably think another pirate did the deed." To Kang, he said, "Check her lung and the lower right ribs, please."

The automat did so while Celwyn straightened and stretched. After Kang listened to the vampire breathe, he said, "That worked well. Finish the others, please."

Valentine managed to say, "What else did you do on the ship?"

"Provided provisions for the prisoners and kept out of sight."

"Good idea." Kang began cleaning the gashes on the vampire's neck. "These aren't knife wounds—I think they used something like an ice pick on her and then ripped it out—" The automat stopped him-self. "Pardon me for being insensitive, Miss McFein."

"You do not mean disrespect," Tara told him. "And I am grateful for what you are doing."

"I am, also." Valentine bowed and said, "To both of you."

Gongs from underneath the *Nautilus* resounded and then stopped.

"I think that means we'll be on our way again." Celwyn regarded Tara beside him and for the twentieth time felt so glad it wasn't her lying on this table. It was uncharitable of him, but he couldn't help it. "How is her pain?"

Tara said, "She twinges, but stays asleep."

"Thank you." Celwyn started to repair the vampire's back, thankful that the damage was limited to two vertebrae. After he pointed them out, the automat added them to the list of things that needed surgery after Miss Redifer left the submarine.

Celwyn cleared his throat and said, "Anyhow, Captain Nemo and the others spoke about the slaves briefly, but there are no concrete plans right now other than staying close to the *Quarto* to watch over them. As soon as the storm eases, things will change."

The automat looked at Miss Redifer's once graceful hands. "Please set her right wrist, then the broken fingers."

"Certainly." Celwyn initiated the task, cursing Dearing and the rest of the pirates. After a few minutes, he shifted to a new position—he still felt tired from his little adventure, but this had to be done.

Tara touched Simone's hair. "When she wakes up, Valentine and I will be here. Jonas has cleaned the blood from her hair." Tara whispered, "I can see deep gouges in her scalp."

"It is on my list to repair, I assure you," Kang patted her shoulder.

"Thank you." Tara stood. "I need to fetch a brush and some pins for the part of it without wounds." Her lips trembled. "And clean clothes so she will feel closer to normal. Excuse me." She kissed Celwyn's cheek and rushed out.

Celwyn studied the deep cuts on Miss Redifer's face. He could temporarily fix anything, but it required real surgery to permanently restore things as delicate as the small bones in a face, the skin, and nerve endings. "Can you repair what they did to her face somewhat?" He asked the automat.

Kang glanced at Valentine as he hovered over the patient. The older vampire said, "I know it is serious. Please speak frankly."

"Let's wait until she is stronger," Kang said as he bandaged Miss Redifer's arm. "All of this... it represents a massive amount of human tragedy for one afternoon."

"Yes, it does," Valentine grumbled under his breath.

"All right then. While we work, I will provide a distraction. As you know, I miss my wife Elizabeth greatly, and talking about her helps." Kang nodded at Valentine. "I write to her every day that I cannot be with her."

"You must have many letters for her?" Valentine asked.

"Yes."

Celwyn said, "We may be stopping in Beirut to hand over the slaves into the care of the church there. We could mail the letters then."

Both Valentine and the magician faced the other way as the Professor examined the rest of his patient. After a few moments, he said, "You can turn around. There is some good news." The message came with a sigh. "The pirates were careful to not violate her or damage her torso for the Sultan's breeding program. Dearing would have killed them if he lost his fee."

Valentine growled his opinion, and Celwyn said, "We will kill them instead. There is no question of it."

"It sounds like you will take turns." The automat listened to her pulse and nodded to himself.

"Those bastards should fry in hell." Celwyn set the first of the vampire's damaged fingers. "I need your usual chatter, Xiau. This is brutal—they must have used a hammer on her fingers—the bones are in slivers."

Minutes of harsh silence went by before the vampire asked, "How long will what you are doing last?"

"For most of it, what I do will not fade until it naturally heals, as long as it doesn't involve other intricate things."

In the following bout of angry silence, the automat did his best to put cheer into his voice. "I wonder what Elizabeth bought for my birthday. It is next month, and I hope we're back home by then."

Chapter 24

A FTER KANG SETTLED HIS PATIENT, he verified her pain medicine. When he returned to the study, he found that they lunched informally on sandwiches by the sofas. The mood of the room was somber with Miss Redifer's situation, and the enormous affront to humanity in the hold of the *Quarto*.

Nemo did not join them and sent Granger in his place. The Lieutenant stood at attention and delivered his messages.

"The storm is abating, and the ships are preparing to set sail again. We moved further off their starboard side and have been observing them. The activity on the *Quarto* appears normal, and they are resetting their canvasses from the storm."

Bartholomew asked, "What does the Captain intend to do?"

"Follow them until they stop at sundown." Granger pointed upward. "After that, we will sink another of the ships guarding her."

Bartholomew's grumble reminded the magician of thunder. "I like that. They are animals."

"When do you want to re-check Miss Redifer?" Celwyn asked the automat.

Kang glanced at the wall clock. "Another hour or so. It will be time for her morphine. By that time, she might be able to tell us if we missed repairing anything." He eyed the big man. "Perhaps a visit from you would lift her spirits, too."

Bartholomew pulled down his vest and sat straighter. "I would be honored to do so. I may treat her to one of my jokes." That last statement brought a few weak smiles; they all had endured the big man's book of jokes intended for Otto and Zander.

To the Lieutenant, Celwyn said, "Please let the Captain know I could cause the ammunition stores on any of the pirate ships to explode ... unless he prefers a more personal touch."

After Granger grinned his preference and departed, Verne wiped his hands on his napkin and waited for someone to talk. Kang selected a cookie from the tray and asked, "What do we know so far?"

"You said that of the three hundred people imprisoned on the ship, many are women and children." Bartholomew leaned back and crossed his ankles.

"Yes. They appear to be safe for now, but the fetid air in the bilge of the *Quarto* is not good. I'll arrange for better air for them. I'm not sure how, though." The magician considered the logistics of bringing in what might be too much cold air as a solution and decided he needed to see the construction of the ship before he would make the adjustment. With a sigh, he went on, "By now, the bastards will have discovered the pirate I killed." The magician lifted a brow and pretended concern. "No doubt they are also wondering how Miss Redifer escaped from where they had caged her, and where she is now."

"I'm sure they are. And they do not know that we have Dearing," the Professor said. "They'll be nervous because they misplaced Miss Redifer."

"True." Valentine's expression had a deadly aura about it, the kind no one would want to meet up with. Long ago, Celwyn had noticed the vampire's presence was not only dramatic but powerful—especially when provoked.

With the slowness of savoring something he enjoyed, Valentine asked, "I wonder what they'd do if Dearing suddenly appeared on the *Quarto*?"

Celwyn laughed. "And ordered them to take the slaves to Beirut?"

Kang clapped his hands. "I love it." He eyed the vampire. "You, sir, have unique ideas."

"Wouldn't it be fortunate if the British Royal Navy was awaiting them when they arrived?" Bartholomew asked as sweetly as he could.

Over the next two nights, the *Nautilus* sank the remaining three ships escorting the *Quarto*. Both times, Celwyn moved the pirate ships further away from the others so that they wouldn't see how the vessels sank, or be able to pick up any survivors if they saw any.

On the morning of the third day, the sun rose hot in a clear and cloudless sky. Along the horizon, hints of land could be seen. The submarine kept its distance behind a wall of mist of Celwyn's making. Pieces of wood, jugs, and pieces of clothing from the destroyed ships bumped against the hull of the submarine.

The magician leaned over the rail of the *Nautilus's* platform and inhaled the fresh clean air. It felt good. So would finishing this business. In the bilge of the *Quarto,* clean air was now filtering in and pushing the bad air out. The magician couldn't recall exactly what he did, but it worked.

From beside him, Bartholomew asked, "I wonder how Miss Redifer is today? Can you imagine what that poor woman went through?" He tossed his cigar into the water. "She was sedated when I stopped by last night."

"Doing better. She will recover, per Xiau. He says she will need specialized medical attention."

Bartholomew held in his anger. "I yearn for revenge, and to stop the rest of these bastards. From what you said, these ships account for half of the men Dearing commands."

"Approximately, yes."

The big man flexed his fists until he could speak. "Do we know which church in Beirut will take the Afrikaans?" As he asked, the automat came through the hatch and onto the platform.

"I don't, but Verne happened to know a few things, courtesy of his constant research. He would be glad to share them and more." Celwyn squinted across the glimmering water. "You realize we no longer need to distract the other ships by using an illusion of the *Quarto*? I am so disappointed." He smiled at the automat. "I'll save what I had planned for another time."

"Of course, you will." Kang grinned.

"What will happen to the slaves?" The big man pulled out another cigar, thought better of it, and put it back.

"Verne said the monks support refugees in whatever they decide and will arrange for them to go home again—if that is what they want. As you can see, we're much closer to Beirut than their home." The magician gestured at the land mass on the eastern horizon. "If this is so, a long journey awaits them, even after they reach the continent." As he spoke, a shadow passed between the *Nautilus* and the sun. Celwyn located a cloud of dark birds skimming across the sea toward the other ship.

"See those birds? Petrels. They fly behind ships when there is a big storm coming."

"How do you know that?" Kang demanded.

"Just something I picked up long ago."

"Do we change our plans because of it?" The big man squinted at the birds.

"That's Nemo's call." The magician shrugged. "I am increasingly worried about how sea-worthy the *Quarto* is after the last storm. She is carrying cargo of enormous weight in her hold. And you'll recall the prisoners are kept next to crates and piles of rubber greater than twenty feet tall."

"They do not need more to worry about." Bartholomew frowned. "The next storm could be even more dangerous."

Kang sent the magician a speculative glance. "Yes, it could."

"I'm glad we are down there." The big man indicated the water below them. "Although I wonder if the trade-off is sometimes worth it. I miss some things very much."

"Such as?"

"Roasted petrel would taste like chicken."

Celwyn grinned back at him. "I do also, my friend. Nemo would find us chicken if we asked. By the way, the vampires are running low on blood. If the *Quarto* heads toward Beirut, Nemo mentioned that we'll stop on Flaxton Island for a spot of hunting, both their kind and ours. Jules says we should be able to find some bird eggs, too."

"Many possibilities." Bartholomew stared at the pirate ship, lost in his thoughts.

"Last night, after I delivered provisions for the slaves, I left them with a suggestion to have faith, and not despair, and that they conceal those supplies from the pirates."

Bartholomew asked, "How long will that suggestion last?"

"Probably as long as we're close by. Thankfully, it isn't too far to Beirut."

The big man regarded him with the same degree of suspicion that Kang sometimes did. "What else did you do?"

"I made sure the pirates who were near the prisoners couldn't be found. Just enough of them not to be seriously missed and be sure there is no retaliation. I left Miss Redifer's cage door open again. Soon, they'll believe their ship has a ghost."

The automat rolled his eyes, and the big man tossed the rest of his cigar into the water after grunting his approval. They headed down the spiral stairs and to the bridge. Captain Nemo was not there. They tried the map room next without finding him. When they entered the study, they discovered the crew setting up the table for breakfast, and Nemo standing in front of the chess table listening to Verne.

"Oh, there you are," the author said.

"Mr. Soriano and his niece are staying in sick bay with Miss Redifer and will not join us. Quite understandable." Nemo watched the crew arrange the chairs and distribute plates. "After last night, I am ravenous."

As they took their seats, Celwyn noticed his appetite had also increased when they caught up to the pirates. Platters of fruit and toast appeared. As they ate, ideas sailed across the table like a birdie in a badminton game—sometimes hits, sometimes out of bounds of logic.

Nemo confirmed that hunting on Flaxton Island would indeed be very good. "I cannot predict when we'll reach there, depending on how fast the *Quarto* travels, and assuming she sails in that direction. If she veers off that course, I assume Jonas will arrange a correction."

The magician nodded his agreement.

"We would catch up with the ship, even after a day of hunting," Bartholomew said.

Kang peeled an orange. "Sir, the plan is to follow the *Quarto* and not attack? Then make sure the prisoners are transferred into safe hands."

"At this point, yes," Nemo said.

"There is a complication." The magician chewed a bite of toast. "We will have another storm soon."

Nemo's frown deepened. "I saw some signs, but how did you come to that conclusion?"

"Petrels."

Captain Nemo nodded. "That phenomenon has always held true in my experience. "You worry about the *Quarto* foundering? I do also."

"Yes."

Kang asked, "Sir, is the solution to take the weight out of her hold?"

"You surprise me, Xiau." Celwyn cocked his head to the side and put a hand over his heart. "Suggesting something so dangerous that I would enjoy doing."

"Pfft." The automat tried not to grin back.

Captain Nemo said, "You mean—ah, I understand."

"Please share. I do not understand," Verne said.

Valentine and Tara walked in and detoured to the sofas. When Nemo and the others stood to offer them seats at the table, Valentine shook his head. "Our news will wait. Please finish your breakfast and conversation."

"As you wish," Celwyn said. "We're about to have a rather large storm. Xiau suggested we unload the massive amount of freight in the hold of the *Quarto* so she will not sink with the prisoners aboard."

Verne listened to every word with his mouth open and then requested the marmalade. Celwyn floated it to him.

Captain Nemo raised a brow at the magician. "It will be a job, even for you. That's thousands of pounds of cargo, from what you reported."

"It also must be done without the slaves noticing. I've been reminded that a display of magic would upset them needlessly." Celwyn did not say he wouldn't use magic, just that they would not see it.

As most of them finished eating, the crew began refilling coffee cups. The exception was the author, who spread preserves on another piece of toast like he painted it with gold and had to reach each edge and corner.

"We can assume the crew fears Dearing. Everyone did, from what we've been told." Kang brushed crumbs from his hands and sat back. "If Dearing was to appear in front of the pirate crew, and demand they take the slaves to the church in Beirut, then it helps the slaves and saves us the need to do so at risk, or the need to attack, possibly with casualties."

As the impact of what the automat said dawned on Bartholomew, the big man put down his cup and gulped. "I don't like this."

Verne squirmed in his chair. "I do not understand."

"You probably recall the effigies that Jonas made of himself and Bartholomew back in Turkey?" To

Valentine and Tara, the automat said, "They were most lifelike, and we used them to draw the Mafioso away from the compound so we could depart."

Verne shuddered. "That entire experience is one I wish to forget.

"This could work well." The gleam came back to Nemo's eyes.

"It will take hours to unload the cargo from the hold, even with my talents, and the storm will be here soon." Celwyn built his plan as he talked. "If the crew of the *Quarto* doesn't realize they are alone ... I've been adding fog all around them, a bit at a time ... since dawn... they will accept a visit from Dearing tonight as a normal occurrence. I can even provide the outline of one of his ships anchored nearby."

"And they won't want to spend too much time with Dearing since they 'misplaced' Miss Redifer," Kang said, with his logic on full display.

"I like it." Valentine looked at his niece. "You, dear?"

Tara nodded. "Yes." Her thoughts lay elsewhere, but she tried a wan smile for Celwyn.

"It would be helpful if the *Quarto's* rudder wasn't operable for most of the day." Nemo raised a brow at the magician. "Perhaps, even better if it sometimes works, sometimes it doesn't; I do not want them to suspect anything."

"That shall be done," Celwyn told him.

"Before we finalize plans to unload the cargo of the *Quarto*, I want to talk with Dearing again." Nemo's expression changed to one of annoyance, probably just thinking about their guest. He left the table and stood at attention. "Please excuse us.

Jonas and I have an appointment with a mad dog." He stopped in front of Tara, bowed gallantly, and took her hand. "Do not worry, we will deliver Miss Redifer to the doctors in Beirut soon."

Chapter 25

THE GUARDS AT THE BOTTOM OF THE stairs saluted Nemo and retreated to the turbine room as he and Celwyn approached the block of cells. Even from a distance, they could see Dearing spread across his bunk like a sleeping bear.

The pirate conveniently faced the other way, and this time no indelicate snoring could be heard. Nemo barked his name. Nothing.

"Allow me." Celwyn sent a collection of red-eyed mice sniffing and crawling over the bastard. Their whiskers undoubtedly tickled. Nothing. Nemo raised a hand to unlock the cage, but the magician stopped him. Loudly, he said, "That is what he wants."

When Dearing didn't move, the magician flicked a hand, lifting him off the bunk and hanging him upside down by the ankles.

"Did you see his right eye open ... just a bit?"

"I did." Nemo frowned at their prisoner. "He doesn't want to talk to us, so," he shrugged, "we can tell him about his ships some other time."

"Fine with me." Celwyn dropped Dearing on the floor, and they turned to go.

The magician had been waiting for the mention of Dearing's ships. The pirate's thoughts went straight to the four ships accompanying the *Quarto*, and then the main ship herself. Celwyn concentrated on how much ammunition she carried and where. He now knew what Nemo wanted from Dearing.

With a nod from the magician, Nemo said, "Let's talk about your headquarters on Manuk Island." A moment passed, and when Dearing turned over and tightened his lips, the picture in his mind centered on a narrow beach in front of a long dock, buildings, and several ships.

"Is that where you keep what you plundered from the churches and the museums?"

Of course, it was, but Celwyn needed him to think about it, preferably in detail.

No answer.

"What about the burning of Frejus?" Nemo regarded the man like he expected an answer; that method had worked to a point when Tara used it. Dearing tried to maintain his silence, but he silently screamed curses at them while still determined not to say anything.

"What about Sultan Mahmud's palace?"

His resolution evaporated and Dearing's eyes narrowed. "I know nothing about that."

Celwyn said, "Yes, you do. Your men killed over a hundred people that day."

Dearing's thoughts skittered to gore-smeared floors and dismembered guards in front of blood-splattered walls. The pirate privately replayed a scene of running a blade through a man several times. A satisfied expression covered his face.

"Did you steal da Vinci's painting of the Codex Mundi?" Captain Nemo asked.

The pirate clamped his mouth shut, yet they were rewarded; Celwyn finally saw Dearing's fond memory of where the paintings hung and listened to his gloating internal commentary as the pirate walked by that and other paintings.

Celwyn silently told Nemo, "*I saw what you need.*"

Nemo's eyes flickered recognition at him, and he stared at Dearing. "When were they expecting you at your headquarters? I'm afraid you won't make it."

Before a deep red color infused Dearing's face and he tried to climb through the bars, Celwyn detected the exact location of his headquarters. A very nice setup from Nemo.

With a glance at Dearing, Celwyn told Nemo in an undertone, "It is interesting. They think he will return within the next month. We shouldn't disappoint them."

<hr>

As expected, the *Quarto* hadn't moved since morning. It seemed her rudder still did not respond. The pirates had dispatched a pair of divers hours ago, but to no avail. They couldn't understand why it didn't work. From a quarter mile away, and behind the fog Celwyn had placed between them, he observed the divers as they climbed back on deck. On the *Nautilus's* platform, they could hear outraged barking from the pirate in charge before one of the divers was shot for his troubles.

Kang and the others relaxed on the platform, smoking, and watching the banks of clouds as they gathered in a mass of deep purple opalescence on the horizon. It neared five in the afternoon, and the storm was racing toward them. The automat studied Bartholomew while commenting on the storm's impending arrival; Kang's cute way of breaking the news to Bartholomew that the time had come. When the big man didn't register the too-subtle hint, Kang raised a brow at Celwyn, refusing to deliver the bad news. The magician glared at the automat.

Celwyn elbowed the big man on his other side. "We're ready to board the pirate ship and dump their cargo."

A puzzled look crossed the big man's face. He asked, "How?"

"Carefully. We also need to visit the prisoners and reassure them they will be rescued. Is there a common language they will recognize?"

"Of course." Bartholomew frowned. "Is that all that is worrying you?"

"Err... no."

Kang leaned around the magician to say, "He is afraid to tell you how we'll do it."

"Oh..."

"Wouldn't it be best if I just do it?" Celwyn asked him.

Bartholomew blinked back at him. Then he closed his eyes and released his death grip on the rail. "Go ahead."

"As you wish." Celwyn changed into a small gull. With Kang and the big man miniaturized on his back, he lifted off the *Nautilus's* platform as gently as he could, skimming low across the water to the pirate ship. As he sailed over the rail and across the deck, he heard a muted squeal from Bartholomew. The magician went straight down the stairs into the fetid hold, reaching the second set of stairs and descending at speed to the lowest deck. He had decided that, like pulling out a thorn, it was best not to prolong the agony.

They sped by the mountains of rubber and crates, past Miss Redifer's empty cell, and to the slaves in the back. The magician stopped before the last wall of crates and by the time they landed, he had reverted everyone to their normal appearance. Bartholomew shook himself and checked his hands. He seemed so relieved, Celwyn expected him to drop to his knees in prayer.

"I must disable the guards," the magician whispered. "Wait here."

Minutes later, he rejoined them, brushing dirt from his trousers.

Again, in a whisper, the magician said, "I hope you can reassure them." The murmur of nervous voices reached them from about twenty feet away. "Before we leave, I'll send in additional supplies to supplement the rations the pirates give them. I can't be too obvious, or the bastards would mistreat them for having food."

"Their rations need to look like what a ship like this would carry." Bartholomew nodded his understanding.

"My version will taste much better."

Kang whispered back, "We can do this."

The magician nodded. "It will be grim. When you are done, stay here until I return. If you are attacked—"

Bartholomew patted the pistol he carried under his jacket. "No problem."

"Hurry, Jonas," Kang said. "I do not want to fly back in the rain."

Celwyn left them to it, and once again lifted his wings. He retreated up the stairs to the main deck and then higher to the crow's nest.

First, he pushed the pirates on deck to the side and blocked them from seeing the center of the deck. With a deep rumble, it opened, the planks shifting and rearranging until they blossomed like the petals of a wooden rose above a gaping hole. Using magic, he brought up the first stack of rubber. It was heavy work that drained his energy, he soon discovered. The initial set went over the side with a loud splash that drew a crowd of pirates to the rail. The second load went over the stern, and they rushed there. He tipped the third installment over the starboard side.

Round and round they went until thousands of pounds of rubber had been dumped in the sea and he felt his exhaustion keenly. After he closed the deck again, the wood appeared as smooth as if it had never been disturbed. Bartholomew would have to figure out what to tell the slaves if they peered too far beyond their cages and saw that most of the cargo had vanished.

The magician flapped his wings slowly, conserving energy, as he swooped back down the stairs and into the belly of the ship. He landed on top of the remaining crates surrounding the slaves and rested. As he leaned over the top, he listened to Bartholomew's baritone. The big man's audience couldn't take their eyes off him, hearing the comfort in what he said, gazing at him as if he was a god. Some wept. Others moaned or prayed. Bartholomew gestured outside and, from his words and their reactions, Celwyn deduced he'd just told them about the storm that would be upon them soon. Lastly, he instructed them not to worry, the extra freight in the hold was gone; the ship would stay afloat.

Celwyn sent the big man a silent message suggesting he tell them that new supplies could be found at the rear of each cell, and to reassure his audience not to be afraid; the sea is benevolent and will take care of them. They must also hide the goods from the pirates. Despite his intentions, this time he couldn't help adding in fruit and other items the pirates wouldn't have given them. They would eat that first. From beside Bartholomew, Kang looked ready to burst with curiosity as he read the big man's expression and listened to his message in their language, a most beautiful one.

By the time Bartholomew finished talking, Celwyn felt strong enough for their trip back to the *Nautilus*.

Chapter 26

THE MAGICIAN SPENT THE EARLY evening sleeping to prepare for his evening visit to the *Quarto*. He expected a spot of magical fun. As he lay down, the last thing he remembered was the murmur of Kang's voice in the study.

It neared midnight when everyone gathered on the submarine's platform to observe the *Quarto* through the mist. The storm had abated, and the pirates swarmed the deck like hundreds of colorful ants. This was the high time of their evening when they drank and brawled, but tonight they also kept an eye on the sea. They were on edge. As they should be. Somehow, every time one of them ventured into the shadows by the rails, they vanished.

The magician increased the fog on the water, despite so recent a windstorm. When he finished, no one on the ship would have been able to see more than a few feet beyond the rail. Much closer, the tendrils of mist that moved across the deck behaved as if alive. Some melancholy music, a dirge perhaps, would have been a wonderful addition, but it would not have matched Dearing's normal entrance.

Far below, the magician tied a small skiff of his own making to the starboard side of the ship. The swells still rose high, and the sea remained rough from the storm. The boat dipped into a trough, and seawater flooded in, soaking him. *Damn pirates.* Celwyn shook his leg and used magic to get the water out of his boot before producing a rope ladder and scampering up the side of the ship.

As he slung a leg over the rail, he hung there. Now that he wasn't flying by in a hurry, he was once again amazed at the filth. A few feet away, a corpulent pirate dropped his bottle and yelped in surprise. If there had been any doubt that Celwyn's copy of Dearing would pass inspection, there wasn't now.

"Captain!" The fat pirate whirled and bellowed, "It's *him*!! The *Captain*!" Voices resounded around the deck in various languages and levels of anxiety. "It's him!" Footsteps thundered across the boards, and others dropped out of the rigging, while the rest of the pirates poured out of every corner of the ship. Their jabbering held as much fear as excitement.

After this afternoon's session with Dearing, the magician had seen in the bastard's thoughts a clear picture of the man he sought right now, a skeletal pirate nearly as tall as Bartholomew. Jakow was the Russian Cossack who commanded the *Quarto* under Dearing. It seemed the Russian sometimes challenged Dearing and got his face cut up for his trouble. The man's complete lack of hair, round head, and long jutting jaw added to the image of a skeleton. Dearing had nicknamed him Skull Man.

From what Celwyn could determine, Dearing didn't fear Jakow and thought it humorous that his first lieutenant hated him. At the same time, Dearing maintained a healthy fear that Jakow could turn the other pirates on the ship against him if he felt like it.

"*Capitán! Capitán! Capitán!*" they shouted, repeating the title like a chant. When the yelling stopped, the deck grew so quiet Celwyn could hear the aromatic pirate next to him breathing. Just like Dearing would have done, the magician caressed the long knife on his belt and posed with one leg splayed forward.

"Well?" He challenged them with a vicious glare.

Slowly, as if he had just awoken from a nap, Jakow emerged from the shadows under the bridge and strolled up the deck to him. He had been there the entire time, watching.

Celwyn waited, hands on his hips and doing his best imitation of Dearing's disdain. While researching the pirate's mind, Celwyn observed the interactions between Dearing and various crew members. They all seemed devoted to him, one way or another. Celwyn hoped it was a recent memory, not just an unfulfilled wish Dearing had conjured up.

In the dead silence, Celwyn waited, his hand resting on his long knife, ready to draw. The eeriness of so many men, so still and afraid, would have fed Dearing's ego more than anything or anyone else could do—if he had been here to see it.

From the look in Jakow's eyes, he didn't regard Dearing in that light, not at all. He waited for as long as he could, dragging out his disrespect, and then dropped to a knee in front of the man he thought of as his captain.

Quicker than the blink of an eye, Celwyn drew his sword and laid it on the back of Jakow's neck. He pressed down as a collective cry went up from the hundreds of pirates. Blood trickled from under the blade and Jakow's gaze grew colder, but he didn't speak. Or move.

"Get up." Celwyn hoped like hell his imitation of Dearing's voice rang true as he whirled the bloodied blade high for them all to see before putting it away.

The skeleton stood. His skin looked quite pale, and the magician wondered why ... in the chill evening air, Jakow only wore breeches and boots, and his torso shone with sweat. Yes, he was sick.

"We have a change in plans." Celwyn sneered at Jakow as he spoke. "Bring your lieutenants over here."

Jakow's gaze warmed a bit with curiosity. He motioned, and four men detached themselves from the others and ran forward. Like a constipated bear, Celwyn swaggered and paced, imitating Dearing while he made them wait. He pushed out his chest and shouted a curse at the nearest pirate, another typical gesture.

When he thought it was time, Celwyn faced Jakow. "You'll sail to Beirut. The other ships are going to Hispaniola. I have already sent them." The magician stopped in front of one of the lieutenants, a nervous one, and backhanded him just as Dearing would. "Pay attention!" Portraying Dearing was a disgusting job.

"Yes, sir!"

"We're no longer in the slave trade," he told Jakow. "We have something better. It pays ... much more gold."

That lit up the skeleton's eyes. "What do you mean? Sir."

Celwyn leaned into his face and yelled, "*I mean what I say*!" Jakow's eyes dropped, and Celwyn barked, "Take the slaves to the monks in Beirut. Leave them there. I've made arrangements with the buyer. Then go to Bintan and deliver the vampire."

Jakow didn't say a word about Miss Redifer's disappearance, but his eyes shifted to the left. It seemed he feared Dearing too much to tell him the truth.

Wisely, the skeleton backed up a pace before asking, "Why not collect money for the slaves? Or kill them?"

Celwyn ground out, "Because I only have part of the money, Fool." He shoved Jakow, and the man fell on his back. The magician planted a boot on his chest as he withdrew his sword again and placed the point at Skull Man's throat.

"If anything happens to the slaves, if I am denied a single guinea because of you, *it will be your neck*! Do you understand?"

"Yes."

He still sounded defiant, but in Jakow's thoughts, Celwyn saw that the gold came first.

"Get up—"

As he dusted the dirt off his pants, Jakow said, "What about the British Navy? I hear they occupy Beirut harbor."

Celwyn hadn't expected the question, but he lied well, as Xiau and Bartholomew could attest to. "Most of them left a week ago for Bangladesh. There are uprisings in India."

Jakow rubbed his chin and nodded but without enthusiasm.

Celwyn moved until there was only a hair's breadth between them and said, "I repeat, if the slaves are harmed, we won't be paid."

Jakow stared back at him. As superstitious as pirates could be, it would be useful to guarantee everyone's cooperation, the magician decided.

He concentrated, bringing a full-sized Wye forward. A collective gasp arose as the wyvern grew larger and solidified, curling and writhing in the air above them, before floating down to recline on the deck. He laid his head on Celwyn's shoulder. Hundreds of pirates couldn't look away as the magician rubbed the wyvern's ear.

Celwyn locked eyes with Jakow. "Feed the slaves and make sure they have water. Take out the waste buckets." He reached and brought another of the dirty pirates forward by his hair. "Make sure no one touches any of them." Wye rolled over the man's shoulder and down his back before the pirate went limp and slid to the deck. "My friend here will remain with you to be sure these instructions are carried out. He will be watching. Even if you can't see him."

Wye rose and streaked by the first line of pirates, slapping them down with his tail before ascending to the top of the masts.

"What are you waiting for?" Celwyn demanded in as nasty of a voice as he could manage.

Jakow goggled at the wyvern. "We... We will set sail as soon as we can chart our location, and our keel is working again."

"Excellent." Celwyn slung an arm around the man. "You can double your share of the gold if every one of them arrives safely. If any are hurt—" He let the threat hang in the air and then grabbed Jakow by the throat, "Of course that goes for that vampire bitch too. She must look like the prize she is."

As he released Skull Man, Celwyn noted how he avoided eye contact, as did the nearby pirates. A few tried to fade into the shadows. Jakow waved at his lieutenants, sending them back to their stations.

Celwyn studied the man, how pale he appeared, and the general air of sickness hanging over him. "What is the matter with you?"

At once Celwyn realized his mistake. The skeleton's gaze narrowed in suspicion. The magician quickly entered his mind and backed out again.

"Still the malaria?"

Jakow's furrowed brow relaxed. "Yes."

The Royal Navy might treat that if they didn't hang him first.

Celwyn slung a leg over the rail.

"Your gold will be waiting for you in Singapore," he lied. "Tell the men what I said."

As he climbed down, Wye floated above the deck and then dissolved. Celwyn left another version of him diving in and out of the top of the canvasses and rowed away into the fog.

Chapter 27

EVERYONE HAD WAITED UP FOR THE magician to return from his trip to the *Quarto*. As he walked into the study, the clock chimed twice.

"You must be slow at rowing, Jonas," the automat drawled and yawned to cover a grin.

"Ha! Perhaps. But a successful evening all around. They will do as we expect and sail for Beirut in short order. The slaves are suddenly very valuable to them."

"Wonderful news," Bartholomew said with his first real smile in days.

"How do we know the prisoners will be safe?" Valentine asked.

"As Dearing, I promised their leader double their purse." Celwyn added, "I'll verify the pirates give the slaves provisions before they sail. Before then, I'll send another load of staples the prisoners can hide, such as fresh fruits, jerky, and preserved fish. It can't be something they have to cook, since they would attract attention doing so."

"I understand, but isn't it too bad we still need the pirates to man the ship?" Bartholomew's brow furrowed. "Otherwise, we would make sure they are gone, and leave the slaves free to roam the ship."

"Yes, it is unfortunate that we cannot." The magician couldn't picture himself running the ship single-handedly and maintaining that illusion for days. He deposited himself next to Tara and stretched out his legs. He eyed Nemo. "Sir, do you have enough men to man the pirate ship and this one?"

"Frankly, no. A ship that size would need at least 250 men to run her, and Beirut is still a distance from here. It would make us vulnerable."

Bartholomew said, "At least we considered it."

"True. I feel like I need a bath after imitating Dearing." Celwyn turned to Tara and asked, "How is Miss Redifer?"

"Better physically, but I worry about her."

Kang poured the magician's tea and handed him a cup. His expression contained a careful sort of somberness and evasiveness that gave Celwyn pause. "Miss McFein and Mr. Soriano and I have been discussing his niece's condition. After that, I spoke with the Captain."

Tara took Celwyn's hands with the kind of regret that alarmed him further. "She needs many surgeries, and a special kind of operation to repair her face and neck, and elsewhere."

With a drag in his voice, Celwyn said, "I understand. My help is only temporary for things such as this." He patted her hand. "What do you want me to do?"

Tara sent Nemo a look. He nodded. "The Captain has kindly offered to take us to Beirut ahead of the pirates. Once there, I will stay in the city with Simone."

Valentine said, "We have a few members of our family there to help, and we'll bring in a special doctor from Rome. My niece's recovery will take months."

Celwyn had no trouble seeing that this had already been discussed and decided. It wasn't his place to make the decision. He did not like it. Kang caught his eye and raised a brow that said, *it is what it is.* When the magician saw the resolution and regret in Tara's beautiful eyes, he knew it was final.

Bartholomew watched the interplay for a moment, and then said, "After Beirut, we would continue—" he couldn't help a shudder, "—underground to the Red Sea."

The magician looked out the aquatic window. Like Qing, he couldn't see anything besides inky water. But Qing never gave up. The bird tapped on the glass.

Celwyn swiveled back.

"If we must do this, we will." He sent Tara a silent message. *"I will miss you terribly."*

The Captain said, "Mr. Soriano will continue with us to Singapore and beyond to Dearing's compound." He nodded at the older vampire. "We both have a score to settle with the pirates, and I heard Dearing's men tried to kidnap another of his family in Milan before successfully capturing Miss Redifer. There is also the attack on Miss McFein in London.

I agree that after she served her purpose in bringing you to her rescue, Dearing would have sent Miss McFein to Bintan also."

"We'll need drawings of Dearing's compound to plan our attack," Bartholomew said.

The magician yawned and politely covered it with a hand. "I must retire for the night. Planning attacks isn't my specialty." He usually just blundered ahead and enjoyed himself. "Tomorrow, I will provide permanent drawings for everyone's use."

"Thank you." Nemo nodded at him.

The kiss Celwyn placed on top of Tara's head lingered. He informed the others, "Before we sail tomorrow, I'll verify the pirates are taking care of the prisoners." He bowed. "Good night."

PART II

Chapter 28

ON EACH OF THE NEXT TWO DAYS, Celwyn flew Bartholomew over to the pirate ship and into the hold next to the slaves. The big man spoke with them and reassured them, while Celwyn verified there were no new atrocities by the pirates, and that they had clean water and food. Where he felt it wouldn't be seen by their captors, he added more elaborate food intended to comfort them.

On each visit, Bartholomew joined them in song, causing a few raised eyebrows and many smiles. Celwyn put a block on anything being heard on the deck above. With the food, the magician included some newspapers and periodicals, and the big man reminded them to hide them from their captors. The magician debated whether to include toys for the children, finally deciding it would be difficult to explain if the toys vanished when he was too far away to maintain them.

Above all, Bartholomew made his message one of patience and hope.

On the morning the *Nautilus* arrived in Beirut's wide and picturesque harbor, Celwyn took one look and decided that it had become a beautiful seaside city, and one that had grown since his last visit. After another few minutes of memories, the magician shook himself; the *Quarto* trailed them by only six hours, and he didn't have time to waste. A few surprises for the pirates must be arranged before then.

Their trip into town was somber as they transported Miss Redifer to the Paix Sérénité Clinic. Once ashore, the Professor and Bartholomew went on ahead to warn the church and the British Navy about the *Quarto* and its large and precious cargo.

Valentine had been his usual solicitous self as he guided them to the clinic. The magician could picture him as a diplomat, albeit with a bloodthirsty side when provoked. They passed a discreet sign outside the clinic that advertised "Rest and Privacy." A fancy place for wealthy patrons, no matter the purpose of their stay.

Later, as Tara walked the magician out of the clinic, they held hands and then embraced. In private whispers, they bemoaned their separation, and she reminded him it would not be for long.

What the hell. Celwyn thought. He had to know. He led her to a bench under a flowering vine that tickled the back of his neck when he sat beside her.

"You know we have very diverse lives."

Tara's eyes lost their sadness and became alert. "Yes."

The magician surrounded them with tiny blue butterflies that no one else walking by could see. With a gentle hand, he caressed her chin and lips and leaned closer. "I want to someday not have to leave you." He cleared his throat. "Can I assume you share those feelings?"

With a fingertip, she held up one of the butterflies and let its wings flutter in her hair. A moment went by, and he had to listen closely to her whisper.

"I do. But I have no idea of how we would be able to." She opened those remarkable eyes at him. "I do not know if we can." At her last words, tears formed and began falling.

"Please." The magician wiped them away. "Think about it. That is all." At her nod, Celwyn smoothed the hair off her brow and did not voice his hunch that it could be much longer until they talked about this again. All kinds of things tended to happen to them. But, as he gazed at her, he knew Tara would be by his side for as much of the time as possible.

By mid-afternoon, Kang and Bartholomew rejoined the magician atop a hill that afforded them an excellent view of the blue sea and verdant hills. They lingered here while the *Nautilus* picked up supplies. It also afforded them a few moments to talk and enjoy the city.

Bartholomew smoked a cigar and continued to scan the water while they awaited the pirate ship's arrival.

"We brought bushels of toys to the church as planned," the automat told Celwyn. "Did you do the same after delivering Miss Redifer?"

"Yes. I mostly bought wooden building blocks, dolls, and balls. They are small and sturdy for traveling. And will last long after I have left them. The clothing will arrive tomorrow." Celwyn asked. "What happened when you warned the Brits about the pirate ship?"

Kang had pulled a small paper bundle out of his pocket. He offered them one of his cookies and then chewed. "We sent in a note with the description of the ship and the pirates and details of the prisoners in the hold. If they do as we suggest," he bit into another cookie, "they'll move their ships away from the dock so that the pirates won't see them and turn tail. And they'll wait until the *Quarto* has unloaded the captives before approaching them."

"That should prevent the slaves from being used as shields." Bartholomew's frown returned. "How do we know the pirates didn't kill more of them?"

"They were told they wouldn't get paid, which seems to be the ultimate inspiration for everything they do. I also spot-checked their thoughts on my visits." Celwyn shook his head in disgust at what he had heard in their heads. "Dearing had the pirates scared before, and I just reinforced the impression that they had better do as 'Dearing' said. Did you hear I took Valentine over for a visit with the pirates last night?"

"Yes. Nemo told us. Seemed he wanted a spot of revenge before the British took over," the big man said. "The agreement was that it would be done discreetly."

"It was. If we hadn't accommodated him, we'd be listening to Valentine for weeks complaining that the actual culprits had not been dealt with, at least by him." Celwyn rolled his shoulders and realized that his wound was finally healed. Was Thales still helping him? He wished he knew.

Minutes went by as they gazed across the bay. The only sound was the Professor chewing until Celwyn realized something. "When the *Quarto* sails up to the docks, I should be there to be sure there isn't a confrontation."

The automat said, "Good idea. But my guess is that they'll pick the least busy dock and unload their cargo without fanfare. And they'll be dressed like regular crewmen, not the pigs that they are."

"Earlier, we delivered a note and funds to the Monastère Sainte Claire, asking them to be ready for the slaves. They'll meet with the officer in charge of the British and be on the quay to greet the slaves." Bartholomew's expression contained a bit of hope for the human misery they'd found. He squinted, scanning the docks, and then the entrance to the bay from the west. A nice breeze arose, tickling their noses and lifting the brims of their hats.

"Very nice to hear. What kind of cookies do you have?" the magician asked the automat.

"Coconut."

"I wonder if Elizabeth approves of your cookie-eating."

"If she knew, she might." Kang shrugged. "On the way here, I sent letters to her and Tellyhouse, and a telegram saying we were on our way to Singapore."

Bartholomew said, "We might have telegrams when we get there. Some of them will remind us to send the boys' science lessons."

The Professor shook his head. "You were there at the telegraph desk when the clerk said it takes four weeks to get a telegram to Prague, plus six weeks back to Singapore."

Bartholomew smiled. "Just my wishful thinking."

Chapter 29

Prague

RICARDO SHOUTED AND RAN AFTER the calèche as it traveled down the driveway away from Tellyhouse.

Edward heard him and pulled on the reins as Ricardo reached them and hung on to the side of the cab while he caught his breath. With his other hand, their chef handed Patrick a package tied with string.

"What's this?"

Ricardo panted. "Sandwiches … for your lunch… and apples. It isn't much, and I will have tea ready at five if you are able to return by then."

"Thank you," Patrick told him. After the horrors of this morning, he realized he had forgotten to eat all day. "It is much appreciated."

"You catch whoever did this." When Ricardo crossed himself, his expression belied the gesture. "Mrs. Kang was a lovely person."

Edward didn't hesitate. "We will." He shook the reins, and they clopped forward again.

Edward remembered the telegraph office on Ovida Street.

During Mr. Swayne's wedding, he'd driven the Professor, Mr. Celwyn, and Mr. Bartholomew there to meet Captain Nemo and another bloke. Although he'd only watched the dark-skinned man with the heavy mustache for a few minutes, Edward could appreciate Nemo's power and presence: he commanded men, campaigns, and explorations. The funny-looking little chap in the grey suit must have been the author. Edward had read a few of his books, but he preferred American Westerns. Someday, he would visit the Wild West and shoot a few rattlesnakes.

As he pulled to a stop, Edward cast an eye over the crowds in the street, and the coaches waiting nearby. Everything seemed normal. A café of petite tables adjoined the telegraph office, and the aroma of strong coffee accompanied them when they entered Dancek's Sweets and Telegrams. The shop appeared empty as they walked by bins of treats to the rear.

Patrick drew the pad of slips toward him, then hesitated.

"Do you need some help, sir?"

The relief on Patrick's face caused Edward to pat him on the back.

"Yes, please." Patrick wrung his hands together. "This is horrible. How can I tell the Professor? How?"

"Keep it simple," Edward said. "Tell them what you know." They both jumped as the door slammed behind them, and a pair of boys no older than Otto entered the shop. Dancek's sold a large variety of candy, and these lads favored water taffy.

"Where are we sending the telegram?" Edward asked as Patrick dipped the store's pen in the inkwell and began writing.

"It is still Singapore. The last I heard was that they would stop there." Patrick labored over the form, wadding it up and starting over. "Any message will take at least twenty-five days to get there from here."

"You worry it won't get there before they do?"

Patrick finished a line. "Yes. We'll arrange for a messenger to visit here every day until there is a reply." He replaced the pen. "Let's send this on its way and tackle the coven next."

Minutes later, Patrick and Edward approached the calèche, and the rain returned with a reminder of who was really in charge of their world. Patrick shook the water off his hat and helped Edward pull the top over the two-seat carriage. Just as Edward made ready to climb into the driver's seat, Patrick exclaimed, "What is this?"

To Edward, it just looked like a woman's black glove, but Patrick had paled, and his hand shook as he dropped it back on the seat. Like a leaf off a dead branch, a piece of paper fell out of it. He didn't want to, but Patrick picked it up.

"Tell the Professor that his wife begged for her life."

"Damnation," Edward breathed as he read over his shoulder.

Patrick mouthed the words again. He pivoted, checking the streets all around them, and raised his eyes to Edward. "This is an abomination. *Sheer evil!*" He shook the paper at Edward. "We need to tell the police."

Edward waited until Patrick settled in the back and said, "Excellent suggestion. If I may say so, we should probably do that after we visit the coven; then we will know what Francesca will do for us."

"You mean ... we do not know how much more protection she would provide."

Edward nodded. "We need to know how much to demand of the police."

With a face of supreme distaste, Patrick put the piece of paper back in the glove and laid it on the carriage floor. "Yes." He blinked several times as emotion threatened to overwhelm him. "Would you mind terribly if I waited outside the coven for you? I don't think I can endure dealing with Francesca right now." *Or ever*, he thought.

"Certainly, sir." Their carriage rolled out onto the street. "I would suggest staying alert while you wait. It is a most interesting neighborhood with odd and fantastic inhabitants."

After holding off while Patrick waited in front of the coven, the rain accompanied the calèche all the way to the police station. In between maneuvers through traffic, Edward called over his shoulder bits of information from his meeting with the witch.

"It wasn't too bad this time, sir," Edward reported. "Francesca was in a decent mood."

The head of Prague's premiere coven ran it as a business, collecting fees for spells, and anything else she could think of. Edward had heard that the witch also had a colorful past with Mr. Celwyn from years ago, and regularly threatened him. If the two of them ever seriously fought, Edward's money would be on Mr. Celwyn.

He slowed the carriage, and they made a turn onto Georgia Street, swerving around a bicycle rider who apparently had begun drinking before noon. "Francesca sends her condolences about Mrs. Kang."

"Will she help us?"

"Yes. In fact, she waved part of her fee. The spells will be—"

Edward pulled hard on the reins. The calèche halted inches from a gaggle of uniformed students crossing the street under the watchful eyes of several nuns who must have believed in divine intervention when it came to traffic and horses. He cleared his throat and lowered his voice while they waited on the flock of children. "The spells will begin later today, and they'll be layered on top of the existing spells."

"Why?"

"Francesca says the spells completely cover the house. This adds another tier of security." When the children, all twenty-six of them, reached the other side of the street, Edward noted Patrick's expression of despair and decided a short interlude was in order. He steered their carriage to the side out of the maelstrom of coaches, horses, and general noise.

"Perhaps we should sample those sandwiches, sir."

"Thank you ... for suggesting this." Patrick unwrapped the package Ricardo had given them and handed Edward a sandwich. "He makes this bread every morning."

They ate in companionable silence for several minutes until Edward said, "We best get on with this sorry mess." He picked up the reins, and minutes later, they rolled down Charles Street, splashing through the flooded intersections and to the police station.

As they came to a stop in front, Edward faced him. "Sir, I can leave you here and return after I hire the guards we'll need."

Patrick sat up straight, his sadness put aside for now. "First, I want to see how many guards the police will provide." He poked at the glove with a fingertip. "Perhaps this will help our case."

"I recommend you ask for a long-term commitment from them." Edward felt sure Patrick was aware he oversaw their security at Tellyhouse, especially with Mr. Celwyn and Mr. Bartholomew away. Before now, it hadn't been too much of a problem. "Until the Professor returns to us, that bastard that killed Miss Elizabeth won't stop." Edward's voice held no quarter. "I swear, I will kill him first!"

Chapter 30

The Mediterranean
Between Beirut and the Red Sea

THE CLOCK ON THE STUDY WALL struck the six o'clock hour as Jules Verne bemoaned, "Two hours before dinner." He cast a forlorn look toward the corridor and the galley beyond.

"Is tonight a maintenance night before Singapore?" Celwyn asked their host.

"Yes, it is." Captain Nemo relaxed on one of the sofas in the study; the stress of hunting and then delivering the *Quarto* was over.

"It sounds like everyone had quite an afternoon," Verne said. "I would like to know what happened, please."

"After the *Quarto* sailed into port, I sent a messenger back to shore. We found our informant on the docks; the slaves were unloaded in good condition without incident and are being cared for by the monks as expected. Like the rest of you, I had my men deliver funds and quantities of supplies to the church." The Captain nodded at the magician. "I understand that you three also added toys for the children, a very nice touch. Our efforts will ensure that the Afrikaans will be taken care of, and I'm sure they enjoy being on land again and in safety."

"When I spoke with them, many intended to resettle beyond their homeland. I wish them well. And thanks to you and the *Nautilus*, they have a good start." The big man addressed the others. "We have had a successful day so far." A nervous tic started in his right eye. "Where are we now?"

"If we were topside, you could still see Beirut in the distance," Nemo told them. "We're passing by the Raouche Rocks."

Strong sunlight painted the water above the *Nautilus* as she traveled at a moderate speed about a dozen feet below the surface. The bay here did not appear to be very deep, and the magician caught glimpses of sand shelves below them, littered with the unfortunate ships who encountered the rocks, or conflicts. As they traveled by, the mounds of debris chronologized maritime history: everything from the curved stern of a Greek trireme to the pointed bow of a Roman corbita, a few quinqueremes, and many vessels Celwyn couldn't recognize. Silvery bonitos and blue-fin tuna darted away from the submarine, much to the consternation of Qing. After a while, the mechanical bird became a touch melancholy. That wouldn't do.

Celwyn concentrated on Wye and cautioned him that no one else should see him. When the wyvern solidified beside Qing, he measured as small as the bird, and lay on the window ledge, gazing up at him. Qing hopped up and down one time before emitting a squeak of joy.

The magician waited, but no one else in the room reacted. The wyvern stared at Qing adoringly and showed his teeth. In return, Qing rubbed his beak across Wye's back and repeated it several times, the sound like a steel bow across the metallic strings of a mandolin. The magician felt a certain level of pride that they could get along.

The automat approached the aquatic window. "No fish here, Qing." He stopped still. "Did you hear that?"

"No."

The automat said, "It sounded like metallic music."

"You don't say." Celwyn blinked at the automat, who stared back at him.

From the sofas, Nemo called over, "To answer the earlier question; we are a few miles from Tyre. We will settle down near Haifa this evening."

"Sir, our dinner will be even more pleasant if we can glean additional information from Dearing first, wouldn't you say?" Celwyn asked as he stood by the sofa, feeling residual hostility at the pirates for causing his separation from Tara. "It would be useful to have a description of what all Dearing has in his vaults."

"True." Nemo seemed lost in thought. "It certainly would."

The magician finished his cup and stood and bowed. "After you."

This time Bartholomew came along, being a most excellent judge of people and a very observant audience. Seeing him would remind Dearing of the big man's part in his capture and make the visit entertaining ... and to the bastard, most memorable. The Captain must have thought so too, and his buoyant mood accompanied them down the steps to the lower deck where the whining of the turbines hummed with comforting regularity.

Celwyn gestured, and three plush wing-backed chairs appeared. They made themselves comfortable.

As Dearing sat on his bunk, he studied them, then licked his lips and concentrated on Celwyn. It took a scant second for the magician to understand. Before they captured him, for most of the pirate's life, he had probably drunk several bottles of wine a day, and the bastard remembered the bottle Celwyn had given him on their last visit. If he had an opportunity, the pirate would slit Celwyn's throat, but right now, he wanted something from the magician, as did Celwyn from him. When the magician shrugged and sent the bastard a bottle, Dearing was so anxious he pulled the cork out with his teeth and gulped.

Captain Nemo glanced at his pocket watch. "Besides everything in the museums that we talked about, what other art did you steal?"

Dearing avoided his eyes while he drank, probably trying to determine why they wanted to know. When Celwyn checked his thoughts, he found exactly that. He also discovered fleeting glimpses of paintings and sculptures. Some objects could be early Greek, from before the Byzantine period.

Nemo demanded of Dearing, "Tell us about your headquarters. I understand your vault is near one of the Nanai graveyards."

The pirate's eyes flamed, and his thoughts confirmed the location while he tried to figure out how they knew of his secret.

Celwyn was not in the mood to drag this out.

The magician signaled Nemo and Bartholomew; he would try something new. After silently detailing a few things for their benefit, he dispatched a fat rat into the cage and at the same time sent an identical rat racing to the vault pictured in Dearing's mind. The rodent flashed its teeth at the pirate as it scurried up a wall and onto a painting. In the pirate's head, he tried to grab it, but it wiggled away and onto the next painting. Dearing visualized the rodent and the canvas in rich detail.

The rat hesitated in front of the next painting, a Fragonard. Celwyn repeated the process several dozen times, cataloging the collection with the rat on the portrait and Dearing supplying exactly what it looked like. After each item, the magician passed along the details of the painting to the big man, who wrote it down. When the rodent scampered down the steps into the sub-basement of the vault and to a smaller room, Dearing became even more alarmed.

His curses grew hoarse as he flung himself across the cell, grabbing at the air near the ground, and then following it upward like a hairy mime.

Every time the pirate leapt toward the rat, it switched its tail at him and ran down the next corridor of treasures. *Ah.* It stopped in front of what Dearing had worried about the most; the painting Nemo had described, the *Tower of Babel,* by Hieronymus Bosch.

Celwyn nodded success to Nemo and directed the rat onto the frame of the painting. As Dearing screamed his rage, the rat scurried away slowly, stopping every few feet to allow the infuriated pirate to keep up. This provided a leisurely exhibition of the surrounding details for Celwyn to absorb. When it reached the far end of the room, the rodent hid under a table and waited for Dearing. The pirate lunged for it, smashing the table into splinters. The rat sat up and emitted a guttural human laugh before darting away again.

In his mind, Dearing followed the rat back to the upper room and then outside into the island sunshine. The pirate roared and sliced at it with his sword, something he wouldn't have done in the narrow space between the artwork.

Satisfied that they had the information they needed, the magician directed the rat in the cell to crawl up Dearing's leg and sit in his lap. When the pirate opened his eyes, he screamed louder and swatted it away.

Oh well, all entertainment eventually comes to an end. Celwyn dissolved the rat in a burst of iridescence.

Throughout the entire performance, Bartholomew watched Dearing with a level of anxiety and fascination, especially when he tried to catch the rat. Sweat poured off the pirate's face, and he shook the bars of his cage.

With a confidential air, Bartholomew asked, "Tell us, those slaves on the *Quarto*... who did you sell them to?"

Dearing jerked his head like a bee had bitten him. He stared at the big man. "How did you—"

"Just tell us," Bartholomew said.

When Dearing clamped his mouth shut, Celwyn applied his own version of pressure; he sent a spotted snake slithering across the floor faster than Dearing could blink and up the pirate's trousers. Celwyn had no guilt about his methods of persuasion... an imaginary snake couldn't hurt Dearing unless he tripped over it.

"Who?" Bartholomew demanded.

"Sultan Mahmud!" The pirate yelled as he jumped and swatted at his visitor. Apparently, abducting and hurting female vampires wasn't enough for the Sultan. Celwyn waved a hand, and the snake slithered out of Dearing's trousers and wiggled across the floor, where it evaporated. In its place, the magician left a bottle of wine. How long would it take before the pirate felt safe enough to touch it?

Bartholomew's anger grew, and he stood, his fists quivering at his sides. "I have no sympathy for you." He spat at Dearing. "Only the vilest of a man would sell another human being." He tried to reach through the bars.

"Don't dirty your hands, my friend," Celwyn said.

Nemo stood and stretched. "I agree." To Celwyn, he said, "Do we have everything we need?"

"Almost." The magician silently reminded Nemo of their curiosity about the pirate's defenses in the harbor, and on land.

"I'd rather eat dinner," Nemo said. "We'll have almost a week to visit with this bastard again."

Chapter 31

A S THE CREW SERVED THE SOUP, Bartholomew inhaled the aroma and said, "I never realized I could enjoy food from the sea so much. Before I came aboard this ship, I had rarely encountered it."

Kang nodded. "Your chef does very well with whatever he attempts, sir."

Once again, there were so few of them that they could fit into Nemo's private dining room. Through a much smaller aquatic window on Celwyn's right, they observed a stingray hovering close by, along with other assorted sea life. Qing had been invited along and monitored the proceedings from atop his perch on the wall barometer.

The automat said, "We should celebrate a victory. Today, we made exceptionally evil men do our bidding ... and saved quite a few unfortunate souls."

"Here, here!" Bartholomew held up his glass for a toast. "I'm sure the pirates still don't realize they were tricked."

On the magician's left, a low growl escaped Valentine. "Those pirates lived. They shouldn't have."

"The British will try them in court and probably hang them." Verne went back to chewing.

Nothing could have made Nemo smile faster. "I had Granger leave the British a list of their crimes ... with locations and dates."

A sudden sadness enveloped the magician as he once again realized how he would miss Tara for weeks ... if not months. The sooner they took care of the situation at Dearing's compound and returned to Beirut, the better.

"She will be waiting for you," Kang said, light teasing coloring his voice, while again proving he knew Celwyn better than he knew himself.

The magician frowned his worry and told Nemo, "That is good news, sir."

The author popped the last bite of a roll into his mouth. "I had a most productive but unexciting day." He spooned soup. "Tell us about your visit with Dearing."

"As you wish. It was as you would expect. We didn't receive voluntary cooperation from him."

Nemo's eyes twinkled, not with playfulness. "Jonas's new method is faster and entertaining."

"We should have a toast." Bartholomew raised his glass, and a collective clinking of crystal went around the room. The big man was in a splendid mood this evening.

Qing took that as an invitation to hop onto the service cart and peck the water pitcher. His form of bird participation.

"So many of us wish our guest ill will." The magician pretended to be concerned. "Perhaps we should draw straws to see who finally takes care of him."

"Humorous, Jonas," The Professor said. "Finish it. What all did you find out?"

"Dearing didn't just sell Miss Redifer to Sultan Mahmud. He sold the *Quarto's* slaves to him too."

"Disgusting." Kang leaned back while the crew served the entrée. "I wonder what else the Sultan is up to."

Several of them shrugged, and Nemo said, "We will find out. Perhaps we can pay him a visit on our return trip."

"An excellent idea, ending in one less market for slave traders," Bartholomew said.

As Celwyn listened to them, he tasted a medley of fresh squash laced with cinnamon and garlic, all of it most likely acquired when they stopped in Beirut. "The remainder of what we learned was not freely given." He relived the process he used with the pirate. "In fact, I enjoyed the experience much more than Dearing did." A bite of fish, a bite of squash. "We needed details of where they stored the rarest and most wonderful of the stolen art."

Kang said, "*Leda and the Swan.*"

"Raphael's drawings of Galatea," Valentine guessed.

"Among others. Knowing they have the paintings isn't enough. We required a detailed description of entrances, exits, lighting, defenses, guards, and many other things," Nemo said and went back to his dinner.

The automat asked, "And ... you found all of that out?"

"Yes. Like I said, not willingly." The magician waited for the crew to remove his plate and speculated about dessert, possibly something cool and citrus-flavored, perhaps. "The first storage room, a vault if you will, had several dozen well-known pieces. Bartholomew has a list of them."

"The list will prove useful for when we return the items to the museums," Bartholomew said.

"Exactly." Celwyn watched the crew push the cart with the coffee service into the room. "At the rear of the building is a door that appears to be part of a tiled wall. It leads down a set of stairs to a smaller vault containing the rarer paintings that Dearing doesn't share with anyone."

Valentine's voice was full of speculation. "I wonder if the Blue Jackal is in there. It has been missing and thought to be resold many times over since Queen Hatshepsut."

"It is there if it is the one that depicts a crocodile eating a god."

Kang's eyes shone with scientific, and in this case, anthropological, enthusiasm. "Can you imagine how wonderful all those paintings are?"

"I can." Verne blinked at them. "I want to see them."

Celwyn stopped himself from picturing the author in the vault chasing Dearing's rat. "Anyhow, we now have a list of the paintings, and know about the security around them."

With a sigh that confirmed that, at times, his curiosity overrode his fear of the unknown, Bartholomew asked, "Explain please how your new method of extracting information from Dearing works? All I saw was Dearing wild with rage and grabbing at the air."

"I'm not sure you really want to know..." When he saw the big man's nod, he continued. "As you wish. It involved my leading his thoughts in the direction I wanted them to go." Celwyn eyed him. "Do you require details?"

This time, Bartholomew nodded like the magician had invited him to cross a shallow stream full of crocodiles.

"I gave Dearing's mind something to chase that threatened his precious hoard, something he feared would hurt his paintings, and it eventually raced into the hidden area in his vault. Each time I had him pursue what he feared so I could study each part of it all."

Kang laughed. "What was it?"

"Just a rat. Sometimes my imagination fails me when I'm looking for something disgusting and repulsive at the same time."

Nemo told him, "This method is one of your more useful talents, Jonas. We'll use it again, I'm sure."

"I prefer you do not use it for me," Bartholomew said with a shudder that vibrated the table.

The crew had been about to set down dishes of pudding and hesitated before doing so. The conversation continued with the magician's description of Dearing's defenses at his compound.

When he finished, Bartholomew chuckled. "Wouldn't it be fitting if we sailed into the bay with Dearing mounted on the prow of the *Nautilus*?"

While the others laughed with gusto, Celwyn absorbed the suggestion as something that might prove useful indeed.

Chapter 32

A HALF-HOUR INTO ANOTHER INTER-
rogation by Major Jardin, Patrick lost his temper.
Two lieutenants flanked the major as he sat
behind his desk, displaying his skepticism and
being annoying. Another stood at the door, leaving
Edward and Patrick in the visitor chairs. The room
felt as stuffy as a barn in mid-summer, and just as
sweet because of the platter of dried pastries that
decorated the desk. A lone fly circled the sweets like
Patrick imagined the flying machine did before it
landed, swooping, and banking, as it headed for a
particular spot. Just like the fly, the taller of the lieutenants couldn't take his eyes off the pastries.

Major Jardin said, "Once again, describe the man
who came into your home."

Patrick shouted, "I've told you repeatedly, I did not see him! My wife and footman both say he was dark-haired, of medium height, and a fussy dresser. Neither one got a good look at him."

With the tip of a pencil, Jardin pushed at the glove with the note that Patrick had put on his desk. He reread the note for the third time.

The other lieutenant, who did not seem to crave stale pastries, spoke up. "What about the boy? The one who had the piano lesson?"

Patrick paused. "No one has asked him. All Otto said was that the substitute wasn't as good as his usual teacher." He hesitated and licked his lips. "Have you verified that his regular teacher, Mr. Baylord, is alive?" Patrick didn't want to ask, but had to know. "What if the murderer killed him to gain entry to our house?"

"Do you have his address?" Jardin asked.

"Not offhand, but I will messenger it to you as soon as I return home."

The major leaned forward and said with more aggression, "We need to talk with the boy and your staff."

When Patrick appeared ready to shout again, Edward put a hand on his arm and told Jardin, "It will be an ordeal for everyone there. I suggest you wait until tomorrow morning. They are too upset today."

When the pastry lover looked ready to object, Patrick stood and said, "An excellent suggestion. When will your guards arrive, sir? From that note, you can understand our concern." Patrick's tone made it clear he wouldn't be refused. If Jardin assumed he wouldn't allow the questioning if the police were not guarding his home, well, so be it.

Major Jardin shrugged. "I can spare two men now, and two replacements for the night. That's it."

Edward told him, "We'll assume they will be armed, and I will be sure everyone is aware of them."

As the sun began her bow before nightfall, the calèche turned down the street and neared Tellyhouse. A brisk wind blew through the trees as if it chased devils, signaling fall would arrive soon to further darken their house of mourning. A few houses ahead, Patrick spied a neighbor walking their dog. He normally would have waved, but instead, kept his head down and studied his hands.

As the calèche headed up the curved driveway to the door of Tellyhouse, two things happened simultaneously.

Twin horseback riders galloped down the street and up the driveway behind him. When the two policemen dismounted and tied their mounts to the hitching post, Patrick noticed they could not have been much older than Abe and Andy. They saluted him before taking up positions on each side of the front door. With a put-upon frown, Sully peered at them through the glass.

A liveried messenger also arrived, parking his bicycle only feet from the police horses. He did not take his eyes off the uniformed guards as he handed over three telegrams, accepted his tip, and climbed back on his bicycle.

"I'll see to the rig and the horses unless you have another errand, sir." Edward's face was drawn, and the bandage around his head sagged to one side.

"You should rest and have Mrs. Thomas redo your bandage, and…" Patrick told him. "I should have left you here to do that."

"No, sir, I would not have rested." He remounted the calèche and jiggled the reins, steering it toward the rear of the house.

As Sully opened the front door and waited for him, Patrick stared at the telegrams. His spirits fell. They were dated long before the tragic news of Elizabeth's death.

"Sir?" Sully called over.

"Oh, yes." Patrick entered the house with a nod to the guards. To Sully, he said, "I assume you'll bring them something to eat and drink as needed." He tried to smile and failed. "I'm not sure what etiquette dictates for when you must guard your own home."

When he entered the parlor, the low hum of conversation stopped. This time, most of the maids and kitchen staff did not occupy the room. Flossy alone remained by the door, ready for requests. There would be some soon as the dinner hour neared, and the house tended to become even busier than usual. Mrs. Pearse had been installed on the sofa next to Annabelle, and Mrs. Thomas waited nearby, holding a clipboard like a club. Her normal take-charge voice had been restored. That alone helped Patrick's resolve.

"Please go help Edward with the coach and horses," he asked Abe. Without a word, the groomsman nodded and exited.

"Good afternoon, sir," the housekeeper said. "We were making plans while waiting for you. I'll see to the tea. I'm sure you can use it, and the boys are ready to bite a table leg."

He thanked her and requested she look at Edward's wound as soon as she could. The floor shook as Mrs. Thomas marched out. Patrick found that comforting, a sign of normalcy in this nightmare.

He took his time embracing his wife. Throughout all this, his imagination kept returning to Annabelle lying in the courtyard outside next to Elizabeth, and it terrified him.

Patrick bowed and said, "It is good to see you, Mrs. Pearse, even under these trying conditions."

It had been longer than a month since the aunt had dined at Tellyhouse. She remained the same; an elderly dowager wearing a permanent frown over bulging, irritated blue eyes. Her fluffy white locks could have used a few hairpins.

Patrick checked Annabelle's expression; if things transpired as usual, it wouldn't take long before the fireworks commenced. He well-remembered how annoyed Annabelle had been when the older woman followed them to Prague and tried to tell her what to do. Now, he was glad the old girl had remained in the city. Her high voice still made his ears ache, however.

"Such a terrible situation," she shrilled. "Simply horrible." She sent Patrick a disappointed look. Another of her endearing habits was to remind her niece she could have married well, especially when the aunt had sacrificed so much to present her to Singapore society.

Before Auntie could launch into her speech, Patrick asked, "Where are the boys?"

"I sent them to the stables to take care of Beastie and help with the horses." Annabelle blinked at him, trying not to cry again. "The Conductor is with them."

He squeezed her hand. "The police have supplied two guards. They are at the front door, and you will not know they are there. Another set of guards will replace them during the night."

Mrs. Pearse dipped her head and rested her chin on her other chins. She glared from under her brows. "Who is Beastie?"

Annabelle touched Patrick's sleeve and said with a touch of steel in her voice, "Our dog. He is very big and is learning his manners. Please do not comment."

The old lady's mouth snapped shut. Patrick spoke up, "There is news. We have received three telegrams that were sent weeks ago. Shall I read them aloud?"

In answer, Annabelle touched his hand again. He opened them. "This one is from Bartholomew."

> *We are in pursuit of the pirate ship carrying Miss Redifer.*
> *Today was a supply stop in Algiers.*
> *Jonas was shot in the shoulder, but it was not serious.*
> *We are catching up to the pirates and will telegraph you when we know more.*

Patrick replaced that missive in its envelope and held up the remaining ones. "The other two are from the Professor to Elizabeth sent on the same day. It will be awhile until they receive our telegram." He wanted to groan withdismay. The Professor would be devastated at the news of his wife's death, especially when he heard how she died.

"I'm glad Uncle Celwyn wasn't badly hurt." Annabelle sighed, and tears filled her eyes.

Patrick continued. Perhaps his patter would distract her. "It will take about three weeks for a telegram to reach Rome, and two more for one to reach Singapore. It has been nearer three weeks since they wrote this. Other than Singapore, we do not know where to send a telegram to arrive before they do."

As she sniffled into her handkerchief, Annabelle asked, "What if they keep missing our messages about Elizabeth?"

Patrick frowned. "My estimation is that they will stop in several cities, no matter what happens. It would take too long for them to *sail*," he caught Annabelle's eye and put up a brow to emphasize the word, "across the Pacific and around South America, and then across the Atlantic." Mrs. Pearse did not need to know about the *Nautilus*. "They're heading east, and they'll come back the way they went."

Annabelle managed to nod. They all gazed out the picture window as Zander ran by, then Beastie, and then Otto. Mrs. Pearse gaped at the sight of the wolfhound and the view of his cavernous open mouth and long tongue.

To distract Mrs. Pearse, Patrick hurried to say, "The Conductor will be dispatched to send the same telegrams we sent to Singapore along to Rome, Palermo, and any place I can think of, in case they stop there on the return trip. We will make sure they know."

Beastie and the boys ran back the way they'd come, each clutching a flower from the garden.

"Why aren't they here?" The old lady asked peevishly. "I thought that hair-brained gallivanting had stopped."

Although not familiar with many Americanisms, Patrick knew what gallivanting entailed—carousing, disreputable acts, and drunken brawls. If Auntie knew what the three adventurers really got up to, she would be in a swoon on the carpet.

Annabelle lifted her chin and proceeded to deal with her aunt as Patrick sighed at the two telegrams in his hand... he had a strong sense of propriety and respect for the privacy of others... But the telegrams from the Professor to Elizabeth could hold clues as to their route and help him find them. He needed a level-headed opinion about this idea, not an emotional one, such as his beloved's.

Patrick excused himself and went in search of Mrs. Thomas to tell her about the guards and to give the Conductor instructions before he and Edward put the horses to bed. He would ask them both about unsealing the telegrams.

As he opened the side door and stepped outside, Patrick couldn't ignore the fact that he also needed to tell the housekeeper to get everyone ready to talk with the police tomorrow morning. Not only would she consider their presence an affront, but the disruption to the household routine an insult to her personally. A potentially explosive morning was indeed brewing.

———

When Patrick returned to the parlor, he found Mrs. Thomas serving tea. His worry over opening the telegrams had been a waste of time; they contained nothing but the Professor's love for his wife, and a careful avoidance of anything else, such as what they were doing and where they were doing it. All Patrick had gained from his invasion of their privacy was a stronger aversion to telling the Professor that the love of his life was dead. She was the one who had worried so much that he would die, and had perished instead.

The boys did their best to answer Mrs. Pearse's questions while stuffing fairy cakes in their mouths. As a mute, Otto had an advantage; he wrote his answers while chewing. Patrick finished his biscuit and had to hurry to keep up with Mrs. Thomas as she strode out of the room.

"Could I speak with you for a moment, please?" he asked before they reached the end of the hall.

Mrs. Thomas stopped short. She eyed him, not without a modicum of pity. "Of course. We can talk in my office."

Patrick held the door open. He had only been in her office once before and again noticed a lack of decoration and personal touches next to the neatly arranged files and a cup of sharpened pencils. A few feet away, faint sounds of kitchen combat came through an adjoining wall. It seemed Jackson had added sugar, not salt, to the gravy. Ricardo's voice rose an octave in fury.

After Mrs. Thomas had settled all six feet of herself behind her desk, he took the guest chair and began, "I need your help."

"Of course, sir."

Patrick rubbed his face. This was such a horrible day.

"I'll be frank with you. We will probably not see the Professor, Bartholomew, and Mr. Celwyn for a month, maybe longer. They are traveling near Singapore. I'm trying to reach them."

Her brows lowered with the kind of irritation the Professor and the others had personal familiarity with. Patrick plowed forward.

"I need to know; should we have the funeral before then? Is it proper to? Or is it possible to hold a body at the undertakers for a couple of months until Mrs. Kang's husband returns?"

"Good gracious."

For the first time since he'd known her, there was something Mrs. Thomas didn't know. She eyed him and straightened her shoulders. "This is a quandary. However, I will find out."

"Thank you." He sighed. "That will help greatly. Now, I must tell you of something that you will not approve, but it will help catch whoever murdered Mrs. Kang."

Mrs. Thomas inhaled and waited.

"The police want to interview everyone here tomorrow. They will arrive at ten in the morning."

That brought a strong reaction, and if it weren't part of catching the killer, the housekeeper would have marched out. She clamped her jaw hard, and calmness eventually prevailed.

"What else is there, sir? I have duties to see to, not to mention the mess the boys made in the water closet upstairs. They said it was a science experiment Mr. Bartholomew sent them."

She waited for confirmation of Bartholomew's or the boys' guilt. Patrick blinked his ignorance. It probably wasn't the best time to ask, but he had to. "I need more of your help ... if you would be so kind."

"Yes, sir?"

Patrick was no coward but knew his limits. He told himself to charge ahead into the minefield. "Mrs. Pearse needs to be told about the witches and spells, and since you have been able to accept them, I am hoping you'll know how to explain it to her. At least enough for us to live through the next few weeks. Arguing with her aunt will upset Annabelle needlessly in her condition."

Mrs. Thomas' eyes widened, and then he saw her stiffen her upper lip. "Once again, I must admit this household is challenging. However, I will take care of it. What else? You are still a tad anxious."

Patrick tried a calming approach. "This is easier. I'll have a talk with the boys, but if you can keep Beastie from encountering Mrs. Pearse, things will be much quieter."

"Consider it done. At least it isn't that damn bird." She stood. Their housekeeper was not a fan of Qing. "We're having Beef Wellington this evening in honor of Mrs. Pearse's visit. The scullery maid has fits of forgetfulness, and I need to go."

To prove her point, Ricardo's voice rose again, echoing through the wall. Patrick thanked the housekeeper profusely. A pot hit the kitchen door as he followed her out again.

Chapter 33

Mrs. Thomas had designated the smaller sitting room opposite the dining room for the police interviews. They used the sitting room rarely, and after today, Patrick would probably avoid it even more.

At breakfast, Mrs. Pearse announced she would remain with her niece in her suite to be sure no one disturbed her. It hadn't taken too much urging to convince Annabelle to go upstairs until the interviews were over. As they climbed the steps, Patrick wondered if Annabelle had told her aunt that she was with child.

Which reminded him of something else not easily resolved. Patrick sighed. He hadn't done anything yet about finding a doctor who knew about unusual things, such as how a small amount of vampire blood from the father would affect the pregnancy. The subject wasn't talked about at Tellyhouse

258

because most of them did not know of his history. During a turbulent time a few years ago, he had partially been made a vampire but continued to live normally. How would that affect their child? After the turmoil from Elizabeth's death had settled down, he must investigate. That thought led to realizing Bartholomew and the others did not know about their blessed event either.

Elizabeth was dead. Patrick stopped short of slamming his fist into the parlor wall. *How could something as wonderful as a baby occur when they were in mourning, or in danger?* He couldn't help a glance out each of the downstairs windows but saw nothing. The grandfather clock chimed the half-hour, a signal that their company would arrive soon.

Promptly at ten, Sully opened the door to Major Jardin and his handsome lieutenant, who carried himself with military authority. His black eyes swiveled, missing nothing when they were led inside. As for himself, Patrick considered protecting his household as his top priority, along with helping the police find Elizabeth's killer. Above all, he wondered why a stranger threatened them. He followed the others into the sitting room with a heart so full of anxiety he couldn't speak.

Jackson delivered a coffee tray and plates of toast points and marmalade and then stood ready for orders.

"I have asked Mr. Murphy," Patrick nodded at Edward on his right, "to be present to help us with details. In front of you is a list of everyone who was here in this house the day Mrs. Kang was murdered."

He pinned the Major with a glare when he would have objected. "If you do not mind, I've asked them to be available to you in the order listed. There will be fewer interruptions to their routines. Jackson, here, will fetch them when you are ready for them."

He could see the man was used to organizing his own interviews, and from his scowl, searched for a way to complain. Patrick kept a smile to himself; if Jardin did so, Mrs. Thomas would be summoned to explain that it would be handled this way, especially since she had organized it.

Major Jardin took off his cap, and his dome shone under the lights. He sighed. "All right. We will do it your way."

Although the sitting room did not get used as much as the parlor, and measured a third the size, it had a pleasant view of the side yard and the fall flowers. Patrick thoroughly wished he were lying in the middle of the flowers and dreaming of bunnies, and that yesterday had never happened. The grandfather clock behind him ticked loudly in the silence.

"Before we start, can you tell me if any progress has been made to find this villain?" Patrick inquired.

"There is none. We expect to learn something today that will help."

"Have you located the original piano teacher, Mr. Baylord? Is he all right?"

Jardin flipped a hand. "Yes. He was found tied up under his bed. Hit hard on the side of the head. He never saw who did it."

Patrick felt somewhat better and asked, "What about the note we found in the glove? That was a direct threat." He didn't want to alarm anyone, such as Mrs. Thomas if she found out about it. Jackson didn't blink; he knew how to keep his own counsel.

The Lieutenant replied, "We are investigating it. We will also leave guards here until we find out who did this."

"Thank you." Patrick felt his nerves relax a bit, but not completely.

Major Jardin said, "Let's get on with this. You're Jackson?" The porter nodded. "Have a seat. State your name, and tell us where you were that day."

By five in the afternoon, everyone except Otto had been processed. If asked, Patrick could confirm that no one knew anything, and few of them had seen the substitute piano teacher. Otto represented their last, and best hope.

When Jackson ushered him into the room, the boy clutched his tablet to his chest like a shield. Patrick glimpsed Zander in the hallway, his eyes full of curiosity.

As he sat down, Patrick clapped Otto on the shoulder. They had built strong mutual trust since he met the lad, and at this moment he felt glad of it. "I'll stay here with you. Just answer their questions as best you can."

Major Jardin said, "Why does he have that tablet? We aren't here to draw."

"This is the police investigator, and this is his lieutenant," Patrick told the mute boy.

The boy nodded and scribbled. He showed the tablet to the major. The man's face reddened as he read. "Please excuse me. I did not know. Yes, we are pleased to meet you, also." He turned to his underling, who had leaned over to see the tablet, and had the grace to look apologetic as he addressed Otto.

"Please tell us what happened the day of your piano lesson. Anything you can tell us will help."

Otto's eyes welled up as he remembered the last day that he saw Elizabeth. He blinked fast as he wrote, and when he finished, Patrick read it aloud.

"'My lesson with Mr. Baylord always starts at ten. The new teacher was late. He was also slow.'"

"How so?" Major Jardin asked.

Otto wrote. Patrick recited. "'He looked at everything on the way down the hall, and in closets and places he shouldn't, before starting the lesson. He didn't pay attention while I played the assignments I'd been given.'"

Major Jardin asked, "Did he know anything about music?"

Otto shrugged.

"What did he look like?" the lieutenant asked.

Otto wrote even faster. He had probably been expecting the question. Patrick read, "He was as tall as the Professor, and he walked like him. This man's eyes were brown, though, not black."

As Patrick read, the lieutenant took notes. "What does his face look like? Any teeth missing or moles?"

Otto wrote and handed the tablet to Patrick. Before he read it, he noticed the boy's angry expression drawing his mouth into a thin line. "He had evil in his eyes. His voice sounded hard, not like a good person. I do not remember his teeth or moles. His ears were little, like the Professor's."

Patrick put a hand on the lad's arm and pulled a pitcher of milk toward them with the other. "Let's take a break."

Jackson offered a platter of scones and refilled coffee cups. Patrick left the scones alone; he couldn't stomach food now. Perhaps later.

When Otto had finished his milk, the Major addressed him, "Please tell us what the man said. Did he tell you his name?"

Otto filled his tablet and handed it to Patrick. "The man said to call him Gaspard. He asked questions, but he did not comment on the piano lesson. He asked if I knew the Professor and if I knew where he was. Then he asked about Uncle Celwyn." Patrick checked with Otto, and the boy nodded to go ahead. Patrick's voice held a measure of sadness for what he had to say aloud. "The man said I was stupid because I can't talk. I let him think that."

Major Jardin leaned back in his chair and pulled on his mustache. "You have been a big help, young man. Don't believe things like that. What else did he say?"

It was Otto's turn to frown. The boy ran a hand through his curls and adjusted his spectacles. Then he began writing.

"Gaspard asked who else lived here. He asked again when the Professor was coming home."

"What did you tell him?"

Otto scribbled and handed the tablet over. "I just said, 'my family.' I said, 'I didn't know.' He made me nervous."

Knowing of Otto's life on the streets before they met him, Patrick assumed the boy thought it best to be quiet about anything dangerous. He would work with Otto to tell them in the future when he felt threatened.

"This explains a few things," Major Jardin said. "Was he a relative of the Professor's?"

Patrick said, "I doubt it. If he had been, he would have introduced himself differently."

"True." Major Jardin stared at the remains of the scone tray. "We'll ask for a sketch to be made from what everyone has said about this Gaspard."

With a sigh of relief that the interviews had ended, Patrick patted Otto's shoulder again. "Do you need anything more from Otto?"

The lieutenant and the major exchanged glances. "No, not now. Thank you, young man."

After Jackson had escorted the boy out, Patrick asked, "What do you plan to do?"

"I will have officers here at night until this is over. Right now, I can't afford them during the day and will assume you will provide your own guards. We will check the train depot and other places to see if anyone recognizes a drawing of this man. I doubt 'Gaspard' is his name."

Patrick stood. "Thank you. Do you know when Mrs. Kang's body will be released?"

The Lieutenant said, "Probably tomorrow. We'll send a messenger."

Chapter 34

El Mullahah before Port Said

IT NEARED DAWN, AND THE LIGHTS IN the study blinked twice.

Bartholomew yawned and made it to his feet before Kang and Celwyn. Valentine already awaited them by the door. Everyone wore rough clothes and boots suitable for a trek through dense brush, or in Kang and Celwyn's case, a day on the beach. Bartholomew cradled a Winchester rifle in his arms and grinned his anticipation at the others.

Verne walked in. "Happy hunting, Gentlemen. Do not forget to look for bird eggs. This island is known for them."

"We will do so," the big man assured him as they headed up the stairs.

Minutes later, the skiff from the *Nautilus* coasted onto the sand. Everyone climbed out and hurried across the beach to the trees, except for the automat. Celwyn followed him to a flat spot in the sand a short distance from the dense green foliage that licked the edge of the beach. They made themselves comfortable, positioned within sight of the submarine as she floated, long, dark, and dangerous, in front of them.

At Kang's suggestion, Celwyn added a bright red umbrella above a table of the magician's invention. For their entertainment, he produced a chess set and did not forget the tea and cookies.

"Oh, really?" The Professor eyed the chess set, then the magician, and laughed. "Too bad Nemo is busy. I will need a worthy opponent soon."

"You must be having a hallucination."

"Of course I am." Kang selected a cookie. "How long will they spend hunting?"

Celwyn smiled at his friend. They had an odd relationship, but a good one. "A few hours, and then take a break before another round." With a yawn, he realized they'd be here all day with nothing to do. Sometimes, he had to make his own theatre. A short distance behind Kang, he sent a half-dozen white unicorns running into the brush. "Who knows what they'll shoot at today?"

The automat eyed him and pushed a pawn forward. "I don't want to know what you did."

In the distance, sporadic rifle shots could be heard. "No, you don't." The magician brought out his rook. The crew could shoot all day and not hit a unicorn, and he also felt certain Bartholomew wouldn't shoot at one anyhow. However, some nice plump grouse would be welcomed at the dinner table.

The game progressed. Every time Celwyn ran out of Earl Grey, Kang finished a plate of cookies. The magician replenished them both and asked, "Another game? You seem to be losing so many games. It must be an overabundance of cookies."

"Pfft."

As they reset the pieces, they heard a deep, drawn-out growl from the brush about thirty feet away. Celwyn stood, spying a well-fed jaguar heading away from the beach and disappearing into the jungle. As he sat again, he asked, "Have you thought about what will become of us all?" A soft breeze played with his hat and caressed his cheek, just like Tara did.

"Such as?"

The magician moved the same pawn again and blinked with innocence at the automat. "Such as; it is unlikely that either you or I will die, at least for a long time. Bartholomew is a part of us, and he can die. I do not want that."

Kang's hand hesitated, and he moved his rook a single space and then two more. "Ah." He regarded the chess piece a moment before his eyes met the magician's. "I have considered this also, but did not want to think too deeply about it."

The magician's rook hopped forward and bowed at the automat. "Your move." He gazed across the water. For as far as he could see, the sea stretched flat and mysterious to the horizon. "I have grown very fond of him."

"As have I." The automat took Celwyn's pawn. "You have an idea, don't you?"

It was not a question.

The magician shrugged. "He could become immortal like us."

This time, Kang's hand froze just as he started to touch his king. "Oh?" He picked up the piece but didn't put it down again. A second passed, and he asked, "Have you asked him?"

"Before I talk with him, I wondered what you thought. There are many aspects to this." He didn't need to vocalize them; Bartholomew's superstitious nature was as well-known as his bravery. The fact he could be in the same room as Valentine marked a tremendous step forward.

Kang continued to stare at the chess piece as the hunting party broke through the heavy brush and onto the beach behind them. The big man led the group, buoyant and happy to be on land again. Nemo's crew came next, with Granger bringing up the rear. Several of the crew carried strings of game.

Bartholomew shouted, "We were quite successful!" With a bit of restraint, he glanced at the brush and added, "We saw something fantastic ... but did not shoot at it." Uncertainty played across his face, but not strong enough to dampen his happiness.

Celwyn asked, "What?"

"White unicorns—I never thought they existed—" Bartholomew told him.

Kang said dryly, "They don't. Do they, Jonas?"

The magician ignored the teasing and told the automat, "Have some more cookies."

"I will." As the big man reached them, Kang asked, "Did you find the eggs?"

"Yes. Some." He checked the jungle as if expecting a visit from the unicorns.

Granger joined him and said, "I say, those cookies look edible."

"Excuse my manners." Celwyn offered him the plate and then gestured. A table with pitchers of water, sandwiches, and beer appeared behind the crew as they talked among themselves. Granger spied the table and didn't hesitate. One by one, the crew stared at the magician and then followed Granger's lead.

Celwyn locked eyes with the automat. "Think about what I said."

"I will." Kang sighed and cast a worried glance at Bartholomew.

Chapter 35

T HE SHIP SPENT THE REST OF THE day traveling south toward Port Said and the Suez Canal. The sea had initially been blue and as clear as a vast unending pool of liquid crystal, but as they neared the canal, silt, and other debris from thousands of miles of the Nile River clouded the seawater until they could make out nothing in it.

If mechanical birds could spit, Qing would have. He was not amused at the murkiness of the water. Celwyn had made him a dozen silver frogs throughout the afternoon, but most of them had been abandoned under the bookcases, minus a few limbs. Qing sat beside them and pecked at them every time they twitched.

Dinner had been as wonderful as usual, and as Kang handed around glasses of port and spirits, Bartholomew packed his pipe and got it going.

He relaxed against the bar and said, "Captain, our hunting expedition was extraordinary. Thank you."

Valentine stood beside him and said, "Mine was also."

A moment of knowing silence greeted the remark, until Verne said, "I will enjoy the eggs you found at tomorrow's breakfast." He included them all in his joy. "Thank you."

A look of remembered amazement lit up Bartholomew's face and he blurted, "We saw white unicorns!"

"That is incredible!" Verne exclaimed.

Nemo bestowed a sarcastic eye on the magician, who grinned.

"Jonas has something to confess." Kang yawned.

Celwyn blew smoke rings at him. "I have no idea what it would be. Wouldn't you rather hear about what the Captain has planned?" Qing flew through the smoke rings as they reached the ceiling, pivoted, and dived through the rest of them.

The tic in Bartholomew's eye kicked in, and he half-looked at Nemo as if it wouldn't come true if he didn't make eye contact.

"All right." Nemo settled back and stretched his legs. "Jonas and I spoke this afternoon, and I've spent some time with the official and unofficial records and maps." He directed a speculative glance at the big man. "For the first few miles of the canal, the water depth for this ship is questionable. After that, it reaches acceptable levels for about another hundred miles to the Gulf of Aden."

Bartholomew had sat up straight at the word "canal," and as Nemo talked, he dropped his pipe. Twice.

Verne asked, "What are we going to do?"

Nemo studied each of them in turn before answering. "We could head west toward Alexandria, go underground, and rejoin the canal near El Mallahah."

The automat eyed the map table but didn't get up.

"However, at this time of year, there's also a drop in water levels by Al Firdan." Nemo gazed at the man-sized globe behind them. "As an alternative, it would take another two weeks to detour back through Constantinople and travel underground to Azerbaijan. There is a series of very deep underground rivers there that eventually reach the Persian Gulf." He nodded at the big man. "I have reservations about this that I won't go into now. Our only other alternative is to double back by Tunis and Algiers and around the horn of Africa, which would be an exceedingly long journey indeed." He regarded their long faces. "Or ... Jonas has another option for us."

Bestowing as much skepticism as possible into his voice, the automat asked, "How much risk is there in your option, Jonas?"

Nemo answered. "Moderate. I normally would make all navigation decisions alone, but because of the risk, I am consulting everyone here."

"This is a bit complex, isn't it?" Bartholomew asked. Xiau and the magician had elected the big man to quiz Nemo if the occasion demanded it. The worried look and lowered brows that Nemo displayed appeared serious, and anything that rattled Nemo couldn't be good.

"Yes." Nemo acknowledged the hunch with a nod. They barely heard him say, "It is imperative that I retrieve that painting."

No one questioned Nemo as to why and his expression had darkened so much that Celwyn debated whether to insist they change the subject.

As if he knew what they had said, or absorbed their feelings, Qing attacked his frog with fervor, the noise of metal striking metal ringing loud. It sounded annoying, and yet at the same time a welcome distraction from their emotions.

"All right. I'll bite. What is the option at Suez?" Bartholomew asked.

After Qing finished shaking the frog leg and settled down, Celwyn said, "When we reach the first part of the canal, it is shallow, as the Captain has mentioned. The best we can hope for there are levels that are only about thirty-six feet deep."

He gazed at Kang to see if he'd figured it out yet. When the automat did, his eyes widened, and his mouth dropped open.

Bartholomew saw his reaction and gulped before switching his attention back to the magician.

Valentine grunted. "Tell us what you are going to do."

"With the Captain's help, and when the canal is as deserted as it possibly can be," Celwyn stopped, and verified Bartholomew remained sitting, "I'll elevate the *Nautilus* as much as we need. With luck,

I'll be able to do so long enough for us to reach the deeper water."

Kang popped up, stalking like an enraged duck to the aquatic window and back.

"Good grief!" He gaped at Nemo. "No wonder we're discussing this."

From his position at the end of the sofa, Celwyn watched the scene play out, well aware that Nemo could do what he pleased, but also that he sincerely hoped for their opinions. He probably wanted that more than any theatrics. The magician nodded at the automat as confidently as he could. Kang goggled back at him.

Verne left his table to join the sparky atmosphere. "If it helps any, I spent a year in Port Said while they were building the canal in 1857, and since then, have made it a point to be aware of the area's commerce."

"Commerce?" Valentine asked.

"Such as the type of ships, who owns them, and what they transported. I've spent time watching the operations there."

Bartholomew asked, "Why?"

Verne colored a bit. "Because of some financial interests I must keep abreast of." He saw their expressions of surprise. "Generally, I know when the least amount of traffic will occur in the canal and other things."

Kang stood in front of him and demanded, "When will that be?" He glared at Celwyn. "You know, it would be quite noteworthy if someone saw this ship rising out of the water like a fantastical sea monster. Good grief!"

Bartholomew said, "The alternative is a trip on an underground river where we may be blocked by shallow water." He gulped again. "And have to back out."

"True." Nemo studied his hands. "Nevertheless, we must finish off the pirates. And I must retrieve the painting from Dearing's lair. I *must*." He met their eyes. "I understand if you do not wish to go any further into Port Said."

"But—" Bartholomew started.

Nemo held up a hand. "I would arrange for your comfort in Cairo, and after taking care of Dearing's compound, we would return to take you to Prague, or Findbar and the flying machine again. Or ..." he hesitated and rubbed his chin. "You could take a commercial voyage to The Hague and await us there. Perhaps you would prefer that your train pick you up by Odessa and wait in Prague."

"There is much to think about this evening." Celwyn hesitated a moment before saying, "No matter what you decide, I'll accompany the Captain to Dearing's compound. Most of what we discovered from the pirate I have yet to record for everyone to use." His eyes hardened along with his voice. "I wouldn't miss blowing that bastard's world apart for anything."

Bartholomew burst out laughing. "I can imagine what you have planned, Jonas."

With a drag in his voice, Verne said, "Attack all those pirates? There must be a thousand or more of them between all those ships, and those guarding the compound."

"It will be done with as much surprise and artistry as possible, I assure you."

"Good grief, Jonas! I'm sure you would," Kang growled at the magician. To Nemo, he said, "Oh for God's sake! Of course, we're going with you." He whirled and barked, "Damn it, Jonas!"

Bartholomew still laughed, now at Kang. "Certainly, we are, Captain." He lifted his chin with the kind of seriousness that made Celwyn suspect him of joking. "I have decided that I want to see this ship rise out of the water. I will not be afraid."

The magician checked with the automat and watched him roll his eyes, whether at Bartholomew's self-delusion, or the prospect of what they intended to do.

"What will happen if you cannot keep the ship high enough?" Kang asked.

"From what Jonas has proposed, I have calculated the time needed and the average speed over the shallowest water." Nemo turned. "Jules, when can we expect the least amount of traffic in the canal?"

The Frenchman shrugged. "Two to three in the morning."

Nemo's reaction could have lit up the room. "Aha! Our optimal time for the tides is two in the morning, gentlemen."

"God help us all!" Kang threw up his hands. "On with it!"

The *Nautilus* surfaced offshore of Port Said at midnight. Minutes later, Celwyn joined Bartholomew on the platform and they lit cigars while glancing across the water at the lights of Suez. Although not large, the city sounded lively and busy. Even during the dead of night, scores of horse-drawn lorries paraded to and from the ships tethered at the docks.

"Have you been here before?" the big man asked.

Celwyn shook his head. "Yes and no. It's been thirty years since my last visit, and there was no canal then. The city would have been much smaller, too." A cool breeze brought a hint of rain riding the sea's brininess. He gestured to the west. "You can almost see the lights of Alexandria."

"I came here for business years ago. Beautiful views, and some of it very poor."

The magician asked, "Had you always been in business until you met us?"

"Mostly." He puffed and thought a bit. "After university, I came home to marry and build a good life for my family. That sent me on buying trips most of the year." His voice dropped to a whisper. "And one day I returned home to find my village burned and my family dead." He swiped at his eyes. "I haven't been back since."

"I am sorry. It is an unimaginable loss, my friend. But now? I'm glad you happened to be in Skudai that day."

Bartholomew tried to smile. "And you bought me a train ticket when they wouldn't sell me one because of my skin." He tossed the butt of his cigar sizzling into the water.

"Of course!" Celwyn relived the encounter. "That night, little did you know you'd see me toss a vampire off the train."

"And so it all began," the big man said. "Are you going to rest before we enter the canal?"

"No. I wouldn't want to get up again if I did. Do not worry; Nemo will be careful throughout the whole operation." He slapped Bartholomew on the back. "He knows every inch of his ship, how she responds, and what to expect. Up to a certain point, we can back out if we have to."

"I wish you hadn't said that."

Chapter 36

B Y PRIOR ARRANGEMENT, VALENTINE, Kang, Bartholomew, and Verne remained in the study while the magician joined Nemo on the bridge. Under normal conditions, the bridge could be crowded, even without extra visitors. If Bartholomew fainted, the others would be sure he didn't hit his head on the machinery, instead steering him to a sofa.

The two aquatic windows on the bridge allowed everyone to view the area as the *Nautilus* moved forward at moderate speed just above the surface. The interior lights had been dimmed except for the instrument panels along the starboard wall. Nemo's crew manned their stations with graveyard faces and barely spoke. Most of them would not look at the magician. *They knew, or suspected, something unexplained was about to happen,* Celwyn speculated. Or they just considered him bad luck.

Granger planted himself in front of the depth gauges located aft of the wheel, and of special importance for their survival. The magician stood behind him. Nemo's lieutenant tapped the largest gauge. "When the needle moves, I will call out the depths. If we're too low in the water, you'll hear the alarms."

"As the water lowers, what will happen?" the magician asked.

"The ship will be visible above the waterline," Granger answered. "If the water lowers too far, we will run aground."

"Thank you."

Tonight's sky might be to their advantage. Granger pointed out the low clouds and murky visibility before they sank below the surface, saying the weather would discourage the number of ships passing through the canal as well.

"Let's hope no one is watching. Or..." The magician thought and thought fast. "Could you have someone use the periscope to spot the ships going into the canal?"

"Yes. There will only be one ship at a time coming or going because the canal is narrow. And the authorities allow passage by appointments only." Granger gestured to a nearby crew member to move to one of the periscopes. "It is only seventy-five feet wide for the next ten miles. After that, the passage is deep and wide enough."

The magician asked, "How fast do the ships go?"

"Only steam-driven ships are allowed in the canal. Top speed, perhaps thirty knots."

The magician thought for a moment; because the pirates sailed a tall ship, how had they expected to get a cargo of thousands of pounds through here? The only thing he could think of was a Confederate ship, powered by steam and set to meet them near here. Or, as Xiau said, possibly they'd have tried steam-driven tugboats... to *tow* them... how interesting?

Celwyn saw some of the crew casting dubious glances in his direction.

"Do they know what we're attempting?"

Granger shrugged. "Yes. Most of them remember when you subdued the Mizuchi last year and have a healthy respect for you."

He referred to last year's battle between a pair of enormous sea monsters as they bashed against the *Nautilus*. "The rest appear ... nervous."

It took all of Granger's control not to laugh—which wasn't allowed on the bridge from what the magician could tell. He settled for saying, "I believe they find magic a bit unsettling."

"Well. I hope not to disappoint them," Celwyn replied with his own smile.

"There is also how you fixed the breach in our hull the other day. They might feel a bit unnerved, but they do have confidence in you."

"I hope so. Did the Captain tell you what I intend to do?"

"Yes."

They watched Nemo at the aft end of the bridge as he conferred with a pair of the crew.

"Let's have a talk with him before we enter the canal. There is a better method than what we initially planned."

<hr />

The *Nautilus* wallowed before the canal entrance, waiting for almost two hours in the shallows. Nemo said they would only stay until three in the morning, because of the tides. If what they needed did not occur by then, they would find themselves in the same position the following night.

Just as the ship rang two bells followed by a half tone, Celwyn saw Nemo stiffen. Then he peered through the periscope and grunted in satisfaction.

"What do you see, sir?"

"A half-ton brig. Heading in. Will that do?"

"Quite well," Celwyn said. His blood quickened— the game was afoot. "Full steam?"

At Nemo's nod, Celwyn strode to the other periscope and swiveled the glass so he could view the steamer. The ship's flag indicated she was American, huge, and proudly lit all around like a massive birthday cake as she squatted on top of the glassy sea in the moonlight. Long columns of steam rose from her stacks, disappearing into the low clouds.

"Catch up to them please, and get as close as possible," the magician requested.

Nemo gave the order, and the gongs resounded as the *Nautilus's* engines grew much louder. Celwyn held on to the periscope to keep from falling as the submarine surged forward.

Dead ahead, the gatekeepers flashed signals allowing the *Atlanta Belle* entry. Although the steamer would only tack about fifteen knots while she entered the passage, it should be enough.

Granger called out, "Sixty-five feet draft and dropping."

"We're about five-hundred feet behind her, and closing," Nemo said.

Celwyn measured distances. "Excellent. Get us as close as you can, please."

"Forty-eight feet." A deep, unnerving reverberation from a gong the magician hadn't heard before echoed from under their feet. About now, Kang would no doubt be cursing him in several languages, but still have confidence in what would happen.

"As soon as you can, Captain." Celwyn stared through the periscope as he squared away, clenching his hands, building, and growing stronger as his music arrived on the bridge in full force, resounding around the room.

The gongs increased in volume, lost in the echoing of the horns and violins as they rose higher.

"Thirty-two feet," Granger intoned, his face set and unblinking in the dim light.

The magician faced the bow and rotated inch by inch in a circle, surrounding the submarine with invisibility. Celwyn brought his hands forward, bringing strong bands from the nose of the *Nautilus* rushing underwater to the *Atlanta Belle's* paddle wheel, wrapping round and round until the steamer hesitated, and then moved forward again, now towing the *Nautilus* along with her.

As they ran out of time and depth, the submarine's alarms became frantic, echoing upon themselves. Celwyn lifted his hands and shifted part of the steamer's forward thrust underneath the submarine so that he wouldn't have to hold them up as much. The paddle ship provided their propulsion.

With everything he had, the magician slowly raised his arms, and the music became thunderous.

The crewman nearest the aquatic window gasped and staggered backward.

Under a galaxy of stars that illuminated everything around them, the *Nautilus* rose out of the water, gliding along on top of the waves as the steamer pulled her forward.

"Forty-five feet and rising," Granger called out.

Nemo eyed Celwyn as sweat poured off the magician's face and his arms shook with effort. Minutes went by. The ship's bell rang three times; still, Celwyn held his arms high as the violins roared around them.

"Fifty feet. We have reached the deeper water—"

Celwyn slowly brought his arms lower, and when the canal water sloshed above the window again, he dissolved the bands binding them to the streamer. In a storm of bubbles, the *Nautilus* sank below the waves and moved ahead on her own power.

"Remarkable!" Nemo exclaimed. The crew roared their excitement.

Granger got to his feet and clapped. Within seconds, every crewman stood with him, and they all joined in. Celwyn was too tired to do more than smile at them amid the relief it was over.

"We'll let that ship remain a bit ahead of us until we pass Al Firdan. The water is deeper after that, and the channel miles wide," Nemo said.

As he slid to the floor, Celwyn halfway heard Nemo, too busy breathing deeply, and very thankful it was done. The violins faded, and the music that had filled the room receded.

Nemo kneeled beside him. "I wasn't sure you could hold her up toward the end."

"She's heavy ... from all of Xiau's books."

"Pfft." Kang bent down to his level and grinned at him.

"Like Xiau said, 'poof'," Bartholomew agreed. "Let's get you to your cabin." Kang and the big man brought the magician to his feet and supported him.

"How long have you been here?" the magician asked.

Bartholomew said, "Ever since we heard the music and saw we were up in the air."

Captain Nemo saluted the magician, and Celwyn returned it before being led away.

Chapter 37

THE MAGICIAN SLEPT THROUGH breakfast, and by the time he reached the study, he found a tea service, Verne, Bartholomew, and the automat waiting for him.

Qing rode on his shoulder as he ducked under the doorjamb, and when the bird saw the crowd of fish in his window, he kicked off Celwyn's shoulder, squawking and flapping his way across the room to greet them. The seawater in the Red Sea could not be described as the clearest, but it did have an excellent variety of fish. Qing seemed to favor the rainbow wrasse for their colors—if his pecking at the glass was any indication.

"Your cup is still hot," Kang told him. "Bartholomew listened at your door until he heard you getting ready. I didn't know you sang opera, Jonas." The automat laughed.

"You still do not," the magician said. "Thank you." He sat and poured, and wished he'd slept longer. "It is early." He checked his pocket watch and compared it to the pendulum clock on the wall. At only ten in the morning, it would be hours until luncheon. He produced a plate of apple strudel.

Verne spied them and put down his pen. Before he could get up, Celwyn sent him one and took another for himself. Bartholomew shook his head as the automat made a selection.

"Thank you. These look lovely." Verne chewed. "The Captain told us exactly what you did to get this ship through the shallows."

Valentine walked in, executed a bow to the room, and stopped in front of Qing's window. "You looked ready to collapse when they brought you out of the bridge last night."

"I was." The magician agreed.

"Thank god that is over. No underground river." Bartholomew sounded so relieved, it cheered everyone else. "The Captain said we'll stop for supplies at the same island where we saw the early version of the flying machine. The one with the hollow volcano."

"Tell me more," Valentine requested. The big man did so.

Celwyn remembered it well. Their first visit to that most beautiful and remote place had not been voluntary. It reminded him of how close everyone had become with Nemo and his crew over the last few years.

Verne brushed crumbs off his tie and said, "The supplies we're picking up there are for the ship, not our dining table. We'll get those in Singapore, from what I understand."

"Could we engage in some hunting there?" Valentine asked.

Verne told him, "I've seen them shoot birds there."

"The Captain may hesitate about that; the last time we were there we heard tigers in the jungle," the Professor said as he made his next pastry selection.

Celwyn covered a yawn. "Where are we?"

Verne said, "We traveled throughout the rest of the night, and I think at the moment we're close to Eritrea, correct?" He directed the question to Kang, who had crossed to the map table even before he finished speaking.

"Yes. And we'll continue into the Gulf of Aden before sundown."

Verne asked, "Would you say it is about a week until we reach Dearing's island?"

Kang pursed his lips. "We'll have to ask the Captain at lunch."

Several days later, they had cruised across the Andaman Sea and entered the underwater volcanic tube that led to the island's center. Bartholomew didn't mind this part of the trip; he'd endured it before. When they came to the end of the tube, the ship ascended, and beyond the window, massive shadows rose in front of a wall of deep darkness.

Riding a cushion of bubbles, the *Nautilus* surfaced in the lake, surrounded by an army of towering stalagmites. What light there was came from the opening in the ceiling above.

Everything smelled dank and salty. They waited while the crew ringed the ship with torches and then emerged onto the platform above the fathomless lake. Both Kang and Celwyn couldn't help leaning over the rail to stare into the opaque surface. They knew what lurked down there. Bartholomew did too, and his face shone with sweat as he purposely avoided the rail.

"I notice Nemo's crew enhanced the railing I made for them," Celwyn pointed to the long walkway and handrail leading to the strip of sand before the volcanic walls. "Watch your step," he cautioned Valentine as he started up the walkway. The magician gave the vampire a short but vivid description of what lived in the water. As he talked, the water below them undulated as if the Mizuchi listened. Kang stared into it with a grave and horrified expression. The Mizuchi had been as big as the *Nautilus,* and wider than the ship the last time they'd seen it. By now, it was probably even larger.

Murmurings reached them, and then a strident voice as Nemo gained the top of the stairs and the platform.

"From the looks on your faces, you must be remembering the experience Mrs. Kang and I had here."

Kang said, "We were." He shuddered. "When the two of you fell in, my world stopped."

"As did mine." Nemo eyed the magician. "I am still in your debt."

"As I am for rescuing Elizabeth," Kang told him.

The magician tamped the air. "Please. I would do it again and again. At the catacombs, sir, you more than repaid the compliment. We would not have survived otherwise."

"I'm happy to assist." Nemo eyed the others. "We'll only be here a few hours for supplies. It is too dangerous to enter the jungle."

Valentine sighed.

"However, if Jonas went with you, along with a pair of armed guards, you could hunt for a short time, or until the tigers discovered you were there."

Bartholomew lit a cigar and waggled the match. "I do not wish to go. There are things out there besides tigers to be wary of."

"Thank you, sir. Yes, I will wait for your guards." Valentine strolled down the walkway a few steps and remained there until the crew and the magician followed him to the opening in the volcanic wall. Celwyn hoped Valentine would be quick. It was one thing to produce a tiger to frighten someone with, but quite another to run from one himself.

Chapter 38

HOURS LATER, THE SUBMARINE traveled away from the island, at full speed to the south. Before dark, they would go through the Malacca Strait, and skirt the Sumatra Peninsula and then onward to Singapore.

As they left the remains of their luncheon behind, Nemo bowed and followed the others into the study.

"I have a treat for you, gentlemen." He glanced at Bartholomew, and his lips twitched. "It does not involve traveling through an underground river."

The automat raised a brow. "From your expression, it is something we'll enjoy. A wreck? An ancient site?"

"Astute as always, Professor. Have you heard of Hagia Sophia?"

Bartholomew stopped short and swiveled to face them. "That is in Constantinople. I have been there. A most beautiful mosque, and a center for Christians, too."

"Even I have heard of it." Valentine added, "The rumors were that Constantine found several secret passages that led to a cache of antiquities."

As they took their seats on the sofas and at the chess table, Nemo said, "In less than two hours, we'll be passing by the Shallows of Miancus. It is a vast underwater site of complex coral architecture that mimics the Hagia Sophia in many ways." He held up a hand. "Please do not ask who made it, I do not know. It is carved from gigantic mounds of coral that are thought to be thousands of years old."

"Fascinating, I'm sure." Kang rubbed his hands together. "I am most anxious to see it."

Nemo nodded. "Most of what is known of the site is from modern divers hired by archeologists, and there has been little damage from earthquakes or other disasters over the centuries. You will be curious why it is so well preserved, and I welcome your comments and opinions. But I know little, other than that the water is unusually clear."

"Shallows?" Bartholomew managed to ask.

Nemo nodded. "Yes. We will be careful. Usually, we're too busy to stop, and I avoid the area because of danger from the coral and water depth. As Jonas well knows, this ship needs fifty feet of draft to have a comfortable passage, and there are parts of Miancus that are considerably less.

"I had heard of Miancus, mostly in obscure journals, but there hasn't been more information about it in a long time—" Bartholomew's frown indicated that no matter the opportunity, he might question the idea of a close-up view.

"Captain, I look forward to seeing this," Valentine said. "It has always interested me."

"We'll do a quick tour of the site—" Nemo sent the big man a speculative look, "—carefully. Traditional divers without a source of air could only go so deep. We'll be able to see all of it."

"This will be incredible!" The Professor's eyes gleamed.

Nemo enjoyed his enthusiasm, and Celwyn appreciated the pleasure Nemo received in providing it to them. He wondered if Bartholomew understood what Nemo meant about seeing "all" of it, and that it meant diving costumes with air hoses.

"The coral fields are extraordinary." Nemo opened his arms wide. "Every color in the rainbow is represented. I've left you some tomes that reference the site there," he indicated the table between the sofas, "and wish you a pleasant hour until we surface."

As he spoke, already the water outside the glass had become clearer, and if possible, of even greater beauty.

Kang and Verne got to the books first, and the fun began.

Chapter 39

GONGS RESOUNDED THROUGHOUT the ship as the *Nautilus* ascended to the surface, where brilliant sunshine welcomed them and transformed the sea into a cerulean world. As Celwyn and the others climbed through the hatch, the magician enjoyed the spectacle, drinking in the warmth and the view.

Verdant islands surrounded the ship, many so close he could have swum to them. On all sides, the jungle quivered with life and the cries of the birds. If Qing heard them, he would be quite interested—as far as the magician knew, he had never met another bird, real or otherwise. To the south, clusters of islands dotted the shimmering water.

Bartholomew and the Professor leaned over the rail next to him. The big man said, "They call this area 'the sea of a thousand islands.'"

"I can see why. It would take years to explore them all." The wonder in the Professor's voice promised he would someday.

"Look!" Bartholomew indicated a whitish area under the water about thirty feet off their starboard side. "It must be the beginning of the coral."

"As beautiful as that probably is, I wager the Miancus is even more so," the automat murmured.

Celwyn ducked as a shearwater swooped low over them, skimming across the water, and splashing down again. In a flurry of spray and wings, it rose upward with its prize. The magician gazed at the midday sun, reveling in the heat on his face and marveling at the cloudless sky only hours from the volcanic island.

Something moved on the periphery of his vision. The magician pivoted and scanned miles back over the expanse of the sea they'd just sailed through. In the next second, he felt thankful for the last of Thales' gifts that remained; the gift that allowed him to see far.

With a frown, he said, "Please ask Nemo not to descend without me—"

He changed into a handsome gull and ascended over Bartholomew's gasp, flying north. Using magic, it only took minutes as he glided over the top of the waves until he reached one of the islands a few miles back. As he rested among the fronds of a palm tree, a dreadful feeling that he needed to be circumspect settled upon him. Soon, he knew why.

A large barkentine sailed silently toward them with a red flag at the top of her mainmast. They were in a hurry, judging from the scurrying men on her deck and rigging. He could make out dozens of men with long swords on their sides, and spyglasses trained in the direction of the *Nautilus* as she basked on the surface. Scores more scampered up the masts and worked the stays frantically. They looked just like Dearing's pirates.

Oh, hell!

Celwyn flew back as fast as he could, throwing up a thick wall of mist between them and the submarine. He landed unceremoniously on the platform and herded Bartholomew and the automat toward the hatch as he waved at the crewman at the other end of the ship. He pointed down. "We must dive—hurry!"

They clattered down the spiral stairs with the magician in the lead and ran to the bridge. When he burst through the doorway, he nearly bowled Nemo over.

"Jonas—"

"Pirate ship—" Celwyn inhaled. "Closing fast. We must—"

Nemo whirled and barked orders to dive. The crew moved fast in practiced coordination, flipping switches and levers. Celwyn felt the vibration under his feet and the aquatic window filled with bubbles as they dove. Alarms shrilled loud over the echoing gongs, heightening the urgency.

The automat told Nemo, "Jonas spied them and flew back to confirm what he saw." He turned to the magician. "What did the ship look like?"

"Four-master. Their crew worked quietly. Not a word, nor did I see a line hit the deck. Damn pirates. Flying a red flag. Their spyglasses were trained on this ship." He looked Nemo in the eye. "No doubt about it." Now he knew why Nemo preferred to only surface at night.

"How many guns?" The Captain asked and swiveled to confer with Granger. He called out, "Turn off the alarms!" and switched back to them.

"Double decks of guns, both sides."

As the magician spoke, the coral outside the window loomed closer, so close it could have scraped the sides of the ship. The *Nautilus* moved ahead by inches, not miles; a wrong move and they would brush against it. It was at this point Celwyn realized they were in the Shallows.

Bartholomew demanded, "*Why* is a pirate ship after us?"

Nemo shook his head and strode back to the wheel. They followed.

Kang asked, "What is the meaning of a red flag?"

"A ship flying it 'takes no quarter.' It is a pirate's warning that they will kill anyone in their way." Nemo rotated the wheel an inch toward starboard.

From behind them, Granger said, "We are at forty-eight feet draft, just above the seafloor. We are riding a fine line right now, and can't dive any lower."

"Why do they want *us*?" the big man asked again.

The infernal gongs confirmed the dangerously low depth, resounding across the bridge with headache-inducing repetition.

With a drag in his voice, the automat said, "I imagine they have caught sight of this ship before, and see her as a prize..."

"Or?" Celwyn asked.

"Or, somehow, they know we have Dearing on board. Pirates are close-knit in their nefarious enterprises, and not necessarily by geography." Kang stared out the aquatic window with a worried frown. "If he hasn't been seen, or there were reports of the destruction of the *Primero* and Dearing being spirited away ... or one of the *Primero's* crew could have survived and seen us."

Hundreds of silvery fish the size of a thumb swam with them at their slow pace. Nemo barked an order, extinguishing all the *Nautilus's* lights and silencing the gongs and alarms. Only the instrument panels glowed with an eerie blue light as the ship crept forward.

The magician did not voice his opinion that the sunlight—which still ribboned downward through the water—also floodlit the sea floor around them with more than enough light for the pirates to spot them. Nemo would already know this. To help, Celwyn layered a darkening film across the water and painted the ship with it. Nemo noticed and raised his eyes to the magician.

They passed heaps of disintegrated wood that had been decorated with bones and skulls and piles of broken pottery, confirming they'd entered a graveyard of wrecked ships. Kang grabbed Celwyn's elbow and Bartholomew's, and they moved to the other side of the bridge to the smaller starboard window to allow the crew, and Nemo, room to watch for obstacles.

"What are the pirates doing? Waiting for us to surface?" Bartholomew whispered.

"Perhaps... I could elevate us with a blanket of invisibility," the magician said mostly to himself. "But not for long."

As he spoke, a sudden shadow blocked the sun, darkening the water above them. In the next second, a concussion reverberated all around them. The forest of bulbous coral they had just passed through exploded, sending thousands of shards into the side of the ship, where it pinged like metallic rain against their armor.

Before they could react, another concussion boomed, and the impact slammed the *Nautilus* hard against the coral. Sea water poured into the bridge where the deck met the outside wall. With the next blast came a loud rending that tore at the ship as the crew scrambled to stay upright. Celwyn inhaled and reached the breach, raising his hands to bring everything he had to force out the gushing water. Just as the water slowed, the submarine shuddered under another deafening blast cut through the air, and with a groan, she ran aground.

Crewmen rushed in all directions. Bartholomew tried to help as Verne and Valentine appeared at the door and were waved back by Granger.

The five notes of Celwyn's music arrived, reverberating across the bridge as he continued to push the water out while trying to close the hole in the ship's side. "I ... can't ... see through the iron ... or whatever is on the side of the ship!" He breathed and pushed. "I need to know where the hole is—"

Nemo had already reached the brass pole and angled the lens backward.

Celwyn's arms shook as he pushed the walls of the bridge closed. He assumed the sea still poured into the deck below them where they couldn't see. Over the next few minutes, as he worked, he knew he had won the battle; he could see less water. The music grew stronger, and the magician sloshed across the bridge to lay his hands on the breached wall.

"Two feet to your right. Begins at eye level to you. Five feet wide and five feet tall," Nemo called out.

While Celwyn methodically sealed the outside of the ship, he listened to the music, reveling in the strength it brought. As if he worked a puzzle, each of the steel panels closed upon themselves. Yet, like an evil cloud, the shadow above them still blocked the sunlight.

"What can we do?" Kang asked Nemo as he ran by them, crossing back to the wheel and flinging it hard to starboard, without result.

"Check on Dearing. Granger went below—"

As Bartholomew and Kang ran out, Celwyn finished the outside of the ship, ready to follow them. He hesitated, hearing only a whirring from the powerful engines; his heart fell, knowing the *Nautilus* couldn't move.

The intercom next to Nemo buzzed. He listened and cursed.

"The lower deck is breached and flooding severely—"

Celwyn didn't wait for more and streaked out of the room, propelled by his magic, and down the stairs. He could hear the yelling and a commotion growing louder as he jumped off the last dozen steps to fly to the wall where the crew pressed whatever they could find against the bowed-out panels behind Dearing's cell. The sea surged across the floor, knee-high and growing higher as it invaded the turbine room. Already it licked the first step of the stairs leading upward... if it reached the bridge, all was lost. Even if the airtight door at the top remained closed, the water would fill the belly of the submarine, and she would never leave the bottom of the sea.

Sweat poured off Bartholomew's face as he helped the crew, handing them sheet after sheet of metal and bundles of something they pushed into the wall. Kang stood with Granger, while he barked orders, and then they both began tossing the bundles to Bartholomew.

The magician had a premonition things would get worse, and when he saw the way the block of cells leaned aft, his worry escalated. He told Kang, "I suggest you get a gun, and guard Dearing." The automat didn't argue and took one of Granger's pistols off his belt. He aimed it at Dearing with both hands.

Meanwhile, Celwyn reached the far wall. He opened his arms and enveloped the outside of the ship in a storm of air. From the amount of water coming in, this breach had to be twice as wide as the one on the bridge—he couldn't keep that much water out and repair it at the same time.

The magician raised his arms as high as he could, welcoming the violins and their music so sweet and strong. Celwyn increased the amount of air tenfold, blowing the water away from the ship as the crew worked. If they heard the violins, they didn't react, just kept hammering the steel in place while other crewmen poured something white around the edges, sealing them. At least, the magician hoped so. Several of the crew pointed to where the leak had stopped and then at the magician.

Granger grabbed a crewman by his collar and yelled, "Get the pumps going—" The man saluted and ran toward the stern.

"I'll seal the outside, although I don't use solder," Celwyn told Granger. "I can only frame the area with it—I can't see it."

Using magic, it only took seconds to slather molten metal all over the outside of the ship. The magician felt himself tiring fast. "It won't last long," he told Granger. "But it should hold until you can repair it." In the silence, the engines of the pumps rumbled and grew louder. Celwyn had two things to do—one more important than the other. Next to him, Granger directed the crew to move faster and check the pumps.

"We're still in danger." The magician caught Granger's arm and held on.

Bartholomew heard him and arrived at his side. "The pirate ship?"

Beyond him, Verne and Valentine stood halfway down the stairs, goggling at the waves of seawater sloshing across the floor, and then at Kang holding the gun.

"Yes, it is still sitting above us, as far as I can tell." Celwyn saw them. He glanced at the author, then jerked his head upward. Valentine took Verne's elbow and dragged him back up the stairs and then returned.

Celwyn almost smiled. They might have to do this the old-fashioned way; Nemo would have to wait to sink a few pirate ships for a while.

To Granger, he said, "We have an option. I can put a buffer between us so they can't see or hear us. If you would like to blow their ship up, you would know where your divers need to attach charges. I can't guarantee my magic would be that precise if I were to do it."

"If we did, it would be on the side of their hull furthest away from us," Granger said.

The automat said, "I assume you wish to make them leave, not sink on top of us."

Granger stopped mid-stride and returned to them. "How do we keep it from exploding over our heads?"

"Yes, I wish to know also." Valentine lowered his brows, for once losing his confident air. "I am ready to help."

Celwyn motioned him and Granger closer. Bartholomew joined them, and Kang pivoted to listen, his pistol still trained on Dearing. The pirate's eyes blazed with excitement and hate as he shook the bars of his cage.

"Stop that!" Bartholomew yelled at him. "You're real close to drowning down here."

"Yes, how?" Kang asked.

With a growl, Granger said, "We need to get this ship off the coral, and then get out of here."

"I agree, but what if they attack us before then?" Celwyn asked. Then a solution dawned on him. He asked Granger, "How close are the pirates?"

"When I last checked, a hundred yards, no more."

"And they can't come further into this shallow water?" Celwyn asked.

Granger grated, "No, they can't, and I wish to hell we hadn't." The pumps grew louder as the rest of them came to life. "They weigh even more than we do and are bigger, too." He eyed the magician. "They can't hear us from above for now, true?"

The magician nodded. "I made sure of it."

"If they think we're dead, they will stop attacking," Kang said.

"Or, if they still want Dearing, they will try to get at us. The question is, do they want to rescue him, or kill him?" Bartholomew asked. "That could have been an attack to disable us. Or force us to surface."

Granger continued to stare at the magician. "What do you have in mind?"

"I'm going to dissolve the coral we're sitting on." He listened to the monotonous thumping of the pumps as they worked. "I'd do it now, but until I rest, I'm not strong enough to keep up the protection on the hull above us at the same time." At Granger's raised brows, he said, "I would have to let go of one to do the other."

"Tell us the rest," Kang requested.

"Simple. We get Nemo's approval and tell him we'll need whatever we can get from the engines to propel us up and forward as the coral disappears."

Bartholomew asked, "What if the hull is damaged getting off the coral?"

Dearing shook his cage and roared endearments at them.

"Stop that!" the big man yelled again.

While Celwyn rubbed his face in thought, Kang answered, "We'll have to take that chance, and hope Jonas can fix it."

"If it were me, I'd approve this," Granger told them. "Let me consult with the Captain." As he started toward the stairs, the ship trembled, then shifted hard to starboard. In the next instant, the *Nautilus* keeled over with a groan from deep within her.

Kang fell and slid across the floor, holding the pistol above his head and the water. Bartholomew rolled after him. The magician held onto a bulkhead. He straightened, pushing the ship the other way, righting her again. That about finished him.

But this wasn't over.

The water on the deck shifted, crashing against the frame holding the cells up. The submarine rolled again, and the frame of the cage cracked and started to fall.

Dearing slammed into the bars, and the cell collapsed. He broke free and charged out of the cage straight at Kang, who'd made it to his feet again. The magician inserted himself between them just as Kang fired. The shot caught the magician in the side, and he went down with a splash. As he hit the water, Celwyn saw Bartholomew lift the pirate by the neck and punch him so hard, he flew across the room.

Chapter 40

UNDER A VOLLEY OF THE AUTOMAT'S heartfelt curses, Valentine helped him raise the magician's head and shoulders out of the swirling water. Bartholomew wrapped a chain around the unconscious pirate and motioned the crew to take over.

Granger barked orders to reset the cells and post guards. "Chain the bastard to the wall!" He joined Kang and Bartholomew as they lifted Celwyn over the water and toward the stairs.

"It's not ... that bad..." the magician said.

"Shut up." Kang thought of all the times he worried about Jonas, and now look what he'd done.

At the sound of gunfire, several of the crew had descended a few steps from the deck above, and when they saw the parade coming toward them, they backed up again. Granger called out, "Get a stretcher!" Kang and the others shuffled through the knee-high water, careful not to drop the magician. The automat kept up a running string of curses, mostly for himself, but some for Dearing.

Bartholomew backed up the stairs after Granger, holding the magician's shoulders and keeping his head from bouncing on the rail. Along with Valentine, Kang held his legs and tried not to look at the blood dripping into the swirling water below them.

Nemo met them at the top of the stairs, where Granger reported what had happened. Nemo's swearing joined the automat's as they made the landing.

"Xiau shot me." The magician tried a playful smile at Kang.

Kang nearly dropped him. "You got in the way!"

"It's all right, Xiau. I'll live—"

Nemo held up an authoritative hand, silencing all of them. "We have to get rid of that ship above us." He addressed his lieutenant, "Ready the divers. We'll blow a hole in her at her waterline, so she'll either head to the islands or sink."

When they reached the main corridor, Kang halfway heard Nemo's instructions to his crew, while he watched Jonas. Of all the times the automat had told the jokester to be careful, it was *he* who had shot him! Then he wondered how long the protection on the submarine would last if the magician lost consciousness. Right now, he seemed alert enough, even amused at Kang's discomfort. The automat rolled his eyes, this time in relief.

Bartholomew waved the stretcher out of the way and strode toward Sickbay with the magician in his arms. It took quite a bit for Jonas to appear small, but the big man managed it. Kang got there first and pushed the doors open.

All the way to his cabin and back to retrieve his medical bag, Kang thought about this new wound. Its location was low enough on the magician's side to not be dangerous, and the automat knew he should be hopeful, but after their scare with Jonas last year, he worried. Any wound could be serious, and it was less than a week since the last time he'd been shot.

"Thank you," he told Bartholomew after he laid Jonas on the examination table. "Hot water, please." The big man whirled and headed out again.

Kang leaned over his patient and said, "Pay attention, Jonas. I need your help." He lifted his bloody shirt and studied the damage before saying, "Stop the blood."

The magician closed his eyes and minutes went by. Loud footsteps in the corridor reached them, and then Bartholomew and Nemo's medical officer, Lieutenant Tiddle came in, both bearing hot water. Celwyn tugged on Kang's sleeve. "It is done."

"Excellent. Now the bullet, I'll help." Kang used long tweezers to hold the skin back until Celwyn expelled the bullet. It pinged off the metal table and bounced across the floor.

Bartholomew picked it up and gingerly placed it in a bowl. "The wound is looking better," the automat told Celwyn as he worked.

"I am going to be fine, my friend." The magician said, "It is mostly a flesh wound located where I ate too many pastries. You never have that problem."

"Pfft." Kang felt better. "You do sound stronger than I expected." He thanked Tiddle for the hot water and told him they could handle things. Tiddle saluted and departed.

"Order some tea, please," the magician requested.

When Kang saw Celwyn was teasing, the automat stopped what he planned to say. "Not now." He fussed a bit and cleaned the wound. "This could have been much worse, and so unnecessary."

"Protecting each other is a habit, Xiau. Dearing was coming right at you, and he wasn't going to give you a kiss."

The automat grunted, unable to speak. "Hush while I examine this."

"Jonas is right. We protect each other and I am so glad it isn't too bad," the big man said.

Celwyn winced as Kang taped the wound. He asked Bartholomew, "Did I see you punch the daylights out of Dearing?"

Bartholomew grinned. "Yes, you did. Our vampire friend will be jealous."

As if by divination, they heard a commotion in the passageway, followed by some of the crew hurrying along as if avoiding someone, and Valentine rejoined them, bringing Verne along too.

"Again, Mr. Celwyn?" Valentine asked as he leaned over the table to see the wound.

"Yes, did you see Xiau shoot me?"

The automat almost smiled but kept working on the tape. "He will be fine."

"Please do not mention this to Tara in any messages you send her."

The vampire nodded while Verne studied the bullet in the bowl. He shuddered.

"I want Qing and some tea please, seriously," Celwyn said.

Kang shook his head. "I'll bring Qing in, but the tea will wait a few hours. And you should rest." He finished listening to the magician's pulse. "I'll sit on you if I have to."

Bartholomew approached them to say, "We will take turns watching you rest. Don't argue."

The magician sighed, partly from pain, and somewhat in defeat. "I have to stay awake to maintain the patches where the water breached the bridge."

Chapter 41

WHEN KANG RETURNED WITH Qing, the automat had a report. "Nemo says his divers are visiting the pirate ship now. We should expect to hear the explosion from the charge in a few minutes." As he deposited Qing beside the magician's feet, he told the bird to stay put. To the magician, he sounded just as annoyed. "Here is some water. That is all for now."

Bartholomew said, "Let's hope—"

A concussion slapped the ship. The automat waited for it to subside and held on to the examination table. "The explosion is supposed to be enough to scare them into moving their ship, not abandoning it." He aimed a thumb outside, although there wasn't a window in Sickbay. "Nor do we need any nasty visitors who look like Dearing."

Granger stopped just inside the door, and Kang motioned him in.

Undisguised fear swam in the Lieutenant's eyes. "The Captain wants to know—"

With Kang's next words, the worry in the Lieutenant's eyes lessened. To a point.

"Jonas assures us he can keep the repair to the breaches watertight. He will be fine. It won't make him more cautious, but he'll be fine." Granger's clenched fists showed his nervousness remained. "Are the panels holding?" Kang asked.

"For now. Our divers are assessing the damage. We're still marooned on top of the coral."

"Not an ideal situation," Celwyn said.

Bartholomew asked, "What does the Captain intend to do next?"

"We're monitoring the situation. I must get back to the bridge." Granger addressed the magician, "Please keep the patches on the hull in place. The Captain's personal request." It came with a sigh of relief.

Celwyn understood. "What will the pirate ship will do?"

Qing defied Kang and walked up the magician's leg and onto his pillow. He rubbed his beak on Celwyn's jaw.

Bartholomew saw him and *humphed*. He and the mechanical bird were far from friends.

Granger's eyes gleamed. "Their ship is taking on plenty of water and has moved away a bit. Not too far. Still within canon distance, if they spy us."

"But?"

Granger's unamused expression matched their own. "The pirates have enough to do not to sink before they reach one of the islands." The smile vanished. "Though they may pepper us with charges to finish the job they started."

The magician sighed and shifted to an upright position. He swung his legs off the table. "It is as I thought. I've rested enough. We need to get to the bridge." When Kang opened his mouth to object, Celwyn continued, "Bartholomew can carry me. This is urgent. I will rest as soon as it is done."

The big man didn't hesitate and scooped him off the table as if he'd been one of Qing's feathers. "It can't wait?"

"The more I think about it, no. Like the Lieutenant says, if the pirates survive, or their ship does, they could spray this area with cannonballs, and we'd have even worse problems."

As they neared the door, Kang called, "What are you going to do?"

"What we talked about; Nemo wants this ship off the coral."

With the magician in his arms, Bartholomew stooped under the lintel, and they headed up the hall. Everyone followed. The mechanical bird landed on Celwyn's shoulder and squawked in Bartholomew's face.

The big man frowned. "It isn't my fault, bird."

Celwyn patted Qing's back. "It is the Professor's." He caught the automat's eye, winked, and added, "Poor Qing is upset, Xiau."

"Shut up, Jonas. That is only the third time I have shot a gun. And I don't like you moving around like this." He checked the bandage. "If you start bleeding again, I will carry you back here myself."

~⌣~

As they came in, the bridge buzzed with activity, and the floor still appeared wet in the corners. No fresh leaks gushed forth.

The chatter between the crew faded when they spied the magician. Still silent, they stood and clapped. Although honored, Celwyn felt very underdressed; he was shirtless and bandaged. After Bartholomew propped the magician against the aquatic window, Qing hopped onto the big man's shoulder, much to his consternation.

"Thank you," Celwyn told them. He caught up on his breathing and faced Nemo. "I assume we still need to get the ship moving before they shoot at us again?" Through the glass, he spied the ragged edges of the coral that resembled erratic rows of teeth—which he knew from personal experience could scrape the skin off a man faster than he could blink.

Nemo regarded him. "Yes. They could start unloading their guns on us any minute."

Granger stood to his right, at attention and ready for orders. He had again developed a sheen of worry underneath his steely control.

"Granger reported you plan to dissolve the coral under us as we gun the engines?" Nemo asked.

"Yes. It will be quick, and is not as tiring as the other excitement this afternoon."

"And your wound?"

"It is a flesh wound." Celwyn shrugged. And a way to taunt the automat.

Nemo strode to the wheel and back while maintaining a deep frown. "This ship should ascend at a moderate degree, or we'd be in danger of dragging our tail through the sand and into more coral."

"That certainly wouldn't do," Kang agreed, with a check on Bartholomew. Their highly superstitious friend seemed fine, for now.

"I'll do my best to prevent that."

Nemo murmured instructions to Granger, who passed them to the crew. Much to Qing's dismay, the vibrations of the engines began, scattering the fish outside the window. Celwyn patted his back; the bird's first visit to the bridge in a while and no fish to watch.

When the engines reached a strong, solid hum, Nemo announced, "We're ready. How will we know when to give the ship full power?"

The magician smiled. He felt fortunate; an opportunity for an artful performance twice in one day! For this instance, Celwyn had a high degree of confidence in the outcome. "You won't have any doubt." He glanced at the automat and the big man. They knew each other so well; the magician didn't have to ask. They took his elbows and held him steady while he did his best to ignore the throbbing pain in his side.

It was time. With each breath he inhaled, he felt stronger as he built his magic and brought forth the music that supported him. He had always loved the five notes; they seemed so much a part of everything he touched or that touched him. They repeated louder, within and without him, until the magician released himself from the support of the others and planted his feet far apart, absorbing the strength of the music and bringing every part of himself to a single point of concentration.

Celwyn raised his arms, and the music became deafening, quaking the ship, and shaking the air around it. The water outside roiled like a giant had stirred it viciously.

Kang saw what he was doing and gulped.

The vibrations grew violent until the coral undulated like a snake, and a low rumbling reached them. The pulsation grew worse, and a loud crack sounded as the coral split open. Blocks of it fell as a long, ominous groan vibrated underneath it, and the ship shifted.

Louder. The magician shook his fists as the roar of the vibrations reached a crescendo. The coral outside the window shimmered and then exploded. Simultaneously Nemo barked the order, and the submarine surged upward. The grinding underneath them reverberated, and the violins roared. Bartholomew caught the magician before he hit the floor, and still, Celwyn reverberated the air.

The *Nautilus* had broken free.

She raised her nose, rising toward the surface. Then she leveled off and lunged forward, flattening and floating again. The roar of her engines moderated as Celwyn dropped to the floor. Sweat poured off his face.

"Captain—leaks?" Kang called out.

"Get us beyond their guns—44 degrees starboard," Nemo barked at Granger.

Again, Nemo had anticipated the need and had pulled the brass pipe to him. He pivoted in a slow circle. Behind him, a crewman called out instrument readings. Nemo announced, "No new leaks. However, I do not like the appearance of the starboard panel."

Bartholomew asked, "Can you see underneath the hull?"

Nemo shook his head as he instructed Granger to station additional men below and to watch for leaks. To the others, he said, "We need repairs, and I know a place for it. The panel should last until we get there."

"Thank god!" Bartholomew sighed.

Nemo saluted. "Well done, Jonas."

"Thank you, sir."

Kang tried not to speculate if the condition of the panel was wishful thinking on Nemo's part, and instead pointed at the magician. "You're bleeding again."

"It was fun, Xiau."

The automat kept the exasperation out of his voice as he replied, "We discussed it, and have come to the conclusion that you enjoy this thoroughly." He took one arm and Bartholomew the other to lift Celwyn to his feet. "And the greater danger, the better." He lost his resolution not to be frustrated and rolled his eyes. "Good grief!"

The magician shrugged and slung an arm around each of them as they headed out the door. "You said you do not like it when I'm bored."

Bartholomew chuckled and kept laughing all the way up the corridor. He had seen the lively decorations just added to the automat's hair. Little bunnies with green eyes.

Chapter 42

T HE *NAUTILUS* STAYED JUST UNDER the surface for the first hour as they headed away from near disaster. Granger's report of their last sighting of the pirates had a certain measure of gratification to it; their four-master leaned nearly ninety degrees leeward, still taking on water.

They traveled steadily north by northwest in the same direction they'd come from several hours before. Kang had patiently explained to everyone in the study they couldn't go back to the island with the volcano to use the lake for their repairs because the Mizuchi would devour any of the crew it found in the lake before they could repair a thing.

Granger stopped by the study long enough to inform them the panels were holding, and the wonder in his voice came through clearly. Bartholomew wasn't the only superstitious one aboard. The

Lieutenant also reported Dearing had finally settled down and remained in chains in his cell.

To keep the peace, Kang and Celwyn had come to an arrangement; the magician would rest in the study and not exert himself. In return, the automat was allowed to fuss over him while Celwyn could be in the middle of everything, and entertain himself. Initially, Valentine sat beside him to keep him company. Or, as Celwyn thought of it, the vampire had drawn the short straw to watch over him.

While Celwyn lay on his good side on the sofa and half-watched the aquatic show out the window, he observed Bartholomew and Verne's chess game. The author liked to talk whenever it was the big man's turn. It could be about anything; Verne chattered like a magpie. The magician suspected he knew it interrupted Bartholomew's concentration and strategy.

Beyond them, the late afternoon sun lit up the Andaman Sea, refracting through it in broad swathes of light. At a slow pace, they traveled through the clear water where, every few minutes, they encountered a parade of fish, much to Qing's delight—until a pack of sharks arrived. The predators escorted them from about thirty feet out, seeming to swim just far enough away to be indistinct. No doubt they would increase Bartholomew's nervousness if he saw them. When the Professor noticed the visitors, he dismissed them because they were the tiger type, not his favorite.

From his position next to the magician, Valentine asked, "How do we know the pirates are not following us?"

"Granger says they won't be going anywhere for a while, and most likely will sink where we left them. Also, we are just under the surface, and the crew is manning the periscope to keep an eye on whatever is behind us," Kang said. "I expect the Captain will increase his security from now on, even in the middle of nowhere."

"If I recall correctly, 'the middle of nowhere' is an American idiom." Celwyn raised an inquiring brow at the automat, who nodded.

When the wall clock behind him chimed, Verne moved his bishop and waited before releasing the piece. "Three hours until our dinner." As soon as Bartholomew started to think about his next move, the author said, "If we're going where I think we are, we'll be there before dinner."

"Where is that?" Valentine gazed at the chess game with semi-interest.

Verne licked his lips and stared at his king. "An uncharted island near Tenasserim. We've stopped there before."

"Uninhabited?" Bartholomew asked.

Verne frowned at the spot where the big man deposited his rook. He even waited in case Bartholomew wanted to reconsider the move. With a huff, he said, "Yes."

Qing's metal feet clicked like a malfunctioning clock as he jumped off the windowsill and waddled across the floor to Kang. They both waited a moment until the automat sighed and handed over his cuff link. With a squeak of delight, the bird tossed it and caught it again before flying to the bookshelves. For an unknown reason, he preferred Shakespeare's *Folio* for company today. The magician wagered that if Qing treated those priceless volumes like he did the whiskey decanters, the bird would have been banished from the study long ago.

Celwyn yawned. The rhythm of the undulating water became hypnotic, and even the occasional fish could be part of an aquatic play... like an expected actor and fragment of the scene. He couldn't stay awake. As his eyes closed, he spotted a dead eye as it swam by the window. He sat up. "Xiau—"

The herd of sharks had drawn closer, easily keeping up with the compromised submarine. Earlier, the magician thought they numbered less than a dozen, but now there had to be fifty or more of them. They swam close, fin to fin, moving as one animal. Every one of the predators trained a soulless eye on the *Nautilus*. The little fishes were long gone.

"Would you look at that?" Kang marveled.

Bartholomew's bottom lip protruded as he pouted at his queen, and then Verne's knight. "Do I want to know?"

Celwyn told him, "Probably not."

"I rather wish I had their teeth." Valentine regarded the sharks. "So even and long."

Verne glanced up and exclaimed, "Oh my—look—"

"I didn't think it possible." Kang tapped the glass. "There's a white shark. See it? In the middle of the pack."

Celwyn leaned on an elbow to see better. "It is as if the others are protecting her."

"The White Queen," Verne said with amazement.

"Are you convinced it is female?" Valentine asked.

As he gazed at it, the magician questioned that as well. There was something familiar he couldn't name about this—and he had had enough rest. He elevated himself over to the window and hovered there, just above the floor. Kang made a hissing noise but didn't say anything about uncooperative, recuperating patients.

For several moments, Celwyn stared out the glass, trying to see details of the white shark, but to no avail. As he watched, the darker sharks escorting the queen faded, dissipating into the shadowy water. Still, the white shark swam with the *Nautilus*. It moved closer until only a few feet of water separated them. A shiver ran up Celwyn's spine when he spied something that couldn't be—or shouldn't be.

From his position at the magician's side, Kang saw it too. "How can that be?"

Celwyn shrugged. The shark's eye looked right into him. A blue eye, not black, as it should have been. As the magician watched, the shark seemed to take on a glow, nebulous and iridescent, until it also faded into the depths. He wondered if it had never been there at all.

Chapter 43

JUST BEFORE SUNDOWN, THEY CRUISED east through a final cluster of islands, and the *Nautilus* limped into a bay shaped like a severely curved half-moon. She submerged for a brief time and re-surfaced in a larger, second bay of pristine blue water enclosed on all sides by a lush rain forest. Only steps from the water, the jungle took over. No one would be able to detect the submarine from the waterside.

Seawater still sluiced off the ship when the crew opened the hatch, allowing Valentine, Bartholomew, and the others onto the platform. That Celwyn had been permitted up the stairs had been a negotiated battle with Kang, who'd finally thrown up his hands and insisted it was only for a minute. During the debate, the automat complained that the magician played upon his guilt for shooting him in the first place. Celwyn just smiled fondly at him.

From macaws to parrots, a storm of birds cawed from the depths of the jungle, and the earthy smell of animals permeated the air. Brilliant-colored lizards ran up tree trunks, and fragile orchids dripped from the nearest branches. Valentine licked his lips. Bartholomew watched a man-size prehistoric lizard as it slithered its way across smooth expanses of sand where nothing, and no one, had trod in a long time.

Verne eyed the birds as if cataloging them for a journal. A wistful expression crossed his face. "Eggs. It has been a week, and I miss my Eggs Benedict very much."

Bartholomew gazed further inland to a rise in the verdant land, a half-mile away. "I hope there will be an opportunity for a hunting party."

"I second that," Valentine told them with the kind of gusto that made Verne's breath catch.

As evidenced in his drawn face and movements, a weary Captain Nemo stepped onto the platform. His gaze traveled 360 degrees around before he spoke. "We'll repair the ship here, gentlemen. It could take a week, even with all my crew devoted to it. My divers are getting ready now to examine the underside of the hull and catalog the damage."

"A beautiful place for it," Bartholomew agreed.

"I hope it is still uninhabited," Nemo said. "And I ask that you wait for my crew to verify that it is before venturing too far ashore." He told Celwyn, "I agreed with the Professor that we prefer you rested— not flying over the jungle. Are you recovering?"

"It is a flesh wound and uncomfortable is all. Xiau agrees when he feels like it."

"Good." Nemo frowned, too tired to join in the teasing. "I'll need your help tomorrow, or the next day, to position the ship out of the water long enough to get the work done. The alternative is to build a frame and pulleys, which would take far longer."

The magician bowed. "It will be my pleasure." He winced as he straightened up again, and the automat saw him. Before he could nag, Celwyn asked, "What will the crew do exactly?"

"Make permanent any patches you made and reseal everything on each deck."

"Excellent." Bartholomew asked, "Do you have the equipment to add to the outer iron braces— to ward off another situation like what we've just gone through?"

Nemo rubbed his chin. "I'd intended to before now. We'll have to obtain the iron and schedule a time for it." He frowned. "The underside of the ship needs that too, after today."

"May I recommend while they are at it, they make a back-up fortification around our guest's quarters, so that I do not have to dirty my hands on him again?" Bartholomew made the suggestion with almost enough seriousness to be believed and then chortled.

Even the automat joined in the laughter, despite his annoyance with Celwyn.

With no trace of humor at all, Nemo growled, "It will be done. God damn pirates!"

Several pleasant days passed by under clear and sometimes humid skies. The magician developed a mild sunburn as he sat in a lawn chair in the sand beside the repair operations. On the second day, he added a blue, green, and red umbrella in honor of the species of parrots perched a few feet away that he admired the most.

From sunup to sundown, Nemo rotated teams of divers and crew to repair what had been damaged. Their work would last much longer than what the magician had done in a hurry.

At one point, the crew utilized the floating pier to hand over buckets of something that more of the crew plastered on the damaged areas. The coral had scraped and gouged deep into the armor. At the widest part of the ship, a second layer of armor was added. Like the big man mentioned, Celwyn hoped they would pick up the iron for the other reinforcements soon.

Each day, Bartholomew loaded himself with firearms and other paraphernalia to follow Valentine, Granger, and several of the crew, deep into the jungle. Although not yet dire, supplementing the larder for hundreds of men had been deemed desirable. The author went with them on the first day to help gather edibles. After a half-hour, a muddy and disheveled Verne was escorted back. Nemo's crew usually practiced deadpan expressions when encountering the guests, and Verne's escort was no exception. Celwyn grinned and wondered what he had done.

That morning, the crew had set up dozens of fishing poles that encircled the bay. Celwyn and

Kang were left in charge of alerting the crew when something took the bait. To facilitate that chore, and not interrupt his peaceful tea solitude, the magician had added a distinctive bell to each pole; if something tugged on the line, the crew would hear the tinkle of the bell and come running. On one of his visits, Nemo had noted the variety of parrot fish and larger fish that they hauled in.

"I assume you could put out fishing nets if we need a greater number of fish," Kang told Celwyn and went back to his book.

"Yes. If the poles hadn't worked, I would find enough fish. What is the matter? You look as pouty as Annabelle does when we do not stop at a hat store."

"We did not see the Shallows of Miancus because of that attack," Kang said. "We only saw the outer banks of coral."

"You should take up that complaint with Dearing."

"Pfft."

As usual, the Professor asked every hour that Celwyn display his bandage so he could check for bleeding. Satisfied, he would return to his book, letter writing, or a checkers game the bored magician had agreed to.

"Tomorrow is our third day here," the automat noted. "Will that be when you help with the ship?"

"Yes. The initial repairs were worse than Nemo thought." Celwyn moved Kang's checkers forward several spots without touching them. "Or it might happen later today." The automat knew he didn't like checkers, and the magician didn't consider it cheating if you *helped* your opponent to win and end the game sooner.

"How?"

Celwyn shifted to a new position and sighed. When Kang jerked upright and gaped at him, the magician laughed. "Just teasing."

"Don't *do* that," he said. "Answer my question."

Celwyn shrugged. "For a short time, I'll use magic to lift the bow end of the ship out of the water while they finish the repairs. They know it can't be for long, and they'll be quick to push the floating framework under her. It will be done at low tide."

Kang fell silent and played with one of the checkers. He raised his eyes to Celwyn and said, "You know, I regret shooting you."

"You have mentioned that several times." He grinned at the automat. "Next time shoot me in the ass ... so that I will have more to complain about."

Chapter 44

ONCE AGAIN, THE *NAUTILUS* SUR-faced on the other side of the Singapore headlands.

It had been two years since their last visit. In the distance, fleets of tall ships and commercial transports crowded the docks of the harbor. It was early in the day, and as Nemo's crew rolled out the floating pier, Celwyn followed the others out of the hatch and off the ship. A cold wind blew over them, attempting to steal their hats, but it couldn't dampen their spirits.

The city, and this part of it, brought mixed memories. During their first visit, Philias Fogg had kidnapped Elizabeth to entice the Professor onto the *Nautilus*. It had all been designed to enlist Kang for Fogg's pet project. Bartholomew and Kang had run after the kidnappers and onto the submarine, while Celwyn landed on top of it, eventually stopping the abduction.

By the time Celwyn and the others journeyed back to Prague, Nemo and the magician had developed a strong respect, including Nemo addressing him on a first-name basis. From what they could tell, no one addressed Nemo by his given name, and they wondered if anyone knew what it was.

On an unpleasant note, Singapore had the distinction of being the location where Pelaez had most likely found them again. Even a whisper of his brother's name elicited a growl from Nemo, and curses from the others. Celwyn didn't blame them.

This morning, their party consisted of a complement of guards in street clothes, and nearly everyone came along except Verne and Nemo. The author had a stomachache, probably from his third piece of chocolate cake the night before, and had begged off. When they reached the city's commercial district, Granger would head toward the market stalls. Celwyn offered to make the lieutenant and his charges a cart to ride in, and Granger had only hesitated a second before accepting.

With a bow and a wave, Valentine strode off toward the docks. Bartholomew raised a brow in inquiry.

"He wanted to find something exquisite from the arriving ships that he can't find in the city." At several raised brows, Celwyn said, "To wear, not eat. He'll meet us back at the *Nautilus* later."

The magician and the two guards assigned to them climbed into a cart. As the big man took the reins and they traveled forward, Celwyn said, "Xiau, I hope we have enough room on the ship for any books you find."

"Ha!" Kang enjoyed himself, in high spirits at seeing the city again, and a probable stop for pastries.

Bartholomew must have thought the same. "We will have a fine day, especially if the sun comes out." He checked behind them. "I say, does Granger know his cart won't last too much longer?"

With a shrug, Celwyn watched the other cart as it trailed behind several other carriages, moving away from them and toward the markets. "Yes. I told him they'd have about another five minutes after they leave us. He thought it would be fine."

As they clopped along Crown Street, they spied prosperous shoppers laden with packages, and hardly any pickpockets. Bartholomew sang something from Don Giovanni in a rich baritone. Some of the pedestrians gaped. Others smiled and waved. A few shopkeepers shook their wares high in the hope the cart would stop.

"What are we going to do today?" the magician asked, already knowing the answer, but it was part of their routine to talk about the prospects.

"First, we stop at the telegraph office," Bartholomew said. "Did you bring your letters?"

The magician patted his pocket. "But of course. Do we expect any responses yet?"

"Xiau tells me there hasn't been enough time, no," the big man muttered as he trailed a look at a rug seller, then a men's tailor shop. "Do you see the vest there, the one with silver buttons? I believe it would look wonderful on me."

Kang said, "It is orange. As unusual as it looks, you can wear it when we test-fly the flying machine again." Bartholomew grinned at the joviality and pulled hard on the reins to steer them onto a new avenue. The automat continued, "I have a dozen letters for Elizabeth, and several letters for each of the boys. Of course, I have some for the newlyweds." The automat licked his lips. "There is one for Ricardo too, telling him how much I miss his Beef Wellington. Do you think he would make it the first night we are home again?"

"We will have to request it." Bartholomew sent a last wistful glance at the vestseller as he faded out of sight. Some things were for the best.

Celwyn studied the windows of a pastry café as they drove by, then noted that at the end of the block, the façade of the Raffles Hotel could be seen above the treetops. "Was that the café where you saw Pelaez?"

As he asked, the magician frowned, remembering that day. He had chaperoned Elizabeth, or she, him, for an unending time while she tried on hats. If he hadn't been recuperating from another blasted gunshot wound, he would not have been left behind when the other two encountered Pelaez. Since then, a debate had raged off and on in the ship's study whether his brother would have approached them with Celwyn in tow.

Bartholomew's face contorted as if he had swallowed a live bee. "Yes. It was quite strange."

"The pastries were very good, though." The automat maintained a blissful stare into the distance where they had seen the cafe.

They exchanged a look, and then the big man glanced at Celwyn. "Do you think we will have time for it today?"

The magician said, "That detour could cut into your book and smoke shop activities. We must be back on the ship by two."

After another glance between them full of anticipation, Bartholomew shook the reins with gusto and said, "We'll take that chance."

"It would be advisable to take a regular taxi the rest of the way. This cart is not exactly fashionable, and not secure for your purchases while we're shopping." Celwyn began looking for a hire cab.

A bit later, a coach driver welcomed them aboard, and soon they bounced along at a good clip, away from Blue Goose Books, passing shoppers and a few near-do-wells lurking in the shadows between the buildings. With a searching look, Celwyn wondered what they had for sale besides opium. He wouldn't buy anything but wondered all the same.

The automat unwrapped his new purchases.

"What did you find?" Celwyn peered at the package.

"*The Violets of Cheshire* and an autobiography of John Dee." Kang caressed the top of a medium-sized book tooled in leather. "Doctor Dee is a hero of mine, of sorts. True, he had an evil side, but his accomplishments overshadow that for the most part. You know, I was quite fortunate; the book proprietor had saved this for me since last year when I expressed an interest." He sniffed the cover and looked as enthralled as a gold miner with a big nugget. "This visit, I left him our address in Prague so that he can let us know of anything else he obtains of interest."

The big man took over the narrative. "I picked up an art book by Georges Seurat. Otto and Zander will love it." He asked Celwyn, "Did you see what else I found?"

"Some of them. I'll look at the rest when we're back safe and sound on the ship." A faint and indescribable touch of unease tickled him; a featherlight sensation without visual substance. Celwyn set his jaw and dismissed it.

As they turned right again on Crown Street, the magician scanned the buildings, looking for the pastry café. The sun had finally emerged from the low clouds an hour ago, and everything seemed clear with illumination that seemed odd, perhaps more intense than normal. The quality of the light emphasized colors and the darkened shadows. A good example of the contrast was the façade of a 13th-century temple they rolled by.

Kang asked, "The book is recent?"

"Yes," the big man said. "And it contains a most comprehensive representation of art, all from the greatest paintings of the last five hundred years. Many of them no longer exist. Some are only rumored to have survived wars and thieves. For instance, the one the Captain intends to retrieve is in the book."

"Is there text with the picture? Telling about its history?" Kang's eyes had lit up just like they did for fresh cookies with a side of Beef Wellington.

Bartholomew said, "I can't remember. The book is in one of the packages we stored in the back. We may have a better source in the Captain, but this should help."

"Perhaps," Celwyn said. "Isn't that the café?" He pointed to a whitewashed building from the last century, its patio busy with a fair amount of business.

Kang gestured. "Yes. From here, you can see the top of the fountain in the courtyard. That is where your brother put the fish he'd tampered with before he approached us." Pelaez was also a magician, and if sometimes Celwyn's antics caused consternation, his tricks paled in comparison to what his brother got up to.

Their coach swerved to the curb, and everyone disembarked with visions of pastries and tea dancing in their heads. As the coach with their guards arrived, Bartholomew began retrieving their packages from the boot. Kang asked the guards to return in an hour. They nodded and wasted no time striding north up the street.

"What is up there?" Celwyn asked, shading his eyes against the light.

Bartholomew stood on his toes. "It appears to be an arcade."

"Interesting." Celwyn bowed them forward. "Shall we?"

⌣

Bartholomew and Kang knew exactly where they wanted to sit, and passed between the tables and beyond the fountain to a spot in the rear that faced the street.

"The scent of the orange trees is just as strong now as two years ago," Kang commented and sat down. "Funny how little sensory memories remain clear in your mind."

Celwyn agreed. He relived the first time he had kissed Tara and how she had looked at him afterward. He couldn't stop himself from remembering the last time he'd seen Pelaez, and growled under his breath. Perhaps a stop in Singapore was not as great an idea as they had hoped if he was constantly reminded of his brother.

They accepted menus, requested refreshments, and quizzed the waiter as to the variety of pastries of the day. Their waiter, a lad of about twenty, did his best and finally resorted to using French to explain the confectionary details. He left them to find their drinks and a few pastry samples.

The automat asked, "Do you know who Valentine went to see?"

"No," Celwyn said and eyed a pastry delivery at a neighboring table: first baklava, then something small covered in pistachios, and another with apple slices.

"He has many friends," Bartholomew said as he also studied their neighbors' plates.

"It is upsetting that the telegrams from Tellyhouse are not yet here." Kang's mood dropped to a melancholy level, along with his voice. "When I sent our letters earlier, I asked how long it would take until they were delivered."

Bartholomew slapped him on the back. "Have cheer, my friend. We will be home sooner than you think. Everyone will be waiting for us."

"Yes. Answers to our earlier messages will be here when we stop by again on the way home. Hopefully," Kang said.

"Including messages from Beirut." Celwyn poured, inhaled the steam, and drank. "Did you tell them exactly what we're doing now with Nemo?"

"No." The automat shrugged. "We shouldn't upset them despite our promises to tell them." He challenged the magician. "You would send very little details with the same result."

"Probably." The magician noticed the other table had forsaken the baklava and were concentrating on whatever the pistachios topped.

As they speculated on the mystery pastry, their waiter deposited a platter of delectable samples in front of them. After they had been admired and tested, the Professor wiped the crumbs from his shirt. "Nectar of the gods. In an earlier telegram, I told Tellyhouse we had captured Dearing, and that we meant to rescue Miss Redifer."

"Our old news," Bartholomew observed. "Things are different now."

"Did you mention our planned stops?" Celwyn asked. He decided upon a tart sprinkled with cinnamon.

"Yes." Kang had to finish chewing to continue. "Also, that we did not know our eventual destination. I say ... these are even better than last time."

The magician had nothing to compare this culinary experience to, as he had instead unwillingly added to his knowledge of women's haberdashery that day. "If we assume that we'll come back here after the Sulu Islands, then so will Patrick." He wondered what to choose next. A chestnut bun? "He knows this area well."

Bartholomew asked, "What if the Captain prefers to go across the Pacific and," he gulped his fear, "then underground by the Panama isthmus?"

"That would be an even longer journey," Kang said.

"Are you sure?" Celwyn asked, mostly to distract the automat from picking another pastry. Self-control should be practiced. The plate moved closer to Bartholomew.

"In my earlier messages, I already told everyone at Tellyhouse we would come back the same way we traveled here." Kang eyed the magician with a bit of suspicion and snagged another galette. "We should expect quite a few messages in Singapore by then."

"This is a wonderful interlude." Bartholomew raised a rapturous face upward. "When we're underwater for more than a few days, I miss the warmth of the sun the most."

If the magician hadn't been looking at the big man at that exact moment, he wouldn't have seen a glimpse, or part of one, of a face in the trees beyond him. When he squinted, he couldn't see anything there at all.

Chapter 45

AFTER A FINE DINNER—WHERE none of them could eat as much as usual—and then the lighting of cigars and pipes, everyone regarded Nemo. He stood in front of the sofas with his hands behind his back and wearing a determined frown.

"Gentlemen, we will perform our maintenance later tonight, and turn toward the Sulu's early tomorrow." To Verne, he added, "I'm sorry, but we'll not have time for a second day here as planned."

Valentine rubbed his hands together in anticipation of the long-awaited mayhem. "Excellent. We will have our revenge that much sooner."

Nemo didn't bat an eye and resumed. "I thought it time to take stock of our preparations and discuss our plans." He regarded the magician. "Jonas has finished the drawings of Dearing's compound and the fortifications around it." He indicated the map table and the wall behind it. "Everything is there for your perusal. You'll notice the placement of the islands, the buildings, and distances between everything, including Dearing's flotilla of ships."

Kang asked, "Is the depth of the sea in between the islands adequate for this ship?"

"Yes. The bays and troughs are deep and would have to be for those ships. Also, there are underwater rock formations, but I'm aware of them." Nemo hesitated a moment, remembering. "I stopped through there twenty years ago and afterward made some rudimentary charts of the seafloor."

As Celwyn poured another cup, he decorated Verne's ears with thumb-size daisies. His gray ensemble needed more color. A cloud of tiny bees hovered over the daisies. Someday, there would be a term for art with interaction with nature; Celwyn just knew it. After he enjoyed Kang's reaction, he asked, "What should we worry about once we arrive?"

Nemo's frown deepened until his brows nearly touched. "We must do a recognizance with the periscopes, both during the day and at night. Until then, I cannot answer the question."

The automat studied Verne's ears with a rather anxious this-could-happen-to-me look and then verified his own appearance with a few well-placed pats. Satisfied, he asked, "Could we hear about the plan of attack?"

"I have some ideas. There is nothing really formed, yet." Celwyn nodded at Nemo. "The Captain will make the final decisions."

"Uh-huh. You make it up out of thin air, don't you?" Kang surmised.

The magician just smiled at him. Without getting up, he brought the drawing of Dearing's vault over to hover between the sofas and enlarged it into a three-dimensional view from the floor to the ceiling. "Perhaps someone has a few ideas."

"This will help." Nemo nodded his approval.

Bartholomew drew closer until he could examine the finer details of the drawing. "If it were me, and I wanted a secret entrance to my treasure house, I would put it here," he stabbed a spot on the far side of the building.

Kang had joined him along with Valentine. "Interesting perspective." The automat moved to stand in front of the adjoining buildings further from the water. "Where do Dearing's guards and staff sleep?"

"Unknown at this point."

"It's possible we would attack at night." Nemo called their attention to a collection of structures next to the first building. "We could come at them from the jungle and the water at the same time."

"And this?" Bartholomew indicated the buildings further inland along a narrow road so thin it looked like a trail.

The Captain said, "When Jonas explored Dearing's thoughts, those buildings contained dry goods and ammunition." He gazed up and back again. "Don't ask me why they do what they do. Their loot from sacking ships is probably stored there also."

"It looks like they have plenty of room for it." Valentine traced the trail with a finger. "We can assume the artwork is all in the vault?"

Celwyn said, "Yes, and the finest pieces are in the sub-basement underneath it. We have a good idea of what the doors and locks look like." He shrugged. "Those are trivial details that can be taken care of. Mostly there are the scores of guards to be aware of, especially if they have hiding places and shoot at us."

Qing chose that moment to fly through the drawing with a chess piece in his mouth. He spun around and flew back through it again. Kang pointed at the magician and mouthed, *"You spoil him."*

"We can hope not all the pirate ships are in port when we arrive." Nemo pretended he didn't see Qing's antics and relit his pipe. "It could make the difference between battling five hundred pirates and a thousand of them."

"I can understand why Xiau asks you what you are thinking," Bartholomew eyed the magician. "What are your plans, even if not final? I assume they involve magic and mayhem?"

"Of course!" Celwyn clapped him on the back. "I am open to suggestions."

"Do they involve Dearing?" Kang inquired.

"Possibly, but just as a distraction." He crossed his arms. "I can't tell you what I do not know."

Kang eyed him. "You *do* make it up as you go."

Nemo paced in front of them. "We will discuss this further before we arrive, and we'll have a few more sessions with Dearing, too." He regarded the magician. "When we know what to expect, we'll know how much support from you will be needed, and where and when."

"If there are hundreds of pirates there, we'll need every weapon we have—" Kang's mouth hung open as the complexity of what they would attempt became clear.

"Agreed." Nemo stopped pacing and faced them. "For weeks, you all have been patient, and you have kindly withheld your questions regarding what I must retrieve from the bastard's compound."

Kang said, "We can wait longer, sir."

"Yes, we can be patient. I can't speak for Jonas, though." Bartholomew grinned. Valentine laughed.

The author said, "I'm curious, but understand."

"Some of you have no faith in my patience. I can't imagine why not." Celwyn enjoyed the frivolity.

"No unauthorized previews in the Captain's thoughts either." Kang stared at him.

"Pshaw. I do have scruples."

"You do?" The automat eyed Verne's decorated ears. "And leave my ears alone."

The big man chuckled and held up his hands. "Not my argument."

Nemo almost smiled at the silliness and joined them on the sofas. He made a face and leaned forward while pulling something out from under the cushion.

"That's Qing's," Celwyn told him.

Nemo flipped the dismembered frog leg into the air and the bird caught it.

"As for the Sulu Islands, I do not wish to be responsible for unnecessary casualties." Nemo's voice grew stern. "I offered before, and will do so again; you do not have to endanger yourselves. Each of you knows the possible cost of this foray and has the option to bow out. I can detour to Beijing to drop you off." He glanced at his feet where Qing had dropped the frog leg and sat waiting for him to throw it again. Nemo did so, and continued, "Although we will be outnumbered by hundreds of pirates, I expect us to prevail."

"I only ask to have the priority on killing Dearing after what he did to my nieces and others." Valentine nodded at Nemo. "I have waited this long out of respect for what you have done for my family."

Verne said, "Dearing killed many of the Captain's crew, too."

"Not to mention the people lost on the ships he sank, and villages he burned," Bartholomew said. "We might be back to taking turns to see who wins the privilege of killing him."

"Letting that go for now, I want to offer you the option of staying here in Singapore as an alternative. You could take transportation back to Prague. Or The Hague, so my crew could transport you to Findbar and the flying machine." Nemo's voice sounded grave, and he made sure they saw his sincerity. Celwyn assumed the Captain was worried about the safety of Bartholomew and Kang. He did, too. Common sense and living in a scientific bubble did not necessarily go together.

"And miss the fun of shooting pirates?" Bartholomew asked. "Never!"

"Even if we did, we would wait for this ship and travel back to Prague and Findbar together," Kang said.

Verne hugged himself. "I, for one, will remain on the ship until this is over." His eyes lit up. "I have begun a new novel ... if anyone wants to hear about it."

"Where Bartholomew and Jonas go, I go." Kang's announcement did not surprise anyone.

"For now, I consider that true also," Valentine said.

"It is settled then. As you know, Dearing has eluded and bedeviled me for years. And he has used up all his luck." Nemo's voice grew colder. "He may be a wicked man, but there are worse in this world."

That statement amazed everyone. The Captain fell silent, and when Verne would have begun telling them about his new plot, Kang held up a hand.

Nemo left them to retrieve a book from the shelves underneath Qing. The bird watched the room with a look in his eye that Celwyn recognized. It wouldn't be long before Qing would be on the hunt for something shiny to peck apart, even if he found it on someone's finger.

"Here is a picture of each of the paintings I am concerned with." The Captain passed the book to them. "If you haven't seen them before, you'll notice that there're hundreds of windows depicted in 'Babel' and the 'Tower of Babel.' The first is by Hieronymus Bosch, the second by Pieter Bruegel."

In fascinated silence, the Professor held the book so close he could have licked the ink as he scanned the print. "I see them. There is a significance?"

Nemo's eyes dropped, and when he raised them again, they held an unexpected, wounded sadness, so rare in his stoic countenance. "Yes." With empathy and embarrassment, the others continued to study the images and waited. He added, "I own a third painting, by Jean Fouquet called 'Sin,' painted fifty years before the other two you see here."

They studied a blurry picture of what seemed to be hundreds of cells, so shadowy it was hard to tell how many were occupied. In one of the cells, a tiny, barred window revealed seawater in the distance.

"Sir, what is the connection?" Celwyn recalled Bosch's themes as either odd or macabre, and yet illustrative of proverbs or biblical adages. He had met the painter in Amsterdam briefly, and although Celwyn had expected the man to be unusual, he was surprised. Bosch did nothing through the entire meal except eat, ignoring all questions and the other conversations. He even disregarded the actress sitting next to him when she put a hand on his arm. At one point, the magician checked his thoughts and found only a collection of skulls and apples. Again, utterly odd.

"In the Bosch painting, there was a new inscription on the back. It could only have been added recently, when the museum decided to sell it, and before I bought it." At their confused expressions, he explained. "There was about a month's wait from when I won the bid, and when my agent picked it up." Nemo pursed his lips and met their eyes again. "The message told of the two more recent paintings. It said they contain the other two-thirds of the information that I need. After we retrieve them and find that information, I will return the paintings to the museum."

Bartholomew still blinked his uncertainty. "How could anyone know you would buy the painting?"

"Well." Nemo inhaled and held his breath before saying, "I will tell you when I finish the whole story. It is a painful explanation." When he noted their hesitation, he went on, "Please do not withhold your comments. I will answer the ones that I can."

The magician felt compelled to say, "Whoever added that clue probably has a nefarious purpose."

"Agreed. What information do you need from them collectively?" Kang asked.

"Something I cannot ever have again." Wounded miasma flooded Nemo's eyes, and his voice filled with despair. "I have an Achilles' heel. An enemy who has eluded me for a long time." He sighed. "I believe it is he who left the trail in the paintings to entice me."

"As a trap?" Bartholomew asked.

"At this point, I do not care." He slammed a fist on the table. "Between the three paintings, I will have found the location of my wife's body."

That was the first time Celwyn and the others had been shocked into silence. Everyone remained that way until Kang asked, "How did she die?"

They could barely hear Nemo's reply.

"I don't know. Excuse me." He marched out of the room.

In the aftermath of the revelations last night, each of them had digested Nemo's news and agreed to retire for the night and think about it before further discussion. Out of respect, they would wait for the Captain to initiate the next discussion concerning the paintings. Every one of them expressed surprise at the news and its being so intimately connected to Nemo.

This morning, the study seemed unusually quiet. As usual, Verne spent the morning writing in his cabin. Before Celwyn arrived, Bartholomew had commandeered the book about the paintings and intended to compare them to the book with the same pictures he had bought in Singapore. While the big man examined the books, Xiau did what came naturally; entertain himself with maps.

That left Celwyn with little to do besides play the organ. He kept it light, simulating raindrops falling through sunlight, tinkling in scales that traveled up and down the minor keys like a circus organ. Then he segued into the music he'd composed for Tara; the same that she had played the night he rescued her. He had named it "Tara's Song" and spent hours recording the notes on parchment and refining the piece. Into the layers of melody, he added Tara's eyes, her voice, her touch. At their next top, he would mail it to her in Beirut. A love letter of sorts. His soft and sensuous thoughts were interrupted by the arrival of their breakfast.

Bartholomew chewed and grunted his appreciation as he held a roll in the air. "This bread is unusually good. But I suspect discussing it cannot sustain our conversation very long."

The magician gazed beyond the big man at a parade of medium-sized fish swimming with the ship. It didn't take long for the *Nautilus* to outdistance them, reaching cruising speed through the turquoise water. They traveled deep under streaks of sunlight that barely stained the water from above.

"One of us should talk with the Captain," the magician said. "We need to know what to expect from his enemies." He eyed the others and saw the big man nod. "Who are now our enemies also."

"I suggest we avoid the subject of his wife." The automat frowned. "But I wonder if Mr. Verne knew of her. We should ask."

The big man said, "The Captain will protect us, but he may be too close to this to prevail."

"True." Kang's frown smoothed out. "If he knows we need unusual help, he will ask Jonas."

Bartholomew nodded, but not with confidence. "Think of the timing of this. Will we have to battle whoever is bedeviling Nemo before or after we liberate Dearing's artwork and prisoners?"

"A very good question," Celwyn said. "We need to know more about the Captain's nemesis to answer that."

"And," Kang said. "What if whatever enemy this is lies in wait for us there?"

PART III
The Sulu Islands

Chapter 46

ON THE FOURTH DAY OUT OF Singapore, the *Nautilus* surfaced about three miles east of Palauen. The clock in the study had just rung the midnight hour when everyone came topside, and except for a few party boats several miles away, they saw no other craft upon the water.

Both Bartholomew and the magician huddled in heavy coats while the automat lit a cigar and leaned over the platform rail, oblivious to the cold breeze washing across the bow of the submarine.

"Will the Captain join us?" the big man asked. "Or is he too busy now that we have arrived?"

The magician shrugged, and the automat shook his head.

In the distance, one of the party boats turned, revving its engines. Strains of raucous music reached them and then faded to nothing as the boat putted its way south.

Kang waved his cigar at them. "I am not nervous, but unsettled."

"It does make things exciting." Celwyn squinted. "How far are we from Dearing's compound?"

Kang waited until Valentine finished climbing onto the platform. When Bartholomew offered him a cigar, he accepted.

"To answer the question, how far away are we from Dearing's compound?" Kang pursed his lips. "My estimation is a bit over two hours, possibly more, due east."

The vampire puffed and contemplated the water. "What is the name of the island we seek?"

"Ankkor," Bartholomew told him. "Nemo reports there isn't any government oversight in these islands, and Dearing commandeered several of them. Further east are dozens of islands of various sizes and uses, but most of the inhabited ones are closer to Babu City. Dearing controls those, also."

"We know he kept some passengers and crews from the ships he sunk. We do not know how many there are." Celwyn had wondered about this for days.

Kang nodded. "He enslaved some villagers from the islands, too."

Valentine dropped his cigar butt into the water and asked, "Has anything been decided since last night?"

They shook their heads, each lost in their thoughts. The sound of the waves lapping against the hull of the submarine sounded loud as the silence stretched between them and the reality of what they faced settled upon them. Before now,

Celwyn suspected the romantic idea of confronting pirates had not been considered very dangerous in the scientists' world.

"Would you say Dearing's compound is close to the other islands? Especially on the northeast side?" Celwyn asked as he popped a peyote button into his mouth and chewed.

"Yes, from what I saw on the maps," Bartholomew said.

"And the distance between them?"

Kang stared at Celwyn, trying to guess his purpose, but answered, "An island of similar size runs parallel to the compound about eight hundred feet away. Then the coastlines diverge."

"I see." Celwyn scanned the water.

The big man told them, "Nemo says that even though we will be greatly outnumbered, we have weapons they do not." He grinned. "The *Nautilus,* and Jonas."

"And Nemo's extensive battle experience. I have a feeling he participated in many of the eastern Ottoman wars and the Russian wars before the *Nautilus* came to be." The Professor flung his cigar butt as far as he could and looked at the magician. "Tell us what you are planning—I don't care if it isn't complete."

The magician shrugged and said, "Just wisps of ideas; I do not know for certain yet. However, it may be that between these islands is the best place for our attack. Or ... perhaps closer to where we would go ashore by the buildings. I am not a tactician like the Captain." He produced another cigar and handed it to the automat. "We will have to wait for the reconnaissance Nemo plans." From his expression, the automat wasn't ready to give up. "You are asking about something that isn't formed in my mind yet. Or in his."

The automat eyed him. "First, we free the prisoners, and then retrieve the paintings, true?" Kang asked, turning to include them all in the question.

Valentine shook his head. "I am here to assist ... and to kill Dearing. End of my opinion." He treated them to a smile that displayed his teeth. "I usually work alone."

Bartholomew tried to pretend he didn't understand the last inference, and said, "We need to sink all of Dearing's ships, and we want to make sure whoever is left does not regroup."

It neared noon, and by prior agreement, Verne remained in the study while the others trooped onto the bridge. Valentine waved them on, saying whatever they decided was fine.

The bridge became more crowded as they did their best to stay next to the lee side wall and out of the way as the submarine approached Ankkor Island. Nemo beckoned, and Celwyn took up a position next to him at one of the periscopes.

After a moment, he asked, "Captain, do you have explosives on board?"

"Yes."

"An earlier suggestion comes to mind. Could your men fashion some of it into hand-held projectiles that would explode upon impact?"

Nemo eyed him. "They could or provide timers if needed."

"Timers wouldn't be needed."

"All right." Nemo squinted through the periscope. "We can discuss this more fully later."

Celwyn continued to study Ankkor, noticing the bay matched the picture in Dearing's mind, shaped like a fat banana that measured a full mile wide. To answer his earlier question, the distance between the main island and the others appeared to be about half a mile.

The magician continued his research. The island appeared mostly flat, covered in jungle, and decorated with a thin strip of coral beach. According to Verne, dozens of species of birds inhabited the islands, along with a serious population of wild boar that had thrived there since Ponce de Leon had stopped by in the 16th century. The author quoted reports that said large sea turtles were so plentiful that, at times, they blocked the beaches. Celwyn did not spy any of the whale sharks also mentioned.

As the submarine drew closer to their target, the magician adjusted the angle of the periscope to see further. From beside him, Nemo did the same, including the cluster of single-story structures that came into view between thick blocks of foliage and lauan trees. Another long, low building lay three hundred yards behind the first buildings. Much closer to the water, the sun caught the glint of metal from the swords and rifles carried by hundreds of pirates as they strutted across the docks and along the beach.

Celwyn knew these were not all the vermin. There would be hundreds more of them not visible here. These pirates looked like copies of the ones that the magician had swept off the *Primero*. He enjoyed the memory of the satisfying crunch of their hull when Nemo sank her a few minutes later.

Nemo adjusted his periscope and growled, "Those bastards."

"My sentiments exactly. What do you think of the two ships at the other end of the bay where we entered?"

Nemo said, "They are roughly the same size as the *Primero*, with a few extra cannons."

"What is their purpose? Just guarding the compound?" Bartholomew asked.

"Probably. Sentinels, perhaps figurative deterrents. There are another seven ships against their dock." Nemo pursed his lips in annoyance as he continued his inspection.

"Let me count them again... yes... seven." Celwyn swiveled, searching until he found what he sought. "The closest island is a quarter mile away, as we thought. Do you concur?" The magician pivoted back and finished his perusal of the main island.

"Yes. What do you have in mind?" Nemo's eyes gleamed.

Celwyn gestured for Bartholomew to take his turn at the periscope. To Nemo, he said, "Let's discuss it, sir." Kang took over Nemo's periscope, and

Nemo and Celwyn stayed close enough for everyone to participate. The magician caught Granger's eye and winked at him. Nemo's lieutenant handed off his post to the nearest crewman and joined them.

"Here is what I would suggest." Celwyn listed his suggestions. Kang and the big man listened in, both contributing ideas. By the time Celwyn had outlined his proposal, Bartholomew laughed so hard he had tears, and the automat fumed with worry. Granger and Nemo conferred, both nodding until a broad—and rare—smile spread across the Captain's face.

"Gentlemen, I think the only question that remains is whether or not we allow Dearing to watch what happens."

Chapter 47

"I LOVE THIS," BARTHOLOMEW SAID AS he strapped a long knife to his calf and slipped a shorter one into his boot.

The four of them, including Valentine, had squeezed into the *Nautilus* armory to get kitted out. The big man continued, "Nemo is certainly prepared. There's still plenty here to choose from, even after all the crew armed themselves."

"Xiau is not allowed to have a pistol," Celwyn said as seriously as he could. "He would just shoot me again."

"Pfft. I will have a knife and my wits," Kang said. "Also the ropes and chains you requested that we bring. Bartholomew will protect me."

As they talked, Valentine selected a nasty-looking pistol and held it up to gauge its weight. "What will I be doing?"

Celwyn leaned close to him and whispered something ending with, "...the welcoming committee."

The vampire seemed a bit surprised, then bowed and, with all the drama of the opening night of *Twelfth Night,* said, "I will most definitely play my part."

Bartholomew told him, "After we capture the docks and beach, you will be with Xiau and me as we breach the main building. It is unknown if we'll shoot our way in or find an alternative entrance. Jonas oversees that."

Valentine shook his silver mane and stood tall. "That sounds like a worthy role." He began loading bullets into the pistol.

"I'll also be carrying spare ammunition," Kang said. "In case we need it."

"Wait—do you have the whiskey?" Bartholomew asked the automat.

"No! I'll ask Granger where the flasks are."

It was times like this that Celwyn appreciated the camaraderie on the ship. The atmosphere reminded him of a festive hunting party, like a royal hunt in the English countryside in place of the volatile and dangerous mission before them, where they were outnumbered by hundreds of pirates.

"What time will this begin?" Valentine asked.

"Nemo prefers late afternoon," Bartholomew told him.

"That is because?" The vampire asked.

Celwyn said, "Nemo wants an ethereal quality in the air when we attack, and it wouldn't hurt if the pirates had all begun their drinking for the night."

He watched the automat and Bartholomew comparing hip flasks and debating if they should carry a spare. He almost suggested they bring something to eat on their picnic.

"My flask is bigger. Do you think there is another one on this ship?" The automat saw the others' amusement and changed the subject. "Granger reports there are about nine hundred pirates. About a third of them are in and around the main building where the treasure trove is located. The majority are either on, or near, Dearing's ships."

"There are seven ships on the dock. For each ship, they would need at least 250 men to crew each of them. Shouldn't we see even more pirates?" The magician asked.

Valentine said, "Perhaps some of the ships are here for maintenance."

"It is possible." The mild-mannered Professor attached a string of ropes to his belt and offered advice to the big man on how to load bullets into a Colt revolver. Bartholomew grinned at him as a series of gongs resounded from below, heightening the excitement in the room.

"Too bad his other ships will never make it back home." Bartholomew recalled their destruction with a somber grin. "Nemo said to watch for the tiger pits with the spikes he encountered when he fought Dearing before. There will be a blanket of leaves covering them."

Everyone nodded.

"How many prisoners are on the island? Do we know yet?" Valentine asked.

"Unknown." Kang turned to the magician. "Are you planning to fly over the island?"

"Yes, as a small bird. I do not want any of the pirates thinking I would be fit for his dinner and shooting at me."

The *Nautilus* cruised to the back side of the island, and Celwyn positioned himself at one of the periscopes, with Granger at the other. Over time, the jungle had swallowed whatever sand had been visible when it reached the seawater. If evil didn't live here, Celwyn would be pleased to visit again someday, seeing an exotic scene and vines that dripped off trees and dozens of streams trickled out of the brush into the bay as a kaleidoscope of parrots swooped between the taller trees.

If he had to describe the bay, he'd assume a whale had taken a bite out of the center of the island. The *Nautilus* left it behind and continued forward at moderate speed. When she reached the halfway point circumventing the island, the submarine ascended to the surface.

By the time the hatch had finished opening, the magician had flown through it, and the ship descended below the waves again.

The afternoon sun seemed pleasant and warm at first, but as Celwyn flew, he soon found it damned uncomfortable.

To the west, the sky was clear and blue with a fine haze covering the water—the mist too thin to obscure the sea, but thick enough to tint what lay below it. To the north, heavy opalescent clouds sat on the horizon for as far as he could see. The *Nautilus* would need to conclude her business and descend again before the storm arrived.

As he soared high over the island, Celwyn spied acres of cultivation, a large swamp, and a cluster of huts between those two points. Presumably, this was where the prisoners lived.

Soon, he reached the docks and bay, and the perspective from above confirmed the picture he'd seen in Dearing's mind with a high level of accuracy—even down to the details of storage bins, water barrels, and small boats. Celwyn assumed the pirates utilized those as transport between the islands instead of maneuvering the massive sailing ships.

Of the seven tall ships, five were three-masters, and two were brigs. Hundreds of filthy pirates snored, brawled, or drank on the decks of the ships. More of the animals lay in the mud at the water's edge, passing bottles around and sunning themselves. Thirty feet behind the mud sty, a door opened in a squat building, and someone threw out buckets of slop. The magician made a face; he had found the pirates' kitchen. The smell reminded him of so many disgusting things he stopped counting.

As he continued toward the east side of the bay, he flew between the crows' nests of the tall ships and counted the guns on each vessel. He swooped low, following a fat and pungent pirate below deck. Within a half hour, he had repeated the process for each ship, at last deciding on the final details of their attack.

By the time he reached the long building containing Dearing's treasures, Celwyn needed to rest. He paced across the flat roof of the structure, waddling along on his webbed feet just like Qing did. While he did his best to see inside, he couldn't. Celwyn cursed. Where had the goddamned pirates found such thick bricks for the walls?

The magician detected the door leading out of the sub-basement and looked for a second entrance.

Ten minutes later, he had his answer. A depression in the dirt about a dozen feet north of the building, camouflaged by rocks, led below. Satisfied, Celwyn returned to the backside of the island once again, diving just below the surface to tap on the aquatic window. This time he scared Kang, who still looked wide awake by the time the *Nautilus* ascended, and he reentered the ship again.

Chapter 48

WITH PLENTY OF CIGARS, TEA, AND spirits flowing in the study, and Qing circling above them, they held a war council. The magician related everything he had seen on his tour, in detail. When he finished, he asked, "Could we cruise by the line of ships again, please?"

Nemo said, "But, of course. What are we looking for?"

"I want to save one of the tall ships for the prisoners to either use for transport or whatever they need. Even to sleep in." Celwyn shrugged. "Some of the prisoners could be sailors from captured ships and might be able to use it to leave the area."

Bartholomew raised a brow as he considered the idea.

Nemo nodded to Granger. He saluted and crossed to the intercom by the bar and issued the order to return to the bay.

"From what I can tell," Celwyn said, "there are several hundred or more prisoners. I flew too high to see details, but they live in huts, perhaps five hundred yards behind the treasure building. The guards sleep in the other buildings, much closer to the water."

As he spoke, Bartholomew took the drawing of the main building off the wall, and the magician enlarged it before floating it in front of them. The big man said, "So, for the treasure building, we could enter either in front or," he tapped a spot at the rear grounds, "use the underground entrance."

"The front of the building will have scores of guards," Nemo said, "and the secret entrance Jonas described could be rigged to explode. Perhaps as a deterrent to the prisoners' curiosity."

The magician nodded; he wouldn't put anything past Dearing. If the bastard blew up his own men, not the prisoners, he wouldn't care. "When we attack, most of the pirates will leave their posts to rush to the harbor. I plan to explode the magazines in all but one ship; the one we reserve for the prisoners' use." He gestured, and a hologram of the harbor hovered between them.

Valentine crossed to the bar and poured a goblet of wine. "This sounds exciting and dangerous. We have waited a long time for this day."

Bartholomew rubbed his chin and stared at the aquatic window as if it contained answers. "Those ships are berthed very close together."

"They are," Nemo agreed. "We only have to ignite one in the middle, and the rest should go, too."

"It will be extraordinarily loud," Verne's expression took on a worried look, "and risky."

"When it blows, it will draw most of the pirates to the dock area." Nemo nodded. "You'll stay here, Jules." He strode to the window and back. "I am anxious to begin. Granger says the storm will probably hold off until near midnight."

"That will help," Kang said. "Are there carts available for transferring the artwork to the ship? We will need many of them."

Celwyn shrugged. "Probably." He thought about the fun they were about to have. "We can't fail." He twisted his mustache and grinned at Kang.

"*What?* Goddamn it, Jonas—"

PART IV

Chapter 49

"Courage is knowing what not to fear."
Plato

AS SOMEONE WHO LOVES USING DRA-matic effects to cause as much chaos as possible, Celwyn had enlisted Valentine, who also loved an audience, for the opening salvo.

When the *Nautilus* surfaced in the center of the bay and cruised toward the pirates on shore, the remnants of the afternoon sun remained, leaving enough light to see properly.

Near the beach, the sea undulated, and with Celwyn's help, it parted as Valentine rose from the depths, walking with magical assistance across the water to the stretch of mud where an assortment of the rogues wallowed. The nearest of them scrambled upright, shouting profanities. The more sober of them backed up. In a halo of red light, Valentine stood tall, regal, and deadly.

His fangs were out.

"Good afternoon, gentlemen," the vampire growled. He grabbed the nearest pirate and ripped his face off. The pirates nearby screamed their terror and tried to get out of the mud, slipping and sliding as they crawled away. The rest reached for their knives as Valentine's weeks of pent-up anger exploded and he shredded them.

Now the submarine displayed a statue tied to her bow: a most disagreeable one behind a gag, and his face purple with rage.

Dearing's men poured out of the nearest building, shouting and pointing as the pirate ship nearest to them broke free. Celwyn propelled it into the middle of the bay, scraping the pirates off the deck as he moved it.

As hordes of pirates crowded onto the sand, they saw Valentine catching the ones nearby like a cat catching mice, and their curses became shrieks. When they checked beyond Valentine, what approached from the other islands was far more interesting than the bloody mess on the beach.

The roar of an engine rumbled like low thunder across the water, growing louder. Some pirates cowered—while others were morbidly fascinated—unsure of what to do.

From within the low clouds, a perfect replica of the flying machine flew low, heading for the mouth of the bay. Its engines growled as it swerved toward the ships guarding the bay and something was tossed out of the cockpit over each of them. As the machine gained altitude and flew on, twin explosions ignited the ships, and then came a deafening concussion as the fire reached their magazines. Frenzied pirates jumped overboard as the ships blazed and rocked in the sea with each successive explosion.

Meanwhile, Nemo's crew rolled out the *Nautilus's* floating pier onto the beach. With Nemo and Granger in the lead, scores of the crew quick-stepped across to shore, stepping over the dead pirates and onto the beach. Nemo gave an order, and the first line of his crewmen dropped to a knee and fired, strafing the mass of pirates. Celwyn stood behind them, checking their flank for attacks, and enjoying the battle unfold. With a baton in his hand, he directed the scene as his music arrived in full force.

The roar from the flying machine intensified, joined by a chorus of trumpets as it flew low, heading toward the remaining ships on the dock. More projectiles were tossed out of the aeroplane into the ships, and when the explosions came, the music rejoiced, rising high in harmony. From the docks, the pirates fired upon the craft, and bullets punctured the side of the machine.

Celwyn frowned. That wasn't supposed to happen.

The magician elevated the flying machine beyond the range of the pirates' rifles and sent it further down the beach, slowing it into a soft dive onto the sand. As the frame and cockpit dissolved, Kang and Bartholomew tumbled out and crouched low when a volley of shots from the jungle peppered the air. The big man pushed the automat down and got off a volley of his own over Kang's head.

The magician rose from the sand, once again as a gorgeous raven of tremendous size. With his own form of protection, he flew above the remaining ships, staring into their holds until the magazines caught fire, the explosions small at first, then a chain reaction of explosions as each adjoining ship blew apart. Flames raced across the canvasses, engulfing the mainmasts as they blazed and fell. Amid a chorus of screams, scores of pirates jumped into the bay, while more of them caught fire under the burning canvasses. If Celwyn hadn't known of the atrocities they'd committed, he would have felt sorry for them.

The magician located Bartholomew and Kang, where they were still pinned down by gunfire from the jungle. He lifted his wings, soaring over Captain Nemo and his crew as they fought their way toward the treasure building. He'd asked Granger to warn his men they might see the raven. From the fright in some of their eyes, it appeared not all of them had heard the news yet. After he landed between Bartholomew, Kang, and the gang of pirates they'd engaged, he removed all the vegetation between them, leaving the pirates exposed.

The big man and the automat had taken shelter in the sand behind some crates—not an ideal situation. Celwyn had just decided what to do about it when Bartholomew yelped and went down.

"*Damn it—*" Celwyn raised the pirates into the air, his anger lifting them into the clouds before he flung them beyond the islands and out to sea. He arrived beside Bartholomew as himself and found Kang covering the big man with his body. "They're gone." He knelt beside them. "How bad?"

"Shoulder." Kang lifted Bartholomew's bloody shirt and frowned. "I need to get him on the ship. Stop the bleeding, please."

The magician did so, and before the automat could complain, covered them both in protection and sent them over the waves and across the bay so fast, Kang lost his hat. The crew guarding the *Nautilus* saw them coming and carried Bartholomew inside.

Now that they were safe, Celwyn could enjoy the action on the beach. He reveled in a most elaborate scene, one artful and dramatic on several fronts. Seconds later, as a monstrous tiger with glowing eyes, he appeared in front of Valentine.

"Care for a ride?" Celwyn expected that a tiger of this size would scare the pirates silly.

The vampire stopped running toward Captain Nemo and came to a stop. "Certainly." Valentine leaped on his back and Celwyn bounded forward under a hail of bullets.

As they neared the jungle from the east, the magician removed the trees in front of the pirates, exposing their positions. Nemo's crew advanced in formation, well-trained and disciplined, as Valentine let out a long blood-curdling cry to terrorize the bastards further. Celwyn leapt over the crew's heads and landed before the group of pirates. He caused the vampire's unearthly growl to reverberate and echo everywhere.

When Bartholomew was hit, Celwyn had decided he'd had enough of sharing the fun and danger with those he should protect. He'd just seen one of Nemo's crew fall under a volley from the pirates, then another. In seconds, he gathered the pirates into a net as big as Tellyhouse. As he lifted them upward, the whoosh of air sounded louder than the flying machine when he swung them round and round, each rotation gaining speed before he let go, and they sailed out to sea. He'd agreed that everyone should participate, but he doubted the Captain really wanted casualties.

Some of Nemo's crew stood rooted to the ground at what they saw until he gestured to them to spread out and continue the assault. In the bay behind them, the charred carcasses of the pirate ships still burned under an acrid cloud of smoke. One of Dearing's ships sank, the flames hissing into the water in a cloud of steam. The magician would remember to check the smoldering ruins for survivors who needed to join the others. As he turned back to the battle, Nemo's crew tossed grenades and advanced. Some gunfire came from the pirates, but it lessened as Nemo and Granger grew closer. When they reached the buildings, a cheer went up from *Nautilus's* crew. Granger barked orders, and they closed ranks again.

The building from which Celwyn had last seen the pirates' cook throwing slop burned merrily. Although a gourmet would agree that burning the building down was an appropriate solution to an affront to culinary sensibilities, the magician stopped it from spreading any farther; they might need some of the equipment.

He could see further inland and spotted a contingent of Nemo's crew combing the jungle while taking sporadic gunfire and returning it.

Nemo waved the magician over. His men had reached the long building known as Dearing's treasure building. Before joining the Captain, the magician changed back to himself, much to the vampire's consternation when he found himself sitting on the ground.

With Valentine bringing up the rear, Nemo and his men backtracked through the jungle until they approached the treasure building directly from the west. To not alarm Nemo's men unnecessarily, the magician cleaned pirate blood off the vampire's face.

"*Stop!*" Nemo and Celwyn shouted at the same time. Nemo pointed to the indentations under the carpet of leaves in front of the door. One of the crew inched forward and lifted the leaves. What he saw caused him to drop them again and back up. Anyone approaching from the direction of the bay would fall into the pits under the leaves.

"We can't enter this way." Nemo paced from side to side. The excitement of battle still filled his eyes; he wouldn't wait long while his crew searched for a way in.

The obvious entrance was from the east end of the building.

Minutes later, with a bark of satisfaction, Granger confirmed they had discovered the entrance. The ground here showed many footprints, most of which stopped a hundred yards away in front of a simple wooden door.

"Please wait a moment," Celwyn recalled the sessions with Dearing and the exact picture in the bastard's mind when he thought about his treasure building. Once again, as a fly, Celwyn flew away. Granger didn't bat an eye; just backed up and verified his crew's reactions.

With more than his usual caution, the magician hovered near the entrance, checking the ground and bushes next to the path for hidden pirates and traps. He slipped under the door and into the murky, weak light. Enough illumination filled the foyer to see what awaited them.

Scores of pirates stood there in perfect silence. He could see the whites of their eyes and dried blood coating the blades of their knives and machetes. The magician flew down a few steps into the first gallery. No pirates hid there. When he reached the other end of the room, he kept going, down more steps to another door set in a tile wall. As expected, it had a solid lock, so he went under the door.

Minutes later, he reentered the main foyer and, with a gesture, put the pirates into a deep sleep from which they would not awaken. Once again as himself, he gazed at them with contempt, remembering the people they killed and what they had done to the survivors from Dearing's raids. He remembered Miss Redifer, Tara, the villagers, and others like them.

"Captain! Don't shoot," Celwyn called out as he opened the door, peeked around the edge, and bowed them inside.

Granger stepped over the dead pirates, grinned at him, and pointed at the pirate at his feet. "You make a wonderful host, Jonas."

Chapter 50

OVER THE NEXT HALF HOUR, IT became apparent to Celwyn that Nemo did not need him as his crew filed into the treasure building and began dismantling it. The magician excused himself and left them to do something he deemed most necessary.

The magician walked the five-hundred feet up the path to the huts. In case any of the hostages became frightened and fired upon him, or they'd missed any of Dearing's men, he made sure no one would see him at all. It would be a shame to spoil the artistic success of the day by getting shot and listening to the automat nag him. But when the path ended, he discovered something that made him forget about the automat and doubt the existence of God.

Scraps of cloth barely covered the first of the hostages he saw. Most were barefoot, and many appeared so emancipated they staggered. Dozens of them were sick, while others lay still in the dirt as if they were waiting to die. Some seemed relatively healthy and were probably the more recently captured. Celwyn's tears fell as he saw pregnant women and stick-thin children in tattered clothes standing in the doorways of the huts. One woman had fresh cuts across her face and arms. Another limped, dragging a broken leg into a hut, and fell face down in the dirt.

The magician's curses escalated. When he discovered a little boy with his arm in a grimy sling, he wished he'd killed all the pirates personally—the hell with sharing the honor! With an angry gesture intended to buy time to think, he covered the sick and lame with something to help their pain.

The pirates must have been collecting prisoners for a long time. Before him was a variety of nationalities, races, and ages, and yet they all had one thing in common. Hunger consumed them, the painful yearning written across their faces.

The magician backed up, and when he reemerged, he drove a donkey and a cart of his own making filled with food. Dozens of eyes watched him as he unfurled a clean expanse of canvass and spread it across the grass. With an encouraging expression, he unloaded boxes of bread, sausages, cheeses, apples, and barrels of wine, water, and milk.

Hungry faces remained close enough to smell the food, but their treatment by the pirates kept them from touching it. In the distance, scattered explosions came from beyond the bay, along with bursts of gunfire. When he finished setting things up, he removed himself from the path and addressed them.

"We have killed most of the pirates. Please eat. You are safe here. Tomorrow I will come back, and we will talk." He bowed to them. "We wish you no harm." He repeated the message in his best French and Spanish. As he waved goodbye, a thin black man stepped forward.

"My name is David." He hesitated. "You must be why the pirates shot at us to keep us here." He glanced at the others, who urged him on. "We are curious."

Celwyn wanted to shake his hand, but the fear in David's eyes showed that would not be a good idea ... yet. In a voice he hoped conveyed peaceful intentions, the magician said, "Pleased to meet you, David. You and the others are safe now." He nodded at them as calmly as he could. "I will return tonight if you think it would not upset anyone."

David conferred with the men nearest to him. One shook his head. The other nodded. While they talked, the handsome woman with cuts on her face approached until she stood only feet away. She had a strong and defiant glint in her eye and spoke with an American accent. "Come back. We want answers."

"I will, madam. Please keep everyone here until we finish clearing the pirates off the island." As he passed the first bend in the path, he healed her wounds and added something to dull any pain. In the fading light and with luck, she wouldn't notice.

By the time Celwyn had gone thirty paces, he remembered his warning to the others; there could still be pirates on the island. God, he needed to rest, but it wouldn't do if one of the bastards took a shot at Nemo's crew or the hostages. Worse, they could use them as shields.

As an exquisite yellow macaw, he flew from tree to tree, finding a variety of what he was sure were dangerous snakes. Despite Xiau's contention that Celwyn was foolhardy, he made a point of checking each branch before he landed.

It took a while to search in a grid through the jungle, across the swamp, and then the outbuildings. Miles away, came sporadic bursts of gunfire from across the water that little by little lessened, and stopped. He sailed on until he spied a pair of wild boars with nasty-looking overbites digging in the dirt. Before he finished his tour, a full complement of stars came alive in the southern sky. To the north, the storm clouds obstructed the stars.

When he felt the pirates were indeed gone, he continued his flight to the *Nautilus*. He landed by Granger on the ship's platform and sighed with relief. Below them, the crew continued to transport crates of artwork. Some pieces went into the largest transport boat—the rest into the submarine.

Celwyn straightened his jacket and smoothed his hair. The activities of the afternoon affected his appearance. "Congratulations on a successful campaign ashore."

Granger said, "Thank you. We're holding some of this trove for the authorities in Hong Kong. The museum pieces we'll take to The Havre, and let the tribunal there handle it." He shook his head. "Nemo calls this a worldwide mess, and I agree with him."

The magician clapped him on the back. "Above it all, the liberation was a productive operation. Your crew is well-trained." He continued to watch the loading of the art. "There is news; I have searched the island, and the pirates are gone. There are hundreds of very scared hostages in the huts." Celwyn headed down the stairs. "Hopefully, by tomorrow, things will be easier for them. I must rest."

The magician continued to sick bay and arrived in time to find Bartholomew trying to get off the examination table with the automat tugging on him—and having a fit about it. The big man's shoulder had been thoroughly bandaged, and his eyes appeared clear and alert.

"I have a solution, my friends," Celwyn told them and stretched out on the examination table next to Bartholomew. "If you stay and rest, I will do the same." He raised a brow at the big man. "Before I do, I'll tell you both what happened after you came back here."

Kang released his hold on Bartholomew's good arm. "I agree."

Bartholomew pursed his lips. "I do also. But only until dinner." He craned his tree trunk-sized neck and checked the clock on the wall. "That occurs in two hours."

"I need to rest and talk with Nemo soon if you'll wake me." After Kang's nod, the magician told his tale. He related the rest of what had happened on the island up to his meeting with the hostages, but his exhaustion overcame him before he finished.

In the corridor outside the bridge, Celwyn had a brief conversation with the Captain before dinner. Nemo planned to bring a medical team in from British Hong Kong. He explained that having them take care of the hostages would be more logical than Celwyn's romantic notion of giving them a pirate ship to sail away in. With a sigh, the magician had to agree. Sometimes his imagination overrode logic.

"Also, we can assume these hostages are from all over the world and include military and political personnel. I cannot afford to be recognized," Nemo said. Celwyn would have loved to know why, and from what, but wouldn't ask. Like Bartholomew had advised, it would be best if related voluntarily.

As they entered the dining room, Qing squawked and flew to Celwyn. He patted the bird's back. "I'm all right." Celwyn asked, "Where is Valentine?"

The Captain couldn't keep the gleam of vengeance out of his eyes as he shrugged, and pulled out his chair. "The last we saw of him, he was dragging Dearing into the jungle." A smile won. "I'm sure he will be back, eventually."

"*'Revenge should have no bounds.'* Shakespeare's *Hamlet.*" Celwyn quoted the bard as he took his place at the table. Bartholomew and Kang already sat there along with Verne. The big man seemed a bit pale but determined not to miss anything.

"Captain, I assume the transport boats will take the hostages to Hong Kong?" the author asked.

"No. Those boats are too small and would not hold up in a storm." Nemo shook his head. "I may have to retract my objection to using the remaining three-master to take them there. We have talked about this a bit before; Hong Kong is at least five days northwest of here. Typhoons can be a problem."

Kang said, "There would also be a question of how seaworthy the vulnerable and weaker of the hostages would be."

Nemo opened the wine, and the crewman poured a sample. "It appears what to do about the hostages will take a detailed discussion." He sipped and nodded his approval to the crew to fill their glasses.

The automat raised a brow at the magician. "You started to tell us about what happened when you spoke with the hostages."

As the crew served the soup, Celwyn related the story of his visit to the huts.

Bartholomew asked, "How much medical attention do they need?"

"Some have cuts, some broken bones, bruises, and other injuries. I temporarily fixed the ones I saw, but they need immediate attention. It is brutal, the way they have been treated." When his anger flared, the magician inhaled and the glassware on the table shook. Verne grabbed his water glass until Celwyn could speak again. "Mostly, they need a great deal of food. I left them with enough provisions to carry them through this evening, but again, they will need more."

"We will visit them, and I'll check them medically." The automat glared at Bartholomew sitting across from him at the table. "You, of course, will be resting."

Displaying both his diplomatic skills and growing knowledge of his guests, Nemo stepped in before they could squabble. "I will accompany you and stay in the shadows. We will need Bartholomew's broad grasp of worldwide languages. I anticipate that it will be an ordeal to help them and figure out what to do. Yes, we must first address their injuries. We also need to answer their questions and see which of them have maritime experience. As Jonas reported, they are from dozens of countries."

Bartholomew tasted his wine, and said, "They could sail to safety on the three-master without us, possibly?"

Nemo's face registered doubt. "Possibly. It would take at least seventy-five experienced men to operate a ship that size, even if they had other men helping."

"I heard that five of your crew were wounded today, plus Bartholomew. It is surprising it wasn't worse." Verne's curiosity surfaced. "What happened? I could see little above the water line from in here."

The Captain cut off a piece of broiled sea bass and chewed. "We were successful." Nemo relived the action, clearly enjoying describing it. "The Professor and Bartholomew flew a replica of the flying machine over the ships guarding the bay and dropped charges inside them. Fancy flying, Gentlemen."

"We took turns," the automat said. "You probably noticed that every time Jonas was distracted, we lost altitude."

"It was still fun." Bartholomew struggled to cut into his fish with only one arm. Without looking, Celwyn fixed the situation and buttered his roll as well. The big man didn't blink, just nodding his thanks. They had come a long way in the last two years with his superstitions.

The magician took up the narrative, relating details of the battle after Bartholomew and the automat departed for the ship.

"Please explain what you will do about the hostages. How many are there?" Verne asked.

Nemo said, "Jonas saw them."

The magician decided Bartholomew needed another helping of yams and deposited some on his plate. "I only saw some of them. My guess is that there are well over three hundred hostages. There may be dozens left on the neighboring islands also."

"We will search the other islands tomorrow for pirates and hostages." Nemo nodded at Celwyn. "Jonas has thoroughly checked the main island."

Celwyn felt an overwhelming somberness pressing upon him. "I saw about a half-dozen children and at least one baby at the huts. And two pregnant women. There were perhaps twenty women of various ages and conditions, mostly suffering from malnutrition." He sighed, reluctant to describe the state of the children. "As for the men, they were of a variety of ages and conditions."

"You left them food?" Verne asked.

"The food I left was nutritious, but not fancy." He looked at Kang. "I assumed they would not be used to rich food."

"Correct." The Professor said, "It will take weeks of solid meals to bring them back to health."

"Are there many serious injuries?" Bartholomew asked as he stared at the pile of yams on his plate, made a face, and then eyed the magician.

"I did not go inside the huts, so I can't say." Celwyn regarded the others. "We might take a look this evening?" He turned to Nemo. "Your chef is very resilient, Captain, to produce such a meal after the festivities this afternoon." When a crewman placed a berry-encrusted torte on the table, he gazed at it, thinking of the human misery in the huts, and put his fork down.

"Bartholomew needs to rest." Kang raised a sarcastic brow at the magician. "Like you never do."

Nemo frowned. "As I said, Bartholomew can help us reassure the hostages and provide a few languages that could be needed. Of course, as his condition allows."

"Why should Bartholomew listen to me when the rest of you don't?" Kang attacked his torte.

Verne nibbled at his dessert like a gopher would have, mostly with his front teeth.

"Could we get back to my question, please? What are the plans for the hostages?"

Nemo said, "Jonas reports they are understandably frightened. To visit them again tonight may frighten them. Or it could reassure them. They heard the battle." His sigh was not from exhaustion but from the situation. "One of the hostages said the pirates shot at them to scare them away from the beach."

"Protecting their ransom prospects." Bartholomew frowned.

"All the more reason they shouldn't see anything odd, such as magic," the automat said as drolly as possible.

"Perhaps it would be best if Mr. Soriano did not come too close to them, either." Bartholomew sat up straighter. "By the way, where is he?"

"He's busy," the magician answered with a blank face. It took Bartholomew a second to understand why he shouldn't ask for details.

Kang asked, "Captain, did you find the missing paintings?"

"Yes. They are safe. We'll look at them when things are settled here."

By the time the crew had poured their coffee, Celwyn had another question. "Did your crew find where the pirates stored their food?"

"Yes," Nemo said, "piles of it. And cases and cases of mediocre wine. We'll take some of it to the hostages in case they have a taste for it." He inhaled. "They should stay by the huts for now. I do not want them to see this ship." He stood and put his napkin on the table.

"Gentlemen, we will go to them now."

Chapter 51

BECAUSE OF THE TEMPORARY BAN on magic, Celwyn carried a lantern and led the way up the path to the huts. Bartholomew walked beside him, his good humor and gentleness on display to quell any fears.

The Professor came next with his medical bag and the ship's medical officer, Lieutenant Tiddle. A large cart, towed by the crew, followed. Guards brought up the rear, with Nemo even further behind them. When the clearing came into view, everyone stayed back and waited while Bartholomew and Celwyn approached the cluster of huts.

In the meager light of the lanterns, the magician found the scene surreal and crueler than in the daylight. Whispering reached them, and then excited chatter as scores of people poured out of the huts. Celwyn would have to revise their total to closer to five hundred. Again, he saw evidence of unbelievable neglect and brutality. Not just broken bones, but proof of old and new beatings. He cursed Dearing silently, controlling his anger before he frightened them again.

"Good evening. We met earlier." Celwyn pointed to the cart behind him. "We have brought food from your captors' storage building." He spied the woman and the man he'd talked with earlier. The light of defiance and anger lit up her eyes—something many of them no longer had.

Celwyn addressed them, making as much eye contact as they would allow. "We also bring medical attention. While we unload the food, would you please find whoever needs medical attention the most, and," he gestured to a row of crates in the grass where Kang and Lieutenant Tiddle stood, "have them wait there, please? These gentlemen are doctors and will help them." In a strong, sonorous voice, Bartholomew repeated the message in German, Spanish, French, Dutch, Portuguese, and Mandarin. He even threw in a few phrases in Tagalog.

The magician bowed and stepped away as Kang and Tiddle set up a makeshift clinic with the clean sheets they'd brought along. The hostages watched in silence. On the way here, it had been decided that they wouldn't use their real names, and most definitely keep Nemo out of it. For some reason, Pelaez's face flashed in Celwyn's thoughts, confirming the wisdom in doing so.

Twenty minutes later, a collection of sheets covered the stacked crates, and platters of food had been set out. Bartholomew spoke.

"Earlier today, we removed the pirates that captured you. We ask for your patience while we determine how best to help you."

David said, "The pirates will kill us—"

"They are *gone*," Celwyn told them. He regretted his hard tone when the nearest hostages gasped and scrabbled behind the others.

Bartholomew repeated the message in a softer voice. "They could be on the rest of the islands, but we will be on guard, so they do not come back here. We will also search the other islands tomorrow when it is light."

"Most of all," Kang told them, "we want you to know that we mean you no harm."

The woman who had been cut said, "Who are you?"

The automat could lie much better than Bartholomew. "Please call me Doctor. This is Mr. Jones." Celwyn bowed. "Mr. Barr." Bartholomew bowed and introduced Granger and the others by their titles.

"We were traveling through this area, and will make sure you are helped before we leave again."

Murmurings grew into a low rumble, like an impending earthquake, reminding Celwyn of how scared they must be. Many of them began weeping and tried to hide.

Bartholomew raised his voice, "We haven't gone through all the buildings the pirates used, and must be sure we found every one of them. That will occur tomorrow when we can see everything. You will be more comfortable there after we clear the buildings. But ... please wait until we check inside them."

He waited for questions. The hostages whispered between themselves and cast doubtful looks toward the shore. The people nearest the food couldn't help staring at it, yet wouldn't touch it. They'd been controlled for a long time. Just watching their yearning broke Celwyn's heart. He wiped his eyes.

"We will bring pencils and paper tomorrow so that you can provide your names and the countries you are from." The big man continued, putting cheer into his voice. "It is the first step toward helping you. We also ask that you list the names of whoever we should notify that you have been found."

"One way or another, we will notify your families," the magician assured them. Fresh weeping spread across dozens of faces, mixed with hope and fear.

"Why?" the woman who had been cut asked.

Celwyn told her, "Because we're assuming you would like to go home, and we need to bring the authorities from Hong Kong here to help you." He noted the rags they wore. "Tomorrow, we will also bring all the clean clothes we can find."

Over their murmurs, Bartholomew asked, "Is there anything you need urgently?" His voice held the same empathy that he'd used with the slaves on the *Quarto.*

"Home," wailed an elderly man through his tears. Others echoed him until their plaintive chant reverberated through the jungle, "*Home, home, home…*"

Chapter 52

LONG AFTER MIDNIGHT, KANG dragged himself into the study and dropped his bag on the floor. Everyone else followed, displaying varying degrees of exhaustion. The *Nautilus* began her descent at the same time and moved north of Ankkor Island and away from the hostages. Per Nemo, she would spend the night in the shadow of the neighboring island to perform her evening maintenance.

Celwyn produced a silvery frog for Qing, a plate of cookies for the automat, and poured whiskey all around for the others. By the time he'd made his tea, everyone had settled by the sofas.

"It is tragic." Bartholomew sounded like they'd just left a funeral procession. "I listened to many of their stories. The worst of it? Those children who saw their parents murdered by the pirates." He shuddered. "Did you know there is a graveyard of dead hostages on the other side of the huts?"

"Yes." Nemo's face darkened. "I could hear many of the stories from my vantage point. It is infinitely sad." His voice and eyes hardened. "We will be sure every one of them is brought home."

Bartholomew asked him, "Did you recognize anyone?"

"Possibly. I think the portly gentleman with the long whiskers is the Count of Daria. The pirates are probably awaiting a ransom payment for him—he would be too valuable to leave languishing here. I saw a few men with military bearing, too." Nemo fell silent.

Kang chewed his second cookie and offered the plate to Verne, who took one and asked, "Will Mr. Soriano join us?"

While the automat grabbed another cookie, Bartholomew shook his head.

Celwyn asked, "Do the cookies help you forget the atrocities you saw?"

"No. Fill up the plate, please."

Nemo told Verne, "Granger reports that Mr. Soriano returned while we were gone, and is resting in his cabin."

"Mayhem and revenge are exhausting," Celwyn said. He studied Nemo. "Did we learn anything tonight that will help with what to do with the hostages?" The Captain shrugged.

As Bartholomew adjusted the sling around his shoulder, he winced. "You know, this is the same shoulder where I was shot back in 1858."

The automat took his time finishing his cookie before asking, "I assume you still do not want any pain medication?"

"Correct."

Kang arched a brow at the magician, a signal of approval for Celwyn to help the big man, despite his intention to brave it out.

Verne asked, "Talk about the hostages you saw tonight, please?"

The automat frowned and replied, "It is horrible to say, but I think we'll find that when the hostages became a bother, the pirates killed as many as they kept. To your question, tonight we only asked for the most desperate in need of attention. We set broken bones, treated infections, and performed one amputation. Then we counseled some of the elderly hostages who aren't handling the conditions well."

They all thought about what he had said for several minutes while Kang continued to eat cookies. The crunching sounded loud in the near-silent room.

"Deciding what to do depends on the hostages themselves," Nemo said. "Did you notice a leader among them?"

Bartholomew said, "I saw a man in the back watching everything. He said little, but the others showed him a measure of respect and deference. Some whispered to him as if consulting him."

"Was he the heavy-set blond man in the green trousers?" Nemo asked.

Bartholomew nodded. "Yes."

Nemo nodded. "He could be a captured ship's captain. He had the bearing of command about him."

"Some of the women were abused by the pirates." Kang looked at his hands and inhaled before he could go on. "We may find that the two pregnancies are from the pirates." He blinked rapidly and stuffed another cookie in his mouth.

The magician growled, and the top row of glasses above the bar exploded, raining tinkling glass over the bar. Verne ducked.

Bartholomew put a hand on Celwyn's arm. "We killed all the pirates. If it would help, we will do it again."

The magician tried to control it. "We'll pick them out of the bay, wake them up, and then slice them in two!"

Verne studied him, wondering if the magician would do so. He managed to say to Kang, "Please continue."

The automat stared at his empty cookie plate and then at Celwyn, his way of bringing the magician back to an equal temperament. After the plate had been refilled, Kang said, "I asked the woman that Jonas talked with how many hostages were really on the island. Her name is Esther Peabody. She sounded most definite about a total of 512 hostages. As for anything else, she said she hadn't been there that long—it had been less than a month since Dearing's men captured the ship she had been on."

Celwyn flexed his hands, feeling his anger rise like a boiling kettle. Bartholomew elbowed him.

"I can't decide which of you is the most worn out after our activities today, but I vote that Bartholomew rests, if anyone cares about my opinion." The automat grunted and considered another cookie. The clock behind him chimed the late hour.

Bartholomew smiled and patted his shoulder. "I agree. It has been quite a day."

"We will wait until tomorrow to examine the paintings," Nemo told them, and his glower faded to sadness. The magician resisted the urge to check his thoughts to discover what bothered him. He might not want to know.

"It is very late," Verne said.

The magician brought forth a quartet of mandolins playing Mahler's *das Lichtung.* The Captain listened, and his melancholy seemed to visibly lift from his shoulders. He nodded his appreciation at the magician.

Celwyn said, "I assume that at first light tomorrow we will verify there are no stray pirates on the other islands?"

Nemo tossed back the last of his drink. "Yes. One of my lieutenants will lead the effort. This ship will remain here, and they'll use the skiffs coming and going to the islands."

"I did not shoot enough pirates today," the big man said.

"We might find a few tomorrow." Celwyn grinned at him.

Kang spoke up. "I suggest that while that is occurring, we speak with the hostages and that Lieutenant Tiddle and I examine the rest of them. Perhaps Lieutenant Granger will accompany me and help with recording what they tell us?"

The Captain remained lost in his thoughts.

"Captain?"
"Oh—yes. It will be arranged."

Chapter 53

UNDER CLEAR MORNING SKIES, TWO skiffs bumped into the dock in front of Dearing's compound. As they tied up, Lieutenant Granger led the way off, with the automat and guards bringing up the rear. Kang sighed. He understood Bartholomew's preference for hunting pirates, but he could have used his diplomatic skills today. God knows Jonas didn't have any.

The crew proceeded to unload a boat-full of supplies from the *Nautilus*, including boxes of clothes, clean bedding, and cases of milk. Kang assumed there was room inside the submarine now for the rest of the paintings, if indeed. They intended to transport the hostages to Hong Kong instead of the other way around.

They stopped at the pirates' storage building so the *Nautilus's* crew could verify no outliers remained.

When all appeared clear, they added more provisions to the carts for the hostages.

Kang asked Granger a question as the guards led the way up the path toward the huts.

"Does a list exist of the ships attacked, or lost, in this area that would help us catalog everyone here, or who was here?"

As they walked, Granger held a frond nearly as big as the automat out of their way. Dozens of birds serenaded them, others screeched and called out in alarm from the depths of the jungle. In the automat's fancy, he imagined the birds celebrated the removal of the pirates. They could also have been signaling the promise of a fine day as the sun rose higher in a cloudless sky.

"The only thing I know is that Lloyds of London lists the names of overdue and missing ships in the newspapers. There are also published stories of people who went missing on ships that are recorded as 'lost.'" Granger's steps slowed, and he eyed the automat. "What are you thinking?"

Kang stepped around pirate trash and empty wine bottles. "I have seen some of the stories, but am superstitious enough not to read many of them. Perhaps I am imagining this, but sometimes months later, there is a follow-up story about the pirates, naming them as the culprits who wrecked the ships." He sidestepped a mud puddle.

"Aye, I've seen a few."

"It may not be just good and decent people that the pirates captured. Wouldn't they take *everyone* with them before learning anything about their backgrounds? Also, some of these hostages may not have generated a ransom demand since they didn't give the pirates their real names."

"Interesting thought." Granger rubbed his chin and stared at him. "Right. The badums could even be the only survivors in some cases." A spotted snake slithered across the trail in front of them. "We will question as many as we can."

With a frown, the automat continued on until they reached the grass before the huts. He cursed. In the clear morning light, the conditions the hostages lived in seemed much worse than they had the night before.

Every few feet, pits filled with sludge and debris patterned the ground, and through the broken roofs of the huts, daylight fell across pure squalor. There wasn't even straw on the dirt floors, only an occasional bucket next to the entrance. No doors kept out insects or the gusts of wind. Tree rats scurried from shack to shack, and the stench increased with each degree of heat from the sun.

Over the next several hours, the hostages lined up in front of a pair of crates Granger had set up as a desk. They gave their names and basic information to crew members, who recorded it in the journals Nemo had provided. If the hostage seemed willing, Granger asked them a few more questions before sending them to the next set of crates to collect clean clothes. After that, they moved on to the provisions.

Their circuit ended with a visit to Kang and Lieutenant Tiddle. Today, they had brought a crewman who functioned as a medic and a third set of hands. By late afternoon, they'd processed the direst cases, or at least those that would cooperate.

Lieutenant Granger stood in front of the prisoners and raised his voice. "Can I have your attention, please?"

The murmurings stopped, leaving only the animal and aviary sounds from the jungle.

"Is there a spokesman for you?" He repeated the question in French and old-style Bavarian.

Esther, the woman who had been cut, and the muscular blond man in the green pants, stepped forward.

"We will," the blond man said. "There is also David." He nodded at one of the men, who ran to the last hut.

Less than a minute went by before David trotted toward them, blinking in the bright light.

"My apologies. I was on guard duty last night."

Granger told them, "We won't keep you long." He indicated the automat who had joined him. Only feet away, the hostages gathered in a large crowd and pressed forward as, once again, their murmurs grew with suspicion and worry. Many of them wouldn't meet Granger or Kang's gaze, so cowed by the pirates they could only stare at their feet.

"We know Esther and David's names. What is yours, sir?" Granger asked.

The blond man, probably forty years of age and average height, possessed more than average confidence. A pair of steely eyes regarded them with intelligence and cunning.

"Captain Horatio Unmann." He spoke with a light French accent laced with a suggestion of lilt and blurring of vowels. "The pirates sank my ship, *The Riviere,* six months ago."

"Thank you," Granger told them. "We will return in a few hours. Until then, please talk with everyone. Ask them if they prefer to stay here, or move into the pirates' quarters temporarily. We would help you clean the buildings first."

"All right." Esther cast a worried eye on the crowd behind her. "What else?"

"Our crew is scouring the other islands for pirates now. Do you know if there are other hostages?"

David shook his head. "They kept us all here, so they could watch us. They used to take some of us to the islands to work the fields." His bottom lip quivered, and he gestured beyond the huts. "We have a graveyard full of those they killed. We call it Tote Freunde."

As he spoke, Esther's agitation grew until she blurted, "Why help *us*?" Her voice broke, and tears streamed down her face.

Kang always felt helpless when confronted with a woman's distress. He glanced at Granger, who answered loud enough for them all to hear. "Weeks ago, we captured the pirate king, Dearing." At the sound of that name, no matter what language they spoke, fear rippled across the hostages. A few stumbled backward and ran to the huts. Granger hurried to add, "He can't hurt you anymore." To the three representatives, he said, "Let them know he is dead."

Unmann did so loudly, and the word spread.

The automat waited until the message had been passed from the front of the crowd to the back. Worried glances still bounced among them, but a measure of their terror had subsided. Kang went on. "We heard there were hostages here, but not this many." He waited until they quieted. "We will not leave until we've helped you as much as we can. We wish you no harm."

Unmann said, "We can see that. What will happen to us?"

The automat noticed the increasing worry and fear on the faces close by. "We are not going to abandon you. We just do not yet know whether to sail to Hong Kong to bring help here or what exactly to do." Kang held out his hands, appealing to them. "We will talk with you as we go. Again," he raised his voice and repeated the message in French and German, "We will not abandon you." A few of them still frowned in confusion, a reminder they needed Bartholomew's language skills.

The underlying hum of their disquiet grew louder and some of the men shoved forward, their eyes frantic. Just as Kang began wondering if they should retreat, Jonas strode up the path, whistling and making as much noise as possible as he joined them. The automat rolled his eyes; he bet the magician would have preferred an even more dramatic entrance.

"Good afternoon," Celwyn called out. "I can see some of you remember me. Please believe what my colleagues have said. We will take care of everyone until we can get you to safety."

"What do you need us to do?" Captain Unmann asked.

Celwyn answered, "Stay here until we completely secure the area. Finish recording your information in those journals." He pointed at them. "We'll pick them up later today when we bring over boxes of food." The magician checked: only a few boxes of biscuits and a half barrel of dried fish remained from last night. After the panic in the crowd just now, Kang was right to ban magic. They would also not understand how hundreds of meals could be cooked without a legion of stoves or campfires. With an involuntary glance behind them, he doubted anyone wanted to use what was left of the pirates' kitchen after it burned. Some hostages, including the man in the green pants, might have explored enough to know the condition of it. Magic was out, but other things could be done.

"What else?" David asked. In him, Kang noted the natural demeanor of a leader. As busy as David had been keeping them alive, he probably didn't realize the others looked up to him.

Celwyn checked with Granger and the automat, then said, "There is much to do. Do you know when, or how, the pirates received their supplies?"

"About once a week, one of their ships would come in full of things," Esther told them. "Very little of it came here."

Kang felt a prickle of nervousness wiggle its way up his back. "How long has it been since the supply ship was here?"

The automat was not the only one who understood the danger. "A little less than a week," Unmann said with a frown at the bay. "We'll make sure everyone stays close here."

Celwyn said, "Thank you, sir," and cocked his head at him. "By chance—"

"Ha! Yes, you know me, you bastard." Unmann glared at him.

"Oh, my." Kang tried not to laugh at the magician and his horrified expression of recognition.

Celwyn waved it off. "In the past, and personal." As he spoke, it seemed the jungle collectively breathed again.

Granger motioned to his guards to move out, some of whom had already begun pushing the empty carts up the path. Lieutenant Tiddle trotted to keep up. Like the magician and the automat, they knew what the arrival of an armed pirate ship meant.

"We will be back later on," Celwyn assured the hostages in English, and in his best French, followed by better Spanish. He returned Unmann's knowing sneer and herded the automat ahead of him up the path. Kang chuckled, ready for more fun with the magician.

"Not now, Xiau. I'm hungry, and we need to warn Nemo about the pirate ship." Nemo's man walked with them, his hand on his pistol, and his eyes swiveling to both sides of the path, on alert. "Do you want to go back with me, or with Granger?"

"I will go with Gra—" Kang stopped as Celwyn transformed into a gorgeous macaw and flapped his way toward the water.

It only took a few minutes for Celwyn to find the submarine floating on the far side of the neighboring island. The *Nautilus* would not be visible to the hostages, even if they obtained a spyglass. But what about anyone else? He circled the island and flew higher. In the clear afternoon sky, nary a cloud could be seen.

He enjoyed the heat as he scanned the water for miles in all directions. Of the six small islands that lay near Dearing's main island, most seemed agricultural, and their docks were nearly empty. Only a limited number of fishing trawlers moored against makeshift piers, and the islands measured less than a few miles long. No outsiders threatened them at the moment. The magician dipped a bit lower, fighting the glare of the sun to complete a 360-degree survey before he descended to the *Nautilus*.

Without fanfare, he landed as himself on the platform next to Bartholomew, who jumped and dropped his pipe. Celwyn caught the pipe before it hit the water and floated it back to him. The big man was still speechless when Nemo came up through the hatch and joined them.

"Pleasant trip?"

"Yes, but there is something you should know," Celwyn told them about the likelihood of a visit from Dearing's supply ship. "Granger heard the news too, and he and the Professor are on their way back."

Nemo paced and scowled. "I could sink anything that sailed into this bay."

"Sir," Bartholomew said. "Excuse me, but we suddenly have about five hundred more mouths to feed. Perhaps we should unload whatever they bring in first?" He gestured toward the main island. "There could be two supply ships, too."

Nemo frowned but said nothing.

"I just scouted the sea within a thirty-mile radius," Celwyn said. "Nothing is out there, but it might be prudent to get everyone back on the ship as soon as possible."

"Of course." Nemo swallowed his ill humor. "It is long past lunchtime. We can discuss this later."

As they headed down the stairs, Bartholomew said, "It would be useful to know how much food is left for the hostages. Perhaps we could provide some fresh fish, courtesy of Jonas?"

Nemo waited at the bottom of the stairs for them. "There are also those wild boars. They could cook those, too."

The magician said, "I will build fire pits for the hostages to use. And provide fish. From what I gathered, the pirates handed out scraps of food they didn't gorge themselves on, only enough to keep those people alive." He joined Nemo as they waited for Bartholomew to descend the stairs.

As Nemo bowed them ahead down the corridor, Celwyn noticed the big man wasn't wearing the arm sling from his wound and grinned when he pictured the automat's reaction.

Chapter 54

Prague

OVER THE NEXT FOUR DAYS, PATRICK did what he could, but it never felt like enough.

Each day, he dispatched Edward to the telegraph office to send telegrams to every port the *Nautilus* had ever stopped at in the past. It had taken hours to gather all of Elizabeth's telegrams and letters from her husband. Xiau wrote prolifically, and she usually stored the missives in whatever she had been reading or doing at the time.

The Professor always started his messages with the location of where the adventurers and the *Nautilus* happened to be. Could they assume he told them the truth? Or did he censor what would upset Elizabeth? Patrick strongly suspected Kang and the others never told them everything that happened, no matter their assurances. With a sardonic grin, he realized he did not find this as annoying as Annabelle did—sometimes it was best not to know.

Each telegram dispatched to the adventurers today, and every day since the tragedy read alike:

Elizabeth has been murdered.
We are in danger.
Come home.

The telegrams sent this morning had been transmitted to ports Patrick hadn't tried yet, or even considered: Muscat, Athens, Antalya, Catania, and Tripoli. After they had been sent, it occurred to Patrick that he didn't even know what happened to the Professor and the others in London. All he knew was that they'd gained a new enemy and a collection of murderous pirates.

How can I find out what happened? He remembered the one telegram from the Professor last week that said little, except that Miss McFein was safe. It ended with the news that Miss Redifer had been captured by pirates, and off they went!

That question occupied Patrick's mind until noon when he arrived at Mrs. Thomas' office. He could admit he had been worried all day ... the housekeeper's request to meet could have been about many things—from Beastie's antics to Mrs. Pearse, or something the boys had brought in from the garden that had gotten loose again. He stood straight and squared his shoulders, then knocked.

Her voice boomed from within. "Come in!"

Today Mrs. Thomas wore an iron-grey dress and a dark expression to match. As he sat down, Patrick decided on his final guess; this would be about the boys' deeds.

"Thank you for coming. No, sit there." She waved a hand at the other chair. "I have some information for you. Whether you would prefer to keep this to yourself or provide it to others is up to you, sir."

Not sure what he would want, Patrick nodded his encouragement.

She eyed him and said, "Just so. I have talked to many of the undertakers and funeral parlors in the city. I have also spoken with the secretaries in charge at St. Titus's, and St. Mary's. Lastly, I met with the administrator of the Greek Orthodox Church." She consulted a notebook on her desk. "None of the churches will allow a body to be held there for two months or more, and most of them wouldn't consider it since the Professor and Mrs. Kang were not church members." She regarded Patrick like she did Zander when he came in with muddy shoes. "I understand that you and the Missus have been too busy to attend church regularly." Without waiting for a response, she said, "Even my minister at the Church of England asked if I was daft."

Patrick managed, "I'm so sorry to put you—"

"No," she waved it away. "I am pleased to be of service. Someday, this information may be useful considering the trouble the inhabitants of this house can get into." She pinned him with a glare that would have stopped Napoleon. "And I do not beg your pardon for that opinion."

"I understand." As he spoke, he promised himself that when they got back, he wouldn't tease the adventurers anymore for being afraid of Mrs. Thomas.

She nodded her approval, his response acceptable. "So, I inquired further. Most undertakers would not consider a request to hold a deceased person for weeks on end. Except one." She opened the center drawer of her desk and produced a card.

As Patrick accepted it, he heard Ricardo raising his voice in the kitchen on the other side of the wall. The man had never been this excitable until he became chef of Tellyhouse. Today, it seemed someone had done something to his fresh basil. While he listened to the cook's shrieks of outrage, he read the old-fashioned script on the card.

Bosephus Crow, Undertaker

"That gentleman will preserve Mrs. Kang's body in ice for us, and promises discretion." She stood, causing him to do so as well. "I would appreciate it if none of the neighbors heard of this. I will *not* put up with gossip."

"Yes, ma'am."

***

Patrick spent the early part of the afternoon writing a letter of introduction for Edward to take to the undertaker, along with a purse of coins and a request to the police to release Elizabeth's body to one Mr. Bosephus Crow. Should they have some sort of ceremony for Elizabeth while they awaited the funeral? Hell, he didn't know. He was more concerned with keeping everyone safe.

What he would do is visit Major Jardin often and pester the man for progress. As he poured ink into his inkwell, he remembered he hadn't received a straight answer as to whether they had found any witnesses at the glove store where Elizabeth and Edward had been attacked.

Although Patrick had asked everyone at Tellyhouse to take one of their newly hired guards with them on errands, enforcing the request became the responsibility of Mrs. Thomas. It would take a brave, or hair-brained, person to disobey her. A fine example occurred when Flossy left early one night for an evening out, without a guard. The housekeeper's bellow of displeasure could have been heard several houses away.

As a rule, the boys did not present a problem. Their play times with the neighborhood children had been put on hold, yet because of their grief over Elizabeth, they did not seem to mind. They did, however, expect a weekly trip to feed the ducks on the river, and hoped for a visit to the street fair every weekend. The muscle-bound twins, Abe and Andy, usually accompanied them, while Annabelle voiced her worry the entire time until they returned.

On the third week after the murder, Mrs. Pearse went home. Patrick swore even Tellyhouse itself issued a sigh of relief.

Things had been rather tense between Annabelle and her aunt since the news of her pregnancy had caused Mrs. Pearse to raise her voice in high trills of disapproval. The old lady still hadn't given up her dream of marrying her niece to royalty, or at the least, an American ambassador. Annabelle made it plain that she loved Patrick and the boys, and her aunt could feel free to go home. Patrick kept his smile to himself, recalling the story he'd heard of Jonas helping the dowager on her way out the door on another occasion.

The only positive result of her aunt's visit was seeing the old fire in Annabelle's eyes when she defended him, instead of being sunk in misery. This also reminded Patrick of one thing they hadn't completely discussed, especially in front of her aunt.

The need for a special doctor for the pregnancy still had to be addressed. Patrick's small amount of vampire blood required more discretion than canvassing the city's undertakers to solve the problem.

His first conversation about this would be with the adventurers when they came home; their new partners, who happened to be vampires, would know. If the Professor and the others did not return soon, he might have to consult Francesca and her coven. The witch knew people and also about things she liked to use for nefarious purposes. The interconnecting network of other beings and unusual entities seemed to be a tight one, and he shuddered just thinking about it.

Just before noon on the first day of October, Annabelle put down her embroidery and announced she needed some fresh afternoon air, and she wanted to go on a boat ride on the river.

"I'll arrange for the calèche," Patrick told her and glanced at the growing evidence of her condition, somewhat camouflaged by a beautiful linen dress. "Do you think it would be too ... err ... bouncy of a ride for you?"

She pursed her lips. "Perhaps. We could always take the carriage and invite the boys along."

"Excellent." Patrick rose from his chair and checked out the parlor window before kissing her cheek. "Please bundle up, my dear. It looks blustery outside."

An hour later, Edward clicked his tongue, and the carriage rolled out of the driveway and down the street. Inside the coach, the boys sat side by side and uncharacteristically quiet. Otto blinked away tears while Zander studied his feet, barely looking up when one of the neighborhood dogs barked.

Patrick regarded them. "It has been weeks since ... what happened to Miss Elizabeth, and I hoped this would be a good outing for us."

Otto and Zander exchanged a nod, and the younger boy said, "We know. Miss Elizabeth used to love seeing the boats."

"I remember," Annabelle said. "We'll have to keep this as one of our special memories of her. Perhaps we could go once a month."

Otto managed a wan smile. Zander kicked the seat and said, "I suppose."

Patrick patted his shoulder. "I'm sure you meant 'Yes, Ma'am.'"

That brought a sheepish grin. He changed his response and asked, "Is it true we are going for a boat ride?"

Annabelle raised a brow of inquiry at Patrick.

"Yes, as long as the baby doesn't object." Patrick looked out the window and confirmed they had just passed through the intersection of Kamyk and Tursko and headed toward the river. "We will have Edward with us. Did you know he was in the British Navy?"

Otto's eyes widened behind his spectacles. He wrote on his tablet and Zander read the one word aloud.

"When?"

Patrick shrugged. "I do not know. You'll have to ask him."

Chapter 55

T HE BLACKWELL ORANGE DOCKS ON the Vltava River housed an extensive variety of private boats that chugged their way upriver, and rental boats heading downriver. In between lay the transport and working boats, making short trips to other docks, and back.

Under a weak, cold sun, Edward and the boys led the way as they approached the ticket seller. All the while, Edward answered a slew of questions about the Queen's Navy. From behind them, Patrick called out a reminder of the worthiness of the Queen's Army, which he knew well. Edward laughed for the first time in weeks. "The 'Army Cheeses' are good soldiers, sir."

They boarded the *Modrá Sonia* at last call just before she sailed downriver toward Braner. Annabelle held onto Patrick's arm as she stepped onto the undulating deck. When an infant breeze captured the ribbons on her hat and tickled her face, her expression told him that they would survive this nightmare and go forward.

Like monkeys, the boys scampered up the ladder the crew used to reach the upper deck and ignored the passenger stairs. Edward followed with more grace and ease, probably born of his Navy years. They leaned over the rail and watched the other passengers, their faces alive again after the tragedy. When the gusts lifted Edward's coat, Patrick verified that he had indeed brought his pistol. It was just as well. Annabelle had decreed that Patrick could not bear arms while she was in a delicate condition, and not at all around the baby. He touched her cheek with fondness and joined Edward in checking the other passengers.

"Where will we sit?" she asked. "I can still climb stairs if we want to go up top."

A series of bells rang from the dock, and the *Modrá Sonia* pushed away from her berth, chugging into the middle of the river under a rather odorous cloud of steam. Patrick gazed upward as the sun broke through the clouds, bathing the ship in a halo of light. Annabelle grasped his hand and led the way up to the top. They found seats on the fore-end and settled onto them as the wind picked up, ruffling the river and trees nearby. Most of the passengers elected to stay on the lower deck.

The *Modrá Sonia's* horn blared as she passed another pleasure boat. All along the north shore, fields of golden grain abutted the river for miles, and near the south shore, pastures and cows predominated.

Annabelle pointed out a pregnant cow.

"That will be me soon!"

Patrick and the boys joined her in the jest. He suspected that as things progressed, his wife would not be as jocular about her condition. From his position on the other side of the boys, Edward wore a polite smile, but his attention centered on the passengers on the deck below them. Patrick wished their driver could enjoy the day, and at the same time, felt grateful he remained vigilant.

Patrick sidled closer to him and murmured, "Is there a problem?"

Edward verified the boys remained busy pointing out ducks, and insisting that Annabelle notice them, too. In an even lower voice, he replied, "I don't see anything, sir. Just making sure. I'd welcome a chance to get my own back against the bastard who killed Mrs. Kang."

⌣

Two hours later, they docked in Branek. Last summer, Celwyn had discovered some excellent teas and tobaccos here. Annabelle wanted to buy flowers, and the boys searched for anything they hadn't seen before; the slimier or odder, the better. Shops framed the docks, catering to the tourists and local people. As they left the fourth shop with arms full of pottery and plants, Patrick asked Annabelle if she needed to rest. When she shook her head, he nodded but kept an eye on her.

The boys had instructions to remain in sight of Patrick and Annabelle and do exactly what Edward said to do. Over the last few months, they'd continued their "wrestling" lessons for self-defense from Patrick and displayed a certain level of bravery, if not common sense. Late last year, the boys had fought off some villains who'd accosted them, and Patrick had been proud of them.

In what seemed like too short of time, *Modrá Sonia's* bell rang, signaling her intent to depart. Everyone returned to the dock loaded with bags of tobacco, candy, and rubbery insects grasped in the boys' hands. Patrick had not forgotten the Spanish saffron Ricardo had requested.

After they boarded the boat again, Annabelle announced she needed to rest, and Patrick followed her into the main cabin to find her a comfortable chair. Edward and the boys headed up top as a light rain fell and the boat backed into the main channel.

With a blast from her horn, she aimed her bow north. The noise caused a chorus of squeals from a group of schoolgirls in prim white blouses and red bows who'd clustered at the stern of the boat. Their chaperone clapped to get their attention and soon led them in song. It was a piece Patrick couldn't place, but he knew it originated in the Alps.

He leaned back and enjoyed their time out. The best part of the trip sat inches away. Annabelle's cheeks flushed with the fresh air, and she had smiled more today than any time since Elizabeth died.

Above all, the evil that had killed their friend had not returned, and around them, he only saw bucolic scenery, and passengers enjoying the boat ride.

As the tower of St. Titus church came into view, Patrick crossed to the cabin window. Annabelle joined him, linking her arm with his. She jumped when the boys ran up to press their faces against the glass before laughing and running back to the stern. Edward followed at a fast pace, still wearing the worried expression he hadn't really lost since they left Tellyhouse.

"The trip was good for them," Annabelle said and buried her nose in her bouquet of roses. "Look—the showers are stopping."

Patrick agreed and watched a ribbon of sunlight bathe the dome of the Opera House as the clouds parted again. In the distance, a church bell rang, and others answered, echoing across a hundred churches. The Professor had informed them that nearly every religion in the world was represented here.

With that thought, his spirits dove: he missed the Professor, Bartholomew, and Jonas. Like an iron blanket pressing down, it weighed on him that they did not know about Elizabeth's death.

A half-hour later, with Zander and Otto in the lead, they walked across the street from the docks to the carriage park, the ground still wet and muddy on each side of the cobblestones. If Annabelle hadn't been behind them, Patrick knew the boys would have jumped in each puddle.

Beside him, Edward's frown deepened.

"Sir? Didn't you ask Jimmy, the guard, to stay with the carriage?"

"I did." Patrick's sense of foreboding twanged, and his breath quickened. "I do not see him."

"Zander! Otto!" Edward called out as they raced the last thirty yards to the carriage. "Stop!"

In slow motion, they came to a stop as Patrick reached them, holding them back, and Edward sprinted to the carriage. From what Patrick could tell, the horses appeared fine and tried to greet Edward as he circled the carriage, pivoting to scan the area between the other carriages. He located Patrick and held up a hand.

It took a second for Patrick to understand why—Edward had not found Jimmy, and the only place left to look was in the carriage itself. Patrick shuddered and felt Annabelle's hand in his as he remembered what Edward had discovered in the carriage before.

Zander began asking questions, but Otto pulled on his arm and shook his head. Then Zander understood too, and both boys' eyes widened in fear.

Patrick couldn't look away as Edward squatted to see under the carriage and then peered through the glass into the cab. He stiffened and called out to Patrick.

"Sir, please fetch that policeman by the ticket counter behind you. Keep everyone back."

A short time later, Patrick put Annabelle and the boys into a hire cab with one of Major Jardin's lieutenants and sent them home. As Annabelle shushed Zander, she kept her expression as neutral as she could before kissing Patrick goodbye.

The hire cab hadn't traveled out of sight before Major Jardin approached with a cigar dangling from his fishlike lips. His eyes were bloodshot, and he had to concentrate as he asked Edward and Patrick if they had remembered anything else. They both shook their heads.

"We found this under the guard's body." Jardin nodded to Edward, who leaned over Patrick's shoulder to read the proffered paper. Patrick noted the same old-fashioned and fussy script he'd seen before.

Mr. Swayne, this time it is a guard.
Next time, it will be someone closer to you.
Tell the Professor that I wish to see him.

"It is signed 'Gaspard.' You still do not know him?" Jardin asked.

Again, Patrick shook his head, numb with the shock of what had happened.

"I haven't heard the name either, except on the day of the murder," Edward said.

"Does this Professor of yours know him?"

"As I mentioned before, I do not know." Patrick wrung his hands. "What about Jimmy's family?"

"I sent someone to the security company he worked at." Jardin regarded Patrick with a measure of pity. "They will take care of it."

Patrick heard him, but he focused on their carriage about ten feet away. He did not want to look inside the cab, yet felt an uncontrollable urge to do so.

"When can we have our coach back?" Edward asked Jardin.

The Major looked away and swiveled back to blow smoke in their faces.

"In an hour or so. This was strangulation, barehanded. There isn't any blood on the seats. You'll just need to give it a good cleaning." He eyed Patrick, and said, "Your wife should not go riding around the city until this is resolved. Two of my men will remain assigned to your home twenty-four hours a day until this is over."

Patrick heard him and thanked him, but his mind had settled on something he needed to do. Writing was not his forte, but he would do it. They left Jardin, and Edward scouted for a hire coach.

"Edward, we'll stop at the telegraph office. After we add Gaspard's name to the daily message to the Professor and the others, I'll send it to every damn city between here and Hong Kong if I must." Patrick felt anger building, overtaking him.

"Hopefully, before the bastard kills again," Edward said and kept a wary eye on the crowd gathered on the other side of the road, who viewed them like a circus attraction.

Chapter 56

DURING A LATE LUNCHEON, ALL talk centered around the hostages. Verne, along with Valentine, peppered them with questions.

"Sir, have you decided what you are going to do about the hostages?"

The Captain finished buttering a roll. "For now, we will listen to what everyone here has gathered, and leave a lookout on duty to be sure we know of any visitors to the islands."

Celwyn hid a grin, knowing full well that wasn't what Verne wanted to know. Nemo had a certain smoothness to him.

Kang took his cue and related what they'd learned that morning. Afterwards, Valentine said, "There has been so much misery caused by these pirates."

"Thankfully, you cut off the head of the snake," Bartholomew said, much to the magician's surprise. As gentle and superstitious as the big man could be, he had a rather morbid and practical side as well.

The vampire smiled. "Yes, I did."

The magician wondered if he meant that literally.

Bartholomew's acceptance of Valentine's dangerous tendencies did not last long. He gulped and changed the subject. "We saw fields of rice and pineapples on two of the islands. That would help supply the hostages. I think the pirates sold the crops to fund their activities instead of feeding everyone here."

"Tonight, I'll gather that up, save some for their dinner, and put the rest in the storage building." Celwyn ate a few bites and added, "Before dusk, there will be fresh fish for them." He eyed Nemo and aimed a thumb out the aquatic window. "What will I find out there that would be the most tasty?"

A discussion ensued between Nemo and the Professor, until Nemo said, "Look for triggerfish and sturgeon." He described them. "They stay near the coral or the rocks just above the seafloor."

"It sounds like we have their immediate needs met." Bartholomew nodded and took another helping of the salad.

As the clock struck a series of bells and their coffee was served, Qing hopped onto the ledge of the aquatic window and tapped the glass.

The submarine rested about two dozen feet below the surface at the head of the circular bay. Here, the water reflected plenty of light on the seafloor and turned it into a surreal scene of sand mounds shaped like melting castles. A single skull lay on its side in the middle of the sand as a reminder of the horrific reality of the last few days.

Celwyn said, "Sir, I'll set up an alert system for anyone entering the bay after dark. We do not want any surprises."

"Thank you. It will save having to post guards ashore all night, also." Nemo told the rest of the table, "We searched all the other islands, carefully, and are satisfied we eliminated all the pirates yesterday."

"That is good news. When I spoke with David, he said most of the hostages want to go home. Many were steerage passengers or tradesmen and are not wealthy." Bartholomew's expression darkened. "David is the only deckhand who survived the plundering and treatment by the pirates. And he has nowhere to go."

"Does he have an idea of where he would like to be resettled?" the automat asked.

"I do not know," the big man answered.

Verne said, "The British will see most of them on their way. Not in excessive comfort, but safely. They will not abandon them."

"Good. I say ... the bread this evening is quite tasty. It goes well with the..." Bartholomew stared at his plate, probably hoping it wasn't something exotic like eel again.

"Angelfish," Kang supplied. The big man blinked, breathed, and continued eating.

Celwyn told them, "I'll be resting for the remainder of the afternoon—preparation for my activities tonight."

"How will you explain the firepits you plan to make?" Kang asked.

"You recall the tiger pits Dearing used as a defense? Cleaned out, they will do nicely, especially since they never contained tigers. The crew is chopping down trees for fuel for them."

As the clock rang sixteen bells, Bartholomew and the magician walked into the study. Kang had already ordered his tea service, and Valentine poured a glass of wine for the big man.

When everyone had taken their seats, Bartholomew announced that besides the food in the pirates' stores, and acres of rice and pineapples that Celwyn had added from the other island, there was plenty of food for the hostages.

"How many fish are there?" Verne asked. "Won't they have to be kept cold?"

"If there are any left, yes," the big man said. "Granger supplied sturdy poles and twine. I showed some of the hostages how to make lures and set the poles. They will teach the others, and supplement fish for their tables daily. We told them we have nets, which will account for the fish Jonas provides."

He continued, "By the way, we cleared out one of the pirates' buildings for them to dine in and meet in comfort. Granger's crew made some plywood tables and benches. The other buildings were swept out."

Bartholomew eyed the magician. "Has the Captain decided how we're getting everyone off the island?"

Celwyn replaced his teacup in its saucer and debated whether to pour more. "No. I'm hoping we will discuss it over dinner."

"If Bartholomew and the crew shoot a few of the wild boars for their tables, it would be a good source of protein and variety," Kang said. "And a measure of safety, too. The animals are vicious and would attack anyone unarmed or in their way."

"We could expect they would soon become emboldened without the pirates around, and possibly surprise the hostages if not taken care of, also," Verne mused.

⌣

After sunset, the *Nautilus* descended under the waves for the night. Celwyn's last glimpse across the bay revealed a line of torches the hostages had lit near the buildings. To the magician, the sight represented signs of hope. Smoke still rose from the fire pits, and many of the hostages had ventured over to the edge of the water, which was now safe to do. In the event someone sailed into the bay, the magician had put the finishing touches on his method of alerting them to unwanted visitors; the gongs inside the *Nautilus* would resound with as much fury as a gaggle of priests would if the devil snuck into an underwater church.

This evening dinner aboard the submarine seemed electric, energized with news of what they had accomplished that day. Per Verne, Valentine remained in his cabin, satiated after another of his own personal hunting expeditions on a neighboring island. On Celwyn's left, the author wiggled in his seat and said, "Mr. Soriano mentioned that he would be 'full' for another day or so."

No one asked for an explanation. Instead, Kang related excerpts of what the hostages had written in the journals. The crew served broiled black-lipped oysters in sauce to accompany the recital.

"I understand the hostages cooked corn over the fires tonight, along with the fish." Kang eyed his plate, checked Celwyn for pranks, and then began eating. His other hand hovered on guard near his food. "They also found lemons weeks ago, and now have something appropriate for them."

Celwyn wondered why Kang appeared so nervous about his plate. It usually meant the automat was up to no good and expected magical retaliation. He gave up speculating and said, "I found a great amount of these oysters and have sent them over, too."

After Kang had taken another bite, he made his report. "The numbers, ages, and genders from Jonas' estimate were fairly accurate. We'll know even more after tomorrow." He picked out another bite. "We have stabilized everyone medically, and they will be fine, assuming we get them professional help soon. Eating regularly will do wonders for them." He sighed. "However, we are extremely lucky it isn't cold right now. We barely have enough clothes for them."

"What about the pregnancies?" Nemo inquired.

The Professor said, "The women are not due to give birth for several months." Before Celwyn's anger could manifest itself in broken crystal, he continued, "They need a calm, stable place to live after what they've been through. For their trip to Hong Kong, we can provide that—providing we give the ship a good cleaning."

Kang checked his plate and then patted his ears. The magician pretended not to notice. The automat hesitated another moment before saying, "Luckily, there are three main leaders: a certain Captain Unmann, who Jonas needs to tell us about, and a Mrs. Esther Peabody of Boston. She is a widow and a most helpful individual. There is also David, the deckhand from the *Fair Lady,* which the pirates sank last year. He is a good influence on the hostages." Kang paused to finish his soup.

"Should we know about Captain Unmann now?" Nemo asked, unaware of Kang's teasing.

"After dinner will do," Celwyn replied and noticed Kang's sarcastically raised brow. "It is more of a personal nature that does not apply to this situation."

Kang left the brow up. "As you say... Anyhow, about the hostages; fifty of the men are still able-bodied enough and have varying degrees of maritime experience. There are another twenty-five or so who could physically do the work to keep a three-master upright and her sails set—with oversight from Granger and his men." He put his spoon down and said, "This presents an interesting scenario ... if we go back to Jonas' romantic notion of having them sail away in the pirate ship we spared."

"What is the name of the ship?" Verne asked.

Nemo said, "The *Cazadore*. It translates to 'hunter.' Dearing's humor."

Verne shivered. "Tell us about the hostages, please."

Kang consulted his notes. "Certainly. As you would expect, there are horrific accounts of how they came to be on the island. Many of them were from the wreck of the *Brown Betty* two years ago, and last year's *Prince George*. Next came the *Fumizuki*, and Batavia's *Lundland*, and others." He flipped pages. "I'd have to verify the rest."

"Could we assume Dearing had ransomed off many more ... besides those we found?" the big man asked.

"Yes, and killed just as many. I saw the burial grounds the hostages maintained." Kang's face worked as he controlled his revulsion. "Miss Esther listed many of the other passengers from the *USS Perry* that she sailed upon. Dearing sank it four months ago, and of the survivors from that ship, she alone had not been ransomed. It is sad."

"Why?" Bartholomew asked.

"She lost her husband during the attack and does not have means. Her husband's family is wealthy, and they disowned her before the voyage."

"Why?" Kang frowned.

"Because she had been studying to become a lawyer."

"I do not understand." Verne glanced at the others in inquiry.

Celwyn said, "I think I do. It is not socially acceptable in high society for women to be educated or to aspire to work outside the home. They consider it embarrassing."

"That is terrible," Bartholomew said. "She is a very personable woman. Strong of character."

Celwyn added, "We can provide the funds to help her become established again. Wouldn't it be appropriate to use Dearing's money for that, and do the same for the other hostages who are without funds?"

"I like the idea." Nemo nodded as he thought. "Most appropriate."

Bartholomew's expression still showed concern. "This must have been an ordeal for her." The magician eyed him, wondering if the big man wasn't sailing into another romantic entanglement.

When their dessert arrived, Nemo said, "We have gutted my ship of all clean clothing. Granger had the rest of it taken to them earlier today. Tomorrow, we'll pick up more in Manuk. And additional medical supplies to replace what we've used and will need." He spooned fruit pudding. "Mango." He licked his lips and finished the bowl. "My crew brought plenty of this fruit on board this afternoon, enough to make desserts for the hostages. You can imagine it will take a while."

Verne asked Nemo, "And the hostages, sir?"

Nemo said, "As we have discussed, it would take us four to five days to journey to Hong Kong. Then about ten days for the British to believe us, get ready, and sail back here. During that time, they would be unprotected unless Jonas, and half of my crew, remained behind."

"Add those fifteen days to the five days for the most seriously ill hostages' journey back to Hong Kong, which some of them may not survive," Bartholomew noted.

Celwyn asked, "What is our next option?"

"Use some of my crew to supplement the men needed to sail the pirates' ship we reserved. The *Nautilus* would quietly escort the *Cazadore* to Hong Kong. Once near the harbor, we'd verify the hostages were safe, retrieve my crew, and be on our way. It would take about five to six days total, under normal weather conditions."

"And I would provide wind for her canvasses if she became becalmed," Celwyn said.

Qing pecked the glass on the aquatic window, greeting a fat fish who hovered on the other side.

"That is the largest frogfish I have ever seen," Kang commented. Qing began a little dance for the fish, hopping to the left, and then to the right.

Bartholomew asked, "Is there a third option?" When no one responded, he asked, "Sir, how many men would you loan to work the *Cazadore*?"

"Unknown at this point. There are also the twenty-five able-bodied who could help... with a bit of training." Nemo rapped a finger on the table. "Remember, we must stay out of sight. On the list of the prisoners, there are two military men from Spain in the group, and the nephew of the American Undersecretary of State." He frowned. "There could be others who haven't identified themselves. Any of them might know of a bounty on the *Nautilus*."

Celwyn wondered about the notable hostages among the group. Either their ransom was on its way, or someone had decided they didn't need their relatives back again.

"How will you present the new crew to them?" Kang asked.

Nemo shrugged. "Granger would be in charge and tell the hostages the men had been loaned to help them."

"Which is true," Verne said.

"Our dinner has ended." Nemo stood. "Let us finish this discussion in the comfort of the study."

Qing flew after them as they marched out of the Captain's dining room, squawking his excitement for whatever the evening brought him—preferably something glittery and energetic he could chase.

After their pipes had been packed, and cigars trimmed and lit, everyone settled in their places and waited. Bartholomew asked the first question.

"Do we have enough food to feed the hostages while we're at sea for six or more days?"

"Yes and no," the Captain said. "In an emergency, Jonas could supply food." He eyed the magician. "Could you devise a fishing net similar to what the Maori use? A larger version that could be towed behind the *Cazadore*? It would need to be something they can see and assume is ordinary when you fill it with fish. In a gradual manner, preferably."

"Yes."

Kang asked, "Is there room for cooking facilities for that many people on the ship?"

"There will be." Celwyn held his hands palms up. "The main problem is how to explain the sudden good fortune to the hostages."

Bartholomew laughed. "Perhaps the hostages not involved in the running of the ship could 'fish' and Jonas attach the catch to their hooks?"

"Possibly." Nemo poured a drink and offered the bottle to the others. "Whatever we decide, Lieutenant Granger must be aware of it."

"That all sounds plausible, one way or another," the big man said.

Verne asked, "Will they have water not provided by Jonas?"

"Good question," the magician told him. "There is a spring deep in the jungle on the other side of the island they'll draw water from before they sail. We have enough coffee and tea, and the same canned milk we use."

"Sounds good." Nemo sipped. "We'll add that to the task list for the hostages before we depart. What else do you suggest?" he asked the room. "Explaining our plan to the prisoners and gaining their trust for the journey is our most daunting task."

Bartholomew sat up straight. "I agree."

"Do we know why Dearing had so many hostages that he couldn't—or wouldn't—feed properly?" Kang asked.

"Greed," Verne said.

"Granger reported finding a ledger in Dearing's handwriting that showed a sale of over three hundred of the hostages as farm slaves. It was dated two months ago," the Captain told them.

Celwyn added the days in his head. "Probably chasing after the Professor with Talos got in the way of Dearing's delivery of them."

"Or…" Kang studied the whiskey bottle as if ants crawled on it. "Or he expected to pick up the money for them in London, and then send word to his crew to deliver them. Or kill them."

"We do not lack possibilities," the big man said.

"True." Celwyn asked Nemo, "We've talked about the weather for the journey to Hong Kong. Will it be a serious problem?"

"We can expect progressively cooler weather and storms." Nemo shrugged. "On another subject, the hostages will find the pirates' bathing facilities here have been cleaned. We're also converting Dearing's quarters for the women; it has elaborate bathing facilities."

"I'll provide flowery soap and other items," the magician said.

"This calls for champagne!" Bartholomew jumped to his feet, his exuberance and relief infectious. "We have a most worthy enterprise, and a solid plan to carry it out."

"Here, here!" Verne joined in.

Nemo excused himself and returned with Granger and the champagne.

"My Lieutenant knows much of what we're decided, but needs to hear everything."

Hours later, after a shortened round of bridge, where Valentine was brought up to speed, they still celebrated. Valentine and Bartholomew prevailed, but politely, while Nemo shuffled the cards and glared at Verne.

At eleven bells, Nemo sent the author one last exasperated look and joined Kang on the sofa where the automat read not one, but three books. One in each hand and one in his lap. Carruthers's *Complete Guide to Birds in the Amazon*, and *The Moonstone*, by Wilkie Collins. Then, *The Count of Monte Cristo*, by Dumas. Food for his brain, a mystery to solve, and an adventure to live through.

From his position at the organ, Celwyn finished a composition and noted a change on a parchment that had so much black ink it resembled a frenzied spider web swirling around the clefs and notes. The magician normally did not record what he authored, but he wanted to present Tara with an offering. To him, the piece recalled the scene at the Tower of London. He hoped she wouldn't have to play it under duress again someday. After a final notation, he stretched and joined the others.

"Sir, things have settled down, and we have confidence in our plans. Do you wish to talk about the paintings that brought us here?" Kang asked.

The happiness drained from Nemo's eyes like a plug had been pulled in a bathtub. He tightened his jaw. "Yes, I must. Let me get them."

When he rejoined them, he brought along all three paintings. Nemo spoke slowly, as if bringing forth something painful hidden deep in his memory, or heart.

"As you can see, the paintings are small: the first one is about forty-five inches by twenty-four inches, and the others are slightly larger. Hieronymus Bosch is known for depicting a spiral building in *The Tower of Babel.* It was painted again by Bruegel the Elder. In 1594, Van Valckenborch painted it. One of the paintings we found in Dearing's vault was Van Valckenborch's, which was the one he stole from the Museum Boyman in Rotterdam just before it burned in 1864."

The automat stacked his books on the table for Nemo to prop the pictures against. After he arranged them, the Captain crossed to the bar and waited there while the others gathered close to study the paintings. Each one had been mounted in ornate museum-quality frames, and the paper on the back of the oldest one had begun to peel away.

Valentine spoke first. "I've seen this before," he indicated Bosch's, "years ago in Rotterdam's museum. It seemed odd then, and odder now. I prefer pictures of flowers."

Celwyn stifled a laugh. Such an interesting combination; a lethal vampire and a bunch of flowers. He agreed, though; the painting seemed strange, and just as peculiar as the other two.

Kang said, "My goodness. What is the story behind them?"

Nemo glanced at Bartholomew. The big man answered, "I read quite a bit about them. Bruegel the Elder's version of 1563 became the most famous. It is based on the bible verse of Genesis 11:4–8. King Nimrod is listed as the builder of the tower along with his entourage depicted at the bottom left of the painting." He pointed it out. "There were many artists around that time who painted the Tower in addition to the three we have here."

Verne said, "In all these paintings, the towers look like they are off-center, or just strange."

"The towers are depicted like the Mesopotamian type of step-shaped ziggurat, which is rectangular rather than round." Bartholomew consulted the book and said, "Bruegel uses plenty of technical and mechanical details. By anchoring the building on the rocky slope, he creates the impression of static equilibrium. Someone viewing it would think it was reaching upward into the clouds. However, the building is optically distorted, and on the left side appears to be sunk into the ground." He frowned. "There's more, but you get the idea."

Verne had moved closer, only inches from Hieronymus Bosch's version. "I see faces in the windows."

Kang crossed to the bookshelves and brought back a magnifying glass. As they continued to study and compare the paintings, Nemo talked.

"If you turn the paintings over, you'll see the message Doctor Lazlo left for me, part of it written on each of them. It reads, '*5 longitude* and *38 latitude*.' I believe that points to the cliffs on the south coast of Espania, between Malaga and Almeria."

The magician whistled. They were finally getting down to it and knew the name of Nemo's nemesis.

Bartholomew removed the painting and rotated it to face the strongest light.

Hieronymus Bosch 1552

Lucas van Valckenborch 1595

Bruegel the Elder, 1563

Celwyn agreed with the others. "It seems more than cryptic, sir."

"It does. But I cannot ignore it." Nemo regarded the paintings with a mixture of hate and curiosity.

Into the pregnant silence, the clock behind them intoned a series of bells that repeated and rang like a funeral dirge. It could be the magician's imagination, but he saw the quick look Verne sent the clock, as if he heard the similarity, too.

The Captain said, "Let us not devote our energy and interest toward this until we have successfully delivered the prisoners. That will take all our time and attention."

"I agree." Valentine nodded. The others joined in.

The automat eyed Bartholomew with speculation. "I'm not going to ask if you over-extended yourself today with your wound. I can see it in your face."

Celwyn covered the big man with something to relax his muscles and block any achiness. "Better?"

Bartholomew opened his eyes at the change. "Much, thank you." To Kang, he said, "I will retire and rest, I assure you. It has been a long day." He clapped the automat's shoulder.

Kang replied, "Good. Before you go, perhaps we can hear a bedtime story." Nemo and the others stared until, one by one, they developed grins. "Jonas promised to tell us about Captain Unmann. I'm sure it will be entertaining."

Nemo's eyes twinkled. "I admit, I am curious."

"As am I." Verne pretended to uncap his pen, and Bartholomew giggled.

Valentine poured another glass of wine. "I simply can't sleep until I hear this."

The magician sighed all the way to his boots. Not because of what he would tell them, but because they would surely enjoy it so much.

He raised his gaze to theirs. "Oh, for God's sake. In Seville, twenty years ago, I attended a party hosted by the notorious Lord Sathos. At the time, I was not as ... discriminating, or careful, in my romantic liaisons."

Kang started to laugh, and the others did too.

"Such things happen," Valentine told him. "However, usually a man of the world learns discretion, does he not?" The vampire asked with assumed self-righteousness. "Did you use your real name?"

"No—" Celwyn shuddered.

The laughter increased until the magician said, "I can't finish the story until you quit that, Xiau." He waited on Xiau's and Bartholomew's riotous guffaws. "Thank you. To go on, I was caught by a much younger Captain Unmann in an intimate situation with the host's wife, Lady Sathos."

In the resulting uproar, Celwyn thought the automat would fall off the sofa, he laughed so hard. With as much dignity as he could muster, the magician executed a full sweeping bow to his audience and marched out. If Wye made an appearance during the night, he'd best be on his good behavior.

Chapter 57

AFTER BREAKFAST, GRANGER accompanied everyone across the bay to Dearing's compound. All except Verne, who preferred to work on his book, and the vampire who agreed that the hostages would be nervous if he went along.

During the night, Celwyn had quietly moved the fully rigged *Cazadore* back to the dock. He'd also sent the debris from the sunken ships and the bodies of the pirates far out to sea. It wouldn't do if the hostages discovered a burned or headless corpse bobbing against the dock. In some instances, they might cheer. For others, it would be traumatic.

Yesterday, Granger mentioned the *Cazadore* appeared sea-worthy, and that they hoped to find new canvasses for her in the storage sheds. The Lieutenant also reported that at greater than 250 feet long, and with a beam of about thirty-five feet, the ship would sleep about two hundred in the crew quarters. They planned to convert the rest of the hold into more beds. With help from Nemo's crew, the hostages would build the bunks.

The magician had seen enough of the ship to confirm its filthiness matched everything else Dearing touched. By the time he'd moved it across the bay, his magic had swept the vessel clean from top to bottom, without a witness. No one from the island could see that far in the dark.

And now, as their skiff docked in her shadow, the magician studied the *Cazadore*. In the clear morning light, the air immediately seemed colder. He asked Granger, "Are the hostages able to help us with the preparations?"

"I would say so." While they prepared to disembark, he said, "We'll ask them to collect as much of the fruit here as possible, now that a bunch of sadistic bastards aren't standing over them to keep them cowed. The stronger ones can gather wood or chop trees for the bunks. There is also small game in the brush that could be dressed for the ship's larder. Our chef has enlisted a regular army to bake enough bread for the trip."

"I saw those make-shift ovens on the beach. However, I doubt Mr. Soriano left much of the game," Bartholomew said as they helped the crew unload boxes onto the pier. "Of course, they'll continue to use the fishing operations Jonas set up."

Kang said, "If Valentine still needs to gather his type of food, I'll ask him to do his hunting on the other islands."

They headed up the dock toward the beach. With the weight of Bartholomew and Granger, the dock swayed, and seawater flooded over the top of it.

"I do worry about one thing, though." The big man frowned and leapt across the sand into the scraggly weeds. "The hostages are not prepared for colder weather."

They walked around mud and through more weeds. As they approached the storage buildings, they saw a solid line of hostages hauling boxes and bags of their meager belongings there. Celwyn listened, hearing their murmurs, and it sounded so wonderful; they spoke with a measure of excitement and energy. He even detected a few smiles.

With Bartholomew in the lead, they reached the first building and asked for Esther, Unmann, and David. An emancipated man put down the box of rat-eaten shoes he held and raised a shaky finger at the building behind them. When they reached what used to be Dearing's vault, they detoured around the cooking pits to the entrance.

"Did the Captain pick up shoes for them when he brought over supplies?" The magician asked. Granger nodded.

David greeted them from behind a row of crates, which had become a large table of sorts. Sitting beside him, Esther wrote in a journal, taking down the whispers from the nervous woman in front of her.

The woman appeared of average height, not young or old, with wild, darting eyes. Sections of her hair had been torn out, leaving angry welts on her scalp. Esther asked a question, and the woman screamed obscenities, staggered, and tried to pull more of her matted hair out before lurching past the magician and out the door. As she went by, Celwyn caught the faint aura of witch about her. He stepped outside long enough to cover her in a measure of calmness and strongly, but silently, suggested that she find her bed and rest.

Esther reached his side and said, "Excuse me, please, while I find someone to watch her."

When she returned, the magician addressed them. "We would like to speak with you, David, and Captain Unmann. Could you locate Unmann for us, please?"

She peered at the huts. "He will come here as soon as he finishes talking to those men." As they watched, her prediction came true. Unmann stepped inside and leered at Celwyn, who ignored it and rejoined the others. One of these days, he would show the man his displeasure, but not now.

After they had settled Esther in the only chair, Kang began speaking. His voice echoed in the nearly empty chamber where hundreds of paintings had once been.

"You have set up this building to dispense information and help everyone?" The automat indicated the boxes of clothes and a tub filled with paper and pencils.

David said, "Yes. They know to come here. It helps everyone to either write down what happened to them, or talk about how they feel, or do it for someone who cannot write."

Celwyn lifted a bag from beside his feet that hadn't been there before. "We found boxes of pencils and some pipes and tobacco for those who use it." He told Esther, "We have soaps for the women to add to their bathing room."

"Thank you." Esther's eyes filled with emotion. "And for all the food you have provided." Her voice wavered with emotion, and her tears fell.

It demoralized Bartholomew to see her cry. He patted her shoulder and said gruffly, "Do not thank us, please. We will do more." He looked at the magician for help. "That is why we're here."

"It is. And things will be better each day," the magician promised her.

Captain Unmann eyed Bartholomew, not kindly, and said, "Why *are* all of you here? What—"

"We have information for you," Celwyn interrupted in a tone that could be interpreted as a warning. Unmann met his gaze, and then he dropped his eyes to the floor. Celwyn nodded at Bartholomew.

The big man continued, his deep voice calm and soothing, "Winter will be upon us soon, and you want to go home. We have a way for you to do so."

David leapt to his feet and gripped his arm. "Please! Tell us!"

"Yes, please." Esther's tears fell anew. "Everyone asks every day, all day long, what will happen to them. What is next?"

Kang took over. "Have you seen the big ship in the harbor?"

David said, "Yes ... we can see the top of it from here. It belonged to the pirates."

"The *Cazadore*," Captain Unmann said. "Why was it spared?" He regarded Kang, and then the magician, not knowing which to suspect, or of what.

Kang lied as smoothly as if he did it every day, "We do not know, however, we plan to use it to take all of you to Hong Kong."

"Hong Kong," David echoed and clenched his fists when his hands started to shake.

Bartholomew said, "Yes. The British authorities there are best equipped to transport you home to the four corners of the earth. And those—" he tapped the pile of journals that had already been filled, "—will be very helpful."

"But, how?" Esther whispered. In her profile and manner, Celwyn saw the same kind of beauty of soul and kindness he had encountered in nunneries.

Granger spoke up. "We will provide about fifty crewmen to work the ship with the same amount from your ranks. That is barely enough. If you have people who are strong enough to help, it would be better." An excited murmur rippled across the score of hostages who had arrived behind them. "We will retrofit the ship to sleep all of you." When Granger saw Unmann's raised brows, he added with solid conviction and authority, "It will work." Celwyn had noticed the Lieutenant did not put up with much, and he loved it. "We'll teach your volunteers what to do to keep the ship running smoothly at full sail."

"The journey will take about six days," Kang said.

"Six days?" David repeated, half in the hope they would go home and half in fear. As they'd discussed, when the moment came for the prisoners to board the ship, it would be stressful for some of them.

Bartholomew saw his reaction, and with the calm gentleness he had displayed so many times recently told the room, "It would take three times as long to go to Hong Kong and convince the British to come to this island. And then wait for them to sail here. After that, it would be days at sea to travel back to the city, anyway."

"We have a list of things you can help with if you approve of our plan." Kang heard the murmurings behind them from the crowd that had grown larger.

David and Esther exchanged a glance. Captain Unmann said, "We will talk with everyone and meet you here again at noon. Will that suffice?"

"Some of the people here are afraid." David watched as dozens of hostages filled the room and surrounded them. "There are those who will not want to go onto a ship again. The rest will be anxious to get away from here. They trust us to a point."

Bartholomew guessed, "But, not beyond that."

"Yes," David agreed. "Each of us," he nodded at Esther and Unmann, "have the trust of a certain amount of the people. And then there are some who will not listen to anyone."

"Because of what they've endured?" Kang asked.

"Yes and no," Esther replied. "Some are ... unsettled, and have been since we've known them."

Celwyn stood tall and kept his voice neutral. "All right. We only ask that you speak with as many as possible. Tell them we leave for Hong Kong in three days and suggest that they go with us. It will be a safe trip. We mean them no harm, and I do not think they will easily survive here after we've gone." He did not have to add that they wanted to leave before any other pirates arrived.

Granger added, "Assure them we will keep them safe against the weather or anyone we meet."

The magician concurred. Little did they know of everything that could be done to protect them.

As they walked back up the path toward the bay, Granger said, "This will be quite an undertaking. It will go better if Unmann understands that I am in charge of the *Cazadore*."

Behind him, Bartholomew swatted away a hanging vine as wide as his leg and said, "He represents a threat to the secrecy surrounding the *Nautilus*; he visits many countries where he could mention the submarine."

They stepped off the path to allow two men hauling a water barrel to pass by. Several small rodents skittered by them and into the thick foliage. When Granger and the others resumed their trek, a collection of parrots voiced their displeasure and retreated into the jungle.

"How can we be sure Captain Unmann understands Granger's status and authority?" the big man asked.

Celwyn stepped onto the sand and the others followed as he headed toward the *Cazadore* where she undulated from side to side in the gentle tide. "I could always scare him into compliance."

"Humorous, Jonas. Another idea. Perhaps you could explore his thoughts when we meet with them later." The automat bent over to study a piece of debris, made a face of distaste, and caught up to them.

"I like that." The big man stretched to his full height and pulled on the ropes, lowering the long plank that allowed access to the ship. As they climbed up the steep incline, he noted, "Some of the hostages will need help getting onto the ship."

Kang scampered onto the deck, and the others joined him. With amazement, he asked, "Did you clean this, Jonas?"

"Yes. I rid the ship of broken bottles, dead rats, and other things I do not care to describe. Pirates are filthy. Apparently, it is a job requirement."

"We can assume that the hostages can't see up here and that they may not remember the cleanliness habits of the pirates... a spot of magic will not be detected," Bartholomew mused as he opened and shut bins on the foredeck. On each side of them, the brass shone, and the wood underfoot had been sanded and waxed. Piles of new stays and lines lay coiled in regulation manner by the masts.

As Celwyn explored, Granger shaded his eyes and glanced upward. "This will save us countless hours. I hope there are enough canvases in storage." He climbed a few feet up the nearest mast and inspected the sail. "These are not exactly new."

The magician shrugged. "If not, I will provide them. I suggest, though, that the hostages see the canvasses being fitted onto the masts."

"Why?" the big man asked. "Ah… so, they will have confidence in the ship."

Granger nodded at his surmise, and they moved to the accommodations under the bridge. Here too, the conditions had been greatly improved. Celwyn had also added soft blankets and toiletries to each cabin, saying, "The women will be staying here."

"Yes." Granger entered a cabin and measured it with his eyes. "They'll be packed in here, too. I'll add bunk beds, too." He backed out again and swung up the iron steps to the bridge with the others close behind. As they watched, he checked the instruments and spun the wheel. "We'll have to bring a few things over. Including lanterns for here, and for their quarters."

Kang had found a bin of maps and rooted in it like a terrier hunting a bone. "These could prove interesting."

"I'm sure," Celwyn said fondly.

"Let's take a look at the galley." Granger consulted his watch. "We have another half hour before we meet with David and the others to hear what they decided."

Celwyn bowed before the steps leading down to the deck. "After you."

As they headed toward the stern, Granger eyed the magician. "If you sent the pallets of dry goods aboard after dark, I believe it will not be noticed how you did it."

"It will be done." Celwyn led the way into the galley. They wouldn't eat for a week if they knew what he'd cleaned out of the galley. "Would you like some equipment for cleaning fish?"

They moved to stand in front of the stoves in the galley. Granger rubbed his chin. "Yes. Can you duplicate the galley again, right here?" He pointed. "What we have isn't big enough. Oh—" He jumped back, as did the others, when a new galley appeared next to the other one. Only inches away, the mizzenmast cast a shadow over everything.

"Err, thank you." Granger blinked and then continued, "I must remember to have them chop a big pile of wood for the stoves. We are fortunate too; there are two hostages who were employed as cooks on the ships they sailed upon."

"I can uproot and bundle a few trees for your crew to find and bring back here to chop up," Celwyn said.

"That will work well. All the food activities should be located mid-deck, as far away from the other masts as much as possible because of the waves and any wind we run into. It is going to be damned crowded most of the time." Granger's frown deepened.

The automat noted, "They'll have to eat in shifts."

As they walked by the long building, a faint aroma from last night's cooking pits reached them. Wearing encouraging smiles, they stepped around a cluster of hostages and went inside. Celwyn counted dozens more, now standing behind Esther, David, and Captain Unmann. Their faces displayed fear, not hostility. The magician considered that a step forward; fear could be more readily dissuaded or distracted.

Beyond them, the unstable woman from their last visit lay rolled into a ball on a pile of clothing and moaned to herself. Drool dribbled off her chin. By the time the automat began speaking, Celwyn had put her into a peaceful sleep.

"Good afternoon." The Professor bowed. "I hope you have had time to talk."

Esther answered, "Yes. I have been asked to present you with some questions."

"Please proceed," Kang said. "We know this is a big step."

"All right. How will we sleep on the ship? There are over five hundred of us."

"The women and children will sleep in the cabins on deck," Granger told them. "If any of you are able, we ask that they help us build more bunks in the hold."

"We can do that, guv'nor!" One of their audience called out. A few of the hostages nodded. The rest still wore their worry.

"Thank you." Esther asked, "You said you would be able to feed all of us. How is that possible?"

"We have brought over the crops from the other islands," Kang announced. "You'll also have fish you catch before we sail, and any fruit you gather from the jungle. The ship will have large nets too, capable of catching hundreds of fish per day."

Bartholomew said, "There will be a great deal of fruit needed, and we request that you immediately begin gathering it from the jungle—we will send armed crewmen with you to be sure the boars do not attack you, and guard against quicksand or other dangers."

One of the men behind David called out, "We lost people who went into the jungle. They were shot when they got back."

"Pass the word please; the pirates are gone, and we will be sure you are safe." The big man told them with steady confidence. "Also, please begin filling water barrels from the springs there." Bartholomew nodded to Granger to take over.

"When we depart, there will be enough provisions for better than a fortnight." Granger added, "We will not run out."

Esther and David conferred. Bartholomew waited and then said, "As you can see, we need your help on several fronts before the ship sails."

Behind Unmann, a skeletal man with an unruly head of red hair asked in a thick Irish brogue, "What if we're attacked, laddie?"

"My men know how to use the guns on the ship." Granger patted the pistol on his belt. "And we will be armed. If any of you are qualified with firearms, we can arm you too in the event of an attack."

In more ways than one, Celwyn thought. He faced Unmann and entered his mind. Once there, he did not find it an unpleasant experience. The man's thoughts had a high degree of organization. The magician backed out again and checked several of the others, finding nothing of note except the various degrees of fear he expected. Most of them had only one thing on their minds; they wanted to return to London, to Siam, to India, to America, and further away.

The magician said, "Please tell the others; we will take you to Hong Kong so that you *can* go home. The British governing body is trained for situations like this. For those of you who are afraid to be at sea again, we understand. There is a good chance that land transportation from Hong Kong can be arranged. We," the magician gestured to Kang and Bartholomew, "traveled by train from this area across several continents to Persia, India, and further west a few years ago." Celwyn maintained a smile and his encouraging demeanor. If they knew what all had happened along that journey, they might prefer a leaky ship.

The Professor asked Esther, "Do you have other concerns?"

She shook her head. Many of the others did the same. "They are ready to go home. Everyone is."

"We'll get started on gathering the fruit and water now." David stood.

Captain Unmann said, "I'll organize the men and send them over to begin chopping wood for the new bunks." He regarded Granger. "Will that do?"

The Lieutenant nodded. "Our crew will help you."

As they motored back across the bay, Celwyn told Granger, "You won't have a problem with Unmann. I suggested something to him. Anonymously." The magician grinned to himself. "He believes your men will only obey you, and he knows he doesn't have enough trained men to sail without you."

"Excellent," Granger said.

Bartholomew dipped a hand in the water and shook it off again. "A bit chilly. Let's hope things do not get colder before we deliver the *Cazadore*."

"Agreed. Thank you, Jonas, for taking care of Unmann," the Professor said. "That is another hurdle we have surmounted."

"We're actually going to pull this off." Bartholomew's smile rivaled the sun's brightness.

Granger agreed. "I have confidence also. My men will be on the ship at dawn to begin assembling the bunks."

A light shower accompanied them, beating a staccato on their hats. Celwyn decided they could tough it out the last hundred feet or so to the ship. "I will have this evening's fish ready soon. Maya maya, bangus, and tilapia. A change from last night." The shower became rain, and with a grumble, he added a canvas over them anyhow. "There is enough corn and bread ready to go with it, and I understand our chef has prepared puddings for the hostages. Tonight, they will have dessert."

He had lost his anger over what had happened to the hostages and instead celebrated each thing that helped them. One at a time.

Chapter 58

OVER THE NEXT TWO DAYS, EVERY able-bodied man and woman worked non-stop to prepare the ship and load supplies. Such was life without using magic. During the day, Nemo took the *Nautilus* to Manat for supplies for both the submarine and for the impending voyage of the *Cazadore*. By request, he brought back additional warm clothing and shoes in various sizes. He also found bushels of bedding.

When he returned, Nemo requested that Celwyn transfer the new supplies to the ship that night, while the hostages enjoyed their dinner. They might think an aquatic St. Nick had visited but would be told Granger's crew had delivered everything.

Bartholomew and a few of the crew had spent the rest of the day hunting on the other islands with Valentine. They found ducks, buttonquails, grouse, and a real find had been a field of wild squash.

Already the evening fire pits had been lit, and they spotted dozens of hostages gathered in front of the buildings as their skiff neared shore.

The Professor had elected to return to the island with them, partly because he wanted to participate, and partly for another reason. Before they docked, he explained, "I need to assess which of the hostages would refuse to sail away from here, and which need more attention because of their fears and physical condition. We need to figure out how to persuade them to go with us." He studied the island as the spray from their boat blossomed on each side, misting their faces. "There is also helping that woman you had to calm down this morning."

"Yes. She appears seriously disturbed by all of this." Celwyn eyed the big man and plowed ahead with what he had to say; they would have to hear it, anyway. "You realize that she is also a witch? Not too active using it, though. From my visits in her thoughts, I found she has been having trouble for a long time, and I fear for her safety."

The automat asked, "Is Esther aware of this?"

"That she is a witch? Possibly. Esther thinks that a greater concern is that the woman will harm herself if not watched all the time."

Both Kang and the big man grew silent for several minutes, the only sound was the purr of their engine and the slap of the waves against the side of the boat. They both remembered Telly's suicide in Prague. Celwyn concentrated on Nemo's small boats that followed in their wake; one tillered by Granger and one filled entirely with fish.

After Bartholomew stopped blinking his nervousness about the witch, and Kang's sadness lifted, the magician continued, "During the day, while she is at sea, I plan to stay with the *Cazadore*. Incognito, of course. I can help keep an eye on the witch and anyone else who is in distress."

Kang said, "That would help."

As their boat slowed and bumped into the side of the dock, they heard rifle shots in the distance signaling the game hunting continued. Bartholomew leapt onto the boards to secure the ropes, and the automat ran to the end of the dock and brought back a cart. He whirled and headed off again. "If you'll excuse me, I want to talk with the hostages."

Before he'd taken two steps, Celwyn put a hand on his arm.

"Wait until this cart is full, and I will go with you. Frightened people are unpredictable, and you can't go alone."

"You fuss too much."

They traded a fond look. "As if you don't." The magician laughed and began unloading baskets of bread.

Chapter 59

November 1870

S HORTLY AFTER DAWN, THE *CAZADORE* set sail, and with an assist from Celwyn, she drifted into the middle of the bay and pointed her nose west. A brisk wind billowed her canvasses and dozens of men scurried across her deck and up the masts.

Every inch of the ship was occupied. Scores of hostages pressed against the rails, silently watching Dearing's island recede in the early morning mist. A few cried. Others quietly remembered much they wished to forget. A few whooped and hollered, cheering their departure while above them; the other hostages hung off the spars, waving their hats if they had them.

On the bridge, Granger moved briskly from side to side, calling out orders to the men in the rigging. He had positioned Captain Unmann at the wheel.

All appeared well. The magician dove off the top of the crow's nest as a most handsome falcon with red-tipped wings. Although they had tramped through the buildings looking for anyone left behind, it wouldn't hurt to take a last pass by. In a marathon session late last night, Bartholomew had convinced the last of the prisoners to sail away with them.

When Celwyn crossed over the main buildings, he flew low, verifying no one remained besides the scrounging rats. The magician checked the other buildings. Nothing. Just as he swerved to the west, ready to return to the ship, he spied something white moving in the brush on the other side of the treasure building.

Well, well. He'd found a near-naked man, quite old, but still wiry as he scrabbled underneath the thicker brush. The magician landed behind him as himself and waited.

The man couldn't have weighed more than Tara, but unlike her, he had no hair at all, not even a single strand. His wispy beard extended nearly to his navel. At least he wore underwear. When he spotted the magician, he stumbled backward in the dirt with his arms over his head.

"What is your name, sir?"

The old man opened one eye and peeked at him like a suspicious parrot.

"Boris."

"Did you miss the departure, Boris?"

The old man treated him to a toothless grin. "I sure did. Found me the bastards' supply of rum in there." He pointed to the long building.

"I assume you would like to join the others?"

"Yes." A tear dribbled out of the same eye. "But I can't ... too late ..." He stared at the top of the *Cazadore's* sails in the distance.

Time was a-wastin', as the Americans say. Celwyn put the old man to sleep and miniaturized him onto his back before flying away. With luck, Boris would blame the rum for his unexpected good fortune when he woke up on the ship.

For the remainder of the morning, the *Nautilus* followed the heavily laden *Cazadore* from a discreet distance just below the surface. The first time Celwyn landed on Granger's shoulder as an adorable fly, the Lieutenant nearly swatted him off until the magician identified himself. He learned to warn Granger about future arrivals.

Like busy bees with clipboards, David and Esther flitted everywhere with answers for the hostages, most of whom remained at the rails or walked the deck. It became a busy intersection; deckhands collided with the prisoners until Granger asked them to keep the area below the masts clear. He pointed at the chairs and benches installed at the foredeck, along with the assorted books and newspapers that Nemo had brought back from Manat. From the way they eagerly scooped up the books and passed them around, it must have been the first printed matter the hostages had seen in a long time.

Celwyn returned to Granger's shoulder and whispered, "The sky is clear, and it is not too cold. Do we expect that to last?"

Granger walked to a shadowy corner of the bridge, away from the others, and spoke.

"Until tomorrow, from what we can tell. The passengers should enjoy the warmth today. It will only become colder the further north we travel."

"Their leaders should know so they can hand out the blankets in an orderly fashion."

"I will tell them." His attention centered on the mizzenmast and, with a frown, he asked, "Is there more?"

"It nears luncheon, and I'm going back to the *Nautilus*. Any messages?" Celwyn hovered in the shadows beside him.

"Yes." Granger stifled a curse. "I don't know how we missed it, but we need to get rid of the pirate flag we're flying. It could get us shot at in the Hong Kong harbor, or even before then."

Celwyn agreed. "Excellent point. I'll ask Nemo for a replacement. If he doesn't have one, I'll still remove what is up there after dark."

"Good. Excuse me." Granger strode to the rail of the bridge and called out orders. Creaking came from above as the foremast rotated and the canvasses flapped their approval in the growing breeze.

The magician held on to Granger's collar while the wind tried to slap him off. "I'll see you later, then."

Granger nodded as Celwyn flew across the deck and over the hostages as they set out tables of food. So many hostages helped with the food—they outnumbered those eating. That reminded him. On his way back to the *Nautilus*, he needed to begin putting quantities of fish into the nets the ship towed.

Chapter 60

J UST AFTER EIGHT THAT NIGHT, Celwyn landed on the *Cazadore* where she lay at anchor. All seemed well. With full bellies, laughter, and smiles of hope, a measure of tentative happiness hung in the air.

Under a dense sky, the dark water of the Sulu Sea extended forever, increasing the feeling the ship sailed in a world all alone. Singing rang across the deck, and the magician resisted the urge to provide music for them. Xiau would complain that it couldn't be explained. Which was true.

Celwyn had opted for the guise of a small sparrow for his evening flight. When he arrived, he streaked down the stairs and into the hold, noting it seemed so much different from the toxic fumes in the hold of the slave ship. Everything here smelled clean, and the scent of new wood from the rows of bunks overlaid the brininess of the sea only feet away.

The magician ascended topside. With the sun taking her bow for the evening, he already felt the cold. The lingering, enticing aroma of roasted corn and fish reminded him of the late hour as he hovered over the cabins on deck. Twenty-five women and children barely fit into the cabins, and from the open doors, he saw so many bunks inside, they would have to climb over the beds to sleep. Even so, they would feel a measure of comfort and security at having their own quarters.

Esther sat on a crate outside the last cabin, a half-eaten plate of food on her lap and a pencil in her hand as she wrote in a journal in the fading light. From above her, nineteen bells rang out from the bridge. After a silent suggestion from Celwyn, a crewman lit the gimbals over the map tables, giving Esther extra light.

All seemed well. He left them and once again found the submarine where he waited in front of the periscope and pecked the lens until the crew let him back in.

On the *Nautilus,* a much smaller group sat down for dinner. Over a platter of roasted quail, courtesy of Bartholomew's hunting skills, and grilled angelfish in a sweet mango sauce, they relaxed after a long day. With an excellent salad, their talk centered on the success of the voyage so far.

From his place on Celwyn's right, Verne asked questions about the freed hostages. The Professor related what he could with contributions from the others.

"There are probably at least a dozen hostages in poor psychological condition and beyond my scope of expertise," Kang told them. "Another sixty of them are not doing well physically, even with more food and improved conditions. The sooner they reach the doctors in Hong Kong, the better. Many need surgery to properly set broken bones."

"There is one woman who is especially not well. Her name is Missy," Bartholomew said.

Kang put down his fork and sighed. "She is the hostage most seriously affected by psychological problems. There are always two other women watching her."

"What about the others?" Verne asked as he caught the eye of a crewman for another helping of quail.

The automat shrugged. "There are scores of them so weak they had to be carried aboard."

"At least we cut off the head of the snake and all its tendrils, Gentlemen," Valentine announced and drank off his wine. No one disagreed with his vivid description and probably wondered if it was a literal description of Dearing's fate.

The magician cleared his throat. "Getting back to Missy—you suspect she will take her own life, and that is why she is watched." Celwyn made it a statement, not a question.

"Yes." Kang nodded.

Bartholomew said, "She isn't the only one who might do so, but is the most likely."

Nemo sat back while the crew removed his plate and poured coffee. "Tomorrow we'll encounter a storm. We've observed it, and the clouds on the eastern horizon indicate it is heading this way."

"Will the passengers be all right?" Valentine asked.

Nemo sipped his coffee and said, "If it is a direct hit, most of the passengers will stay in the hold, at Granger's request. The pumps are in good order. Either the cabin doors on the main deck will be nailed shut, or the women will be herded into the salon. Granger will decide." He regarded the magician. "I assume you will help without them seeing you do so."

Celwyn steepled his hands. "Correct. The *Cazadore* will weather that storm, one way or another."

Verne waited until everyone had taken a bite of their dessert, and said, "I love chocolate."

"So does Xiau." Celwyn eyed the automat. "Especially in the form of cookies."

"Pfft." Kang told the table, "After the hostages reach safety, I look forward to sending letters to Elizabeth and everyone at Tellyhouse. We'll have to wait until Singapore for answers to our earlier messages."

Celwyn said, "Did you know my father regularly took trips to Singapore? Before he went insane, of course."

"That is interesting." Verne's face lit up with interest and he uncapped his fountain pen.

Nemo regarded Celwyn with a measure of pity before saying, "Most likely, we'll stay in the city for at least a few days." He glanced at Bartholomew and Kang as he sampled his cake.

"Excellent." Kang's eyes lost their spark and took on the kind of melancholy Celwyn rarely saw. "I miss Elizabeth very much."

There was a solution to that. While the magician decided how to leave the automat behind in Prague the next time they ventured abroad, Qing hopped on to the ledge below the aquatic window and fluffed his metallic feathers, the sound like metallic wind chimes. Outside the glass, the water had darkened when night fell, and little could be seen. The bird pecked the glass in irritation.

"Captain," Celwyn asked, "could you talk about security on the *Cazadore*, please? I hate to suggest it, but Dearing's supply ship could still be out there and may begin tracking us."

Bartholomew said, "From what I heard, Dearing's rivals avoided the Sulu Islands, which is good news."

"We are about eight hundred feet behind the ship." Nemo dabbed his lips with his napkin. "My crew is stationed above us on both platforms. One scans the water, and the other watches for a signal from the ship. There will be someone in the crow's nest of the *Cazadore* all night."

"Thereby able to see beyond any fog or mist," the big man concluded.

Nemo picked at the crumbs on his cake plate and eyed the others. "I see I am the last to finish my cake. Shall we adjourn?"

Valentine said, "Perhaps we can discuss your plans beyond Hong Kong, Captain? Although I owe you a great debt for your help with Miss Redifer, I believe my usefulness to you has come to an end for now."

As they stood by and watched the crew disassemble the table, Nemo said, "Perhaps not. However, I would like to talk with everyone later this evening. Excuse me, I have duties on the bridge. Even more so without Granger." He bowed and marched out.

Chapter 61

WHENEVER HE HELPED THOSE IN need, Celwyn always felt a sense of pride. Over the last few days, they had successfully moved a mountain of people. Soon, the hostages would rejoin their families. God damn those pirates—they shouldn't have had to go through this.

When the clock chimed the eleven o'clock hour, Kang put down his book and motioned to Bartholomew to join him at the table for their evening bridge game. Verne sat nearby and moved too slowly to beat Valentine to the other vacant chair. Which was just as well. Nemo returned a salute and crossed the room to the game table. Everyone knew which chair he preferred. With a shrug, Verne went back to writing in his notebook, and Qing edged closer to his fountain pen.

All seemed well.

Normal.

When the magician felt his skin twitch and his nerves come alive, he left the sofa to stand in front of the aquatic window. The seawater looked opaque, and the reflection of the room was like a mirror of it. He removed the reflection so he could see outside.

"Captain? Is there a full moon tonight?" As Celwyn asked, he noted that they floated on top of the water, and the muted sparkle from the stars decorated the surface. The sea glowed under an intense and beautiful silvery sheen.

"Yes. Almost full." He eyed Celwyn. "Why?"

The magician studied the sea below them, unable to see through the depths to the floor, and concluded that the sea must be deep here. If so, the *Cazadore* with its much bigger draft and weight, would have had to use a wind anchor to sit still. While the surface remained glassy, the current barely undulated against the hull of the *Nautilus*. He shivered, and it seemed like a cold hand wiggled its way down his spine.

"Just a premonition, perhaps it is nothing—"

Gongs resounded from the belly of the ship, and the lights blinked. Captain Nemo shot out of his chair on the run and called back, "Trust your premonitions—"

The iron eyelid outside the window closed, interlocking into itself.

Verne looked up. "That only happens when the Captain expects to do battle." He grabbed his pen away from Qing. "I suggest we all find a good position and hang on." As the author spoke, Valentine made himself comfortable and waved a hand at

Kang, Celwyn, and Bartholomew as they headed toward the hall.

When they entered the bridge, they ducked to the side, hoping to keep out of the way. Celwyn addressed Nemo.

"Captain, would you mind letting me out before you dive, please? I will block what the hostages see and hear."

"Certainly." He gestured to a nearby crewman, and Celwyn trotted out again.

As he climbed the spiral stairs, Kang caught up to him and tugged on the cuff of his trousers. "Nemo says there is a large ship about a mile to the south coming this way. It is traveling silently and without lights."

Celwyn nodded and pushed the hatch open. Before he had flown a dozen feet, the *Nautilus* sank below the waves again.

The magician swerved, climbing high into the night sky and realizing it was damn cold. A playful breeze buffeted him as he lifted the wings of a swallow, all the better to blend into the darkness. He flew at an unnatural speed toward the huge shadow materializing out of the fog.

The ship could have been a sister to the *Cazadore*, a three-hundred-footer with dozens of guns spread across both sides of her deck. In case one of the hundreds of pirates on her became anxious, the first thing the magician did was plug every one of her cannons. He circled her masts, dipping low across the desk, and hearing whispered conversations about Dearing's missing ships and the empty island.

The whispers also wondered what Dearing would do to them if they did not retrieve the hostages. As Kang had guessed, one of the more nervous pirates confirmed Dearing had indeed already sold many of the hostages as slaves. No wonder they had come after them.

Minutes later, the pirates below him grew excited. They had seen the *Cazadore*. In the distance, her lights twinkled in innocence, reminding him of the magician of her precious cargo, and how much they needed to be protected. He had heard enough from these bastards. Like the rest of Dearing's lot, they were just as bloodthirsty and deserved what Nemo had planned.

Before they could move any closer to their prey, he locked the tiller on their ship. Instead of sneaking up on the *Cazadore,* the bastards soon found themselves drifting away from their intended target. It did not take long for the pirates to react with whispered and frantic cursing. When he propelled the ship a bit faster away from their target, their curses increased.

The magician streaked across the waves to the *Cazadore's* bridge, searching for Granger. It took nearly three passes around the deck until he found him climbing down the mizzenmast. Celwyn hovered in front of him and said, "Pirates. Do you see their ship?"

Granger almost lost his grip on the mast. When he could speak, he said, "Yes."

"Nemo is getting ready to sink her. I've disabled their guns and made sure she is heading away from you."

Granger jumped the last few feet to the deck. "That will work. But it will still be loud."

With as light of a touch as he could manage, Celwyn landed on his shoulder; a moment to rest. "I will block the sound. Did you tell the passengers to go below?"

"Already did. But Unmann won't leave the bridge."

A dozen of the hostages passed by, heading to the hold. A few hurried toward them from the aft end of the ship. The magician's laugh sounded a bit strange on the near-empty deck. "He will."

Celwyn gave Unmann a simple and uncontrollable urge to sleep in his bunk in the hold.

As Unmann yawned and descended the steps to go below, Celwyn ascended to the top of the main-mast to perch on top of the crow's nest. Except for Granger and his crew, few passengers remained on deck and none on the bridge. The magician made sure the women had gone into the salon and sent anyone remaining on deck a strong suggestion that they needed to join the poker game in the hold.

He spied one holdout. Boris.

The old man had found another bottle and had curled up in between the bulkheads. This time, he wore clothes. Granger's crew ran by, not seeing him. Celwyn decided to leave the old rascal where he hid. Would anyone believe him if he said he heard something unusual?

It did not take long. From several miles to the east came a loud grinding and even louder rendering. Faint shouts carried across the water. Then another loud concussion. The fog had cleared, and the moonlight grew stronger. When Celwyn spotted the bow of the pirate ship, it pointed to the stars above. A second later, the ship slipped beneath the waves.

Chapter 62

AFTERWARD, WHEN THE PASSENGERS emerged from the cabins and the hold, the magician searched for Granger. As he flew across the foredeck, he verified no one had heard the destruction of the other ship. Celwyn found Granger alone on the bridge and landed on the map Nemo's lieutenant studied.

"It is done," Granger said.

"We shouldn't have any further trouble from pirates before Hong Kong. From their conversations, I confirmed that ship sailed alone. We've finally wiped out Dearing's operations. Anything else before I leave for the evening?" Celwyn asked.

Granger checked the glassy sea. He relaxed and shook his head.

A chilling scream sailed across the *Cazadore's* deck like a bird on fire. They rushed to the side in time to see several of the women and Esther gesturing and hovering under the canvasses as scores of hostages poured up from the hold and dozens more rushed to them.

Two-thirds of the way up the mainmast—a good two-hundred feet or higher—the unstable woman, Missy, extended an arm as she scrabbled off the mast and onto a spar. The canvasses had been furled for the night, and their lines hung loose like puppet strings, swaying from side to side as the sea rocked the ship. Even from this far below, the magician could see the woman's hands shaking as she edged further out along the spar until she stopped, crouching high above the dark water. In the stunned silence, she crooned incoherently to herself.

Celwyn faded back into the shadows of the bridge, saying, "I will handle this." He felt a growing sense of guilt; he should have done something before now.

When the magician landed next to her hand, Missy didn't flinch. She gazed at him with the intense inward stare only the insane understood. Underneath them, waves lapped in rhythm, glistening in the moonlight. The woman gurgled, and drool dripped off her chin as she took one of her hands off the spar.

Celwyn could not keep her from falling without resorting to magic that everyone would see—if they saw a bird holding her up, there would be an even greater reaction. By now, every hostage and most of Granger's men clustered below them. A few of the crew started climbing the mast until Granger called them off. Celwyn took that as a sign of confidence in his abilities.

The audience's murmurs rose as the woman wobbled and stood upright on the spar.

"...of me ...me." She eyed Celwyn. "You ain't a bird." She watched him with a circus smile. "I know things," she whispered. "Know things ..."

Missy gazed at the sea—and the magician realized her intent as clear as day.

"Look at me." Celwyn made it a command.

"What are you?" Missy whispered, "What—"

"A magician," Celwyn told her. "It is time for you to come down."

She shook her head. "No. I can fly too. I can..." She raised her arms wide, and the murmurs in the crowd on the deck swelled.

"Are you a witch?" Celwyn asked her.

An icy wind blew between them. She tilted her head coquettishly. "I used to be."

"Could you fly then?"

"No." She swayed over the water and back. "No."

"I will help you fly if you promise you won't come up here again."

A shy expression crinkled her face, and her hair blew in wild circles around her. "Would you?" She leaned over the water once again, trying to see further. Her tears began slowly, like the birth of a small stream. With a sob, she gripped a line, then let it go again.

"We have a deal, do we not?" Celwyn asked her.

She tried to nod through the misery in her mind.

"Here we go." As gently as he could, Celwyn miniaturized her and put her on his back. At the same time, a full-size effigy of Missy, complete with the same billowing white dress, edged her way off the spar, scooting back toward the mast.

"Hold on," he told her as he took his time floating in and out of the canvasses and soaring over the water. All the while, the effigy climbed down the mast to the cheers of the crowd below. By the time the effigy reached the deck, Missy had been returned to them, replacing the effigy. She still wept, but was at peace.

As Celwyn flew away, he reminded her to remember their agreement.

After sinking the pirate ship, the *Nautilus* surfaced to perform her maintenance. When the magician walked into the study, the aquatic window remained closed, most likely because the bodies of dead pirates still drifted by like colorful toys in a morbid bathtub.

He beheld a cozy scene. Valentine and Bartholomew played chess while exchanging opinions about Stuart Robson's performance in *The Forty Thieves*. While in Rome, Valentine had seen Edwin Booth's run of *An Ardent Heart*, and he posited that Booth's skills could be comedic too. The big man disagreed as he gave his captured rook a sad look. Or ... his reaction could be part of his strategy. Everyone aboard took their chess games quite seriously.

"Where is Jules?" Celwyn asked.

Kang raised his nose over the top of a book. "In his room writing. He said we were too distracting.

"Ha!" Celwyn laughed and regarded him. "You might be, I'm not. Do you think there is any laudanum, or something similar, in sickbay?"

"Possibly. Why?" the automat asked.

Celwyn told them about the situation on the mast, his flight with Missy, and why the drug might help. "There is no telling if she won't be successful next time." When he got to the part about the effigy, Bartholomew clamped his lips together and went back to his chess game.

"Perhaps we can give her some until the Hong Kong doctors look at her," Kang suggested.

The magician produced a tea service and relaxed on the sofa as the clock chimed the midnight hour. "Will Nemo join us again for bridge, or is it too late?"

The automat shrugged and stuck a finger in his book. "I think so. We haven't seen him since he sunk that ship. It was a horrible noise this time."

"But deserved. Before it was destroyed, I toured their ship and heard the pirates' plans. They talked about taking back the hostages, and not gently. A few discussed punishing them. If the pirates couldn't retrieve the hostages, they planned to sink their ship."

"With all 512 hostages?" Verne asked. "Why?"

"So, they couldn't tell the British where they'd been found, most likely," Kang said. "Or have to explain themselves to Dearing."

Bartholomew asked, "How did they find us?"

"They stopped at the island, then decided where the hostages could go—Singapore or Hong Kong? They also assumed that Dearing's hoard of art must be with them, which was the only reason they hadn't yet fired on the *Cazadore*. A few of them assumed Dearing himself was aboard, and planned to cut them out of their share." The last brought a smile to Kang's face.

"It must be terrible to be a confused villain," the big man said and moved his knight forward.

"Those bastards." Valentine's good humor evaporated. "I am glad there are less of them in the world tonight."

"Agreed … and fewer people will die," Bartholomew said. "They'll never get that hoard back, and Nemo will return the paintings to the museums they came from."

With a self-satisfied yawn, the vampire said, "They may or may not have found remnants of Dearing in the jungle." As he pushed his bishop across the board to sit next to Bartholomew's rook, the others' expressions demonstrated they couldn't help but picture that for a moment.

With a spring in his step, Nemo entered the study. He stopped at the bar first and then settled next to the Professor on a sofa. Bartholomew thanked Valentine for the game, and they adjourned. Everyone exchanged glances—the unspoken sense that Captain Nemo wanted to talk colored the air— and they collectively waited.

"Mr. Soriano, I had said earlier that we would need to confer. We will do so now, and afterwards, you might prefer to stay in Hong Kong or continue with us."

Celwyn sipped his tea. "Sir, will it take the full six days to reach there?"

"Probably not." Nemo shook his head. "It depends on the storm tomorrow." He drained his glass and balanced it on his knee. "It is even possible that we will arrive late on the fourth day."

"How will the *Cazadore* arrive in port, and Granger and his crew return here without the authorities noticing?" Kang asked.

"I wondered about that, too," Valentine said.

Celwyn sent the whiskey bottle to the Captain. After he poured a refill, Nemo said, "By the time the ship reaches Hong Kong, the passengers working on it with my crew will know enough to sail a short distance, especially with Captain Unmann in charge. The *Nautilus* will travel ahead of them and arrive on the lee side of Hadley's Island, about five miles out. Once they arrive there, my crew will use some of the *Cazadore's* lifeboats for the rendezvous." He nodded at the magician. "If a catastrophe hit the ship in the short distance between that point and the harbor, Jonas would be sure they didn't need the boats.

"That sounds most logical," Bartholomew said. "How will the hostages be received?"

Nemo paced to the window and back. "I have given this much thought. For obvious reasons, I cannot introduce the hostages and explain their rescue. Neither can any of you; you are remarkable separately and memorable when seen together.

Whoever presents the hostages needs to be both believable and of enough stature not to be dismissed."

"Captain Unmann," Kang said.

"Exactly," Nemo agreed. "Who better than a hostage himself to explain what happened?"

Celwyn said, "We've been careful not to use our full names. Unmann has not seen this ship. He knew me as a wastrel named Pennyman when we met at that infernal party."

"Let us hope that is enough." Kang frowned. "Of course, the Brits will be busy resettling everyone, and those journals by the hostages will assist them in that." The automat lit a cigar and wiggled the spent match. "Their navy should have no time to spare to look for us."

"Don't put that in the ashtray. Qing digs in there for toys," Celwyn told him.

"Spoiled, spoiled, spoiled." Kang changed the subject. "For the hostages with families, or who have means, resettlement is feasible. Sadly, we've discovered there are many who do not have either."

Nemo spoke with a certain amount of satisfaction, "But we have the information to retrieve Dearing's money and give it to the hostages." He looked at the automat. "Did you keep a copy of their information so we may contact them later?"

"But, of course."

"Excellent," Nemo said. "I'll have my lawyer arrange the transactions. It may take a while to distribute, but shortly after they return home, the hostages should receive a windfall."

Like he expected to be the center of attention, Qing walked across the back of the sofa, stopping to study each of the occupants. He pecked the frame of Verne's spectacles but did not receive a reaction. When he stopped behind Bartholomew, the big man wouldn't turn around, but his eyes bounced, indicating he knew the mechanical bird waited there. One by one, everyone checked to see what Qing would do. The big man couldn't take the suspense anymore and leapt to his feet.

"Come here." Celwyn waited until Qing hopped over to him and rubbed his beak across his chin before saying, "When I next visit the ship, I'll leave temporary funds with Granger for those who will need them. It might help."

Bartholomew deemed it safe enough to sit again and did so with an eye on the mechanical bird. "Has anyone considered what the hostages would say about us? Even if they do not know our names, they'll probably be asked about us, and about the artwork we liberated."

After a few headshakes indicating they did not have an answer, Valentine asked, "Did the hostages actually know about the paintings? There would be no reason for the pirates to tell them." Qing caught a flash from one of the vampire's rings and flew to him, but not too close. Usually, the bird displayed little patience. As they talked, he edged closer to Valentine's hand.

"It is possible someone saw something when the pirates returned to the compound after a raid."

Nemo watched Qing as he studied Valentine. "The risk is minimal."

They drank in silence for several minutes until the Captain spoke. "When we are in Hong Kong, we'll obtain supplies and allow some of my crew leave ashore." He eyed everyone in the room like he wished they were under his orders. With a sigh, he settled for saying, "Your time there should be highly circumspect."

Celwyn laughed. "I hope bookstores and pastry shops are considered discreet."

"I enjoy the city." Valentine stretched. "The theatres are unsurpassed, and the Kunqu operas are worth seeing." He addressed Nemo. "Sir, should I make plans to go to Beirut overland, or?"

"Well." Nemo set his jaw. "Now we get down to it. Excuse me while I fetch Jules, so he can listen to the rest of our discussion." On the way to the door, he glanced back. "If he suggests a game of bridge, do not encourage him. I'm not in the mood for it."

Qing flew to the bookshelves and settled. His eyes still glittered in anticipation; he never gave up.

While they waited for the Captain, Celwyn produced a plate of cookies and put it directly in front of Kang. The automat stared at the plate, suspecting a trick. Bartholomew chuckled and grabbed a cookie. He hadn't taken his second bite before Verne arrived with his notebook and curiosity. When he saw the cookie plate, he picked a spot opposite Kang and helped himself. The automat snuck a look at the magician, just before Nemo rejoined them and began speaking.

"As you all know, according to the clues left in the paintings, my wife's remains should be on the southern Spanish coast."

Several of them had adopted his somberness. Bartholomew asked, "Sir, you mentioned a certain Doctor Lazlo as the source of this information. Would you tell us about him? What can we expect?"

"Will he attack us?" Nemo continued, "It is possible." He leaned back and closed his eyes. When he spoke again, his voice sounded stronger. "For years, I have occupied my time with scientific and archaeological explorations, and correcting political situations that perpetuate evil. Most of the time, my response is to guarantee that the evil cannot grow back."

Celwyn thought that was a fancy, but accurate, way of describing the destruction of pirate ships and the like. He approved.

Qing chose that moment to prove he hadn't forgotten the vampire's rings. He dove off the bookcase and landed on the sofa arm, inches away from the vampire. They were on eye level as the mechanical bird edged forward and clicked his tongue. Valentine gazed at him. Qing stopped clicking and backed up until he fell off the sofa arm. Celwyn suppressed his amusement and opened his collar. The bird hurried to him and burrowed inside. *Smart bird.*

Nemo said, "I and the *Nautilus* are wanted by the British, but they do not know precisely what they are looking for. They have a vague description of this ship, but cannot fathom how it works, or confirm it is real."

"From what I can discover from my contacts," Verne said, "most of the United States Navy is also looking for us. We have been avoiding their territories for the last few years."

Nemo frowned. "I will not be intimidated by them if confronted. Nor any of the Queen's Navy." He growled, "I am afraid of very little, which brings us to Doctor Lazlo."

The echo from the clock's bells seemed loud in the room.

Kang said, "A long time ago, I heard of Lazlo of Vienna. Is it the same man?"

Nemo nodded. "It is. In the 1840s, he was known in the Pontic Mountains of Romania as the 'Butcher of Sfantu.' Then he settled in Vienna. He was a medical man who did more than just medicine."

Celwyn rubbed his chin. "He killed his patients?"

"Worse," Nemo grumbled, the fire in his eyes growing to a blaze. "He experimented upon them first. Lazlo believed in genetic superiority. Also, he studied patients after he infected them with bacteria and disease. The worst part? He believed in the mass killing of races."

Nemo kept his eyes on the aquatic window until he could continue. "Doctor Astrid Nemo worked with him until she couldn't stomach what he did anymore. She tried to leave—" The room waited, and Celwyn could hear Verne breathing like a nervous rabbit beside him. "She escaped for a time." Nemo's eyes watered. "Until he found her."

In the ensuing silence, the sound of Qing chewing on the magician's collar could be heard.

The magician unbuttoned it, and the bird flapped his way to the bar to sit beside the decanters.

"My wife was Lazlo's sister."

That statement stopped the conversation for an even longer time.

"Sir, are you sure she died?" Celwyn asked.

Nemo said, "It has been twenty years without a word. Before these 'clues,'" he gestured to where the paintings had sat, "I had searched everywhere. She would not have left without telling me." He tossed off the rest of his drink. "For years, I paid agents to explore likely locations to find her. Nothing."

The automat guessed, "And then you found the message on the painting."

"Yes. Last year. It was as if Lazlo knew of my efforts and enjoyed torturing me. He also remembered my fondness for Bruegel's art."

Valentine wiggled his empty glass at the magician, and Celwyn sent him another wine bottle. He even uncorked it first. As the vampire poured, he asked, "Captain, does the location pinpointed by the three paintings seem logical to you? Why tell you of it, even indirectly?"

"Perhaps like a cat with a mouse." Bartholomew regarded Nemo. "It is a game. At worst, it would be a deadly trap."

Celwyn stretched and walked to the chess table and back. At times like this, when he wanted to think, he wished they were on land so he could move around, kick a pebble, or cause a thunderstorm.

"At best, you could retrieve your wife's body—" Kang started to say.

Nemo threw his glass against the bookcase. Qing screeched and streaked across the room to dive into Celwyn's open collar. The magician patted his back and sat again.

"Apologize for me, please," Nemo requested.

Celwyn did so, not sure if it was for the bird or the others in the room.

Valentine watched them for a moment and asked, "What is our plan?"

Like the magician, Nemo paced. On his third return trip from the window, he stopped to pick up the glass shards, but the magician had already beaten him to it.

"Calling it 'our plan' may be premature. I don't really have one," Nemo told them. "However, as stated before, after Hong Kong, we will sail south to Singapore. Then we'll retrace our route from a few weeks ago, this time heading west toward Espania."

A faint sheen of perspiration appeared across Bartholomew's forehead. "Err ... the *same* route?"

Kang bestowed a sympathetic glance on him. "The Captain has said we'll assess the Suez Canal again before then."

"Are you all right?" Celwyn asked Qing. The mechanical bird edged his way onto his shoulder and checked the room before flying back to his window. He let out a healthy squawk.

Nemo's frown relaxed when he saw Qing had reverted to normal. "Yes, which brings us to this; you are all welcome to stay in Hong Kong and travel at will. When I hunt Lazlo, I will not expect you to go with me, or request you do, other than to say that

I could use your talents and would welcome your assistance."

Without hesitation, Bartholomew got to his feet. "I speak for myself, Jonas, and Xiau. We are with you."

"Here, here!" Kang held up his cookie.

Verne said, "I am also, of course."

As Xiau pushed the empty cookie plate toward Celwyn, Valentine drank off his wine and stood beside Bartholomew. He slung an arm around the shoulders of the superstitious man who had been so afraid of him months ago.

"I am also with you, but request to be dropped off in Beirut to be with my nieces when this is over." When he removed his arm from Bartholomew's shoulders, the big man kept a jovial expression on his face ... and didn't faint.

"Certainly, that will be arranged," Nemo said. "With this decided, I can finish describing our plan, at least what we have at this point."

Everyone took their seats again, but not before a commotion drew their attention to the bookcases. With a bit of frustration, Qing bashed a frog leg against the books, then tossed it in the air and caught it. When no one congratulated him, he did it again.

"Don't encourage him," Kang remarked.

"As you wish," Nemo said. "The Castell de Ferro is on the southern coast of Spain. It is a fortress built into the cliffs by the Moors. You can assume that it will take us several weeks to journey there." As he spoke, a series of gongs resounded from the belly of the ship. Before they stopped, the clock on the wall began chiming the hour.

"Once we arrive," Nemo addressed Valentine and the magician, "I'll need the unusual and extraordinary talents of you gentlemen to scout the enemy while we plan our actual attack."

Verne crossed to the bookshelves, made a selection, and returned to his seat. "There is a picture of a fortress here. Ah—" He laid the book open for them to see.

Qing landed beside Nemo and pecked at the brass button on his jacket sleeve. Without hesitation, the Captain removed the button and handed it to him. A peace offering, bird style.

"That will be an interesting place to scout." Celwyn raised a brow at the vampire. "If you are going with me, probably the only way inside is to fly."

Valentine frowned at him, trying to determine if the magician was serious. Kang enjoyed his dilemma and then jumped into the discussion. "Sir, what can you tell us of Dr. Lazlo?"

The Captain listened to a set of gongs. He sighed. "It is a fairly long story. Perhaps we can save that for tomorrow evening? I must visit the bridge before retiring." He stood. Qing waited at his feet and dropped the button in front of him.

"Excellent suggestion," the magician stretched. "I must rest too. Hopefully, Wye will keep to himself tonight. You wouldn't believe the racket they make while Qing cleans his scales."

Chapter 63

Hong Kong

THE NEXT DAY, THE EXPECTED STORM blew itself southeast, before heading across the Pacific, and the wind from the storm's perimeter filled the *Cazadore's* sails, propelling her toward the British colony.

Celwyn spent most of the day in the crow's nest of the *Cazadore,* holding on during the stronger gusts. He still felt an obligation to be sure no other ship, whether friend or foe, approached the hostages; a cloud of frailty still surrounded them after their confinement and mistreatment.

By mid-morning, the magician had grown tired of his perch and descended to the bridge. When he landed on Granger's shoulder, he whispered in his ear, "It is teatime. I have some messages from Nemo, and assume you have some information for him also."

Granger had gotten used to the magician's habits and didn't flinch at Celwyn's arrival. Things appeared quiet, and the magician scanned the bridge while two of the ex-hostages conferred with Captain Unmann on the starboard side.

Granger had the wheel and murmured, "Give me five minutes, and I'll meet you in the first mate's cabin. This time of the morning, my bunkmate should be busy on deck. Be sure you avoid the Captain's cabin—the women occupy it."

"Which one is it?" the magician whispered back.

"Right next to the salon. I wouldn't go in the salon either, that is where many of the women have congregated, and they are nervous about most everything." He eyed Celwyn's feathers. "Including odd visitors, sir."

Celwyn chuckled and left the bridge. As he flew into the shadow of the bulkhead, he became a much smaller fly, tiny enough to fit under a cabin door. By the time Granger arrived for their meeting, the magician had reverted back, drank a cup, and poured his second cup, plus one for Granger.

Nemo's lieutenant sat heavily in the only chair and said, "I'm not as young as I once was. Thankfully, this will be over tomorrow."

Celwyn floated a cup across the cabin to him. "Sugar?" At his nod, he sent that over as well. "We arrive tomorrow?"

"Yes." Granger gulped the tea, and the magician sent him another. "We will pass by Hadley Island about ten in the morning, where the crew and I will leave the ship." He spread his hands wide, indicating the width of the ship. "The *Cazadore* will be visible to their Navy before noon."

"I see."

"Could you make about four good-sized lifeboats like the existing ones? If we use yours, and only a few of theirs, to transport ourselves to the island, we can leave most of the originals strapped to the ship for the hostages, and for the Brits to see."

"Yes, it will be done." Celwyn debated whether to make another pot. Perhaps oolong this time, in celebration of their arrival. Or Darjeeling... Such a wonderful quandary over such a pleasant subject.

"There is no chance of the ship sinking during the last few miles, but I would feel better if there were boats for them."

Celwyn said, "I understand. The ones I make will be located next to the stern." He poured. "You've answered Nemo's first question as to whether you need any help with transport. Scone?"

Granger eyed the plate. "I'd better not, I have work to do."

"What will happen when the Brits board this ship?"

"We're flying a white flag, and the women and children will line up on deck along with some men to show them that the ship has civilians and to prevent any accidental shooting. They've elected Unmann to represent them, so there shouldn't be any trouble. Of course, they are not armed."

"I see." Celwyn rubbed his chin as he thought. "So, once we confirm that the Brits have boarded the ship, the *Nautilus* will continue the rest of the way into port?"

"Yes and no." He sighed, either about the task ahead … or just being dead-dog tired. "We will turn north to the headlands. It is a few miles from there into town." Granger stood and stretched. "What did you say to that disturbed woman on the spar last night?"

"I talked to her and gave her the flight she wanted."

Granger's frown became one of confusion. "That wasn't her climbing down the mast, was it?"

"No."

"I figured. It won't happen again. I have men stationed at the base of each of the masts." Granger said, "Don't tell me any more about it, I don't want to know how you did it." He smiled readily, unlike the taciturn Nemo. "Anyhow, is there anything else I should know right now?"

Celwyn got to his feet as well. "The Captain asked if you need anything."

"Nothing needed." Grangers stared out the porthole. "The hostages who are helping sail this tub are trained enough to do it by themselves for a couple of hours. Unmann is asking why we are getting off the ship."

"What did you tell him?"

"That the island was our base, and we preferred not to deal with the British Navy."

"Sounds logical. He's a man of the world, and knows there are other forces besides official ones out there, and other operations, such as what he probably thinks ours consists of."

Steps sounded as several men quick-stepped by the cabins. Granger's attention became divided.

"You'd think so, but Unmann has said he doesn't believe me." He shrugged. "I need to get back to the bridge."

He stopped at the door. "The fish delivery is working well, and tell the Captain there is plenty of water and food."

"I will."

The magician flew out of the cabin behind Granger as he headed for the bridge.

Everything transpired as Granger predicted.

A few miles outside the Hong Kong harbor, the *Nautilus* surfaced behind the cliffs of Hadley Island and a safe distance from the *Cazadore*. The loaned crew reboarded the submarine, and she descended again to follow the ship as she continued on her way.

Nemo and Granger used the periscopes on the bridge to observe the *Cazadore* as several gun boats from the Royal Navy approached and encircled the three-master. When they boarded the ship, it didn't take more than ten minutes before one of the boats turned around and made haste back to the harbor. In time, several larger Navy ships joined the *Cazadore*, and Nemo pushed the periscope aside to say, "The hostages are cheering and hugging the British sailors." His voice lowered and became hoarse. "Some are crying."

"Thank God," Verne intoned.

Captain Nemo pivoted and regarded Bartholomew, Celwyn, Kang, and his crew. "A most successful operation." He saluted Granger. "And all with a show of excellent seamanship."

Bartholomew called out, "Here, here!"

"Congratulations, Lieutenant." Celwyn asked Nemo, "What are our plans, sir?"

"We'll travel to the headlands as planned. After dark, if you'd be so kind as to provide carts and horses, many of my crew will go on leave in town. I assume you will make a night of it, too."

"Yes, we will. How will they get back?" Bartholomew asked. "What Jonas makes won't last if we are too far away."

Nemo said, "They'll be told. Some will elect to stay in town, and a few will elect to return with you, if you arrange a place and time to meet."

Kang rubbed his hands together. "That will do nicely. I've been dreaming of a rare steak."

"With cookies on top?" The magician asked.

PART V

Chapter 64

A S HE STOOD IN FRONT OF THE aquatic window, the automat adjusted the collar of the formal suit he wore. He eyed Bartholomew beside him as he did the same. The big man's skin no longer had the color of rich coffee. Instead, he appeared as pale as Kang, and so much like him he could have been his slightly taller brother with precisely trimmed white hair.

Celwyn fussed with his own tie and studied himself in the window's reflection. Qing sat below him, eying the three of them with his head tilted the way he did when he tried to understand something.

"It's me, Qing," the magician assured him. To the mechanical bird, he would appear as a slightly taller relative of the Professor, and that could be confusing. "These are just our costumes for tonight."

"Why isn't Mr. Soriano or Mr. Verne coming with us?" Bartholomew asked.

Kang replied, "Verne is afraid of the city at night from a prior experience, which has not yet been explained. Valentine is already out hunting and enjoying his cultural pursuits."

"He mentioned how there is one of those Kunqu operas every night of the week." Celwyn patted Qing's back and noted the festive air of the room for the trip ashore. It had been years since he visited Hong Kong.

Bartholomew licked his lips. "We're having steak. I can taste it now."

Celwyn laughed. "Your carnivore side is showing, my friend. Perhaps you need a set of canines like Valentine's."

Kang shot the magician a look full of meaning, remembering their conversation about something very similar while they sat on the beach a few weeks ago. He changed the subject. "I understand the need for being circumspect until we're sure the British Navy isn't looking for us. However, you two..." He eyed them. "You make me feel odd with those disguises."

"You'll get used to it," the magician told him as he ushered them out the study door and toward the stairs leading upward.

***

Argentine steak houses seemed plentiful in the city, and Bartholomew had pointed out several of them along the way. Their dinner at the Tango Mooloo Steakhouse was everything they had hoped for. They sat in a private room full of congeniality and comfort and fragranced with seared meat. Celwyn chose the wine, and the others approved. Initially, Kang enjoyed being on land again and looked forward to their outing. Yet, as he relaxed and drank his wine, he reminisced how much he missed Elizabeth.

"You know, today is our eighteenth wedding anniversary. I think of her very much."

Celwyn said, "She will understand why we are not in Prague."

"I suppose." Kang's mood did not improve. "I will do my best to make it up to her."

Bartholomew said, "Buy her something exquisite tomorrow."

"A hat?" Kang suggested.

The other two groaned and waited for their waiter to return with the kabobs they'd ordered.

"Do we know where the hostages have been taken?" Celwyn asked.

The automat replied, "Nemo says most likely they will be at the Tamar Yard. He reports the accommodations are extensive there, and they are decent and warm. You two were shivering earlier; evidence that November is becoming a very cold month."

"Yes, it is. Being a British installation, I imagine the food will be bland, but nutritious," Bartholomew said.

The magician waited while the kabobs were set in front of them. "Where is the yard located?" He agreed with the big man and would add to the hostage's tables before the night was out. Of all the varieties of food, British was his least favorite.

"Granger said it is north of the commercial docks." The big man chewed a bite of marinated beef and savored it. The angelic look of bliss on his face would never appear on Nemo's in exactly the same way.

"That would put the yard close to here, would it not?" the magician asked.

Kang regarded him. "You intend to visit, discreetly, and verify all is well?"

"Yes."

The automat told Bartholomew, "I do not fancy a ride on Jonas's back to accompany him. We would be more comfortable here in the bar, would we not?"

"We certainly would." Bartholomew smiled at Celwyn. "Bundle up, Jonas. It's cold out there."

As the two of them settled in the bar and ordered a bottle of champagne, Celwyn departed. It neared the eleven o'clock hour, and they expected to meet some of the crew and return to the ship at midnight. The magician's errand would have to be quick.

He elected to travel as a smaller raven once again, black as the night sky. When he gained altitude, he found the evening air had a spicy quality to it, overlaid with the scent of rain. On the streets below, he found hundreds of bicycles, and in contrast, only a few ornate carriages pulled by fancy teams of horses. By soaring high above the coastline, he located the shipyard and the Queen's ships, all freshly painted and decorated in pristine canvasses. Compared to them, it wasn't difficult to spot the *Cazadore*.

As he approached the rows of barracks, he discovered only the British within them until he reached the last two buildings. In those, he saw a flurry of activity and familiar faces of some of the hostages as they smoked and talked, and a few even laughed. Celwyn still felt a sense of pride that they had been rescued. He flew to the next building and again noticed recognizable faces. In front of the door, one woman brushed the hair of another. Through a window, he saw Missy, the distraught woman, sitting on a cot, talking with several of the other women. She appeared somewhat calmer.

Celwyn searched until he determined Esther was not with them. It took nearly ten minutes of buzzing in and out of open windows until he heard David's familiar tenor explaining life on Manuk Island to a group of grave-faced English officers. Unmann sat on his right, and Esther on his left. The magician made himself comfortable in the rafters to listen.

Chapter 65

A SHORT TIME LATER, CELWYN USH-ered Bartholomew and the automat, with plenty of hilarity, out of the steakhouse and into the night. While the big man sang a loud version of the opening song from *Faust*, Celwyn searched for a hire couch and finally flagged one. Kang wandered back into the steak house, and the magician pulled him out again. As he poured his friends into the cab, he directed the driver north, leading out of the city. For this time of the night, he decided he'd accomplished something highly convoluted.

"I miss Elizabeth," Kang said with palpable melancholy.

As they rolled forward, Celwyn patted his shoulder and changed the subject. "I found Esther, David, and Unmann. Nemo will be pleased. I also heard all the hostages will be repatriated or taken to wherever they want to go."

Bartholomew goggled at him. "You did? How is Esther doing?" The big man had trouble focusing, and he'd started to revert to his normal appearance. His muscled shoulders strained at the seams of the smaller suit, and his skin had darkened. The magician changed him back to his normal appearance in an appropriately sized suit.

"Yes, and Esther is well. Everyone seems comfortable, and the Navy interviewed the three leaders as I watched." Celwyn stopped his recital long enough to finger back the coach's curtain and verify no one followed them. "During the interview, David did not describe us in detail. And he glared at Unmann to do the same. Esther did her best not to describe us, either."

Kang's amazement showed in his voice. "We did not even have to ask her or David to do so. That is impressive."

"They knew we would prefer to avoid attention, and are grateful for our help."

Their carriage bumped onto a street of newer cobblestones, and Bartholomew had to raise his voice over the clatter. "What about Unmann?"

Celwyn inhaled to control his irritation. "He told them about dropping the 'extra' sailors on Hadley Island. After David frowned at him, Unmann added that the sailors had other obligations."

"Will that be enough?" Bartholomew asked.

Kang said, "The British are overwhelmed with processing and helping the hostages and too busy to look for us. Tomorrow, we may plan our excursion as ourselves." He raised a brow at Celwyn daring him to contradict him. The magician let it go, for now. The Brits weren't the only ones who would find the sight of them memorable or who could be looking for them.

"Wonderful." Bartholomew rubbed his hands together. "This is my first time in Hong Kong, and I want to see everything!"

After breakfast, several skiffs motored away from the *Nautilus* toward the shoreline beneath the headlands. Long before their boats neared the rocks, the magician had covered them in invisibility while he scanned the cliffs and the ancient forest behind them. Satisfied, he checked south to the green fields before the city.

While the crew concentrated on maneuvering their boats onto shore, the magician made the carts. As usual, Bartholomew stepped off the boat first and splashed through the surf to the edge of the trees. A bit later, Celwyn led a pair of horses out of the brush, with more "horses" following. If one did not look closely at their eyes, the confused emptiness in them wouldn't be disconcerting.

The carts held a score of crewmen who would spend hours replenishing the ship. In the cart in the lead, Granger, Kang, and Verne sat in the rear behind Celwyn, and Bartholomew, who drove. The magician dried the big man's trousers and shoes; no point in inviting a cold.

Granger said, "Your party is free to spend the day without worrying about the crew. We keep the carts we rent hidden there," he pointed to the trees, "to use until we leave. It usually works well."

"That means," the big man jiggled the reins, urging the horses up a rise in the track, "we'll have the day for bookstores, tobaccos shops, and perhaps an art gallery or two."

"Don't forget the pastries." Celwyn directed a conspicuous smile at the Professor.

Kang patted a yawn. "My, oh my. Hong Kong is known for its tea shops, is it not?"

They all laughed.

"Actually, the Captain suggested I go with you. He wants to be sure you return." Granger kept his face as serious as he could.

More laughter erupted, partly born of relief after a tricky mission, and some at being on land again. Most of it came from good company.

With a furtive look in each direction, Verne said, "We must be back before dark."

"Why? What happened before?" Kang asked.

Verne licked his lips and shook his head. "I will tell you later."

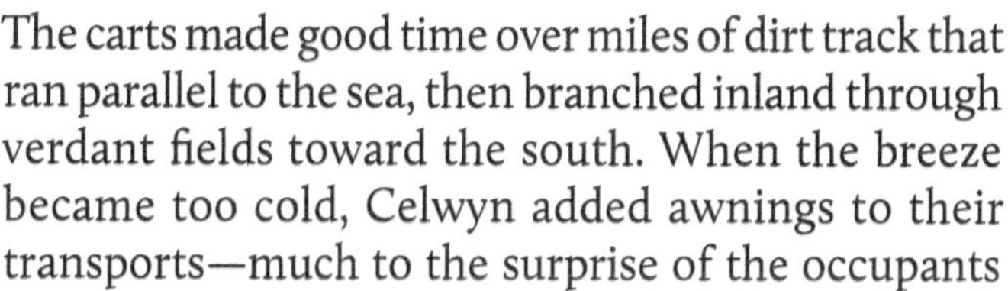

The carts made good time over miles of dirt track that ran parallel to the sea, then branched inland through verdant fields toward the south. When the breeze became too cold, Celwyn added awnings to their transports—much to the surprise of the occupants in the other carts. In another few moments, a light rain began.

"I love the smell of wet earth, especially after not smelling it for a long time," Verne commented.

It seemed as if the weather gods had heard him and wanted to see if he truly thought so. It rained harder, and in the distance, a rolling rumble of thunder radiated from under a bank of dark clouds and grew stronger. Bartholomew watched the storm a minute before saying, "I hope this doesn't last all day. We prefer to have our luncheon outdoors." The big man shook the reins in irritation and took the left fork of the road that angled toward the beginning of the farms. The other carts followed until they paused, allowing a collection of busy chickens to move out of the way.

"Does the Captain want us to pick up anything in town?" Bartholomew asked Granger.

"He gave me telegrams to send, and I need to stop at the bank. Otherwise, he made no requests."

Kang said, "This will work well. I have a series of letters and telegrams for my wife and everyone at Tellyhouse." He tapped Bartholomew on the shoulder. "Do you have the science experiments ready? Zander and Otto are probably waiting for them."

"Yes." He patted his coat pocket. "And I also plan to look for books for them." Bartholomew told Granger, "They are twelve and fifteen, and have a serious interest in art, birds, tigers, and all animals."

"I see. They must miss you when you are not there."

Kang said, "They do." His expression fell, and he grew wistful. Celwyn wondered why the automat seemed exceedingly homesick this trip.

Hoping to lift Kang's spirits, he added a pair of guitars playing a light ballad. The music grew playful, one guitar asking a question, and the other answering it. When he sent the music to the other carts to enjoy, he realized how good it felt to do something magical that did not involve catching fish or alleviating human misery.

"I must write to my publisher, too," Verne said.

"Which telegraph office to you prefer?" Bartholomew asked Granger. "I understand there are many of them."

"Half a mile up ... Haishan Road. North to Wutong Road. The bank is nearby, too."

By luncheon, they had strolled through the Aplei market and observed the antics of a trained monkey and its flamboyant owner. The costumes worn by these performers displayed a variety of colors compared to those in Prague where they had more bells. Celwyn especially liked the small man dressed as a green dragon who fed an imaginary friend. When the dragon spit a column of fire, the magician enlarged it until the crowd exclaimed in amazement. Celwyn felt Kang's eye on him and decided not to produce a small dragon for the act. Imaginary would do.

Everyone agreed that Zander would have enjoyed the sight very much. Otto, too, but he became nervous more easily. At one of their stops, Bartholomew bought the boys miniature animals carved from teak, similar in size to the magical ones Celwyn had made for the lads a few months ago. Wearing a reverent, yet excited, expression, the big man directed their attention to a questionable tie. Celwyn held back a remark the tie deserved.

With their arms full of packages, they headed toward an outdoor café that met Bartholomew's approval. Kang lifted his nose and sniffed. The others did too, enjoying the mature Katsura trees that shaded the courtyard of the Royal Bee café, and inhaling the fragrance of the Mandarin oranges decorating the trees. The rain had stopped an hour ago, which restored their party's joviality.

As they neared the entrance, Kang said, "It is not possible for those oranges to be ripe this time of year. They would have ripened months ago."

"That is true." Celwyn grinned at him. Sometimes they noticed his enhancements, sometimes not.

"Ha!" The automat whirled and led the way inside.

According to Kang, the courtyard and café dated from the 14th century and the Southern Ming Dynasty. It held two dozen tables surrounding a weathered stone fountain. Children sat on its ledge and tossed silver pieces into the bubbling water.

After again thanking the magician for the sensory cloud of oranges, Bartholomew and the others took a table just steps from the fountain. Of all of them, only Granger wasn't burdened like a donkey with packages. He carried two: one from a tobacco shop, and one from a spice shop.

"What spice is that?" the big man inquired as he opened a menu.

"Yellow paprika for our chef. He prepares scrabble for me if I provide the paprika, the pig brains, and other parts."

Bartholomew made a face. "Intestines?"

Granger nodded. "It is an acquired taste. Usually, I prefer plain food."

While Celwyn studied the menu, he became aware little by little of the hair on the back of his neck rising. He closed his eyes, all the better to decide what alarmed him in such an innocent setting.

He couldn't hear anything unusual, and when he dropped his napkin as an excuse to check the area to the side of them, he didn't see anything, except several tables of businessmen in shirtsleeves, and a family with children. At the nearest table, a young man and woman held hands with glazed expressions. The magician doubted they would notice anything except an earthquake.

Bartholomew leaned to his left and asked Verne a question. Celwyn took the opportunity to search the other side of the courtyard. Nothing, yet now erratic butterflies chased themselves in the magician's stomach. The only place left to check was between them and the street.

"What is it, Jonas?" Bartholomew's frown replaced his usual good humor.

With a look at Celwyn's face, Kang stood and scanned the tables. In a murmur, he asked, "What do you suspect?"

Granger's hand went to the pistol on his waistband.

"I do not know," Celwyn said. "Just a sense of danger. Usually, it comes from something unnatural ... not a garden variety villain, such as a robber."

"Good grief." Kang dropped back into his chair and rubbed his face so hard the magician wondered if the automat's leathery skin would come off.

Verne asked, "How do we know it is a danger to us specifically?"

With another growl, the magician said, "We don't."

Again, Celwyn searched the courtyard. This time he spied a pair of heavily bundled men with their hats pulled low, who sat in the corner furthest away from the fountain. Bartholomew had spotted them, too. He narrowed his eyes. "Would they account for your reaction?"

"Perhaps. If Valentine or Tara were here, they could confirm my suspicions."

"Which are?" Kang asked.

"That those are a pair of daemons up to no good." He asked Bartholomew, "Discreetly check their eyes, please—" He leaned toward Kang and said, "Not you. You are not discreet."

"Pfft."

Granger's frown drew his heavy brows down. "If I shoot them, what will happen?"

The automat shrugged at Celwyn, who shrugged back and raised a brow at Bartholomew. The big man said, "We don't know."

"I have seen them dismembered by vampires and set on fire before, but that is it," the magician told them.

"What are they?" Verne asked.

Bartholomew's eyes hopped from patron to patron with apprehension. "In Bengali, they are called Dimana. In the rest of Africa, it is as you said, daemons." He shuddered. "And nothing I want to meet up with."

"Shall we order our lunch and see what they do?" Granger asked. "Or leave?"

The magician was not convinced the daemons accounted for his unease, but a spot of tea might help him figure out what caused it. "I suggest we stay for now." He signaled their waiter, and when he arrived, Celwyn requested, "A pot of Earl Grey, and another pot of Darjeeling, please."

"We'll also need a bottle of red, two beers, and one of white to begin with." Kang asked Granger, "Is there a local appetizer you enjoy and recommend?"

While he thought, Verne said, "British sausage rolls and Chinese shrimp balls."

"Chicken skewers are good." Granger cast a glance over his shoulder.

The daemons now regarded them openly. Celwyn felt a shiver travel up his arms. He pivoted and saw another table full of daemons near the entrance. Like the others, they hunched over with their collars up and hats low.

"Oh, hell."

Bartholomew nodded. "I count another five of them." He leaned back as the waiter poured their wine. When he departed, Bartholomew said, "I see what you mean about the eyes. Reddish around the irises."

Verne grabbed the big man's wrist. "Is it safe to stay here?"

Just as Celwyn decided they should either take the offensive or forget their luncheon, he saw Xiau's face change. His brows went up, and he pointed with his eyes.

Everyone in the courtyard gazed at the entrance.

In a beautiful new silk cape and floppy hat, Valentine strode into the courtyard like Charles Fechter, the Shakespearean actor, as he entered the stage on opening night. His mane of silver hair waved in the breeze and added to the theatrical aura. With a glance at Celwyn and company, he held up a hand to wait and swiveled. He purposely slowed as he neared the first table of daemons. Before he reached them, they knocked over their chairs and ran. One hurdled a low wall, and the others bumped into waiters and then the fountain as they scrambled to get away. The commotion alerted the remaining daemons, who jumped to their feet, unsure which way to flee.

Before Valentine reached their table, the daemons' bodies rippled, undulated, and turned to smoke. Their images shimmered inside the smoke and then disintegrated.

The vampire studied the patrons in the courtyard and switched to the magician. Celwyn shook his head at him, and stood also, his defenses up and quivering. The other diners had glanced away after the vampire's entrance and seemed oblivious to what had happened as they continued to eat, drink, and laugh. The couple at the next table kissed passionately, like they were alone in the courtyard. Not only were the reactions odd, Celwyn *knew* he hadn't blocked them or suggested anything to anyone there.

In a blur, the vampire joined them, pulling out a chair between Bartholomew and Kang. He nodded at the others and asked Celwyn, "That was not you?"

"No."

Celwyn continued his scrutiny of the area, only this time he took his time, person by person. In each instance, he saw what he expected: yawns of boredom, expressions of humor, and a pair of elderly ladies in conversation who seemed giddy with naughty anticipation. None of it seemed nefarious enough to account for what happened.

"What are you looking for?" the Professor asked, and his voice dropped. "...it can't be."

"Can't be what?" Verne twisted around in his seat, half afraid, but always curious.

Celwyn ignored the questions and gazed at Granger, who had stood also, his hand on his pistol. Valentine growled in his throat, threw back his cape, and made himself comfortable.

"You may as well sit down. They are gone." The vampire helped himself to the wine and added, "One way or another."

Bartholomew dropped back into his chair, causing it to creak, but it held. He eyed Valentine. "It is most fortuitous that you are here. Especially with what just happened."

Valentine patted a yawn. "I saw you crossing the street between Kent and Aplei. It was only a matter of deducing where you'd go for your lunch." He smiled at them. "I, too, enjoy this café, although it has been more than a dozen years since my last visit."

The magician listened to Valentine with one ear as he continued to scrutinize the courtyard. Kang had deduced what Celwyn had feared, and he really did not want to talk about it. Yet, he couldn't help searching, fearing to discover what he wouldn't acknowledge.

Granger pursed his lips, made a decision, and told them, "I do not know what just happened, but it hasn't affected my appetite."

"Here, here!" Bartholomew agreed. "I plan on having the British chicken cottage pie with plenty of potatoes and buttered beans."

"Chinese spareribs for me ... although their kidney pie reminds me of the best pub in London." Verne frowned at the menu.

As they chattered, Celwyn calmed down. He even grinned at his companions so he wouldn't have to answer any questions, such as 'Did he feel safe again when the daemons were removed?'

If they had asked, he would have said, "No. I do not."

Chapter 66

WHEN IT WAS TIME TO RETURN TO the submarine, they walked by the Queen's Navy Yard. They did not have to ask directions; the smell of the bay reached them riding a breeze that stirred the air with purpose. By squinting, Bartholomew confirmed the *Cazadore* still lay at tether there. He also spotted at least a dozen large Navy brigs and an impressive array of transports filling the available berths.

The author shaded his eyes and tried to hold on to his hat at the same time. "If it mattered, we could speculate what the British would do with the pirate ship we brought them. Scuttle it without ceremony? Or turn it into a floating prison in Tasmania? There are dozens of them there already. Some of them are for *women*," Verne added with a bit of awe.

"My vote is to burn it," the automat said.

"What about that one? She is a beautiful ship," Valentine indicated a white frigate pushing away from a berth and steaming its way out of the harbor.

As she bleated her horn twice, Kang murmured, "I wonder if some of the hostages we rescued are on her."

"I do, also." Celwyn looked at the ship for a moment. "If you'll rent a carriage and await me on Bonham Road, I will check."

By the time Bartholomew opened his mouth and closed it again, the magician strode away.

"Have a good flight, sir," Granger called after him.

"Thank you." Celwyn darted between the two storage buildings and emerged again, flying straight for the bay.

It took several minutes to reach the British ship; it had put a healthy distance between itself and the docks. When he drew closer, he noted that even with her array of canons, she had far more cabins on deck than expected. He circled the ship twice, noting the clean dress uniforms of the crew and the general atmosphere; this was not a warship, although it could become one. The ship also appeared pristine, as if not used often. When he toured the bridge, he found out why.

Long ago, the magician had seen a picture of Disraeli in the *Morning Post*. Although smaller than advertised, the Prime Minister was recognizable as he stood in front of the wall-to-wall map table, tapping a particular spot on it, and arguing with an officer. Celwyn had no interest in politics and continued on his way to the cabins. He landed on the flat roof and walked across it fore and aft, and listened to the thoughts inside. He finally heard a voice he recognized and had hoped for, that of Esther, deep in discussion with the disturbed woman, Missy.

When another woman took over calming Missy down, Celwyn sent Esther a strong urge for fresh air. She excused herself and opened the cabin door. It was good to see her without a frown of worry. He followed her along the deck long enough to drop a purse of coins in her pocket along with a rather cryptic note of best wishes.

Esther felt the weight of the purse and pivoted in a complete circle as she dug out the message and read it. She scanned the deck to the rear and raised her face to the wind. Hong Kong suited her; she seemed rested, and the welfare of hundreds of hostages had been lifted off her shoulders. She wore a plain, but clean, frock of green, and her eyes sparkled.

"Where are you?" she called as she paced to the rail, searching the water nearby.

The magician realized the ban on magic in front of the hostages had expired when they arrived safely into British hands. After verifying no one hovered nearby, he landed on the rail so close she could have ruffled his feathers.

Esther eyed him and then stared.

"I ... am not afraid."

Celwyn said, "I would not expect you to be. Good afternoon, Mrs. Peabody."

With narrowed eyes, she regarded him until she slapped the rail in recognition. "I know which one you are! No bird has such green eyes."

Celwyn dipped his beak in a bird's bow. "A bit of vanity on my part. How are you?"

"Much better." She gasped. "It was you!" She tapped her cheek. "You heeled my face that day!"

"It was my pleasure."

"I'll never be able to thank you and the others enough. Oh—" She blinked rapidly. "I must apologize to Missy. She insisted she met a bird who talked to her while she was on the mast the other night. I convinced her she did not."

A healthy breeze lifted her hat, and she clamped a hand on it. Celwyn increased his grip on the rail and said, "That would be best in her condition. Did she mention her, uh ... flight?"

She eyed him, not unlike Xiau did at times. "No. What did you do?"

"You are aware of her impulse to harm herself? I couldn't talk her out of jumping off the spar—she wanted to fly. Nor could I make her descend again. So ... I accommodated her."

"That doesn't make sense. I saw her descend the mast. Hundreds of us did."

Aware that Bartholomew wouldn't take his response with calmness, but that Esther probably would, Celwyn said, "That wasn't Missy ... until the last foot or so above the deck." Not only would Esther understand, but he might as well be honest with her. He had a hunch they would encounter her again.

"I see." After a long moment, she looked him in the eye and said, "I won't pry, but I hope to see you all again." She blushed. "I admire Mr. Bartholomew greatly. He told me his name just before we sailed." Her eyes twinkled. "He has a wonderful innate serenity that is infectious."

The magician could have told her Bartholomew found her wonderful too but didn't go that far, in case it was a while until they saw her again. "We all admire you also for what you've done. Where will you go?"

"They are taking me to Bombay. A few weeks after that, and I'll be on a ship for either Lisbon or Marseilles."

"And then?"

"It is up to me. I'll decide according to my studies."

"Periodically, we will leave messages for you in both of those cities. If you could check General Delivery there, please? How are David and Captain Unmann doing?"

At the sound of their names, worry clouded her eyes.

"Excuse me, but what is wrong?"

She glanced around them and said, "It is David. He is such a good person, and I fear for him."

It was the magician's turn to check their surroundings as a pair of uniformed British officers passed by, both acknowledging Esther and inquiring about her health. They did not ask about the bird sitting on the rail beside her.

When they had passed out of earshot, Esther again faced the water and said, "I fear for him because he has nowhere to go, and Mr. Unmann is telling lies about him to the authorities."

"Do they believe Unmann?"

She hesitated, and her voice grew angry. "Some do because David is uneducated and not a white man. Before I boarded this ship," she gestured around them, "I told him not to sign anything without a friend looking at it. There are several in our group who would do that for him, besides me. But—"

Celwyn waited. Her concern had a basis, and as intelligent as she could be, she wouldn't guess at something so serious.

"I fear the worst."

"Where is he now?" A plan sure to upset the automat and surprise the others had already occurred to the magician.

She whipped around at the sound of voices approaching, but the quartet of officers touched their hats and continued along the deck. She said, "He is in Barracks Four with everyone else ... unless they have arrested him."

"I wish you well on your journey." Celwyn squinted at the harbor behind them. "I will leave you now to make sure of David's safety. You have my word, madam." The breeze around them grew stronger. "One last thing that you should know; we've arranged funds for all the hostages." This had been facilitated this morning when he copied the manifest the British had made of all the hostages and their home ports. "Please do not give away the coins in your pocket—we want you to have them."

As he rose from the rail, she whispered, "Thank you. I will not forget your kindness."

It did not take long to find David. As Celwyn approached the walkway to Barracks Four, the door opened and two guards led David out, each holding onto one of his arms.

The magician did not hesitate. In seconds, the guards released David and curled up under the nearby bushes. Before David could speak, he too was asleep and much smaller on Celwyn's back. As the rain clouds moved back in, the magician flew around the barracks one more time before shivering his way to Bonham Road and the warmth of the hire carriage Kang had found.

"We had almost given up on you," Kang told Celwyn as he climbed into the coach and settled next to Verne. "What is that?" the automat pointed to a plain wooden box Celwyn held in his hand.

"A friend in need." He regarded them. "I saw Esther, and she is well, and on her way to Bombay. Then either Lisbon or Marseilles."

The big man rubbed his chin and hid a secret smile at her name. "You don't say."

"Yes, I do." Celwyn grinned at him. "She mentioned your serenity, and her expression was just like yours right now concerning her." Kang giggled and elbowed the big man as the magician continued, "I also told her she might expect a few letters to General Delivery in those cities in case someone cares to write to her."

The big man patted a pretend yawn. "I think I know of someone who most certainly will do that."

Celwyn enjoyed seeing his happiness. It had been a long time since his disastrous liaison with Crazy

Mary. He asked Granger, "I understand you lost one crewman during our raid on Dearing's compound, and four more who are recuperating."

Granger eyed him with surprise, and a touch of the automat's chronic suspicion, when he heard Celwyn's seemingly innocent questions. "That is correct. Why?"

Kang's suspicious gaze switched from Granger back to the magician. Celwyn blinked at him and patted the box in his lap. "Just curious." He watched out the street as they passed an elderly couple walking hand in hand along the sidewalk. Another couple from a younger generation walked behind them. Further along, the road ended in front of the last of the small, well-tended houses.

"I say, it looks like we've reached the end of the line for this hire coach." He descended from the cab, saying, "I'll make transportation for the rest of our trip."

As he walked into the nearby woods, Celwyn chuckled, feeling Kang's gaze on him every step of the way.

Chapter 67

AFTER EVERYONE TROUPED ABOARD the *Nautilus,* Celwyn sought out Nemo. He checked the bridge and learned the Captain could be found in the map room.

At Nemo's, "Come in," Celwyn entered and laid the box on the table next to the chart Nemo studied.

"Sit down. Yes, Jonas? You appear a bit apprehensive... more daemons?" Nemo continued to use a magnifying glass on the page in front of him.

"Err ... no. A pleasant day all around, sir." The magician saw that Nemo had been studying the waters between Gibraltar and Spain. They would soon need that information.

He cleared his throat.

"Sir, I understand you are short a few crewmen at the moment." At Nemo's nod, he continued, "I might have a candidate for you."

Nemo put the magnifying glass down. "Oh?"

"Yes." The magician told him of Esther's concerns, Unmann's uncharitable actions, and the arrest of David that he had interrupted. "So, I was wondering if you'd consider David as a new member of your crew?"

Nemo blinked at him. "I suppose it is possible, but our process is usually one of not letting anyone see the ship until we're sure of them. Where is he?"

Celwyn touched the box and waited.

The Captain wasn't slow. His eyes grew wide, despite his worldly experiences. He raised his brows.

"I could arrange for a neutral setting for Granger to interview him. If it is not to be, David would not be aware of where he was before I took him back to the city. Then he would find he had funds to put distance between himself and the British. If you mutually—"

"I understand. Please arrange it with Granger." Nemo poked a finger at the box. "I think it will be interesting."

That evening, the atmosphere seemed tentative, yet hopeful.

The Captain relaxed in front of the aquatic window, enjoying their gathering before dinner. He raised a brow at the details of the incident at the café but did not comment then. From the scrutiny mixed with pity he subjected the magician to, Celwyn had no doubt that Nemo, like the automat, wondered if Pelaez had been present and responsible for the daemons' demise.

After the salad had been served, Verne asked Nemo, "Do you have any reservations about us visiting the city again after what occurred today?"

"I do. However, tomorrow is our last day before we begin another long journey. We were able to restock the ship much faster than expected." He asked Bartholomew, "How do you feel about the encounter? Was it random or planned?"

The big man finished chewing and took a deep breath. "I found the scene strange, but then Mr. Soriano," he shot Valentine a look, who returned it with a show of teeth, "approached them, and the creatures left. In fact, they couldn't get away fast enough."

Kang remarked, with as much sarcasm as he could, "What happened next to the rest of them did not fit with the daemon's level of fear." From across the table, he eyed Celwyn with pursed lips. "Jonas didn't even have a chance to do anything flamboyant."

"He didn't need to, as it happened," Bartholomew said. "What were they doing there in the first place? They arrived before us, and it appears they had been there a while."

With care, Nemo put down his fork and sighed. "Months ago, when we were in Palermo, we encountered that warlock right after Thales and your father." He nodded at Celwyn. "Do you remember your comment?"

"Certainly. I said that it seemed strange that witches, vampires, warlocks, daemons," he tapped his chest, "and immortals, all seemed to be gathering in that part of the world."

"I remember." Kang sounded even more irritated, if that was possible. "We couldn't decide if Thales or your father was the attraction, or if it was the flying machine."

Qing chose that moment to fly above the table and drop a cufflink between the butter and the rolls. Before anyone could react, Celwyn dissolved the cufflink. Nemo's lips twitched, but he said nothing.

Verme blinked around the table and then addressed Celwyn. "And now?"

"Ah. That is a good question." Celwyn produced a few new cufflinks and scattered them under the aquatic window to keep Qing occupied while they finished eating. "I think we can rule ourselves out. As Bartholomew mentioned, the daemons were already seated at the café when we got here. Also, it's been months since Palermo. Would we find a proliferation of entities there now?"

Bartholomew said with Kang's type of logic, "On the way here, we went by Palermo so fast in our pursuit of the pirates, we didn't stop. And months have gone by since then. Nothing untoward occurred in Prague or Findbar before that, so why would they be tied to those entities?"

"In my opinion, the daemons we met in London happened to just be there at the time." Valentine shook his mane of hair and smoothed his mustache. "In Hong Kong, I did not detect anything unusual."

"That doesn't explain everything." Nemo's expression hadn't lightened—if anything, he looked even more concerned as his lips tightened and he put his fork down.

"When we are in town tomorrow," Valentine said, "I'll telegraph my family and colleagues in Palermo to see if they know of anything." He regarded the others at the table. "You'll remember that my nieces traveled there with me at Thales' request."

"I am very glad you were there, sir," Celwyn told him, remembering Tara's eyes, her lips, her scent.

The automat understood his expression. "We know why."

Valentine skipped it and said, "Anyhow, we could expect responses from some of them by the time we reach Beirut."

Kang's amusement deserted him. "I hope I have letters waiting for me in Singapore. It has been almost two months since we left."

Time for a diversion. "The boys will expect new books from our travels, too," Celwyn reminded them.

Nemo began eating his cake with a distracted air. "So, it is the consensus that today's incident at the café has nothing to do with us?"

Glances and shrugs passed between them until Bartholomew said, "Confirmed. It was strange, but not planned."

Kang said, "I hate to dampen that thought, but there is also the importance of the finale. The remaining daemons disintegrated—into smoke."

"When that happened," Verne mused, "for some reason, it reminded me of the warlock."

Valentine finished off his wine and said, "Witches and warlocks are natural enemies of daemons." He smiled like an angel with plenty of teeth. "However, it is usually left to vampires to deal with them, as is proper."

"Even so, what we saw did not remind me of a witch or warlock. None of us detected either of those." The automat stared at the magician and waited. The silence at the table grew along with the expectant looks at the magician.

"Oh, for god's sake. Yes, it reminded me of someone."

"Who?" Bartholomew asked.

"Pelaez."

The table became so quiet, the magician could hear Bartholomew's breathing increase. After a short discussion about Pelaez, Nemo stopped the conversation.

"I want to give you some good news."

Verne asked, "Yes, sir?"

"When the British questioned Dearing's hostages, Unmann did a serious disservice to David, another of their leaders. Unmann tried to discredit David and put him in jeopardy. Esther was concerned. When Jonas visited her earlier today, she told him about it."

Kang's mouth dropped open. Verne's brows lowered in consternation because he didn't understand, and said so.

"When Jonas went to talk with David, he found him under arrest and brought him here."

"In that box..." Kang whispered to himself.

That news caused the big man the kind of consternation that went way beyond the usual. "In ... in that box!"

Celwyn raised his hands to placate them. "Please understand, I did not know if he and the *Nautilus* would be, er, a match. Plus, he shouldn't see this ship until things became clear. I also didn't want to argue with any of you until we knew. So, I chose that method to bring him aboard."

"Pfft!" The automat seemed a bit huffy.

Nemo waved it away. "Granger has taken David through our vetting process, and he is now a member of the crew for as long as he cares to be with us."

Without touching him, Celwyn closed Kang's mouth and grinned at him.

Chapter 68

BY ELEVEN THE NEXT MORNING, Celwyn and the others had arrived on shore and traveled into the city. Their first destination had been voted upon last night, while Bartholomew and Kang prevailed over Nemo and Valentine at Bridge. They would visit the Jinzi Museum, known for sculpture and antiquities. Later they would once again luncheon alfresco, but not at the café where they discovered the daemons.

Valentine acknowledged the time and place to meet again when everyone would return to the submarine. He intended to visit a few friends, one of which supplied specialty blood to the vampire; the impending first leg of their journey west would be a long one.

"I am relieved David has a new position and one that will afford him security," Bartholomew said.

"He may want something else for his life, but for now, he is safe and employed."

"True. Although with Nemo, he may find it more exciting than he is used to." Celwyn tapped a finger on the windowsill of the coach. "He will let us know if he intends to leave us."

Their carriage rolled away, gaining speed over the cobblestones, but hadn't gone far when Kang spied Toads and Mallards Booksellers. Although billed as a quick stop, a full hour passed before they climbed back into the carriage with several parcels.

"What did you purchase?" Verne asked the automat.

"The newest journal on blood clots, and *The Vicar of Bullhampton*, by Anthony Trollope."

"I've heard of Trollope."

Kang unwrapped the book and handed it to him.

Bartholomew asked Celwyn, "Do you know why Granger did not come with us today?"

"I know he and his officers are welcoming David, but nothing else."

"What happened when David saw the submarine?" the big man asked.

Celwyn shrugged. "I was told that he handled it well. The new position will probably work out for him. Not only is he handy with tools, but he also felt relaxed with Granger, which helped."

"What happened when he woke up ... from being in that box?" Verne asked. "Was he aware of where he was?"

Celwyn pursed his lips. "No, that is why I was invited to his ... er ... debut. But I explained enough, and he felt calmer after that. The crew will probably tell him of Valentine and other things."

Kang raised a sardonic brow. "I wager David already knows, and can tell them of some of the things that occurred on the island that they didn't see."

"What did he think of the *Nautilus*?" the big man asked.

"Granger says he had the usual wide-eyed reaction. There is good news too; David can cope with closed-in areas, such as a submarine, and Granger thinks he will do fine."

The automat said, "Talk about risky and flamboyant, Jonas. What if Nemo had said no?"

"Then I would have taken David back to Hong Kong and given him funds and wished him well on his journey."

"You could have told us first," Kang pouted.

"So that you could tease me or question what I wanted to do?"

Bartholomew laughed. "But of course."

"Stop!" Kang yelled at their driver. The carriage swerved to the curb. Kang scrambled over the others and out the door. He paused long enough to say, "Today is my wedding anniversary!" He pointed to the shop behind him, whose window displayed bushels of feathers, ribbons, and other adornments atop a variety of hats. "I must get her a hat." He whirled and trotted across the sidewalk and on inside.

Bartholomew watched him. "Does he know that is not considered a romantic present?"

"No." Celwyn wished he could implant ideas in the automat's mechanical mind. "Not remotely."

They chatted about the merits of Ceylon tobacco over Spanish tobacco until Kang ran back to them carrying a large hatbox. The coach rolled forward again.

"What kind did you purchase?" Verne asked. "I usually bring my wife a present when I return home." He eyed the hatbox tentatively. "Perhaps a hat would be a good idea."

Kang told him, "A nice toque. It is supposed to be the latest fashion." He puffed up his chest in pride. "Elizabeth will be so pleased."

"Did you meet her in a hat shop?" Bartholomew asked.

Celwyn grinned. "Did she ask you to model one for her?"

Kang took the jesting well, and then said, "We met on the Embarcadero in San Francisco on a Sunday afternoon. She was leaning over the seawall and watching the sea lions."

"Were you afraid to talk to her?" the big man asked.

Kang shook his head. "I thought she was the most beautiful woman I'd ever seen. I couldn't speak at first. A few minutes later, I did."

"In the last three hundred years, she was the only one you have found?" Celwyn asked.

The automat unwrapped one of his books. "Well, no. But the only one in the last fifty years or so. Anyhow, I happened to knock her gloves into the water. You should have seen the look she gave me."

Celwyn could picture that and chuckled. Bartholomew asked with a smirk, "What did she do?"

"A month later, she married me." His own smile showed he remembered the occasion well. "She couldn't understand why I owned so many books, but eventually she stopped asking and just found places for them." He sobered. "When she and Nemo fell in that lake with the Mizuchi, I thought I had lost her."

"Never." Bartholomew slapped him on the back. "We are heading home soon."

They passed a peddler of pearls and a vendor of hot chicken, and when another bookshop loomed ahead at the end of the block, Celwyn sent their driver a silent suggestion to go faster when he hurried to say, "Nemo mentioned something before we left the ship." The others looked at him, not at the bookshop. "He trusts that we would avoid daemons and cafés of ill-repute." The magician popped a peyote button in his mouth. He only had three left and hoped his new supply would arrive by the time they returned to Prague.

Verne asked, "If that was Pelaez yesterday, wouldn't he be far away by now?"

"Unknown." Kang eyed the magician with pity. "How did he find us?"

Inside the cab, a thoughtful quiet descended over them. Everyone jumped as a siren blared and its wail traveled by them at speed before dying out.

"I don't know," Kang said.

"Neither do I." Bartholomew hesitated. "You knew him best, Jonas. What do you think?"

The magician had pondered this throughout the last evening until he fell asleep. His mood had not improved since. As he scanned the street, three tots, a nanny, and a harried mother hurried along through a light rain that had just begun to fall. The children were pushed under an awning. Beside them, a street musician had set up a table of tiny drums. He twirled silver-tipped sticks over them and began his concert. Through the shop window behind the children, a vintage train chugged by, ready to travel across miniature hills and valleys. Before Celwyn could make it do something else, the automat cleared his throat as a reminder they waited.

"I am flattered that you think I would know, but all I can offer is guesses."

"That is a start," Bartholomew said.

Their carriage slowed for a turn, and Verne leaned into him and straightened again. "Your brother frightens me."

"Remembering what happened in Turkey makes me afraid, too," Bartholomew agreed.

"Justifiably so, if he killed them." Celwyn noted the sidewalks seemed more crowded this time of day, perhaps because it was a market day. "Anyhow, one guess is that despite his disappearance, he never has really left us. Instead, he follows us."

That got a reaction. Kang's eyes widened, and he sputtered, "He could know about Findbar!"

Verne had paled, and Bartholomew puffed hard on his pipe as he imagined what Pelaez had seen, or how close he had come to them and the new version of the flying machine.

Celwyn inhaled and waited until their reactions died down. "It is possible, but—" another fire brigade passed by, heading toward the bay. When things quieted again, he continued, "We must ask ourselves if Pelaez can travel great distances underwater."

"Can he?" Bartholomew demanded.

"Yes and no. I am not up to date on everything my brother can do. Only what he displayed last year when he journeyed with us. Yet..." He saw Kang relax again as his analytical mind took over. "Weeks ago, I saw something strange after we repaired the submarine and headed toward Singapore." He reminded them of the incident with the pack of sharks and described the blue-eyed white shark in detail. "If that was Pelaez, then yes, he could have followed us. But not for hundreds of miles."

They digested the implications until the Professor asked, "Does Nemo know of this theory? Of the possibilities?"

"Yes. We discussed it last night."

After they had traveled another block, Verne inquired, "What are your other guesses?"

"Ah." The magician sniffed the air, detecting rain again. He closed the carriage window and shivered. "I would like to think this scenario is more likely; assume Pelaez took himself out of Turkey to any of the various cities in the Mediterranean. At that point, he changed his mind and wanted to find us—or," Celwyn showed a hard smile, "perhaps something seriously frightened him ... or found him, and he decided the safest place is underwater. Even with us."

"Oh, my." The big man intoned something several times, perhaps a chant to ward off evil.

Kang said, "Or he respects your magical ability enough to believe you would help him if he were in danger. He has the ego to think he could talk you into it."

"It is possible." Celwyn shrugged. "We can assume he spent some time at the docks in one or the other of the cities we stopped at—from Algiers to Beirut, and that he promised the disreputable reprobates and drunks in these ports a fat purse if they spotted us. He'd give them a pre-paid telegram to the cities he intended to visit for messages. Their fee would depend on getting a message to him."

"That sounds fantastic enough to be true." The automat glared at them.

The magician couldn't argue the fact. "Considering the bribe Pelaez would offer, it isn't hard to imagine the cooperation he received. All he had to do was describe a medium-sized automat in the company of a seven-foot African and a tall, handsome Englishman—which is probably the closest description of myself." He started counting the times they'd been visible together and stopped. "Pelaez couldn't be sure Jules would be with us in public, so I doubt he was part of the description. My brother would have only paid out the bribe if all of us were spotted together, guaranteeing he had the right trio."

"Handsome, eh?" Bartholomew chortled.

"And so modest, too." The automat rolled his eyes. "Anyhow, Peleaz probably would have given them a demonstration of his magic should they try to trick him," Kang said.

Bartholomew repeated, "Oh, my," and regarded the others. "They could have found out everything about us for more gold, too."

"I concur," Kang said. "This is not far-fetched. Pelaez knows our habits when we're aboard the *Nautilus*, and at which cities the submarine will surface for supplies."

Celwyn nodded. "Exactly. Even if he traveled at a sedate overland route, or by ship or both, at each of the ports, his informants would report when they saw us, and each account would show our progress eastward over the last few months. It would be logical that we would eventually stop in Singapore."

Verne tapped his chin and glanced at them. "And when he didn't find us there, or even if he arrived after we left for the Sulu Islands, he would continue to Hong Kong with the probability of that being our next destination. This reasoning is solid. If he didn't find us there, he'd try Manilla next."

Kang cursed.

Celwyn held up a hand as their coach swerved to the curb in front of the museum.

"Remember, this is all conjecture. We do not know for certain."

"No, we don't," Bartholomew growled. "God damn Pelaez."

Kang prepared to disembark and eyed the magician. "Since we do not need the extra entertainment," he pointed to the museum entrance, "Jonas, please

refrain from befriending any wyverns or other entities in the exhibits."

Their visit to the museum, and the luncheon that followed, did not include any daemons, but Celwyn's sense of foreboding remained alive and well. Something was about to happen, and he knew it as distinctly as if Thales stood before him and told him so.

As the afternoon wore on, he had also caught glimpses of something in the peripheral of his vision several times. Yet, when he turned, he could detect nothing untoward. Just a suggestion of something watching. He reminded himself it did not have to be Pelaez, although his companions would probably disagree with him.

Celwyn barely heard the conversation bouncing around them as their boat neared the submarine. Night had fallen an hour ago, and in the distance, the lights of Hong Kong twinkled brighter than the stars above. With their fishing done for the day, the last of the working boats headed toward Aberdeen Island.

The magician continued to worry about Pelaez, or whatever could be causing his unease. Verne, Bartholomew, and Kang relived their shopping excursion and nattered about their plans for more. Valentine had rejoined them and smoked from his corner of the boat, contributing a comment here and there. The scientists could be the true targets because of their knowledge of the flying machine, or again, it could be Kang's work on atomic power. The magician believed in many things, yet the incident with the daemons smelled like the malicious playfulness of Pelaez. Or, it could just be a coincidence.

Going forward, Bartholomew would be disguised, as would the automat, whether they liked it or not. To keep the complaining to a minimum, Celwyn would disguise himself as well. Nemo would approve too—he did not believe in coincidences either.

Like the big man had said, *God damn Pelaez.*

Chapter 69

S EVEN DAYS LATER, AFTER WAITING
an extra day for ship maintenance and the last
of their supplies, they neared Singapore once again.
Just after dawn, the submarine surfaced near the
headlands.

Everyone enjoyed a hearty breakfast, a modified
one intended to stave off hunger until the pastries
party later in the day. With an anticipation of a wonderful outing, everyone climbed out of the *Nautilus*
and walked across the floating pier to the beach by the
high rock formations. Once they rounded the headlands, tall ships in the harbor could be seen in the distance, floating like skeletons wearing fluffy petticoats.

As they approached the path leading to the city,
the automat asked, "Do you think the *Zelda* still
docks here?"

Three years ago, the ship had taken them from
San Francisco across the Pacific to Singapore, and

their adventures and friendship had begun. Along the way, their detour into the Artic Sea had been most memorable and much too flamboyant, according to Kang.

Bartholomew said, "I never saw her. A three-master?"

"Four." Kang sidestepped a pile of rocks and watched Bartholomew as he stretched to his full height to see further out.

To the south, heavily forested land descended to the sea. "This is only my third trip to this city. It is beautiful." He smiled. "And I want another pastel de nata like what we had last year. I can still taste it."

As they left the last of the rocks behind, and approached the short field before the road, Granger told them, "I remember your first visit here, right on this very spot."

They stood in a circle facing a stand of red pine trees leading into town. Celwyn sniffed and decided the spicy perfume of the trees should be bottled and pumped into the *Nautilus*. Valentine wrinkled his brow and asked, "Why was it memorable? Did something unusual occur?" He blinked innocently at his attempt at humor.

Granger eyed the automat and magician before saying, "Mr. Celwyn could explain better than I, sir." His face remained studiously blank.

The magician said, "Elizabeth was kidnapped and taken aboard the *Nautilus* so that the Professor would follow. It was an exciting time."

"Ha! How understated can you be?" the automat exclaimed. "After Jonas followed us aboard and sabotaged the ship, there was a stalemate, until a good-size python squeezed the stuffing out of Nemo."

The big man told Valentine, "It didn't take long, though, until things between us improved."

"I am so glad they did," Verne murmured.

Celwyn regarded him. The author hadn't exactly been forthright during that escapade. Verne caught his expression and changed the subject as they began the walk toward town. "What are we doing first today?"

The Professor said, "I do not know, but I find these britches are too tight and the sweater itches, Jonas. I do not like wool."

Celwyn had dressed the automat as a student with a thick mustache, and dusted his hair with ashes to lighten it. Bartholomew now appeared much shorter and pale-skinned, like Kang, while the magician had once again adopted the disguise of an elderly professor. He hadn't thought it necessary to do much to Verne's appearance—the author could pass as another fussy professor any day.

Other than adding a hooded cloak to hide the vampire's silver locks, Valentine did not require special attention. Celwyn entertained himself, thinking of what Pelaez would do if he ran into the vampire on the street. Valentine would have a quicker reaction, and Pelaez would have to do more than smirk to get away.

"Sorry to hear that, sir." Granger referred to the comment about itchy wool. His face transformed every time he changed moods, and there was no need to disguise him.

Valentine said, "The telegraph office I prefer is on the north side, near Parliament, and I hope to find answers to my telegrams. The ones concerning our discussion the other night."

They stood at a fork in the road: the left turn led downtown, the right followed Royal Street, which dissected the government and banking districts.

Verne swiveled to Valentine. "What discussion?"

"We talked about the phenomena where it seemed that an unusual number of witches, vampires, magicians, and warlocks seemed to be congregating near Palermo," Bartholomew answered.

"Ah, now I remember. Thank you."

"Our telegraph office is downtown." The Professor asked Valentine, "We will do some shopping, and I assume you also have errands. What time for luncheon would suit you?"

Valentine shrugged. "Two? Where?"

Bartholomew had no trouble with that question. "Pearson's Café. They have good food." He smiled. "And I do not believe Pelaez has the nerve to bother us there twice." His brows lowered. "He wouldn't dare."

Wouldn't he, though? Celwyn thought. The automat caught his eye with a slight bob of his head, disagreeing with the big man. He, too, believed in Pelaez's audacity. The magician set his jaw so as not to think about his brother. It was too fine of a day for that.

"Two it is." Kang bowed to Valentine, and they parted ways.

Chapter 70

Unlike Hong Kong, carriages seemed as plentiful as chickens in Singapore, and they flagged one down in seconds. Their Pakistani driver, who introduced himself as James Goodfellow, beamed at them and enthusiastically displayed his command of the Queen's English—all without stopping for any punctuation or breathing.

They climbed in. A faint whiff of excellent tobacco, both exotic and robust with hints of musk, surrounded them with a delicate touch. Celwyn tapped the glass and told the driver the address of the telegraph office. "If you should happen to stop at the same tobacco shop that your last passenger patronized, we would be most appreciative."

"I am from Jaipur, and know Singapore well, sir. You will have your tobacco, sir."

The magician thanked him and told the others, "I want to purchase some for the Captain. He puts up with a great deal. Of course, it is all Xiau's fault." At his teasing, the automat put his nose up in the air. The magician continued, "An idea for when we arrive at Bartholomew's café; we could buy as many pastries as we can carry for the crew."

"They would like that, at least those who are not on leave." Granger checked his watch and nodded to himself. "The rest of the crew, those who did not have shore leave in Hong Kong, will get their turn here."

Their coach bounced across Imperial Street, passing the Convent of the Holy Infant Jesus, and the Thian Hock Keng Temple. The automat sighed. "Elizabeth will want to come back here soon. As you know, her mother lives nearby." He stared at Celwyn. "Do you know she still mentions those bulls in her letters to Elizabeth?" For the others' curiosity, the automat provided an abbreviated account of the incident in the front yard of Elizabeth's mother's house that featured a certain walrus-like policeman.

Bartholomew chortled. "Even though I'd heard the story before, I can still imagine Xiau's face when he saw the bulls and knew you were there, Jonas. I wager he loved nagging you about it."

"He still does."

"Why French horns?" Verne inquired.

Celwyn heard the question, while keeping a distracted eye on the streets they passed by. In the last few minutes, his premonition had come back, stronger than before. He observed a plump woman in silks and sequins trailing behind a thin man with her head bowed. "That day at her mother's, everything fit the circus atmosphere caused by that policeman. First the braying, and then the French horns answering." The magician wished things were as simple now as their first visit had been. He hated the nervous feeling in his stomach that felt like a wolf chasing a gazelle back and forth in circles. And it made him angry because he couldn't control the sensation ... or destroy it.

Verne, as usual, unaware of anything amiss, asked, "How much further is it to the telegraph office?"

The automat kept his eye on the streets around them for bookstores and other pleasures. "About—" he stopped as they slowed in front of Palameri's Fine Tobaccos, a narrow shop with clean windows and a red door. "I see we found our first tobacco proprietor." He winked at the magician. "I am sure we'll find something in that teashop next door, too."

As they alit from the carriage, Celwyn verified the area all around them. Bartholomew and Granger did the same. Verne and Kang scurried into the shop without a care in the world.

Hours later, with a glazed look in his eyes, Granger led the way out of the Jouet Museum they'd discovered on Somerset Street. The toy trains had not interested him, and he appeared not quite asleep, but not quite awake either. Celwyn and the automat exited next, discussing the model Pinkerton train they had seen. The magician insisted he was correct, and that Rolan had also built a replica of it. Kang maintained it was his imagination.

When they had gathered at the bottom of the stairs, Bartholomew rose on his tiptoes. "Jonas, I do not like being so much shorter for this disguise. I cannot see all the way down the block."

"It is a bother." The magician used his elderly scholar's shuffle to wobble into the street, tapping the cobblestones with his cane. "I do not see our cab driver yet." He eyed the others. "Please humor me. Today is the last day for disguises for a while." They would soon be inside the belly of the *Nautilus* again for several weeks and not need them.

"Do you really think Pelaez would approach us?" the big man asked and couldn't help a glance at the rear. The act was reminiscent of Bartholomew's careful checking for Qing when he couldn't spot him.

Granger displayed his opinion by caressing the pistol on his belt and canvassing the avenue in all directions. The tembusu trees and stately colonial buildings of the district couldn't have looked more innocent.

They started across the street. "Perhaps I will feel better when we're on our way again." Celwyn put cheer and hope into his voice that he couldn't come by naturally right now.

What was bothering him?

The Professor pointed down the street. "The telegraph office is only four blocks east of here. We are well protected, and Lieutenant Granger is armed— which is quite useful for non-magical defense in crowds." He nodded at Celwyn. "You are armed in your own way."

Bartholomew said, "I brought my pistol along, also." His smile boded ill for an enemy. "I haven't shot anyone in a while."

"Since Dearing's island?" the Professor laughed.

Verne said, "It is settled, then." He caught up with Kang and they headed up the street. Granger shrugged and fell into step with the others.

"This is a main thoroughfare, and our driver will find us soon." Granger stepped into the street and back again. "We'll need him to reach the rendezvous with Mr. Soriano by two."

Celwyn hoped so. A pair of matrons waddled along in front of them, taking up most of the side-walk and making it impossible to pass by. That could be a tactic to contain Kang and the others in a small space for an attack, but the magician didn't see any-thing untoward, such as the telltale signs of Pelaez—grotesque fish and nasty pigs. When the women stopped to watch a mime, Bartholomew and the others did not hesitate and detoured around them.

"What are you brooding about?" Kang asked.

"Nothing." Above it all, Celwyn worried that when something happened, it wouldn't be because of the normal signs of Pelaez—his brother could devise something new to enhance his element of surprise and success anytime he pleased.

On another level, the magician realized Captain Nemo had done something subtle and admirable when they arrived: knowing Pelaez had been with the *Nautilus* when she departed from the Singapore headlands last year, Nemo had purposely parked the submarine in the same spot, again displaying that he welcomed confrontations and did not run from them.

As if the automat could read his thoughts, Kang slowed until he joined Celwyn, pace for pace. He asked, "What do you think Pelaez would do if he found us?"

They had passed three storefronts, a discarded bicycle, and a mother reprimanding a crying child before Celwyn responded. He chose his words with care, aware that the others listened as raptly as if they were in church and the priest had just confessed to a fondness for opium and geishas.

"If Pelaez still considers the flying machine evil, he will want to destroy the source of it; you and Bartholomew. If he regrets what he did at the compound in Turkey, he might wish to reconcile with us. At the least, he is probably looking for the new version of the flying machine."

"Or, if someone is after him, he might want yours or Nemo's protection," Granger said.

"True." The magician noted Granger had become comfortable enough with them to participate, and that was a good thing. They needed to be prepared and all thinking alike.

"We do not know definitively that he murdered everyone there." Verne pursed his lips. "He could have done some of it, to get close enough to set the machine on fire. Then Ginnie, the witch, destroyed the rest."

"It could be," Kang allowed. "Or he killed them all and intends to kill us." He stared at Celwyn. "I'm not going to state the obvious."

The magician laughed, and it sounded hollow to his ears. "You are referring to the fact my brother would have to kill me also if he harmed any of you."

"Yes."

As they approached the telegraph office, Kang's mood lightened and his eyes gleamed. "Look—Barstow's Books! I had forgotten about them."

"In the interest of time, we'll retrieve telegrams while you and Jules browse." The magician raised his chin at Bartholomew and received an affirming nod.

"I am sure you do not need me for either activity. I will remain on guard out here," Granger told them with the relief of a non-book lover.

It did not take long to claim the dozen messages, half of them addressed to Professor Kang, and dated more than a month ago. They also included a surprise. As a rule, Patrick never wrote to them, but this time had sent them each a message. As they made haste back to the sidewalk again, Celwyn remarked upon it.

"Curious. This must be good news since Patrick usually leaves the family correspondence to Annabelle."

They ripped open their envelopes at the same time and read.

Celwyn gulped air. His anger and grief discharged, shattering windows in every direction.

More explosions scattered the rest of the pedestrians as if a bomb had blown up.

"My god—" Tears streamed down Bartholomew's face.

Another storefront window imploded into a whirlwind of tiny pieces just as the tree next to them flew apart. Bartholomew grabbed the magician's arms and squeezed. The remaining trees flew upward, and the big man wrapped his arms around Celwyn. "Stop! You'll hurt someone! Stop!" Bartholomew put his head on the magician's shoulder and sobbed. "We have to tell Xiau... oh... how *can* we?"

That helped; the big man needed him. Celwyn inhaled and started to think again. Yes, he had a duty he couldn't ignore. The magician breathed again and nodded at Bartholomew, who released him. "We will do what is necessary."

"*What will we tell him?*" Bartholomew's sobs grew louder. "This is *horrible!*"

Granger saw them and stepped around the fallen tree and glass to them. He saw their expressions, but ever proper, said nothing until he reached them. "Sir?"

"Mrs. Kang has been murdered." Celwyn handed him the telegram.

After he read it, Granger said, "I am sorry. She was a most gracious woman." He raised his eyes to theirs. "The message says murder, but nothing else. Do you know who would do such a thing?"

Bartholomew emitted a bark of gallows laughter. "At one point, it could have been several villains. But lately, there would have been no one." He slammed a fist into a brick building. "No one!" He began punching the building as hard as he could.

It was Celwyn's turn. He restrained the big man and wrapped his fists in something to kill the pain.

Granger had been watching the bookstore. "Here they come."

First Verne, and then the automat, backed out of the bookstore door, balancing packages in their arms, jabbering and heading toward them.

Bartholomew hid his face from the automat while Celwyn scouted the street. Not two-hundred feet away, a beautiful park had been wedged between two office buildings. It would do.

"Come on." He grabbed Kang's elbow and took some of the packages. The others followed with questions. The magician called over his shoulder, "We are going to see a new species of koi. One of the shopkeepers says it is enchanting."

The grumbling faded away as they trooped down the street.

Before they crossed an expanse of green velvet-like grass, a new koi pond appeared in the quietest corner of the park. As they gathered in front of it, Celwyn checked Bartholomew's thoughts. As expected, the big man preferred Celwyn to give Kang the news.

"What is the matter?" the automat demanded peevishly. "Why is Bartholomew crying? There aren't any koi here."

God, Celwyn hated this. He glanced behind them, not seeing anyone, but blocked the area anyway before he made a pair of benches facing each other.

He sat across from Bartholomew, and Kang and Verne lowered themselves onto the other. Granger stood between them, hands behind his back, at attention.

"Do it, Jonas," Bartholomew requested as his tears fell again.

Celwyn breathed deeply and encountered Kang's suspicious and anxious eyes.

"Elizabeth is dead. She has been murdered."

The automat's mouth opened, and Bartholomew reached for him and held on.

"Xiau, I am so sorry," Celwyn told him.

The automat blinked and then lowered his head into his hands. His shoulders shook, reminding Celwyn of their conversation so long ago on the *Zelda*. Xiau had told him that automats had emotions. That they could love.

And now grieve.

In the silence, they could hear nothing except Xiau's painful sobbing. "How?" he whispered.

Bartholomew said, "We do not know." He handed his telegram to Kang and fished in his pocket for the other unopened missives. "Here are the ones from Tellyhouse." Kang kept reading and rereading Patrick's telegram. The big man stuffed the others in the automat's pocket.

"We need to get you back to the ship," Celwyn told him.

Bartholomew grunted. "And retrieve Valentine."

When Celwyn had lost control, all their disguises left them too. It helped settle the magician to see the big man as himself. Yet, as his grief waned, his anger grew.

"It nears the two o'clock hour now." Granger said, "Mr. Celwyn, if you'll take everyone back, I'll find Mr. Soriano and meet you at the ship." He set off across the street at a quick pace.

"Come on." The magician brought Kang gently to his feet. While they waited for him to compose himself, Bartholomew handed the automat his handkerchief.

Kang wiped his face and Verne patted his shoulder, saying nothing, for once sensing the mood of the situation. He raised his brows at Celwyn, asking silently, *what next?*

Two things kept the magician calm and from destroying everything in sight: he had to take care of Xiau, and in the last second, cold fingers of premonition had wrapped themselves around him with an overwhelming sense of danger.

"We have to get out of here—" Celwyn told them. "*Now!*"

Bartholomew's stance changed to one of defense, his eyes alert, and his movements quick. "Which way to the ship?" He put protective hands on the automat and Verne's shoulders as they followed Celwyn across the grass toward the street.

Celwyn's nose twitched, and his steps slowed as he detected something cloyingly sweet, yet rotten. It reminded him of decay... he stopped still as the weight of dread slowed his movements further. Thirty feet away, masses of shoppers and tourists had rebounded and buzzed around the sidewalk like colorful flies. He pivoted.

Nearly on his heels, Bartholomew was there with Kang, and Verne, so close he could have tied the big man's tie.

Behind them, a ball of fire approached. In seconds it grew larger than a carriage, expanding until it licked the leaves of the trees above them. There it undulated, solidifying, as Celwyn gathered Bartholomew and the others to him, and the horror of what he saw was worse than any nightmare.

From within the fire, a man of tremendous size formed with wild black hair and the blazing eyes of Wolfgang Augustus Griffin. Celwyn's father. Distantly, Celwyn could hear screams from the street. His ears roared, and the magician narrowed his energy to concentrate on the one thing that would help.

They must survive.

Verne fainted, and Bartholomew started to pray. The big man swayed, and Kang caught him as Celwyn slung the three of them behind him. He enlarged himself until he was the same size as his father and spread his arms wide. When a cloud of green mist thickened between them, the wyvern arrived, massive and enraged, snapping his tail, and hissing at Wolfgang.

Wye's eyes burned with fury and when he roared, more screams came from the street.

"Run! Goddam it—*run!*" the magician yelled at the others.

The wyvern howled in rage and stayed between Celwyn and Wolfgang as his father's bellow shook the buildings and bricks fell. The magician had never seen Wye so fierce, or even imagined him like this. Bartholomew herded Verne and Kang toward the street, backing away with his pistol trained on Wolfgang. When Celwyn swiveled back again, his father reached for Wye, wrapping his fingers around the wyvern's neck. The magician willed Wye to go, and he evaporated in Wolfgang's grip.

"Your pet—is a coward!" His father laughed; his malicious grimace became what Celwyn's terrors had always been made of. "Are you?" He approached, and with each step, the ground shook. "Are you, o' son of mine?"

The smell of decay choked the air, and Celwyn wondered if his father bathed in it or slept in it. He also had no trouble reading the madness and murderous intent in his father's eyes. Celwyn had never known true fear, except in his dreams, and he couldn't stop his terror now. The magician did what he didn't have to think about; in the blink of an eye, he climbed toward the sky as a green-eyed raven once again.

An unseen hand slammed him down, face-first, into the dirt. The magician reverted to himself and crawled away as his father tried to stomp him.

No. It will not end like this...

The five notes began, repeating in Celwyn's mind, centering on survival, and filling him with strength. They grew louder as Celwyn staggered to his feet, flexing his power into a narrow focus.

For what seemed like an excruciatingly long time, his music roared as Celwyn confronted Wolfgang, pushing him away as his father hurtled him backward and advanced. The dance continued until Celwyn exploded the dirt between them, and dove, burrowing into the earth as something so small he could not be seen. He tunneled an erratic path to the north, eluding his father and drawing him away from Kang and the others.

He had reached the edge of the sidewalk when the ground in front of him blew apart and his father lifted him by the neck high in the air and then brought Celwyn so close he felt his father's hot breath. It smelled like a burning grave.

"My son, the worm! Ha—you still have your insidious music, I see—"

Celwyn's anger deepened as he tried to break free.

When a series of pistol shots rang out, Wolfgang yelped and slapped his thigh. Bartholomew had advanced, despite all his fears, firing rapidly. It was what Celwyn needed. But when he broke free, Wolfgang already had Bartholomew in his hands. Celwyn threw flames into his father's hair until he screamed and dropped Bartholomew.

It was then that something he had expected and feared occurred.

Pelaez's pig waddled up to Wolfgang Augustus Griffin and bit his leg.

His father roared in pain. Celwyn brought Wye back and the wyvern wound himself around his father's torso as Celwyn landed in front of him. A second more, and Pelaez stood with him, shoulder to shoulder. They raised their hands and spread their feet apart.

"Now, Brother?"

Celwyn nodded.

With everything they had, they pushed Wolfgang back, as he fought them and struggled in his madness and rage.

"We'll gather … the others on my back…" Celwyn threw lightning bolts at his father and watched in horror as he changed into a massive dragon. The magician willed Wye to disappear as the dragon opened his mouth wide. Wye obeyed, but the magician couldn't tell if Wolfgang ate him or if he got away before his father rushed toward them, spitting columns of fire.

"…When I'm ready … make us invisible … to Father?"

"But, of course." Pelaez pushed but only managed to rock Wolfgang from side to side. With each second, the madman drew closer. "Now is a good time. He is going to charge us—"

The dragon's tail switched violently, knocking down the remaining trees.

"Cover us—" Celwyn demanded.

As Pelaez did so, Celwyn changed once again into a raven. In seconds, he gathered Verne, Bartholomew, and Kang onto his back. He swooped low across the ground to Pelaez.

As his brother climbed aboard, he said, "You'd better hurry, Brother."

"Of course." Celwyn panted and could feel himself fading. He hadn't had to battle anyone, or anything like this, in hundreds of years. Seeing his father made it worse because of the hurt that came with him.

As they flew over the market, Pelaez tossed one of his shoes off the back of the raven. "Higher. And in a circle."

"I know what to do," Celwyn growled, realizing how good it felt to be so irritated at Pelaez again. They passed over the top of a high spire. He asked, "How long until he can see us?"

Another shoe tumbled over, then a sock. "No more than five minutes." His coat sailed out and over and drifted downward like an erratic kite. "Higher."

As the magician made a near-vertical ascent, Verne maintained his grip on Celwyn's back while Bartholomew and Kang did the same. It had to be five miles to the *Nautilus*, and with the four of them on his back, the magician knew this would be a chore. Pelaez flung his shirt over and started to undo his trousers. Bartholomew raised a brow but didn't say a word.

After his britches sailed downward, Verne managed, "Why are you almost naked?"

Pelaez gestured, and a new suit covered him. "My clothes dropped in a circle. Father will follow my scent from item to item in a broad circle. Before he gives up and looks upward for us, we'll have you back on the submarine. I hope." He called over his shoulder to Celwyn, "He will see us within another minute, Brother."

Bartholomew yelled, "I see the bay! There are the headlands—"

Celwyn skimmed the top of the trees as they neared the water. From this height, he prayed he would find Granger and Valentine. He scanned the ground and wondered if they had already gone aboard. No matter. He flew faster, exceedingly afraid of his father. *How had he found them? And for god's sake, WHY?*

As he raced between the trees, directly toward the ship, the magician's wings clipped branches and Verne yelped in fear.

"We are visible again," Pelaez announced.

"As expected."

When Celwyn reached the last of the trees, he flew as low as he could, and pushed Kang, Bartholomew, and Verne off his back, tumbling them into the canopy of branches. They would be safer there and, more importantly, he had to distract his father before he discovered the *Nautilus*.

Celwyn called down to Bartholomew, "Get them to the ship!"

Without a word, Bartholomew swung down a branch and landed flat-footed next to a very surprised Valentine and Granger. Kang and the author followed him out of the tree more carefully.

"What are you going to do?" Bartholomew called upward where Celwyn hovered, his wings moving just enough to keep aloft.

"We'll draw my father away from here—tell Nemo to go to the first island he finds and stay submerged." He began moving away. "We'll join you—"

Pelaez called out with what Celwyn rarely heard in his voice. Fear.

"Jonas—"

Celwyn turned to the west and saw what Pelaez had. A low roar of thunder rumbled and grew louder above the rooftops as an undulating wall of fire emerged from the sky, rushing straight at them. The flames flared as Wolfgang's rage intensified.

"*Do something!*" Pelaez shouted before a great force hit them, knocking them head over heels downward.

When Celwyn stopped rolling, to his surprise, he saw a pale image of Thales descending to the ground beside them. More thunder shook the sky. Behind Thales, Wolfgang reared up, his fury tangible. The ground shook once more as he approached.

When Celwyn glanced toward the water, the last thing he saw was Bartholomew, Kang, and the others as they sprinted across the floating pier and disappeared into the belly of the *Nautilus*.

Book club questions

1. Did you expect the pirate ship carrying Miss Redifer to be easy to catch?
2. Did you enjoy what Nemo did to the pirate ships? Did the pirates deserve their fate?
3. How would you handle being in a submarine with an angry vampire?
4. Do you want to see more of the Wessex Club from book 3 in the future books?
5. Do you want to see more of Jakow in future books in the series?
6. Between the slaves Celwyn rescued and the prisoners they later found at Dearing's complex in the Sulu Islands, what would have been the difference in their futures if Nemo and company had not intervened?
7. Is Celwyn evolving into a softer person? Does it suit him?

8. If you could talk to the author, what burning question would you ask about Celwyn?
9. Which character did you most relate to and why?
10. Do you enjoy cross-genre books (the Celwyn series contains multiple genres like mystery, fantasy, adventure, romance)? Why?

Author Bio

LOU'S EARLY WORK WAS HORROR AND suspense. Later, her work morphed into a combination of magical realism, mystery, and adventure, painted with horrific elements as needed.

Lou is one of those writers who doesn't plan a plot—no outlines, no clue, and she sometimes writes herself into a corner. Atmospheric music in the background helps, especially "Black" by Pearl Jam.

More information is available at LouKemp.com. She'd love to hear from you and what you think of Celwyn, Bartholomew, and Professor Xiau Kang.

Milestones:

2009 The anthology story Sherlock's Opera appears in Seattle Noir, edited by Curt Colbert, Akashic Books. Available through Amazon or Barnes and

Noble online. Booklist publishes a favorable review of my contribution to the anthology.

2010 The story, In Memory of the Sibylline, is accepted into the best-selling MWA anthology Crimes by Moonlight, edited by Charlaine Harris. The immortal magician Celwyn makes his first appearance in print.

2018 The story, The Violins Played before Junstan, is published in the MWA anthology Odd Partners, edited by Anne Perry. The Celwyn series begins.

2022 The partnership with 4 Horsemen Publications begins. Book 1, The Violins Played before Junstan, is published.

2023 Book 2 of the Celwyn series, Music Shall Untune the Sky, is published.

2023 Book 3, The Raven and the Pig, is published.

The companion book, The Sea of the Vanities, is published June 2023.

The companion book, Farm Hall, will be published in 2024.

Book 4, The Pirate Danced and the Automat Died, will be available in 2024

MORE BOOKS FROM
4 HORSEMEN PUBLICATIONS

FANTASY, SCIFI, & PARANORMAL ROMANCE

AMANDA FASCIANO
Waking Up Dead
Dead Vessel
The Dead Show
Dead Revelations

BEAU LAKE
The Beast Beside Me
The Beast Within Me
Taming the Beast: Novella
The Beast After Me
Charming the Beast
The Beast Like Me
An Eye for Emeralds
Swimming in Sapphires
Pining for Pearls

CHELSEA BURTON DUNN
By Moonlight
Moonbound
Bloodthirsty

D. LAMBERT
Rydan
Celebrant
Northlander
Esparan
King

Traitor
His Last Name

DANIELLE ORSINO
Locked Out of Heaven
Thine Eyes of Mercy
From the Ashes
Kingdom Come
Fire, Ice, Acid, & Heart
A Fae is Done

J.M. PAQUETTE
Klauden's Ring
Solyn's Body
The Inbetween
Hannah's Heart
Call Me Forth
Invite Me In
Keep Me Close
Heart of Stone

KAIT DISNEY-LEUGERS
Antique Magic
Blood Magic

KYLE SORRELL
Munderworld
Potarium

LYRA R. SAENZ
Prelude
Falsetto in the Woods: Novella
Ragtime Swing
Sonata
Song of the Sea
The Devil's Trill
Bercuese
To Heal a Songbird
Ghost March
Nocturne

PAIGE LAVOIE
I'm in Love with Mothman
Dear Galaxy

ROBERT J. LEWIS
Shadow Guardian and the
Three Bears
Shadow Guardian and the
Big Bad Wolf

T.S. SIMONS
Project Hemisphere
The Space Between

Infinity
Circle of Protections
Sessrúmnir
The 45th Parallel

VALERIE WILLIS
Cedric: The Demonic Knight
Romasanta: Father of
Werewolves
The Oracle: Keeper of the
Gaea's Gate
Artemis: Eye of Gaea
King Incubus: A New Reign
Queen Succubus: Holder
of the Crown
Val's House of Musings: A
Mixed Genre Short Story
Collection

V.C. WILLIS
The Prince's Priest
The Priest's Assassin
The Assassin's Saint
The Champion's Lord

CRIME, DETECTIVE, AND NOIR

A.K. RAMIREZ
Secrets & Photographs

JOE DAVISON
Journey to Hell

MARK ATLEY
Too Late to Say Goodbye
Trouble Weighs a Ton

Fantasy

D. Lambert
To Walk into the Sands
Rydan
Celebrant
Northlander
Esparan
King
Traitor
His Last Name

Danielle Orsino
Locked Out of Heaven
Thine Eyes of Mercy
From the Ashes
Kingdom Come
Fire, Ice, Acid, & Heart
A Fae is Done

J.M. Paquette
Klauden's Ring
Solyn's Body
The Inbetween
Hannah's Heart

Lou Kemp
The Violins Played
Before Junstan

Music Shall Untune the Sky
The Raven and the Pig
The Sea of the Vanities
The Pirate Danced and
Automat Died

R.J. Young
Challenges of Tawa
The Witch of the Whirlwind

Sydney Wilder
Daughter of Serpents

Valerie Willis
Cedric: The Demonic Knight
Romasanta: Father of
Werewolves
The Oracle: Keeper of the
Gaea's Gate
Artemis: Eye of Gaea
King Incubus: A New Reign

Kyle Sorrell
Munderworld
Potarium

Discover more at
4HorsemenPublications.com